To: Ellie
It was so nice
to meet you today

Bob Craft

DREAMS OF DARKNESS AND DESIRE

B.L. CAGLE

with

S.J. BROWN

SONDER PRESS

ISBN: 978-1-7379822-0-3 (EBook)

ISBN: 978-1-7379822-1-0 (Hardback)

ISBN: 978-1-7379822-2-7 (Paperback)

ISBN: 978-1-7379822-3-4 (Audiobook)

Printed in the U.S.

This is a work of fiction. Any resemblance to actual events, locales, or persons, living or dead, are used fictitiously. Names, characters, and places are a product of the authors imagination.

For more information about this book or the author, please visit: www.blcagle.com

✳ Created with Vellum

PROLOGUE
CONNECTED

Deep breath in. Exhale out.

Kira focused on two intrinsically linked and instinctive acts. She could no longer trust anything. Him. Herself. As second nature as it might be, she also no longer trusted her lungs with the simple act of breathing.

The fall should have killed her. It didn't. For a moment, she thought it was another nightmare. But the feel of her scuffed knees spilling off the rug onto the hardwoods and the bite from trace amounts of asphalt digging into the back of her bare thighs as she knelt against her heels told her it was not.

It was real.

He was real.

Deep breath in. Exhale out.

With her eyes clamped shut, she lowered her hands. They were still outstretched high above her head, reaching for him, for someone to pluck her from thin air when she finally felt the ground beneath her.

She wondered how long she had fallen. Seconds? Minutes? It

could have been hours. At the time, it felt like floating. Despite the gravity that sent her soaring over the cliff's edge, the sensation of weightlessness still clung icy to her bones. From the rush of the wind that whipped against her skin, raw and cold, to the sight of his face as it disappeared amongst the stars above told her she was falling.

But that was over. Kira knew where she was now. Her arms hung at her sides as her fingertips gripped into the worn rug beneath her shins, grounding herself back to this place.

Back home.

Shame overtook her. She sunk further down, dropping her chest against her upper thighs. Her stomach dipped as agony welled deep down into the pit of it. Her hands dug deeper into the fibers of the rug, desperate to cling to something.

To someone.

To *him*.

The realization of how she still wanted him sent another torrent of pain, causing her to wrench and twist tighter into herself. A soundless cry floated in the silence. She rested her forehead against the floor as tears pooled onto the hardwoods. Her heart and body were betraying her mind. Perhaps they were betraying her soul. The things he did to her should disgust her, but instead, she found herself crumpled on the floor, aching for him.

Needing him. Still wanting him.

Time passed. It was impossible to determine exactly how much, but the tears had stopped, leaving her skin blotchy and dry. Kira remained on the floor, her cheek pressed against the hardwoods in the dim room. She focused on the beam of light radiating from the hallway through the crack at the bottom of the door. The faint sounds of music lilted through the walls. She briefly saw her roommate's bare feet patter past. But none of those things could pull her attention.

She was somewhere else entirely. It was a perfect illustration of the culmination of the past year. Kira, trapped in hushed darkness while all that was light and good sat just out of reach, taunting her with the possibility of something different.

And then she heard it.

Breathing.

Kira squeezed her eyes shut as a shudder skittered down her spine like the tiny legs of a spider. When she heard it again, she sat up quickly, scanning the four corners of the room. There was no one. Turning slowly, her eyes met her reflection.

It was the mirror.

The mirror was breathing.

Deep breath in. Exhale out.

ONE
DARK SECRETS

S pring made way for summer early. Kira sat perched on the open ledge of the window seat in her room, basking in the day's waning light. It was warm and sticky from the humidity outside, but she enjoyed these quiet moments looking out over the blooming Magnolias. The scent of freshly mowed lawns lingered in the air, and she could hear her neighbors' children as they jumped on a trampoline next door.

As brief as the moment was, it served as a much-appreciated distraction. It was right around this time last year when things shifted, when the pieces of her life began falling out of place. Like any puzzle, you rarely realize that one piece is missing until multiple pieces are gone.

It happened slowly, starting with dreams. Dreams turned into nightmares. Nightmares turned into late, sleepless nights. She tried to distract herself by taking on a heavy course load at school, but it only added to her dilemma, piling additional stress and anxiety onto her already burdened mind. Fatigue set in making it difficult to concentrate.

It wasn't in her nature to complain or to unload onto others. Instead, she fabricated a pretty veneer, lying through her smiles, further insulating herself. It affected every aspect of her life. Her friendships. Her love life. And despite every effort she made, the denial was becoming destructive to her dream of dancing professionally.

Kira thumbed through the pages of her brown leather journal, not landing on any specific page. The dreams started several weeks before she ever committed to putting her memories of them down on paper. Even then, she ripped out the first page once it was written, embarrassed by her own thoughts and words. And for added measure, she burned it in a desperate act of reducing the memory to nothingness. The jagged edges of that first missing page along the center of the binding were still visible. Eventually, as the dreams persisted, she talked herself into opening the journal once more. Sitting here now, peering down at countless tear-streaked pages, she could feel the heavy weight they carried.

The abrupt sound of Kat's voice startled her. "Hey, you! I'm excited about tonight! We're gonna get our T Swift on!" Kat beamed, dancing into the room, tossing a scrap of black on her bed. "Wear this! You're gonna look amazing!"

Kira watched as her friend sauntered out of the door singing her own version of "I Did Something Bad" with a hairbrush serving as her makeshift microphone.

Kat was not only her roommate, she was her one saving grace. They became instant friends after she moved to New Orleans her junior year in high school. And after the unexpected death of Kira's parents their senior year, Kat's family took her in to live with them. They also helped her navigate the will and even co-signed on the loan when she purchased this house. For all the hurt and confusion Kira had experienced this year, she knew she had the greatest friend in her corner. A part of her knew she held back from

6

sharing any of her difficulties because she did not want to taint the one untarnished part of her life.

Kat was a bright spot in a world of gray.

Kira tucked the journal under a pillow on the window-seat and crossed the room, picking up the slinky, black dress. She frowned and shook her head. Admittedly, Kat was a little more fearless in the fashion department. Accepting defeat, she changed, slipping the dress over her head. She stood in the center of her room with her bare toes digging into the rug, inspecting herself in the mirror. She tugged at the dress in an attempt to create some additional length only to cause her cleavage to become more pronounced. She fought the high low battle several times, trying to strike the right balance.

"Legs! You've got great legs, girl," Kat said, poking her head in the door.

Kira looked back over her shoulder, but she'd already disappeared from sight. "I look slutty," she yelled back.

"Good! Colin can thank me later!"

She took a long look at herself, plastered a pageant-worthy smile across her face, and smoothed out the edges of the dress. Her type A disposition was fracturing, but she was determined to fake it till she made it. "You got this," she murmured to herself.

More lies.

"WELL, HELLO, LADIES!" Eric whistled as the girls made their way down the sidewalk.

As practiced, Kira smiled brightly, took an animated spin, and struck her best pose to model the look Kat had given her. She sauntered over to Colin, mimicking his own nod of approval. "You like?"

"Very much. You look gorgeous as always," he said, wrapping his arms low around her back, kissing her forehead.

"You're welcome!" Kat called out, jumping on Eric's back, planting a big kiss on his cheek from behind.

"Just let me know when you can't walk anymore in those things, and I'll give you a piggyback ride around the club," Colin joked, opening the door for the girls.

"She dances around on point shoes all day. I think she can manage some stilettos," Kat countered, patting him on the chest before crawling in behind Kira in the backseat of Eric's car. "Gosh, I really need to blow off some steam tonight. I had my calculus exam today. Brutal. I have two more finals next week and then it's over! What about you, what do you have left?"

She wasn't wrong, they both needed to blow off some steam. She had packed in a lot during this semester and this last week was punishing. "Just my ballet jury." Her smile was unconvincing. There wasn't anything *just* about this exam. This was *the* exam.

Kat reached across, giving her friend a reassuring squeeze at the knee. "You got this girl. You'll dance circles around those clowns."

Kira shifted uncomfortably in the tiny space, once again attempting to adjust the dress. She wished like hell her friend was right, but all the evidence as of late pointed to the exact opposite. As they drove, she remained quiet, semi-listening to the three of them discuss finals and plans for summer. In the darkness of the backseat, she allowed her facade to fall, wilting back against the headrest, watching the streetlights as they passed.

Colin cleared his throat. "Hey, you okay back there?"

Her tone was as hollow as her vacant stare through the window. "Yeah, just a little tired."

For once, it wasn't a lie. She was always tired. Upon glancing up, she caught Colin's eyes in the rearview mirror, but he immediately diverted his gaze. Guilt crushed into her. Though she hated to admit it, she knew he was more aware of her mood swings than she would like him to be. It was hard to continue a semblance of happiness and normalcy twenty-four hours a day. Of course, he was beginning to notice the cracks in her disguise.

Kira bit at her lip, catching glimpses of strangers passing by on the sidewalk. Invisible in plain sight; physically present, but any true emotion or thought was securely veiled. It made her wonder what their lives were like, and if they, too, had dark secrets.

She envied their anonymity, thinking she had it under control, but the look she just glimpsed on Colin's face pained her. The sudden realization that she wasn't as invisible as she once thought landed hard on her heart.

As they got closer to the club, there was more tourist foot traffic, and the rows of houses turned to businesses, restaurants, bars, high-rise condominiums, hotels, and casinos.

Upon arriving, Kat immediately tugged Kira across the center of the dance floor towards the DJ booth to browse song titles. It was karaoke night. Together, they made their way through the crowd, walking across the vivid multicolored carpets and through the brightly colored faux leather couches and booths. Kira squinted against the luminous neon flashing laser beam lights as she followed in behind Kat to find the karaoke songbook.

Kira smiled to herself, watching her friend hum and bounce to the beat of the music as she ran her fingers across the page, searching for the perfect song. She spent several minutes browsing, occasionally glancing up to gauge Kira's opinion on a particular song. As a musical theater major, Kat took karaoke very seriously.

Kira nodded in approval as she held the song book proudly to her chest, pointing to: "Look What You Made Me Do" with a cheesy grin across her face.

"You have to sing with me," Kat demanded, writing both their names on the paper and tossed it into the fishbowl before Kira had a chance to refuse.

"Um . . . no."

Kat ignored her friend and quickly selected another song, scribbling Eric and Colin's names onto another slip of paper before flashing it to Kira. "Beastie Boys!" She excitedly dropped it into the bowl and then linked arms with her friend, leading them back across the room to find the guys. "You don't want me to get my T Swift on without you, do you?"

Kira shrugged. "You know I suck." *I really do. No lies there.* But there was a day when she loved jumping on the stage and making a complete fool of herself alongside her friends while belting out their favorite songs. It had become somewhat of their Friday night ritual during their freshman year. "Plus," she added to keep the mood light, "you just make me look bad."

Kat pursed her lips and nodded. "It's true. You screech like a cat being tortured." She paused, and then patted her on the hand. "Maybe you should just stick to dancing."

She's letting me off the hook. Kat would only back down if she knew something was majorly bothering her. Giving free passes was not her forte. For the second time tonight, she knew she wasn't fooling the people around her and would have to work a little harder to maintain her front. With a bright, equally faux smile, she and Kat approached the table where they found the guys.

Another false smile. Another lie. It was beginning to take its toll.

Kira crawled into the booth next to Colin and curled into his side. He smelled good. Old Spice and peppermint. It was familiar and safe. It was what she needed more than anything, and as close as they were physically at this moment, she still felt like they were a million miles apart. She snuggled a little closer, trying to fill the gap between them.

Kira zoned in and out over the next hour, trying to watch for visual cues to laugh or nod. It was already hard to hear with the volume of the music. And concentrating on a conversation that bounced around from how Colin jokingly planned to grow a goatee to how much weight Eric was currently lifting at the gym didn't make it any easier. Heavier thoughts weighed down her heart and her head. She fidgeted with her hands, growing more restless by the minute. *Is it hot in here?*

Colin must have sensed the growing tension in her body. "You okay?" he asked, leaning down into her neck so she could hear him over the music.

There was that question again. How many times had she heard it now?

"Of course," she chirped, attempting to sound enthusiastic. "I've been working overtime on my fouetté turns." *That's true. Not everything has to be a lie.*

Unfortunately, she was having to work harder to maintain her skill. Her loss of sleep and thus, her concentration had started to wreak havoc on her once flawless technique.

Colin seemed to buy it, murmuring some words of encouragement into her hair as he pulled her in tight. He really was the best boyfriend. They'd been together since their junior year of high school. And though he had originally planned to attend an out-of-state school, he chose to stay and follow her to Tulane. He was loyal and dependable and far more patient than she deserved over the past few months. It's probably why she said nothing when she watched him order his third beer.

Colin wasn't a big drinker. Until recently, it was a rare occasion for him to have more than two or three drinks in one night. Somehow, at some point this spring, that changed. It was still early in the night and at this pace, he would leave there well past drunk. She glanced down at the stamp on her hand. Maybe Colin was on to something. A couple of drinks might lighten her mood and serve as a much-needed distraction.

Kira snapped back to attention at the sound of Kat cheering loudly, her hands applauding high above her head. "Yeah! Get it, boys!"

Eric and Colin cautiously rose from the table and slid out past Kat. "What did you do?" Eric laughed, giving Kat a playful poke in the ribs. Colin resisted a bit, but Eric pulled him along. "No way, dude, you're going up there with me."

Kira couldn't help but smile as they made their way to the front. She watched Colin grab another beer from the server midway, carrying it with him to the stage. Her smile faltered a bit. *Liquid courage, indeed.*

At the sound of the music, Eric bounced up, leg in the air and yelled, "Kick it!"

Both he and Colin jumped into a stirring rendition of "Fight for Your Right" a song from well before any of them were born, but a classic, nonetheless.

Kira and Kat sat close together and cheered the two of them on. It was good fun, and for a moment, she felt herself relax. Towards the end, Kat was standing in her seat, never taking her eyes off Eric. Kira watched them for a brief minute, glancing back and forth between them. She could see their connection. She could feel it. With her eyes on Colin now, she watched as he chugged the remaining beer during a break in the lyrics. *That's four*; she mentally tallied.

The crowd was exuberant, to say the least. Fighting for your right to party apparently resonates well with drunk college students on the brink of final exams. Eric and Colin were clearly proud of themselves, fists pumping in the air. Eric quickly made his way back to the booth and lifted Kat, who still stood tall on her seat, spinning her around in jest. Yes, their chemistry was undeniable.

Kira's smile disappeared entirely as she watched Colin make a beeline to the bar. *That's five.*

She felt her heart sink. She loved him. He loved her. Suddenly though, love didn't seem to be enough to bridge the distance between them. The distance she'd created. Sitting alone in the booth, the walls seemed to close in tighter, stealing all the oxygen in the room. Her hands balled into fists in her lap as she tried to find her breath. *I need a break.*

"I'll be back in a minute. Just going to grab some fresh air," she managed to get out as she slipped out of the booth behind Kat and Eric.

Kat placed a sympathetic hand on Kira's shoulder; concern written across her face. "Do you want me to come with you?"

"No. I'm fine. Promise. It just feels a little stuffy," she answered quickly, trying to get away before Kat could insist or follow her.

Kira pushed through the crowd, hastily making her way to the exit. Her chest tightened, her breath becoming quick and shallow. The panic built faster and faster with every step she took. She centered her attention on the exit just ahead as she continued to focus on her rapid breathing.

Passing through the doors, she felt the sudden release of pressure and basked in the coolness of the night air. With her eyes closed, her head fell back with her chin to the sky. *You're okay;* she told herself, taking a few deliberate and deep breaths. Folding her hands across her stomach, she opened her eyes and released a final long-winded sigh. *A panic attack?*

She had never experienced fear or loss of control like this. The onset was sudden and intense. And then it was gone as quickly as it had come.

Kira smoothed out her dress and brushed her hair back, tucking it behind her ears in an attempt to regain her composure. She walked herself across the parking lot to Eric's car and relaxed against the hood. With her lips pressed into a thin line, she scanned her surroundings. Not focusing on anything, her expression blank, she silently compartmentalized the entire episode, burying it somewhere deep down. She didn't have the time, the energy, or the interest to over analyze any of it. It was a skill she had become well-practiced in. *Take a deep breath, bite back the tears, and smile. Everything is fine.*

"Everything okay?"

She jolted at the sound of a male voice behind her and whipped around, her hand clasped to her heart as she let out a shaky laugh. "You scared me." Her eyes drifted up as she took in the toned, statuesque frame of the man standing in front of her. Her gaze rested there for a moment before lifting her eyes to meet his. Her mouth went dry.

She stood there bewildered, words escaping her.

The man smiled softly; one eyebrow lifted in question. "Are you okay?"

Words. Say words; she chastised herself, swallowing down the huge knot in her throat.

None were to be found, so she nodded, a tight-lipped smile on her face. Icy blue eyes deeper than the oceans stared back at her. The man inclined his head as if he doubted her. His smile widened, showing strong teeth. Kira felt warmth spreading through her with the sudden thought of those teeth grazing her neck. She silently scolded herself for the bizarre nature of those thoughts.

"I should head back inside," she finally managed, taking a step backward, but never breaking eye contact.

The mysterious man acknowledged the space she created, and took two steps forward in response, closing the gap between them even more. "Now, why would you want to go back inside, when you clearly want to stay out here and talk to me?"

He was tall. And so close. She had to crane her neck back to look at him. His scent invaded her senses. Sandalwood and citrus. It was oddly familiar. She inhaled again, her heart racing.

The man's body shifted imperceptibly. Kira almost didn't notice until she felt his touch. She looked down at her hand as the tip of his index finger trailed the inside of her open palm. It was the lightest of touches, but the sensation from it slammed into her. Those tiny strokes lit up all her nerve endings. It seemed all her senses were betraying her.

"You're afraid," he whispered, leaning in as his lips grazed her temple. "Don't be."

Her face still pointed to the ground; she clamped her eyes shut. The sound of his voice raked through her like ivy tendrils, slowly creeping through her soul and wrapping around her heart. She swayed slightly as her body floated on the sound. She still couldn't put words together but found the strength to meet his eyes again. Soul-crushing blue eyes that pierced right through her.

Everything melted away. The lights and sounds coming from the bar disappeared. At this moment, only they existed. Her breath caught in her chest as everything around them faded into blackness. It was a welcomed abyss. She would happily drown in those pools of blue that looked back at her.

No. No. Somewhere deep down in her subconscious, Kira could feel a flicker of herself. *Fight it.* It was no more than a whisper, but it was there. The light slowly started to creep back into the corners of her sight. Outside sounds began to penetrate the stillness that he'd created.

The man nodded, his features tightening along his jaw, clearly recognizing the faint shift in her control. He smiled again, but it didn't meet his eyes entirely. He pulled back half a step, allowing himself the room to view her fully. With his arm outstretched, the pad of his finger still trailed along the inside of her open palm, continuing to ignite her skin. They were connected by the most infinitesimal of touches, but she may as well have been wrapped up tightly in a full intimate embrace. In that one touch, she could feel his hands tangling into her hair, his lips on the nape of her neck, and the warmth of his hard body pressed firmly against hers. She could feel him entirely.

With the slight curl of his finger, the connection was broken, his arm dropping to his side. Kira released a strained and audible breath, her body aching from the loss. The electricity that had been brewing between them dissipated into nothing, leaving a hollow place in her heart. She was still enthralled, but that little flicker she had sensed earlier was getting stronger.

"It's okay, though." He took another half step back. "You are not yet ready."

Kira tilted her head, confusion across her face. Words once again were nowhere to be found. She searched for the flicker inside. It was there, but it wouldn't let her protest his retreat.

"But you will be . . . soon," he said, his smile widening, confidence blazing in his eyes.

Soon? Her arm hung limp at her side as she rubbed the pads of her fingers together, trying to revive the sensation. *Soon isn't soon enough. Don't leave.*

The man continued to pace backwards, inclining his upper body forward, bidding her farewell. He silently mouthed the word, soon. His eyebrow arched high, that wide gleaming smile returning in full.

Still rooted to the spot where she stood, she watched him as he slowly strode backwards. Their eyes remained locked on one another. The flicker inside that seemingly stopped her from reaching out to him was fading. Kira fought for her words again. *Soon.* She wanted to call out to him, but before a sound could leave her lips, he bled away into the darkness. *He's gone.*

For several seconds, she was a statue. She didn't realize the amount of tension in her body until it was released in a rush that left her gripping onto the car to keep from crumpling to the ground. Hunched over, her palms flat against the hood, she blew out a deep breath. Her entire body ached, and she could feel the cold sweat on the back of her neck. Unsteady on her feet, she balanced herself between cars as she made her way to the edge of the parking lot.

Nausea rolled through her. Kira crouched down and put her head to her knees. With her hand holding back her hair, she heaved, sending the contents of her lunch onto the gravel. She remained crouched low, balancing herself against the ground with her free hand. The crunched-up pavement and gravel dug into her palms, but at least her nausea was subsiding. After several seconds, she pushed herself back up to her feet with her arms wrapped around her waist. Taking slow and measured steps, she walked back to the bar with the intention of leaving this strange and intimate encounter behind.

Entering back through the doors, she was tossed into sensory overload. The music's volume, the loud voices of patrons, the flashing stage lights, and the smell of stale beer were all overwhelming as she made an immediate escape to the ladies' room.

The cold splash of water on her face settled her, soothing her achy chest and panicked mind. She rinsed her mouth out, bracing herself against the porcelain sink, dropping her head back in relief. She exhaled deeply. Her emotions were raw, laid bare by a man who barely spoke more than ten words to her. *What the hell happened to me out there?*

Kira shifted her weight and looked down at the palm of her hand, running her finger across the center. In that one simple touch, she felt something crash into existence. Something that wasn't there before. There was that ache again. The ache of losing something that she never even had a chance to know or understand before it was gone.

She glanced up to face herself in the mirror as the prick of tears threatened to unleash themselves. She stood there for far too long, willing herself into a state of calm. "Get your shit together, Kira!" she ground out beneath her breath.

"There you are!"

She jolted to life at the sound of Kat's voice, and quickly put on a practiced smile. "I'm sorry I disappeared for so long," she answered, fanning herself with her hand. "I felt really hot. Is it hot in here to you?"

Kat, ever the caretaker, placed a hand to Kira's forehead and cheeks. "You do look a little flushed. Do you feel sick?"

Kira shrugged. *I could be sick,* she thought. As far as excuses go, being sick is an easy one to play up. She was just puking in the parking lot only minutes before. Yes, she would go with that. "Maybe a little . . . but, but I'm sure it's nothing."

Kira stood there silently as Kat gave her a once-over, and then nodded cautiously. "Okay. Do you want to go home?"

Yes, her inner self screamed. "No. I'm sure I'll be fine." She bit her lip, tapping the toe of her heel nervously on the tile. Lying to herself was one thing. Lying to Kat was an entirely different thing.

"Okay then," Kat drawled, a lack of certainty in her voice.

There were many reasons why she didn't like lying to Kat. One was that she was her best friend, but more importantly, she was terrible at it. But at this moment, with what she was feeling, she couldn't afford not to be convincing. Kira smiled, straightened her spine, and firmly planted her frantic, dead giveaway foot to the ground. "Okay! Let's go get our T Swift on!" she exclaimed, linking arms with Kat.

The look on her friend's face was worth it. It felt less worth it when she was finally on stage later that night. She did sound like a tortured cat. Not surprisingly, singing on stage in front of strangers also felt like torture.

On the way home, Kira shrank back into her seat. Her heart and mind were straying to a place she didn't want or need to revisit. She needed to let that moment live in the past. Leave it in that dark and dank parking lot.

She glanced up at the front where Colin was passed out. The guilt was a two-ton box of lies sitting heavy on her chest. She couldn't budge it. It was here to stay for the time being. Anger was also taking up residency.

She was angry at Colin for turning to alcohol to find comfort.

She was also angry at herself.

Angry because she knew Colin's behavior was a direct consequence of her own actions.

Angry for allowing a strange man to touch her.

Angry because it felt so real.

It was real.

TWO
FADING AWAY

A strip of bright light hovered across Kira's face. She squinted against the harshness of the sun that peaked through the opening in her curtains, using her hand to block it. Seeking a dimmer spot, she shifted her body and nestled into the cooler side of her pillow.

Kira laid there for several minutes, willing her mind and body to again retreat back into sleep. Back into deep, uninterrupted sleep. It was the first time in weeks she had slept through the night. She felt rested and relaxed. Cool composure wasn't a hallmark she'd been acquainted with recently, and this new feeling set off an alarm bell inside.

Her eyes popped open, glancing at the clock on the nightstand. It was nearly noon. Her brow furrowed. Under normal circumstances, she would have launched herself out of bed much earlier. Instead, she just pulled the covers up closer to her chin. She continued to stare at the clock as it slowly ticked the seconds away. One. Two. Three. The room was quiet. She listened to each tick echo through the room, an emphatic reminder of time lost. Four. Five. Six.

Somewhere in her silent count, she began to recall events of the night before. She was at the club. She danced and sang alongside Kat. She watched Colin drink. And drink. And drink some more. More time passed. Twenty. Twenty-one. Twenty-two. She remembered a sensation in her body. It was an indescribable tension mixed with dread and heat that flushed her skin. *Was it a panic attack?*

Kira dug back into the corners of her mind. There was something here. Her thoughts poked, prodded, and pried, silently willing her memory to let her see it. Thirty-three. Thirty-four. Thirty-five.

There were cars. She could hear the muffled sounds of music. The air was fresher and less suffocating. *Outside . . . Outside in the parking lot of the club.*

Kira held onto it. It was right there. Beneath the covers, she clenched her fists and held them tightly to her chest, her body coiled into a ball. Her eyes remained steadfast on the clock. Forty-seven. Forty-eight. Forty-nine.

As she neared the minute mark, everything faded into black. The cars were gone. Infinite silence replaced the music. The air felt lighter and cooler against her skin. And within a blink of an eye, her thoughts ripped away the wall, revealing a current of blue staring back at her.

It was all she could see; oceans of blue waves crashing into shallow pools that seemingly floated in the dark. He was faceless, but his eyes promised her everything, focusing all her attention there. The clock was irrelevant now. Time was irrelevant. Fifty-eight. Fifty-nine. Sixty.

One minute gone.

Kira rolled onto her back, reveling in this contentment. It was a change of pace from what she had grown accustomed to. She was happy to lavish in this feeling for an entire day, but a sudden knock on her door pulled her from it. A small pang immediately settled in the pit of her stomach. Annoyance. She glared at the closed door.

"Kira?" Kat cracked the door slowly, sliding half her body through the frame. "Are you okay, sweetie?"

"Yeah, I'm fine," Kira grumbled. She could feel that magic sensation fleeing her body. She wanted to chase after it, but her judicious side reminded her that Kat was in the room.

Kat nodded in response, appearing to be unsure of what to say. "I checked on you earlier today before lunch. You seemed dead to the world."

Kira eyed her profoundly, brows furrowed. Kat seemed off. *Is she concerned?* She propped herself up on her elbows to try to get a better read on her friend, who still stood plastered against the frame of the door. One foot in, and one foot out. The Kat she knew would already be lounged across her bed right now.

"I had some errands to run, and I just got back. I was surprised to see you still in bed."

Kira's brow furrowed deeper. Her eyes glided across the room in confusion as she considered Kat's words. It took a few seconds before she noticed the light, or the lack thereof. That blinding beam of light that had woken her from sleep was now replaced with the softer glow of the moon. She whipped her head back to the clock; it was now after nine pm. Her confusion was suddenly growing into something more, seeping into her body with a swiftness she couldn't control. She tried to shake it off, to ignore it altogether.

Kira looked back to Kat, giving her a phony smile. "Oh, my goodness. I didn't even realize what time it was." She laughed and fell back into her bed.

Her change in posture gave Kat the assurance to enter the room.

"Do you feel sick?" she asked, crawling up beside Kira on her knees. "Can I get you anything?"

Kira shook her head, a silly smile on her face. "Oh, no. I'm fine. I woke up earlier and read for a while. I guess I laid back down and fell asleep again." *Professional liar. I should get business cards made up.* "I haven't been sleeping well lately. I guess my body was playing catch up." That was the key. Simply insert a bit of truth into the lie, and you were golden.

Kat returned her smile, nodding along with her. "Yeah, I've noticed. I'm glad you were able to finally get some," she said, reaching out to pick up Kira's phone from the nightstand. "Speaking of getting some." She held the phone up for her to see.

Kira glanced at the screen. *Colin.*

She had nine missed calls from him and even more texts. That was the last thing she wanted to deal with. She put her hands over her face, exasperated by the thought of having to talk to him. *Why do I feel that way? I love him.* They shared everything. She tried to recall the events of last night again. A vision of him passed out in the car on the ride home flashed through her mind. *Oh yeah, because he sucks.*

Something else was also there. Something fleeting that she wasn't ready to give up, but her focus was thinning. What had she been thinking of before Kat came into the room? She couldn't remember. She felt a light brush in the center of her hand. Glancing down at it, she squeezed her palm tight in an attempt to hold on to it. She opened it as if she half expected to find something tangible. There was nothing. That brush against her skin was an obscure goodbye. The sensation of contentment and bliss was gone. She swallowed hard, feeling the tension in her muscles grow.

"He called me about an hour ago asking if I knew where you were." Kat placed the phone on Kira's stomach. "He thinks you're mad at him for getting so drunk last night."

23

Kira said nothing. She only glared at the phone.

Kat's brows arched in question back at her. "Are you?"

It took her a moment to answer. She wasn't sure. Her emotions were all over the place. It was as if they'd all been stuffed into a jar and violently shaken. She couldn't nail down one specific feeling. "Yes. No. I don't know," shaking her head, flustered. "Maybe."

Kat only smiled, placing a comforting hand across Kira's knee.

Kira frantically searched for words in her muddled mind. Before she could find anything, her phone began to ring. Colin's name, along with an image of her planting a big kiss on his cheek appeared across the screen. A twinge of guilt fluttered in her stomach.

"I'll leave you to it," Kat muttered as she made her way out of the room.

Kira took a deep breath. "Hi," her voice was soft and unsure.

"Hey. Hi . . . um," Colin stammered, clearly surprised to hear her voice. It took him a few seconds. "Are you home?"

"Yeah. I'm home."

Another several seconds of silence followed. "Can I come in?"

Confusion registered across Kira's face. She scooted across her bed, quickly making her way over to the window seat to peer behind the curtain. Down below, she could see Colin's truck parked on the street outside. The flutter in her stomach was forming into a heavy stone. "Yeah, of course . . . I'm in my room."

Kira hung up and tossed her phone to the side. A glance in the mirror revealed the state of mess she was in. She moved to retrieve her brush but stopped mid-reach, realizing she didn't care. Instead, she curled up on the window seat and used these last few seconds of alone time to search for that sensation again. *What was it? Who was it? Who?*

She'd only been focused on the idea of what. But as her

thoughts lingered, the idea of *who* it was now seemed like a better question. Was a person responsible for those feelings?

Kira dug deep within her subconscious. Blue eyes began to materialize. That sense of euphoria was creeping back into her fingertips, but before she could cling to the image, she heard her door creak open, breaking her contact. Once again, she felt it escape. She knew she wouldn't get it back now.

"Hey," his voice was cautious and apologetic. He lingered halfway into the room and watched her warily. "I'm so sorry about last night, babe. I'm not sure what got into me. It was me, but it wasn't me," he tried to explain. "Do you know what I mean?"

Kira said nothing. She simply stared back at him, her expression blank. The stone from earlier was now a boulder weighing her down. They were only a few feet apart, but it felt like a canyon. By the look on Colin's face, she knew he felt it, too.

He sighed heavily, rubbing his hands across his face and through his hair. "Please say something."

The boulder kept her rooted to the spot, unable to form words. A numbness wrapped around her heart. She couldn't look at him anymore. Her eyes now focused on the distance between them.

Colin quickly closed the gap, dropping to his knees beside her, and buried his head into her lap. "I'm so sorry, babe," his voice cracking.

The feel of his body on hers jolted her emotions awake and shocked her senses. Tears pricked her eyes, but she still couldn't find the comforting words she knew he needed. She placed a hesitant, unsteady hand on the back of his head. It was all she could manage, unable to offer any additional comfort.

He wrapped his arms around her calf, his head still resting in her lap. "I miss you."

Kira's heart dropped as she felt a tear roll down her leg. Colin wasn't a crier. He was her rock. She had never seen him cry. She sagged, releasing the tension in her body, her own tears now breaking through the dam. The emotion welling inside finally allowed her to give Colin the reassuring gesture of stroking her fingers through his hair.

It was the invitation he'd been waiting for. He grasped onto it, immediately lifting his body at her touch, taking her hands in his, pressing several small kisses across her knuckles before grabbing her and pulling her down onto the floor with him.

He held her tight, his face buried in the crook of her neck. "I know why the drinking bothers you. I know what it means to you," he stumbled through his words, but he seemed determined to get them out. "I'll be better."

Kira shut her eyes, trying to push back the visions of her parents' mangled car, heaps of twisted metal being pulled onto the banks of the river. More tears leaked down her face at the feel of Colin's hand stroking along her lower back.

"I don't know why," he continued, pulling her hand to his cheek, "but I can feel you slowly fading away from me. You're always there, but it feels like I've lost a piece of you."

Kira stilled, her head resting against his shoulders as she listened to him speak. She suddenly recalled the look on his face last night when she'd caught his eyes in the mirror of the car. She'd felt it then, that the veneer she had so carefully crafted was wearing thin. At this moment, she knew it had been cracking far earlier.

He gently shifted his body to look at her. "The harder I try only seems to make it worse. I don't want to lose you." Holding his hands to the sides of her face, he twined his fingers through her hair and pulled her in close. It was so intimate.

They sat on the floor, their legs tangled together, looking at one another so closely that their noses touched. Kira mimicked Colin's earlier touch, gently rubbing her fingers at the base of his shoulders. She did love him. Her heart crumbled as it silently asked whether that alone was enough anymore. Her body quaked as she felt Colin's thumb wipe away her tears. It only unleashed more.

"Please don't tell me I've already lost you." It seemed impossible, but he pulled her even closer and tighter to him. He couldn't let go. "I can't lose you."

Kira didn't answer; she just cried.

He cried.

They sat that way for a long time, saying nothing. Their tears finally calmed, silence filling the room.

Kira could hear the faint sound of the clock ticking.

Time still irrelevant.

Kira woke to a dull ache in her neck. It was still dark, but enough light lit the room for her eyes to roam across Colin's face. She'd been sleeping soundly in the crook of his arm for the past hour. They hadn't said much more after the tears. She only remembered saying, "I love you" before he swept her up and carried her to the bed. Their bond was stronger than one fight. It was stronger than a million words spoken. At least that was what she was telling herself right now.

Reaching out, she swept a stray strand of hair back. *He's good to me, more than I deserve.* He had been the one apologizing, but she knew deep down that she was the one who should have been asking for forgiveness.

Kira gently and quietly eased herself out of bed. As she made her way across the room towards the bathroom, she caught a glimpse of something in the mirror.

She stopped dead. It was dark; she could see nothing, only the ornate outer edge of the mirror. Taking a measured step forward, her reflection faint in the dimness of the room, she glanced back to Colin, who was shifting in his sleep.

Her eyes now meeting her own back in the mirror; she didn't know why or how, but she could now feel it.

Anger.

She didn't move.

She couldn't move.

One. Two. Three.

Kira counted the seconds as they ticked away.

THREE
HE IS REAL

Kira took one step and paused to take in the scene around her. She stood alone in a dim room with dark walls and floors. It was empty, except for a small circular stage that rested in the center of the room. The enticing yet familiar scent of sandalwood and citrus hung in the air. Inhaling deeply, she took another cautious step. She did not know this place but didn't find it unnerving either. Instead, she felt sanguine and strangely fearless.

Slowly, she crossed the room, her eyes fixated on the vertical steel pole standing in the center of the stage. Her fingers softly grazed her exposed outer thighs as she walked toward it. The sensation sent chills straight to her core. Standing at the base of the stairs, she glanced at her hands as her fingers slid up across her hips to her center. They continued, tracing the outer line of her body before reaching her collarbone. Her fingers worked their path up her neck, where they deftly worked to remove the pins, allowing her to shake out her long dark hair.

A hazy smoke billowed down low across the stage, illuminated by an array of faint blue and green lights. The music was instrumental but not familiar. The sounds were rich and visceral, but oddly somber all the same. If she closed her eyes, she could feel her entire body vibrate on the melody.

It was calling out to her.

With another step, she made her move up the stairs and onto the stage; her eyes remained steady on the pole. She was a dancer. A highly trained one at that, but she had never danced the way her body was enlisting her to do at this moment.

Her fingers curled around the cool steel. A surge of electricity seeped into her skin, causing any lingering inhibitions she may have to melt away. Her breath quickened as she slowly sauntered around the pole, one hand gripping it firmly while her free hand explored the lines and contours of her body.

The creamy sheer mesh of the bralette and thong she wore highlighted the golden tone of her skin. Her fingers glided over the delicate lace details of the bustier, feeling her own heart beating wildly beneath it. Her hands continued the journey up her neck before she traced a single fingertip across her lips.

Moving closer in, her right hand floated high above her head, still gripping the pole as she leaned her back against it. Her eyes rolled shut at the sensation of the chill against her bare skin. She lingered in this feeling for several seconds before slowly sliding her back down towards the ground, her one hand still high above her head as it slid along the pole. She liked this feeling; the way it made her feel sexy, confident, and even a little reckless. She liked it a little more than she wanted to admit, wanting more.

Upon opening her eyes, she caught sight of something across the room. She froze. Everything seemed to pause. The music. Her breathing. Her heart.

It was a man.

He sat at a small table no more than ten feet away from the stage silhouetted in darkness. She could only make out the hard line of his jaw and strong hands that rested firmly on the table. Dominant, strong hands. She felt like she knew them . . . like her body knew them. She watched intently as he curled one finger, the pad of it skimming ever so slightly across the linen cloth, causing her breath to catch in her throat.

Fire. It now blazed in the palm of her hand. It was a warmth that radiated outward, setting her entire body ablaze. She inhaled sharply. She was feeling confident moments before, but a new boldness was penetrating deep into her bones.

She was valorous.

Her lips settled into a playful, sultry smile before she arched her back, her hips rolled to the front. The stretch allowed all the tension to release from her muscles, leaving her in a state of bliss. She dropped her weight, her body leaning at a slight angle as her right arm stretched out, gripping the pole, sashaying around it. She moved slowly at first, allowing the man the time to drink in her movements before taking two quick steps in succession, and hooking her right leg around the pole and spinning through the air.

Kira had never done this before, and the success of one move gave her the confidence to try another. The mysterious man often rewarded her, offering the curl of his fingers across the tabletop. She could feel them now, moving across her jaw, down the line of her neck, and brushing across her collarbone. She didn't question how he did it; how she could feel this seemingly magical touch from across the room. She didn't care. It only inflamed her more. Kira would master this piece of steel and wield it as a means to get what she wanted. And at this moment, she only wanted those hands on her. Everywhere.

With her back now to his table, she reached a single finger up to her shoulder, playfully tugging at the strap before sliding it down. She repeated the movement with the other strap, briefly glancing over her shoulder, a knowing smile on her face. She skillfully unsnapped the back closures, allowing the bralette to fall down the length of her arms, and tossed the scrap of lace to the floor.

Any sense of the controlled, rigid Kira was completely abandoned at this moment. A new energy had taken hold, enveloping her body, heart, and soul. Dancing made her feel free, but this was a freedom she had never experienced. She held her arms high above her head, slowly traipsing her fingers down the line of her right arm and across her décolletage as she twisted her body towards him.

Her hands slid to the center of her body, clasping together over her heart. The electricity evaporated at the sight of the empty chair. He was gone. Her lips parted in protest, but before she could form words, she felt the energy surge back into her body, twisting around her heart as his hands slid in from behind her, pulling her into his chest.

Her breath hitched, and her mouth went dry. She melted into him, his hands exploring every inch as his teeth grazed the hollow space of her neck.

Those hands. She knew those hands. She knew this touch. His touch.

"We will be together. You will be mine." His presence alone was dominating, and there was so much control in his voice. He was unrelenting in both his words and his movements. He slid his hands down her torso, down between her now parted legs, his fingers working in soft, slow circles over the scant scrap of lace that separated her from his direct touch. "Soon," he whispered.

Kira sank into total unabated euphoria, ready to give herself over entirely. "Yes," she whispered back, almost breathless, barely able to form an intelligible sound.

"Kira . . . Kira."

Startled, she blinked rapidly, snapping back to attention. With her hand to her chest, it took several seconds to gather herself. She looked up at the girl calling her name, a fellow dancer who sat across from her on the studio floor where she'd been stretching out.

"Are you okay?" she asked, genuine concern plastered across her face.

Kira swallowed hard, her mouth still dry. She nodded, forcing a weak smile.

"They just called for you."

Kira craned her neck, glancing at the door the girl was pointing towards and the clock above it. *Damn it!* She scrambled to her feet, and quickly made her way around the corner just outside the larger studio where she was about to perform in front of the final exam jury.

She waited for the monitor to signal her through the door, taking these precious extra minutes to continue stretching and recall the movements in the choreography. She practiced moving into en pointe from relevé several times, only to lose her balance after just a few seconds. From the corner of her eye, she saw the monitor wince at the sight. This was not going to go over well.

Taking a few deep breaths, she pressed her hands along the wall to support her weight, toe box planted to the ground, while she mindlessly stretched the arches of her feet. Scenes of her body whipping through the air around a pole flashed through her memory. Staring blankly at the wall, she attempted to process her thoughts.

Kira let the entire scene play through her head. The smoke, the soft glow of lights, and the steel pole that stood tall like a beacon in the center of the room calling out to her, she could see it all. She closed her eyes, resting her head against the cool wall in front of her as she recalled the way her skin lit up when it touched the pole. She remembered the surge of energy and the unabashed confidence that rolled through her as she moved around it.

And then there was *him*.

Even as she stood in the starkly white hallway, she could feel his hands wrapping around her torso. She inhaled deeply, taking in the scent of sandalwood and citrus. It was as if he'd never left; that they were still together at this very moment. She exhaled, releasing the tension, her nerves melting away.

"Kira."

With one more sobering breath, she pushed herself from the wall before looking toward the monitor, who was now holding the door open for her.

"They're ready for you now."

As Kira made her way across the floor, she didn't take much time to register the faces of the three professors sitting behind the table at the front of the room. She wanted to hold on to the feeling that had settled into her core. She never saw his face, just the hard line of his jaw. That was the image she worked to hold on to, along with the sight of his hands as he curled that one intoxicating finger. A smile rested on her lips as she felt that finger trace a line in her palm at that very moment. *He's here.*

She didn't care how, only that he was.

She settled into fourth position, and on the third beat of the music, she exploded into développé, her leg extending out high above her head. At the same time, her arms stretched into beautiful open lines. She deliberately and gracefully moved across the floor, matching the melody as its intensity moved from soft measures to more impassioned tones.

Throughout the rise and fall, her confidence continued to grow. She seemingly floated on air while leaping into grand jeté; her technique was pristine. The dreams she'd been experiencing over the past several months had been nothing more than a barrier. They disconnected her from herself, from the people around her, and any form of artistic expression. Now though, as she glided across the floor, she felt more connected to her own body and soul than she ever had.

In the days prior, she had changed the choreography to remove five rotations in her fouetté turns. It was a movement that stood as the highlight of the entire piece, but as this day grew closer, she found it increasingly difficult to perfect, despite all the additional training and effort she poured into it. Instead of twelve rotations, she'd chosen to only do seven.

Kira had been disappointed with the decision, finding it to be a clear indication she may not have the career in dance she had dreamed of since the day she slipped on her first pair of ballet shoes at the age of three. But that was before this newfound confidence. He was here with her. He would support her through this moment.

Kira found her center and dropped into a deep plié before rising into relevé and whipping her extended leg to propel her body into a quick and succinct turn. She repeated the motion one, two, three times. As she approached her seventh rotation, she knew she could continue. She beamed as her body spun in place, completing her twelfth turn, and not stopping there. Her chin lifted a notch as she felt that familiar touch in the center of her palm, encouraging her to continue. She whipped her leg out again and again. The music came to a halt seconds before she finished her seventeenth rotation and falling back into fourth position. Her chest heaved with excitement and exhaustion.

For the first time, she looked directly at the faces of her professors on the exam panel. Her smile widened as she watched Professor Clendening, a particularly harsh teacher, give her a quiet nod of approval. She quickly made her way out of the studio, wiping the sweat from her brow with the back of her hand. It was over; she could relax.

As she walked back to the holding room where she'd left her bag, she allowed her successful performance to sink in. She performed amazingly. She knew it. She more than knew it. She felt it. Kira could still feel the sensation of spiraling in place while gracefully extended on her toes en pointé. It was like magic.

Her dreams had been haunting her at night while she slept. They were often fervent and carnal, and always frightening. Mostly, they were confusing. They distracted her from everything important. Today was different. This dream was different. For the first time, she had drifted into a dream while wide awake. She hadn't felt scared, confused, or unsure of her own emotions. Instead, she was bold and clearheaded.

In her previous dreams, she'd often felt someone else's presence. Someone who was always on the outer edges, orchestrating the scene to play on her worst fears and anxieties. This was different. This man was different. He lifted her high, and took her body to new heights, making her feel things she didn't know her body could feel. He made her soar. He may have been in her dream, but he felt so real.

Kira looked down at her palm, feeling that little twinge.

She smiled. *He is real.*

FOUR
THAT'S HIM

It was the morning after Kira's contemporary ballet exam. She stood silently in her bathroom mirror, applying a finishing touch of gloss to her lips. Pulling her hair back in a neat ponytail, she examined her appearance, smoothing out the lines of her camisole tank, pivoting back and forth, scrutinizing herself even more. Using her fingers, she pulled a few strands of her hair around the edges to frame her face.

Kira pushed out a heavy breath and dropped her head in defeat as she held herself up on the edge of the sink. *What the hell is wrong with you?* She lifted her chin to stare herself down. This wasn't her. She'd spent the better part of the morning getting ready because she hoped to impress a man who only existed in the constructs of her mind.

And hands? She glanced down at her hand and swiped a finger across the center. She hadn't felt him since yesterday afternoon. Closing her eyes, she searched for the feeling; it had been so strong. She'd been so sure of herself, so sure of him. She carried that feeling with her the entire day. Even as she went to sleep last night, her trust in him was steady. Whole.

She took another long look at her palm. There was still nothing.

Irritated, she pulled the tie from her hair and slung it at the mirror in protest. All the positivity that had flooded her mood since yesterday vanished in an instant.

"I'm so fucking stupid," she chastised herself and stormed back to her room, where she gathered a few of her things and dumped them into her leather bag.

Kira could hear Kat and Nadia giggling downstairs. She paused for a breath, brushed her hair back, and applied a well-practiced smile before heading down the stairs. With any hope, she would leave this new obsession behind her.

"Hey girl," Nadia beamed as Kira entered the room.

As always, Nadia was picture perfect. Her bright blonde hair was sleek and polished to perfection. Her cheeks were delicately dusted in shades of pink that matched her nails. And Kira couldn't help but notice the cute sundress she wore. It was a far cry from the gothic black wardrobe Nadia was known for in high school.

"I like your dress," Kira teased, dropping beside her on the sofa. Her faux demeanor was artistry in action. *And the Oscar goes to*.

"Oh yeah," Nadia squeaked. "I may have gone through your closet last week and borrowed it."

"Keep it. It looks better on you," Kira insisted. "But you do look like you are going somewhere special. Trying to impress someone?" she joked. If the words hadn't escaped her own lips before she'd realized it, she would have choked on the irony.

Kat didn't hold back her laughter. "Um . . . yeah, she is," snapping her fingers back and forth through the air for added emphasis.

Kira pursed her lips and leaned in. "You two have tea? Spill!"

Nadia was a bit of a flirt, so it wasn't a surprise to hear of a new love interest, but she was a dear friend. So, if it were important to her, then it was important to Kira.

Eric waltzed in from the kitchen and settled in behind Kat. "She's talking about the hotties with the bodies down the street," he informed, stumbling through a mouth full of cookie.

Kat twisted in her seat towards him; her brow arched comically. "Eavesdrop much?"

Eric swallowed as to clearly emphasize his defense. "*Listen.* Listen much. Good boyfriends listen," he mused, tapping at his ear.

Kira laughed. Genuinely laughed. Eric was good for the soul. Even better for Kat. "Hottie with a body, huh? Didn't know you swung that way, Eric."

"Yeah, should I be jealous?" Kat faked a pout; her bottom lip stuck out.

Eric snuggled closer. "No way, baby. You've got nothing to worry about," planting a kiss on her cheek. "But if I was gay, I would totally break down the closet door for those guys," he affirmed, taking another bite from his cookie.

"Wait!" Nadia raised her hands to halt the conversation. "Guys? There's more than one? And how do you even know who I'm talking about anyway?"

"I heard you talking about a guy who moved into the old Calloway Estate. I saw him and his friends the other day when I was walking by," Eric told her, snuggling into Kat's neck, growing bored with the girl talk.

"That place is under construction. There are guys walking in and out all day. What?" Nadia paused for a moment before shrugging at the judgmental eyes all pointed at her. "Geez, guys. I drive by there almost every day on the way to school."

"Stalker," Eric whispered jokingly, before ducking back behind Kat just as Nadia launched a pen at his head.

"Says the heterosexual who's coming out of the closet."

Kira sunk back into the sofa, finding enjoyment in the friendly banter. She missed this. She looked to Eric and waited for his response as she absentmindedly rubbed the center of her palm.

"Look, I don't know who they were, but they were definitely not construction workers. They were," he lingered, trying to find the words, "I don't know. Definitely not construction workers." The girls narrowed their eyes at him. "And one of them had a sweet ride."

"Not a construction worker . . . and has a sweet ride," Kat repeated her boyfriend's description, patting him on the knee mockingly. "Well, babe, I think you summed it up. I'm going to have to leave you now and run away with this non-construction worker." She put her hand up just as he started to protest. "No, no. You can't stop me. I think I'm in love with him now."

Eric nodded, lips pursed. "I understand. The heart wants what the heart wants."

Nadia and Kira exchanged glances as Eric pulled Kat in closer, tickling her sides and nuzzling further into her neck, ignoring them both, making her giggle wildly.

"I think this is our cue," Nadia said flatly, tilting her head towards the door as their friends went horizontal on the sofa.

Kira smacked at Eric's leg. "Get a room, guys," she teased as she made her way around the coffee table to follow Nadia outside. "I hear the one upstairs and down the hall is fantastic!"

IT WAS EARLY, but the air outside was already balmy. Summers in the south were brutal. Kira's hair felt hot against her neck. She immediately regretted wearing it down. She wanted to go back inside and retrieve the hair tie she'd slung across the room, but who knew what state of dress Eric and Kat would be in by now. No, she would suffer through the heat.

Nadia slinked her arm into Kira's. "Thank you for helping me get this done today. Finally, it's my last paper. How about you? What do you have left?"

Kira shook her head. "Nothing. I'm all done," she said matter-of-factly.

Nadia jumped in excitement, her hands gripping on to her arm. "Oh! You had your ballet jury? How was it?"

Kira immediately felt a knot form in her throat. She nodded stiffly as she tried to swallow it back down. "Good. It was good." It was all she could manage.

The fingers of her free hand splayed, trying to shake off the feeling. Or, in this case, the missing feeling she had worked so hard to revive since yesterday. She wasn't looking directly at Nadia, but she could sense her smile.

"Yay! That's awesome! And your fouetté turns?"

Kira looked directly at Nadia this time. This was her friend. Her true friend. Nadia wasn't a dance major and knew next to nothing about ballet, yet she clearly remembered how hard she'd been working on this specific movement. She cared enough to listen. To truly listen. *She deserves more than a brush off.* "I nailed it."

Nadia reached up and gave Kira an enthusiastic high five. "Yeah, you did!"

Kira laughed. She could feel that Nadia's excitement was genuine. It was enough to allow her to finally shake off the bad feelings that lingered in her heart.

As they continued their walk to the coffeehouse around the corner, Kira felt her mood ease. This is what she needed. She'd felt the same way earlier at the house. It made her a better version of herself when she was with them. It helped keep the bad feelings at bay. *Why do I push them away? Why do I shut them out?* Kira glanced at her friend. *Because they will think you are a crazy person if you tell them an invisible man holds your hand while he helps you dance.* Yep. There was no way she could share that bit of information. *Padded cell for one, please.*

As much as she loved her friends and as much as she knew they loved her, this was something she needed to keep to herself. Kat and Nadia were amazing. She was lucky to have them. She'd known them both since high school.

Kira and Kat had clicked instantaneously, but her friendship with Nadia was a completely different animal. They met her junior year in AP chemistry. Kira was late on the first day. When she arrived, all the seats had been taken, except for two. One was free at Amber Brooks' table. Amber may have been beautiful, but she was also bitchy, judgmental, and slightly stupid. Kira was surprised to even see her in an AP class.

The other free seat belonged at Nadia's table. Kira knew very little about Nadia, only that she had jet black hair, wore tattered black tights under black shorts and combat boots. Plus, she had multiple piercings and clearly liked to layer on the eyeliner. Sure, other students called her a witch but what were the chances that the school accidentally placed *two* stupid people in an AP chemistry class? Witch or not, she wanted to pass the class.

Her judge of character had paid off. At the teacher's instruction, students at the same tables were automatically lab partners for the year. And fortunately for Kira, Nadia was incredibly brilliant. They formed a quiet friendship, often extending invites for Nadia to join her and other friends, but she rarely ever accepted. Nadia was a loner. It wasn't until their senior year that she showed any desire to socialize. It was also when she slowly changed her outer appearance, seemingly conforming to what others deemed appropriate. It had somewhat saddened Kira, but she never said it out loud.

The changes were modest at first, but by the time she showed up at Tulane their freshman year, she had physically morphed into a new person entirely. Kira smiled at her friend, her pretty, dainty friend with an enormous spirit and sweeter soul. That fact had just become abundantly clear in the moment they just shared. Kira felt slightly guilty at the realization of how she'd forgotten. Same Nadia on the inside but wrapped up in a very "Amber Brooks" exterior.

Kira's silent walk down memory lane was suddenly interrupted when Nadia grasped her arm, stopping her from making the turn through the courtyard. It was the route she always took when walking to their local coffeehouse.

"What the . . . where?" she gestured to the path that was now in her wake.

"No, we need to go this way," Nadia insisted.

Kira glanced back. "The courtyard is faster. And dude, it's hot as Hades."

Nadia was hesitant, clearly trying to find the right words: "Yes, but . . . but I need the exercise. Bikini season, *hello*."

She arched an eyebrow and glared down at Nadia's body. "I think you're safe. Does your body even know what a carb is?" Kira chided, still following along before it suddenly dawned on her. "Oh, you little liar! You are so busted!"

"What?" A tight-lipped smile tugged at the corner of Nadia's lips.

Kira nodded her head. Even though she was hot, she was even more amused. "Eric was right. You are a big fat stalker."

Her smirk widened. "Skinny stalker. Skinny stalker with good boobs. And don't tell Eric."

Kira erupted with laughter. "Deal, but you are buying."

A few minutes later, as they rounded the corner, the Calloway property came into view. Nadia gripped onto Kira's arm in excitement, stretching her neck to catch sight of the mystery man. The house was across the street from where they stood. They took a few measured steps before pausing under the shade of a massive oak tree, an aged stone wall at their backs. Kira took in the sight. Something heavy pressed into her heart. She reached a hand back against the wall for support.

She had driven past this place many times, remembering it as dark and dilapidated. The roof was sagging, and the windows broken and boarded. The massive trees and foliage around the house were overgrown and ominous. What stood in front of her now was far beyond what her memory had served her.

The house loomed over the property. It was easily six, maybe seven acres, which was significant in this neighborhood. It was a massive two-story house with large Doric columns that stood tall and framed the grand covered veranda that wrapped the entire home on both levels. In true antebellum style, the grounds featured an alley of large moss-covered oak trees leading up the center drive. There were eight, with four on each side of the path. The entire home was surrounded by a low masonry wall that featured manicured hedges and flora. Sturdy stone columns gated and flanked the entrance.

It was a breathtaking sight.

She glanced down at her hand hanging limply at her side, confused by the unease and her unwillingness to let it go. She looked back to the large estate. It seemed to hang over her as if it would swallow her whole. Both mesmerized and anxious, she curled her fingers gently into her palm. This house made her feel the same way he had.

Kira felt something as she stood there, instinctively flexing her hand, only to roll her eyes at the mindless movement. *What is wrong with you? He isn't here. He never was.* She wrenched her hand again. *Damn it.*

"It's insane that it's the same house."

Nadia's voice grounded Kira back to reality and closed her sagging jaw. "Yeah. It's . . . it's something alright."

"Look! Construction dudes, gardeners, and movers. Sure, they're okay, but none of these guys have anything on the hottie I saw," she said emphatically, taking Kira by the arm to continue to the coffeehouse.

Kira followed along, her friend practically dragging her away. She didn't say anything, but her eyes remained fixed on the house, her neck craned uncomfortably in its direction until it faded from view.

The coffeehouse was just around the corner, across the street from the courtyard. She frequented this place several times a week, but always cut through the courtyard. Always. She hadn't walked past the large estate in months. She was still in awe of its transformation as they entered through the doors. Nadia headed straight to the counter to grab an iced coffee and a frappuccino.

Not focused on anything around her, Kira immediately waved at her friend, Jade, standing behind the counter. She paused to take in the scent of coffee grounds and baked goods before walking over to a little corner where two free chairs sat, plush and inviting, in front of the fireplace. There was no fire. Instead, the firebox housed a small fan with orange and red ribbons tied to the face. The ribbons blew wildly as the fan oscillated back and forth. Kira leaned back in her chair, eyes closed, enjoying the breeze and the escape from the outside heat.

She was comfortable, relaxed. Her mind was blank. The sounds of the ribbons rustling together soothed her. The breeze was gentle, a whisper on her face. She soaked in the moment. And then, there he was. She felt him stroke a finger across her palm. The corners of

45

her mouth tipped up slightly. *I'm losing it, but I don't think I even care anymore.*

The peace he brought with his touch was vivid and electric. It was a raging fire amid a velvet black sky lit with stars. She would willingly live in this feeling forever if she could.

The feel of Nadia's hand on her own sent a small wave of irritation through her, but she kept that feeling in check. "What?" she asked, keeping her eyes closed.

"O—M—G! Don't look now . . . seriously, don't look. Just act casual."

She notched an eyebrow, her eyes still closed. "Who am I *not* looking at?" She could hear the excitement and nerves in Nadia's voice. "Hmm . . . is it possibly the non-construction worker?"

"Yes," Nadia half whispered, half squeaked. "It's him and his very non-construction worker friends. Holy hell. I can't blame Eric for wanting to come out of the closet."

Kira giggled. "Can I look now?"

"Um. No. Maybe. Okay. Just be super casual."

Kira slowly opened her eyes, nonchalantly looking up, and immediately locked onto shades of blue staring back at her with a depth she couldn't fathom. Her mouth went dry and her breath hitched as all the oxygen in the room seemed to evaporate. Even from across the room she could see swirls of sapphire and cerulean mixed with flecks of silver. She could feel a warmth radiating in the pit of her stomach, spreading low between her thighs. Her hand lit up. It was on fire. She gripped it with her other hand, holding it close to her chest, but never shifted her gaze away from him. The sensation was almost painful, but it eased quickly, radiating into a dull ache before fading back into gentle strokes.

"Okay, you suck at casual. Geez," Nadia scolded, pulling at her wrist to get her attention.

46

Kira broke eye contact and looked back at her friend, a failed attempt to shake it off, still rubbing at her hand. "Which one?" It seemed like the right question. *She did say there was more than one, didn't she*? She'd only seen the one; his form still burned into her vision. She was scared to look back, fearful he was looking deep inside her soul. *Inside me?*

She took a moment to comb through the thought, pressing her palm to her chest. It pulsed lovingly as if it were giving her the answer. She looked back across the room, not truly hearing the words Nadia spoke.

His eyes were steady and sure as he continued to stare her down. A million unspoken words danced between them. She could feel all of it. He cocked one eyebrow and smiled as he stood from the table. Familiarity slammed into her. She knew that smile. His eyes never left hers as he and his friends walked across the room, exiting the front doors of the shop.

Kira blinked wildly as her eyes readjusted to the reality around her. *That's him.* Suddenly, multiple fragments of her memory flooded her mind: the parking lot, the dream, the ballet exam. He was there for all of it. *He's real.* "Ow!" Kira whimpered at the light punch in her arm.

"What is wrong with you? I said, be casual. That was *so* not casual," Nadia continued to scold.

Kira looked back at her incredulously. "I'm sorry. I don't." Words were not going to explain this. She glanced back over her shoulder at the entrance. He was gone, but the feelings he stirred deep within her lingered. She sank back into her chair, releasing an audible breath.

"Seriously, though," Nadia agreed. "I told you. Sex on a stick."

Kira continued to hold her hand against her chest, but that gentle stroke was gone. She'd been so encapsulated in his eyes that it was hard to remember the expression on his face as she attempted to replay the scene in her head. At first glance she thought he'd looked confused, startled even. His eyes were narrowed, and brows tugged in. Several long seconds had passed between them before his face twisted into something else. She searched the corners of her mind, recalling how his nostrils flared and how his lips tightened in a straight line. *Anger? Why would he be angry with me? He doesn't even know me.*

That expression hadn't lasted long before it softened into something else entirely. This time her heart, not her hand, lit up as she envisioned the cocky smile he flashed her. He had expressed so much to her in that brief encounter. They both seemingly had just run through a gamut of emotions. Kira glanced down, her fingers still firmly held to her chest, and exhaled as the realization hit her. *I felt everything he felt. It was like we were connected.*

"I'm kind of digging the Native American guy with the long hair," Nadia mused. "Although, his hair is better than mine. I don't know if I could date a guy who's prettier than me."

"Are you guys talking about Armand?" Jade asked as she slid onto the arm of Nadia's chair.

"You know them?" Nadia exclaimed, nearly choking on her iced coffee, slapping Jade on the arm in a playful motion. "You've been holding out!"

"No. He's actually very sweet. A big flirt, but sweet. He and his friends have been coming in fairly regularly over the past few weeks. Apparently, one of them owns the old Calloway Estate around the corner," Jade informed.

"Yes, we know that much. We walked past it on the way over here. It looks amazing," Nadia said, jokingly rubbing her thumb and forefinger together. "Somebody has some major dollar bills y'all!"

Kira sat silently, listening to her friends gossip and presume the nature of their mysterious new neighbors. She tried to keep her face neutral by laughing and nodding at all the right moments as they reveled in their good-natured light fun. She, though, was still reveling in the gaze that had set her body on fire. The source of that flame was gone, but the embers continued to burn.

"I don't know much about them. Armand is always the one that orders and pays. We've been engaging in some light flirtation," Jade announced, a smile brightening across her face. "I'm expecting a proposal any day now."

"Okay, point taken. Armand is off-limits. What do you know about the others?" Nadia asked, propping her chin on her hand, leaning in, excited to get all the details.

"Vincent is the black guy. He seems really quiet," Jade said with a grin. "Yeah, he's definitely the strong and sexy silent type."

Nadia's shoulders animatedly danced up and down. "Oh yeah! I like a man of few words."

"That's because you never shut up," Kira teased, laughing as she dodged a swipe from her friend.

"Larz, the really muscular guy with the wavy blondish brown hair is basically the total opposite. He talks a lot, but you won't hear me complaining. He has the sexiest British accent." Jade swooned ever so slightly. "And then the other guy, the tall dark haired one, has these insanely gorgeous blue eyes."

A little flutter danced inside her stomach at the mention of him. "Do you know anything else about him?"

Jade nodded. "Yeah, his name is Blake. He paid once and I saw his driver's license in his wallet. He's from Massachusetts," she added matter-of-factly.

"Wow, you're like a little hot guy encyclopedia. I'm gonna have to put you in my back pocket and go man-hunting," Nadia joked, elbowing Jade playfully.

Kira relaxed further into her seat, only half listening to her friends as they continued to discuss their beautiful new neighbors. The hushed sounds of the fan and the memory of that impossible touch lulled her into a state of contentment she hadn't felt in months. She inwardly groaned at the buzz of her phone ringing in her bag before scrambling for it. *Colin.*

She allowed it to ring two more times before silencing him to voicemail. That conversation would take her to a place she had no interest in visiting at the moment.

Kira wanted to stay here and linger in those shades of blue.

FIVE

INITIATION

His muscles were tense, his body rigid. He felt Larz's eyes on him. "Say it," Blake managed through gritted teeth, his elbows on his knees, and his hands steepled in front of his face.

Larz, always a picture of calm and relaxed indifference, said nothing, only offering a shrug of his shoulders.

Blake's eyes glanced up beneath stressed brows. His brother's lack of words didn't surprise him, but he needed to hear something. Anything. He waited as anxiety vibrated through him. It was a foreign sensation. He was methodical, practicing restraint and precision in everything he did. He wanted to have control over every encounter with the *Supra Virtutem*. But then there she was, staring back at him from across the room. His guard was down.

His guard was never down.

"You should really work harder if you want to hide those thoughts, brother," Larz finally managed, pushing himself off the wall he'd been resting against.

Blake immediately re-built the barrier around his mind. Brick by brick, he shoved Larz out. He wanted his brother's advice, but he didn't want him foraging through his thoughts either, especially not now. He eyed Larz with caution, curious as to how much he'd already uncovered.

"That's better." Larz dropped into a chair across from him, propping his ankle across a knee. "She blindsided us all."

Blake remained quiet. He needed to monitor his words.

Larz let out a laugh, working hard to break the tension. "But man, I felt her. Bloody hell!" He paused, taking a moment to find the right words as he ran a hand through his hair. "Man, you were right. She's the one. Her power screamed at me. I'm surprised I didn't feel her walking down the fucking block."

Blake felt an odd twinge of ire reel through him. *Jealousy?* It wasn't a sensation he was familiar with, realizing he didn't like the idea that anyone felt anything she put off. He glared across the space at his closest friend, making a mental check that the walls around his thoughts remained firmly in place. He shook his head slowly, and lowered his gaze to the floor, afraid that direct eye contact would give away all his secrets. "It's prodigious."

"So, what do we do now?"

Blake took in a deep breath before standing tall, pushing any and all thoughts of Kira and her power into the far depths of his mind. "It's time to finalize Vincent's initiation and his place within the Brethren. We do it tonight."

They had spent years searching the world for the *Supra Virtutem*, a witch born with a vast reserve of natural power.

That search had now ended. The three eldest of the Brethren had taken all the necessary steps in order to harness their own power and absorb this newfound source. Now it was time to bring their newest brother, Vincent, into the fold. It was vital. They needed a fourth to call upon the four corners and to be able to enact The Order of Three.

Blake stepped out onto the veranda alongside Larz, where Armand and Vincent were draped across loungers, beers in hand.

"It's time," he announced as he walked past them, his face resolute and lips pressed into a hard line. He wrenched his fists at his sides in an attempt to stave off some of the adrenaline that coursed throughout his veins.

His brothers said nothing, immediately following him across the lawn and through the gardens toward the center of the property. The estate's outer edges, save from the front portion, were surrounded by a tall stone wall to ensure total privacy. The walls were aged, brittle, and mostly overgrown with creeping fig. Massive oak trees and cypress further bolstered the walls with attempts at seclusion.

He squinted against the sun as he made his way across the property. It was a beautiful sight with carefully tended gardens of white roses, camellias, and anemones. Rows of perfectly manicured boxwood hedges lined various flagstone paths waiting to be explored amongst the grounds. Antique stone fountains served as elaborate centerpieces throughout. Larz had fashioned it from the gardens at Mapperton Manor in Dorset. He and Larz both had fond memories of their time there before they journeyed back to the U.S. together.

Blake slighted his chin, glancing over his shoulder as he passed underneath a long arbor tunnel cloaked in wisteria and clematis. The brief shade was welcome in the New Orleans heat. His brothers continued to follow but still said nothing.

He wondered to himself if Vincent was nervous. He was still so young. He had also never taken a human life. It would change him.

Death changes you. It awakens something deep within that most strive to keep hidden. Blake had discovered that a very long time ago. Today, he thrived on that once dormant part of himself. It was that same part that was now creating the conflict in his mind. He wondered if it was because of her?

Walls up. Larz sent him a silent reminder.

Fuck. Blake visibly flinched. Immediately, he shoved the thought down, boarding up the walls in his mind once more, but he could still feel Larz's eyes on the back of his head.

Once the four had exited the shaded tunnel, they found themselves at the center of the grounds, where a lengthy rectangular pond separated the front portion of the home and gardens from the back section of the property. It was narrow and glistened a greenish-blue hue and was dotted in flowered lilies. Beyond it stood a newer version of the stone wall, cutting a line through the estate grounds, secluding nearly one third of the property behind it. The new wall was built in the same old style as the outer edges, but the rocks were not as weathered, nor did it have the same invasive foliage that had taken over the older portions of the wall. Instead, tall Italian cypress trees lined the length, flanking two gated entrances, one at each end of the pond.

The gates were made of iron, narrow, but ornately designed. At a glance, the elaborate bends and spirals of metal seemed insignificant. But for someone like Blake and his brothers, they knew the intricate patterns were highly powerful runes. The shapes that took form across the gates were a binding spell. It was a form of magic that bound people from entering and, when necessary, bound them from escaping.

Without pause, Blake held out a firm arm, palm towards the gates. *"Ingress."* It opened at his command, allowing the four to pass, before closing behind them.

The world behind the gates, behind the stone wall, was vastly different from the lush and manicured gardens. The grounds in which the house rested and where guests were free to roam were vivid signs of a modern world reviving what was once old and worn. A piece of history brought back to life. But behind the gates, was a whole other world, one forgotten by time. It was older than the plantation house, the gardens, or the aged stone walls that surrounded the property. The only living thing here that knew this place's true age were the seven-hundred-year-old oak trees whose moss-covered branches hung low and heavy, stretching across the grounds. They stood tall and unyielding, canopying the area from the outside, as watchful, and vigilant protectors of something as old as they were.

Less than two acres, this area, protected by the four stone walls, was much smaller than the other part of the estate, but it was breathtakingly beautiful. Beneath the stately oaks, wood ferns and moss blanketed the ground, creating a majestic panorama of emerald green. But it wasn't the trees nor the stunning hues of the foliage that made this place sing to life; it was the ancient ruins they attempted to veil.

In the center of all the beauty, surrounded by nature and an eerie quiet, stood the remains of a grand stone staircase. Open arches supported it, where one could pass beneath and wrapped into a curve as it ascended into the air. The structure itself appeared sound, but its age was shown in the moss patches that covered the steps and the ivy vines that weaved and clung to the stone arches. But even more intriguing than the stairs themselves was where they led.

Nowhere.

A staircase this impressive and built so strong would have had to lead to a commensurate building or home. But where this phantom structure stood, there was nothing. Not a single stone suggested something was once there. No ruins. No foundation. Not one lone stone.

Blake and the others made their way directly to the base of the stairs. Larz opened a large trunk hidden underneath one of the archways. Inside were nothing more than simple white linen pants. Larz tossed a pair to each of his brothers, already peeling off their own clothing and kicking off their shoes. The ritual required purity and outside contaminants could never be risked.

"Do you know what needs to be done?" Blake asked, tying the strings of the pants that now fell at the base of the rigid V-shape that formed along his abdomen, his eyes watching and waiting.

Vincent took a moment to answer, taking a steadying breath before nodding, his face stoic and certain.

"We can't help you," Larz added, tying back his hair. "You must do it on your own. Entirely on your own."

"Her magic isn't strong, so you shouldn't worry," Armand laughed, slapping a hand on Vincent's shoulder as a reassuring gesture. "She's definitely no, *Supra Virtutem*!"

Blake felt himself flinch and locked eyes with Larz. His mental guards were all intact, but he knew Larz could read his face no matter how many walls he built around his thoughts.

But Armand's joke landed perfectly. Vincent visibly relaxed and nodded as he took the first step up the stairs, leading the way for his brothers to follow. They appeared as four torturously beautiful men, shirtless and soberly climbing their way to their impending deaths.

They marched on at a steady pace. Four steps. Three steps. Two steps. Vincent took a steadying breath. One step. He reached the final stair, and with no hesitation, eyes wide, he took another perilous step into the open air. One by one, they each vanished with a single step onto a vacuous cloud.

Gone.

No. Not really gone. More like, somewhere new. Unseen.

Vincent stood, his feet firmly planted to the stone floor beneath him. He waited as his brothers came into view one by one. Behind them, the faint glow of the sun penetrated the portal they had just passed through, casting a sheen across the haziness. You could still see the outside landscape, the stairs, and the trees, but they were distorted as if you were viewing them through the lens of a water-filled glass.

"Are you ready?" Blake asked, looking toward the door leading inside the cistern.

"Absolutely," Vincent answered, eagerness in his voice as he strode towards the door. Surviving a leap with nothing but thirty feet of air and hard ground beneath you has a way of invoking confidence.

The wood groaned loudly against the hinges as the doors opened. Sunlight poured in from above through a massive circular hole cut into the roof. Vines from centuries of overgrowth hung down in tendrils while others wrapped around the opening and clung to the tall domed ceiling, sprawling out in all directions, like roots searching for water. The four men stepped out onto a small balcony. Ten feet below, rested a large circular pool around eight feet in diameter, slightly larger than the roof's opening directly above. The water was clean and clear, save from debris from the foliage, but its inky dark color suggested that this hidden reservoir was deep.

The room was small. It was amassed completely of sandy-hued stones that were polished smooth and felt cool beneath their bare feet. The balcony was flanked by two staircases that wrapped down to the sides of the pool below. In front of it sat a large carved stone slab marred with dark stains. The temperature was easily fifteen degrees lower than the outside, and the scent of a recent rain hung in the air.

Blake gripped the edges of the balcony railing and looked down upon this incongruous edifice. It was quiet. He could hear his own breathing. He could hear *her* breathing. In the far-right corner, less than eight feet from the base of the stairs, he saw the young witch.

Her legs were curled in tight against her body. The threadbare shift they gave her was smudged with dirt from the floor. She stared back at him with an attempt to exhibit rage, but Blake saw it. It was in her body language. In the depths of her eyes and in the rapid sound of her heart beating. *She's terrified.*

Blake gave his brother an indicative nod and remained up top in the center of the balcony. Larz and Vincent took the right staircase down towards the witch they had captured only one day before. Armand mirrored them on the left staircase.

The witch saw them and quickly got to her feet. Her arm bent weakly, palm out towards Vincent, she cried out: "*Subsisto!*"

"*Averto,*" Vincent swatted his hand, deflecting her incantation before she could even choke out the last syllable. He was on her now, their faces only inches from one another.

Her eyes were wide as she looked up at him, remaining silent. She only sobbed as she shook her head in defiance, a pleading last attempt to avoid what she knew was coming. She backed away slowly. Vincent followed.

The witch stopped at the feel of something low and hard against the back of her legs. The stone slab. Gripping her hands against it for support, she risked a look back, knowing what those stains were.

Blood

"*Requiem.*" His voice was soothing and melodic.

The fear inside her did not dissipate, but her body relaxed. She was unable to run. Unable to protest. A prisoner in her own form. For a mere moment, her breath hitched in sweet relief as Vincent turned and walked away. Blake continued to watch. He saw confusion settle upon her face as she watched Vincent kneel at the pool, stretching a hand into the dark water. Her eyes rested squarely on his, fear bubbling back up inside of her at an alarming rate. Knowing not to look, knowing what was coming. She closed her eyes.

Vincent stood, his hand lifted from the water, a blade now in his fist. He stood in silence for several seconds. From above, Blake wondered if he was relishing the moment and committing it to memory. He watched him closely, listening for the beat of his heart. It was strong but composed.

Without a sound, Vincent took several slow but unwavering steps toward the witch, the blade hanging down at the side of his body. He stopped at an arm's length away as he continued to wait and watch.

Blake looked to Larz and then to Armand, who both remained at the base of the stairs on each side, before turning his attention back to Vincent. Over his brother's shoulder, he could see the witch's face. Her eyes remained closed; her lips moved ever so slightly but made no sound. If possible, the room seemed to grow even quieter. His eyes narrowed as he tried to comprehend the movement of her lips. *Is she praying?*

Understanding finally dawned upon him. Vincent wasn't savoring the moment. He was gifting this tiny witch with a few more seconds of life. He was granting her the opportunity to find clarity and peace.

Blake looked on as the witch's lips finally came to a halt. She took a deep breath and imperceptibly inclined her head. Within a second, Vincent's right arm stretched across the small space between them, dragging the blade across the delicate curve of her throat.

Blood sprayed.

Vincent lowered his arm, liquid, warm and red, dripped from the knife and his body. He watched silently as the witch fell backward onto the stone slab. She was alive for a few final seconds, but she felt no pain. He saw to that. Her eyes opened one last time to meet his before he witnessed the light within them fade. Blood continued to pour from her neck, further staining the stone with her death.

He placed the blade on the slab beside her before lifting her into his arms. He carried her to the pool and gingerly released her. She floated on the water for a few seconds, her hair drifting like a golden crown around her head as he recited an incantation: "*Omnes the invocamus . . . di immortatales inteerr omnes tee inveocamus. Omnes te invocamus.*" He bowed his head as she slipped below the surface. "My gift to you, Khalida."

It was done.

SIX

MIA

Kira stared up at the ceiling, her face blank as she lounged across her bed. Her mind raced as she mindlessly rubbed her thumb across her palm. Her thoughts weaved a twisty trail between images. She saw his beautiful face with those pools of blue and the cocky arch of his brow. She remembered the fiery sensation that pulsed in her hand, thinking back to her dreams and the words he'd spoken.

She glanced at her clock, scowling at the realization that she'd been agonizing over this all afternoon. She searched through all her thoughts, her memories, her visions but failed to hold onto anything concrete. Her mind ran amuck, unable to focus. She squeezed her eyes closed in frustration and slammed a fist into the bed.

"What is wrong with you?" she muttered to herself, her eyes back to the ceiling, silently willing it to write out the answers she needed across the blank white space. The answers didn't appear, but a few deep breaths did make way for a brief moment of clarity.

Kira jumped up and reached for her journal tucked away beneath a pillow on the window seat, quickly scanning through it.

She searched for details and pieces that would hopefully help her form the larger puzzle. The pages flashed before her eyes as quickly as the images of him appeared in her mind. She huffed and tossed it to the floor. A beautiful stranger who magically makes her hand tingle had suddenly stricken her with a case of attention deficit disorder.

Taking another breath, she closed her eyes, and attempted to block out everything, focusing only on that night. Over and over, she played it through her mind. Outside. In the parking lot. Dark.

Are you okay?

She could hear him now. See him now. His face was beautiful. His eyes cut through her. She felt him deep down in her core. Deep within her bones. Not wanting to let the images distract her, she pushed them back in her mind, and focused on his voice.

You clearly want to stay out here and talk to me.

Did I? She couldn't remember and concentrated harder, directing all of her attention to that moment. The smell of sandalwood and citrus filled her nostrils. She wasn't sure if she could truly smell it or if she simply recalled the memory of his scent.

It felt real.

Kira pulled back the edges of her mind a little further. It was all there. She watched him lean in ever so slightly and then felt the caress of a single finger across her palm. The sensation ripped her from her stupor. Her eyes opened to inspect her hand, feeling him now. It wasn't in her memory. It was here with her now in the present. It was a light tingle, the faintest of touches, but it seared her.

Kira smiled. She felt absolutely insane, but she smiled.

Closing her eyes again, she centered her attention back on his voice.

You're afraid . . . don't be.

Her brows twisted as she tried to recall her own emotions at that moment. It was muddled, but she had a distinct feeling that there was something important in those memories. Something important in those words.

You are not yet ready . . . it's okay, though. You will be. Soon.

She looked down at her palm again. He was gone now. She craned her head, not looking at anything in particular as her eyes skimmed the room, hoping answers would suddenly materialize out of thin air.

They didn't. Nevertheless, she was happy.

She had finally been able to center herself enough to play through the events of that night fully. She hadn't been able to completely delve into her own thoughts, but her memory of him was suddenly becoming crystal clear. He was no longer a hazy set of blue eyes floating in the corners of her mind.

He was real.

She had started to feel like he wasn't. That he was only a dream brought to life by an overactive imagination and an incredible lack of sleep. But then there he was, sitting in her favorite coffeehouse. Those blue eyes that stared back at her were indeed attached to the face of a living, breathing man.

Kira silently questioned herself; *Yes, Nadia and Jade were there. Definitely yes.* She nodded to herself definitively as if her body needed to convince her brain. She eyed the journal at her feet for several seconds before scooping it up. *Just in case.*

She proceeded to write it all down, carefully noting all the details that she was finally able to uncover. She was almost done when she heard her phone chime.

It was a text from Colin: *Just wanted to give you a heads up that I'll be there in about half an hour. I Love you.*

A tidal wave of guilt pulled her out to sea leaving her to drown in her shame. She had forgotten about her date with Colin. "Crap!"

She tossed the phone on to the bed and tucked her journal out of sight, before running to her closet and rummaging through the items hanging before her. She clamped a hand across her forehead, uncertainty, and reluctance settling in the pit of her stomach. Bouncing on her toes, Kira tried to shake off this new feeling of discontent.

It was emotional whiplash. She was happy just moments before. It was a happiness so light she felt like she was floating. But Colin was her gravity, a weight that brought her crashing back to earth, back to reality. The sudden thought turned her annoyance to sadness. Where sadness lives, guilt creeps in.

Her phone chimed again. Another text. *I really love that little pink dress with the skinny straps.*

She clamped the phone tightly in her hands, closed her eyes, and released a deep breath.

Minutes later, she stood in her mirror, adjusting the straps of the dress, remembering when she'd bought it two years ago to celebrate their first week at Tulane together. She'd worn it several times since then. It was his favorite. Kira pulled her hair up into a messy bun, and then turned to check the time. She made quick work of her makeup, applying a generous layer of mascara, and dusting a light shimmer of blush across her cheeks. She was looking through the makeup tray in front of her to find a complimentary shade of lip gloss when she heard Colin's voice downstairs.

Kira paused to take a long moment to stare herself down in the mirror, silently coaxing herself into girlfriend mode. She applied the lip gloss to finish off the look, and then gave a self-assured nod to the mirror.

"Hey, babe."

She turned to see Colin easing through the door, a bouquet of blush-toned peonies wrapped in kraft paper in his hand. She flashed a well-practiced smile. "Hey, you." She crossed the room, planting a kiss on his cheek before taking the flowers. "My favorites. Thank you."

"I remember," returning her greeting with a kiss on her forehead. "And that's my favorite dress," he mused, pulling her a little closer, wrapping an arm tight around her waist. "Thank you for wearing it."

Her hand burned. She squeezed it tight. "I should get these in water." She pushed away from Colin's hold, quickly heading towards the door. "Where are we going?"

If he'd noticed her discomfort, he didn't show it. "Wherever you want. It's your special night," he said, following her down the stairs.

"Kat, do you mind putting these into a vase for me?" Kira asked, handing the flowers over to her friend before turning back to Colin with a frown. "My special night?"

Colin tilted his head as a bark of laughter escaped him. "Yeah. You aced your exam. I know you were worried about it."

There he was again. The Colin she'd fell for in high school. The one who taught her how to drive a stick shift. The one who took her to prom. The one who gave up his dream school to stay close to her. The one who remembered she hated roses and loved peonies.

She smiled, nodding her head. "I was."

He was also the one who listened to everything she told him. The pit in her stomach called out to her. She knew deep down she wasn't doing the same for him.

———

Colin raised a questionable brow. "Are you sure this is where you want to go?"

Kira pursed her lips, nodding as she took in the scene. "Yeah, even though we might be a little overdressed." The pub down the street from her house was a former fave. It was a small dive with cheap beer, pool tables, and the best-fried food. She looked back to him, leaning in with a veritable smile on her face. "But I love the cheese fries here."

"Really . . . cheese fries? Let's not get too crazy now."

It felt good. It felt familiar. There'd been laughter and flirtation. They talked about future plans, including the internship he wanted to take for his junior year and if they should plan a trip over the summer.

They hadn't spent any time together since the night he came over to apologize. That night hadn't yet been settled entirely. She kind of allowed herself to sweep it under the rug, to tuck it away somewhere unknown and forgotten. She wasn't sure if she did it because she decided to forgive him and move on, or if she was too emotionally unavailable to deal with it. Maybe it was a little of both.

"Hi, guys," the bubbly blonde chirped, tray and notepad in hand. "What can I get you?"

"Ice water. I'm so thirsty," Kira answered, looking up at the server, fanning herself with her hand.

The walk over had been nice, but it was still hot as Hades outside. Her smile faded slightly. Her lips twitched, and her eyes narrowed a bit as she noticed the look on the girl's face as she eyed Colin.

Leaning in a little closer, she asked, her smile growing a little brighter as he looked up at her. "And you?"

"I'll have a Corona," Colin replied, barely giving the girl a full glance before looking back to Kira. "No. Um . . . I'll do water as well."

Kira shook her head, reaching out across the table to place a hand on his forearm. "Babe, it's okay." She watched his face tilt in question. "Seriously. I don't mind. Promise."

She meant it. A beer didn't scare her. Two beers didn't scare her. It was when one or two quickly escalated into five or six; that was what upset her. And unfortunately, that habit had been gaining ground over the past couple of months. Worse, she was afraid to ask him about it. Afraid because deep down, she felt that it was her fault.

Colin had never been a big drinker before. To her knowledge, nothing major had changed in his life to cause such a shift. Then again, she had been emotionally and often times physically absent over the past several months. Kira had always thought it was her that was creating the problem, but now wondered if she was missing something important in his life.

For a moment, her mind drifted back to how she had spent her day. Lying in her room, desperately seeking out answers about a mystery man she spent a grand total of five minutes with. A man who had taken all her time and attention over the past week and had just recently caused her to forget about the date she was currently on. *I forgot about him. I'm such a bitch.*

"You're sure?" he asked, waiting to get that one last nod of approval before glancing back to the server. "I'll take the Corona and two orders of cheese fries."

Kira bit back a laugh as the server sauntered away. "That girl was totally flirting with you," she mocked him with a disapproving look.

He feigned ignorance. "I have no idea what you are talking about. I was only looking at you."

She smiled back. Colin wasn't lying. He did barely glance at her. It had been that way forever, even after being together for over three years. He only ever seemed to have eyes for her. Another pang of guilt. She quickly pushed that feeling aside.

The server was as swift as she was eager. The girl's scant regard struck Kira as she continued to eye him, leaning in close across his shoulder in her attempt to place their drinks on the table. It was an audacious move. It was also a clumsy one.

Kira's ice water immediately tumbled into her lap. She jumped up, ice and water splashing to the ground. "Awe! Damn it, that's cold!"

Colin jumped up and fumbled around, clearly not knowing what to say or do. There were no towels or napkins in sight.

"I'm so sorry! I'll go get some napkins," the girl exclaimed, clearly embarrassed.

Kira shot her a look but thought better of it and nodded. "Thank you." She waited for her to disappear before looking at Colin, who was trying not to laugh. "Really?"

"I'm sorry." He was still choking back his laughter. "You okay?"

"This is your fault. Maybe if she'd been watching what she was doing instead of pushing her boobs in your face, I wouldn't be soaked right now."

"She had boobs?" Colin joked as if his interest was suddenly piqued, looking back to find her.

"Oh, shut up!" Kira smacked playfully at his arm as she walked away. "I'll be right back."

She made her way to the ladies' room, cursing under her breath as she passed the server who was frantically searching for a towel behind the bar. Kira frowned once she caught sight of herself in the bathroom mirror; her dress was soaked from her chest down to the hemline. She blotted at it with paper towels. It wasn't working.

"Damn it." She blew out a deep breath, glancing around the bathroom for a solution. Her brow arched at the hand dryer on the wall. "Hmm . . . well, there's a first time for everything," she mumbled and pulled the wet dress over her head.

Kira stood for ten minutes in nothing more than her bra, panties, and sandals in the small two-stall bathroom while attempting to dry out the dress. Fortunately for her, only one other patron walked in on the scandalous scene. Even more so, the girl took the incident in jest, laughing with her over its ridiculousness.

Her dress was still slightly damp, but dry enough to shimmy back into comfortably. On her way back to the table, she stopped by the bar to grab another water. She was still horribly thirsty and wasn't sure she trusted the server at this point. At the moment she placed her order, she caught sight of something. Someone.

Her head and mind did a double take as her heart leaped into her throat. *It's him.*

He was leaning against a pillar across the room in a small group of other guys. He seemed to be listening to someone and laughing, but he was clearly looking at her. Directly at her. She squeezed her hand. A new habit. She mentally scolded herself for it.

Three seconds. Five seconds. Ten seconds. His smile was beautiful. Kira kept her face neutral, unsure of how she felt. Not unlike the last time she saw him, she was experiencing a wide range of emotions. Confusion, surprise, happiness, shame. Lust? *That's a new one.*

"Miss?"

Kira turned to the bartender and took the glass, barely able to form a clear "thank you." When she turned back around, he was gone. Her head spun back and forth, scanning the room. He wasn't there.

Looking toward the ground now, bewildered and eyes wide, she wondered if she truly did see him. She looked back to where he'd been. Still gone. *Did I just hallucinate a man I don't even know?*

Kira took a few additional minutes to find some composure. She took a deep breath, pulling her shoulders back and lifting her chin. "You don't need to manifest a man into existence, you have a perfectly good one waiting for you at the table," she muttered to herself before walking around the corner.

She sat back down in her seat, smiling brightly. "All good now."

Colin was mid-swig of his beer when she sat down. "Good! Looks better . . . you okay?"

Kira nodded, happy to see their food was now at the table. "Much better."

She was about to put a fry in her mouth when she noticed it. It took her a few seconds to process it, but it was there. One, two, three bottles. Her eyes darted from bottle to bottle and then back to Colin while he ate. She held her fry in suspended animation, and then dropped it. Her appetite instantly bottomed out.

He was taking another drink before he realized she was watching him. It only took a few seconds for him to register what she was thinking. "It's 'two for one' night."

Her eyes drew together, and the lines across her forehead creased as she shook her head, trying to form a response. "What?" It was all she could say. She could feel her cheeks flushing with anger.

Colin could see it. He lowered his tone in an attempt to soothe her into understanding. "Two for one. She automatically brought two when she brought the drinks over." He was stammering over his words a bit. Not drunk, but seemingly nervous. He waved a hand in her direction. "I don't think you noticed because you jumped up and then left."

Kira's face twisted even further. "Okay," she gestured to the bottles, "but there are three here."

Colin leaned back in his chair, a long leg stretched out in front of him, his third beer still in hand. He opened his mouth and closed it again. He looked at her for a long moment. "I don't want to fight about this."

"I don't want to fight about this either!" Kira was surprised by

70

the sharpness in her own voice. She took a steadying breath and lowered her tone. "There are two empty bottles and a third one in your hand."

He immediately set the bottle to the side. "I'll stop drinking it. It's done."

Kira shook her head, her eyes fixed on the trio of beers, anywhere but on him. "That's not the problem, Colin."

He pulled his leg back into his body, leaning his chest into the table. "Then please tell me what the hell it is," his voice on edge.

Her eyes flared. This wasn't normal for him. She searched his face. He looked different. His eyes seemed empty. She couldn't decipher if it was anger, frustration, or sadness. She only knew it wasn't him. The way his hands gripped the edge of the table made her heart clench. A part of her wanted to reach out to them, but she couldn't bring herself to do it.

He eased back into the chair a little, clearly trying to settle the tension in his body. "The server brought another beer over. She felt bad for spilling a drink on you, and she wanted to give us a drink on the house," he explained. His voice was still tense. He had gone from apologetic to annoyed.

Kira said nothing. She didn't know what to say. He was still the same boy who took her to prom. The boy who remembered her favorite flowers. She brought her eyes back to his, searching for that boy, the one she fell in love with. She couldn't see him. His eyes were cold.

"I was gone for ten minutes, maybe fifteen tops." She again made a weak gesture to the bottles. "In that short time, while I was in the bathroom, you drank almost three beers. Does that not seem like a problem to you?"

Colin swallowed hard. "I ordered water when I got here, Kira." His voice was lower and softer now. He was undoubtedly being cautious with his words. "You said you didn't mind if I drank. I don't understand why you are upset."

Kira could feel the heat in her cheeks again. *How does he not understand?* She fought back the tears that were threatening to spill. She dug deep to find the same soft tone that Colin had just used. It was hard. She was screaming on the inside.

"A drunk driver killed my parents. You were there. You know what that did to me. You saw what I went through. I cried in your arms night after night." She looked at him again. Those tears were desperate to come out. "I'm not upset because of the beers. I'm upset because you had three in a very short span of time. How many would you have had tonight? Would you have even been able to walk home with me? Would I have had to call Kat and Eric to help me get you home again? Do you even remember how many times I've had to do that lately?"

Colin's face was blank. She couldn't decipher what he was feeling or thinking as she spoke. He looked vacant. Kira took another deep breath to gather herself. She wanted to keep her voice calm and steady, but her heart was racing, and her stomach fluttered.

"Mostly, I worry you don't see the problem, that you could be another person who gets behind the wheel and devastates some other family." Her voice cracked slightly. One small tear finally managed to break free. "How many times has Eric taken you home? It was only a week ago that he had to. We had a long talk about it . . . I . . . I," she stumbled through her words as she felt that emotional wave take over the solid wall of calm she was trying so hard to hold on to. "I don't know that I could forgive you if you hurt someone."

Colin looked at her for a long moment. It felt like an eternity passed between them. "What did you expect?" Again, his voice was sharp as he leaned in across the table so that others couldn't hear.

"My girlfriend is MIA . . . all the fucking time." His last few words were clipped and soaked with disdain.

Kira flinched.

"You've been moody and distant for months. You cancel plans. You're late to everything. You forget things. You've gotten to a point where you don't even answer my calls."

He rattled through his list of grievances with an urgency. It was as if they'd been living on his lips forever, and he was finally getting the opportunity to speak them. Her chest tightened. The air was suddenly harder to breathe. He was calling her out, and the hardest part was that he was speaking the truth. She looked away as the onslaught of shame consumed her.

"You constantly make up excuses to not stay with me. We sure as hell don't sleep together anymore. The other night was the first time we were together in weeks." He rubbed his hands across his face as if he were trying to scrub away his current emotions. "Son of a bitch . . . I was crying that night. What the hell was that? A pity-fuck?"

Kira's eyes darted to his, her face incredulous. She blinked rapidly as she searched herself for words, her heart threatening to burst from her chest. In one quick motion, she stood from her seat, grabbed the glass of ice water, and tossed it into Colin's face.

Startled with wide eyes, he stared back at her. He started to speak but appeared to think better of it.

"I'm leaving. Don't you dare follow me." Her words came hard and fast. The anger, disappointment, and hurt were plastered across her face.

Her earlier tears had retreated.

She was too incensed to cry now.

SEVEN
DOES HE FEEL IT TOO

Kira's arms were wrapped tightly around herself, a feeble attempt to soothe her fragile emotions after walking out on Colin. She was angry and hot, but after a few steps outside of the pub, the flames of anger inside her turned into a cold stone in the pit of her stomach. The tears broke free then.

It was dark. The day's heat was finally beginning to subside, making the walk a little more comfortable. Young people and couples alike strolled the sidewalks alongside her, hopping in and out of bars and restaurants. She eyed the couple in front of her holding hands and stealing kisses. It made her stomach clench.

She'd been walking for some time now. Her tears had finally dried up. That cold stone was slowly turning back to that previous flame as anger wedged its way back in. She never expected Colin to speak to her in such a way. He'd always been nothing less than a gentleman. The perfect boyfriend. He was kind, funny, and loyal. He was sensitive and attentive.

The Colin she'd witnessed tonight was cruel and bitter. She

replayed it over and over in her mind as she walked along. His tone, his body language, the words he used. He wanted to hurt her. He wanted her to feel that shame. It wasn't her Colin. He was someone else. Someone she didn't know at all.

Kira dropped her head in her hands. She knew she deserved it on some level. Most of what he'd said was true, but she winced as she thought of those last words. It stung just as hard as her mind replayed it for the hundredth time during the walk home. It was the one thing he said that wasn't true.

She thought about all her lies. They were plentiful. She shook her head at the sidewalk, a physical nudge to remind herself that they were only meant to protect the people she loved. Not hurt anyone. His lie, however, was meant to cut her wide open. "Damn it, Colin. What the hell were you thinking?"

"I hope you are talking to yourself and not to someone I can't see."

She stopped mid step, jumping slightly. Gasping, she clasped her hands to her chest, and barked out a small laugh. It faded into silence as her eyes met his. Her mouth going suddenly dry. She swallowed hard, trying to work past it. What had he said? Her brain was a muddle.

"We've already heard enough haunted house rumors."

What? She couldn't process words. Her body was working overtime to manage other feelings. The angry fire from earlier had transformed into an entirely new type of flame. She remembered it from the coffeehouse. By reflex, she flexed her fingers and squeezed her fist. She didn't feel anything there, but it didn't matter. She was feeling a lot of things in a lot of different places. "Are you following me?" she finally managed, shifting her weight, pressing her thighs together.

The flame burned a little hotter as she watched him arch that cocky brow and push off the stone pillar he'd been casually leaning against.

"Following *you*?" He had a comically incredulous look on his face before gesturing behind him. *"I live here. Looks like *you* are following *me*."*

Her eyes left his, realizing she was standing directly in front of the gate at the Calloway Estate. She looked over her shoulder, retracing her steps in her mind. She hadn't meant to walk there. She turned back to him. The flame emerging inside left her mouth dryer than the desert sand. If her brain ever allowed her to form the words, she wasn't sure her mouth could speak them.

He smiled a wolfish grin. It was sinful. "I bid you my apologies as it seems I have forgotten my manners. I'm Blake Michaelson," offering his hand, "and you are?"

His voice was riveting. It played in her ears like a beautiful melody. She tore her eyes from his, glancing down to his open hand. He had opted to take a step closer to her instead of stretching out his arm. He was so close. Too close.

She craned her neck to look up at him as the image of him standing over her in that dark parking lot flooded her mind. She peered back down at his hand, remembering the last time he physically touched her. The memory of that touch had been haunting her ever since. She swallowed hard, attempting to ground herself. "Hi . . . I'm Kira."

His strong hand wrapped firmly around hers. The electricity from the contact sent shock waves of awareness through her system. Every part of her body tingled and pulsated with the contact. She felt herself stiffen in response but attempted to keep her facial expression neutral. She searched his face as they stood there, hand in hand. She couldn't be sure, but she sensed he was also struggling to keep his composure. *Does he feel it too?*

He released her hand far too quickly. It left her feeling cold and achy, but she pushed the negative feelings down, replacing it with a smile. "It's nice to meet you," she said, finally able to latch on to some clarity. Kira allowed her gaze to drift over to the gate and the house behind it, fearful she would lose her calm if she stared at those eyes for too long. "The house looks amazing."

"Thank you." His words were quick and clipped, backing away a couple of steps. "It's been in my family for generations, and I decided it was finally time to put it to good use."

Kira didn't bring her eyes back to his. Instead, she surveyed the additional space between them, and how the distance made that amazing rush of electricity between them fade even further. The absence of it felt like it was physically beginning to hurt. She sucked in a breath, willing her mind and body to keep control, watching him retreat another half step. Yes. It did physically hurt. She squeezed her hand at her side but felt nothing in response.

She needed to escape. "Well, I should get home."

Kira risked a glance back at that beautiful face. Those blue eyes felt like they were impaling her, rooting her to that spot. She watched in surprise as the man with the cocky eyebrow and the lazy smile struggled to keep his face reposed.

He took a breath, effectively shaking off whatever issue had caused it, and returned to that sinful smirk laced in arrogance. "I'm sure we'll see each other again. Soon."

Soon. The word bit through the distance, lighting something back up temporarily. She flexed her fingers. Kira forced a smile and nodded, but she couldn't speak another word. She turned and walked on.

Her body was rigid and wary as she walked away. She didn't want to risk turning back, because somehow, she knew he was watching her. She quickened her steps, feeling an intense need to put some distance between them. Once she rounded the corner, she collapsed against the stone wall that surrounded the courtyard.

She clamped her hand to her chest. Her breath heaved. She was somewhere between a fierce desire to sprint back and jump into his arms and racing home to hide under her covers. Either way, she was fearful of the impact he had on her.

"What the hell is wrong with you?" she grumbled to herself, just as tears made a sudden reappearance. With her hand still pressed against her chest, she flexed her fingers again. There was nothing.

Kira paused when she reached her driveway. Colin's truck was still parked outside on the street. It hadn't moved. She glanced around, wondering if she would spot him walking back, or worse, was he inside waiting for her? The thought left her with an uneasy feeling as she reached the front door.

"There you are!" Kat nearly leaped over the coffee table. "Where have you been? You didn't answer your phone. Eric just left to pick up Colin. He said you guys got into a fight a couple of hours ago, and that you walked out on him."

Kira stared back at her friend, her face blank. Her emotions were raw. She couldn't bear to explain anything at this moment.

Kat hugged her tight before stepping back to inspect her more thoroughly. She used her hand to rub away at something on her cheek, and then tucked her hair back, her inner mom taking over. "Are you okay? Have you been walking around crying all night by yourself?"

She sucked in a breath, shaking her head. *Two hours? Have I been walking that long?* "Eric went to get him?" Her voice was shaky.

Kat seemed to understand what she was asking, answering her with a weak nod.

"So, he's drunk?" Kira asked, nodding in response to her own question. She didn't need Kat's confirmation to know why Eric had gone to pick him up. That scenario had played out more than a few times over the past couple of months. She paused for several seconds, the silence ripping at her heart. What must her friends think? Her behavior had clearly not gone unnoticed by Colin. And if that was the case, then Kat was far more aware. Her stomach dropped at the thought. "I'm going to bed," she finally managed.

Her friend gave her a supportive nod, keeping her thoughts to herself.

In the darkness of her room, she allowed herself to relax, collapsing against the closed door. She thought she would cry again, but her eyes were seemingly all dried out.

She slipped out of her shoes, prepared to toss herself onto her bed and sleep in her clothes, but as she made her way to it, a sudden pain sliced through the bottom of her foot. "Ow," she cried out, hopping backward in the dark, fumbling for the light switch.

Her immediate reaction was to inspect her foot, but the light revealed the full scene as her eyes fell into focus. It took her several seconds to understand what she was looking at. She opened her door and called out to her friend: "Hey, Kat. Can you come up here for a second?"

Kat bounded up the stairs in a rush, a questioning look on her face. It shifted to surprise and concern, looking back to Kira. "What happened? Did you do this?"

"No! Of course not." Kira was offended that Kat would even suggest it. She looked back across the floor of her room, glaring at the glass and flowers that covered it. Water from the vase puddled in small pools and droplets on the hardwoods and soaked portions of the area rug.

"I'm so sorry. Of course, you didn't." Kat shook her head, embarrassed. "I put the flowers in a vase and brought them up here." She again shook her head, searching for an explanation. "I don't know . . . maybe there was a crack in it?"

Kira looked back to the floor. It hadn't simply fallen. It looked as if it had exploded. She could see tiny shards on the other side of the room. With her back against the wall, she lifted her foot and glanced down at it. Blood trickled from the cut.

She started to take a step, but Kat pulled her back. "No, sweetie. You don't have shoes on. Come on. Let's get your foot bandaged up first." She helped ease Kira to her bathroom.

She sat silently as her friend cleaned and wrapped her foot. The urge to share the encounter with their new neighbor clawed at her thoughts. "I met that guy, Blake tonight." She instantly regretted saying the words the moment they left her mouth.

Kat only looked back at her, blinking. "Who?"

It was too late to take it back now. She played it up casually. "You know . . . that guy Nadia was so excited about." She watched Kat's confused expression grow even more so. "I walked by the house tonight. He was outside. I think he saw that I was upset. He was just being nice." Kira bit her tongue, realizing she was rambling.

Kat only nodded. "That was nice of him." She paused as if she were waiting to see if Kira would share anything more. When she didn't, Kat jumped to her feet. "Okay, sweetie, go and get in my bed. I'll clean up the mess."

Kira was about to protest, but Kat stopped her, raising a hand to shush her before pointing to her room down the hall. "Go. I've got it. You're upset, you're exhausted, and the last thing you need is to be on your knees in glass, cleaning up the flowers Colin gave you."

Her heart swelled as she lurched into Kat's arms, her tears making a comeback. "Thank you."

After pulling on one of Kat's t-shirts, Kira settled into the covers. It felt odd not to be in her room, but she was grateful. She closed her eyes. The sound of the vacuum humming down the hall lulled her to sleep quickly.

No amount of sleep could heal the amount of hurt Kira was feeling. She was angry, confused, and sad. She wanted to share everything with Kat, but the need to keep her secrets about the dreams along with this unexplainable connection to their new neighbor kept her quiet. It would be easier to talk to someone who couldn't judge her for the many nonsensical thoughts and choices. For that reason, she now found herself walking alone amongst rows and rows of burial tombs.

Her mother and father were buried here. It had been some time since her last visit. She felt some guilt in that, but she honestly hated being here; hated that they were here. It wasn't fair. She continued along the path, eyeing the stones, looking for markers that seemed familiar. Because New Orleans is mostly below sea level, St Joseph's is primarily made up of above-ground mausoleums and tombs. It could be rather difficult to navigate.

The sound of thunder in the distance stopped her. Kira spun around, silently checking the clouds. They appeared to be far enough away; she had time before the rain rolled in, using this moment to take in the view of where she was and get her bearings so she could find her parents' burial site. Nothing looked familiar. Had it been so long?

At a fork in the path, Kira realized she'd gone too far. Just as she turned, she caught sight of a large black bird out of the corner of her eye. It swooped down low, causing her to flinch and stumble backward. She tripped over the edging along the path and fell back against a stone wall – hard.

Pain shot through her body as she gripped the back of her head. With her hand firmly in place, she glanced up to see the black raven perched upon a cross that topped a large granite sepulcher. *Is it staring at me?*

It screeched in her direction, its wings stretched out, only emphasizing how large and menacing it seemed.

Kira pushed herself to her feet, flinging her hand in the air at it. "Shoo!"

The bird wasn't fazed at all by her ill attempts, cawing at her again. That's when she noticed the smear of red on her hand. *Blood.* She reflexively put her hand back to her head. It stung at the touch. "Damn it."

Kira looked back at the stone tomb she'd fallen against. There was a small smudge of her blood across it. She started to turn away but did a double take back to the tomb, her mind finally catching up to what her eyes had seen. She stepped closer and crouched down to where she'd fallen just moments before. Her chin tipped toward the sky as the thunder crashed, vibrating through the cemetery.

The storm was moving in faster than she'd thought. She needed to leave now if she was going to avoid the rain, but something important had caught her eye. She glanced over at the tomb again. It was old, weathered from centuries of exposure, causing the marked etchings to be faint. Her eyes finally rested on the spot where that small smear of her blood clung to the stone. With squinted eyes, she leaned in even closer. Her fingers ran along the surface as if she were reading it from touch.

Kira Lockwood.

She inhaled deeply, brows knitting together as she pushed herself up, stepping several feet back, eyeing the tomb in disbelief. She looked around, desperate for an explanation. Thunder sounded again. The sky grew darker by the second as ominous clouds moved in with a fury. She took two deliberate steps back to the stone, needing to know what else it said.

She wrapped her arms around herself, her head shaking in absolute denial. Her eyes roamed lower. The dates were just as faded, but legible enough.

Born December 24th, 1999–Died December 24th, 2020.

Kira released a ragged breath, one she didn't even realize she was holding. That was not her birthday. A spine-tingling shiver danced across her skin as her eyes searched the stone once again. The date of the death wasn't in the past, it was in the future. Almost six months in the future. "That's not possible," she whispered to the rain that now poured down. Her hand traced the etched markings once more before forcing herself back to her feet. She watched the rain wash away that small stain of red, still silently denying her own eyes.

Malefic streaks of lightning lit up the black sky, shaking her out of her stupor. She took one long look at the tomb and the surrounding mausoleums. It was hard to tear her eyes away, but the rain itself had now darkened the stone, making it impossible to read. She would come back tomorrow and prove to herself that she was wrong, committing this spot to memory before running back to her car.

She was soaked once she finally made it inside the warmth of her car. She checked herself in the mirror, wiping away the moisture from her face. The rain was coming down harder now. It was so hard, it bounced off the metal roof like hail stones, nearly drowning out her own inner thoughts.

Once she pulled out onto the road, she hoped to make it home before the storm got worse. Her hopes were not answered. The rain came down in sheets, making it hard to see. She was so focused on staying on the road that she didn't realize she'd missed her turn. In an attempt to backtrack, she found herself on the Pontchartrain Expressway about to cross over the river.

Lightning lashed against the sky once again, followed by another loud clamor of impending thunder. She hated this bridge. Lightning flashed again, illuminating the sight of a man and a woman standing in the middle of the road just as she crossed onto it.

Kira choked on her scream as she gripped the wheel and slammed the brakes. The car hydroplaned and skidded off the road, crashing through the guardrail, plummeting down toward the river below. She didn't make a sound as the water in the river grew closer and closer. Even the sound of the rain seemed to have disappeared. There was nothing but silence.

Just as the car was about to hit the unforgiving water, she violently jerked, jarring herself awake in a cold sweat. Her breaths were short and ragged. "What the hell?" Kira mumbled to herself, with her hand across her chest, feeling her heart pound. It took her a moment to gather herself. *Kat's room.* The memory of her earlier night filled her conscience. She tiptoed down the hall, glancing over the stairway banister to see the glow of the TV in the living room. *Kat must have fallen asleep on the sofa.* She peeked inside her room. It was empty and perfectly clean. No glass. No flowers.

Kira scribbled down her latest encounter, recalling all the details she could remember, almost wishing this was one she could forget. She thought about the faces of the man and woman on the road. It had happened so fast she didn't see them clearly.

Kira relaxed her head against the wall, resting the journal in her lap. "It was just a dream," she murmured to herself, a quiet reminder that her parents were gone.

It didn't matter if it had been them on the road or not. *It wasn't real.*

After finally unleashing a few final tears for the night, she curled up in her own bed.

The nightmares from earlier finally gave way to something much happier – dreams of Blake.

She was grateful for the reprieve.

EIGHT
THE SUPRA VIRTUTEM

K ira was long gone, having turned the corner more than half an hour ago. Blake had stood there watching her until she disappeared around the wall that surrounded the courtyard park. Even now, he remained rooted in that same spot, working to make sense of the thoughts swimming endlessly in his head.

He was losing his focus, and he didn't like it. Centuries of sharpening and honing his skills should have made this easy. She was shaping up to be so many things, but easy wasn't one of them.

Blake finally turned on his heel and pushed through the gates, making the walk up the path beneath the canopy of oaks and Spanish moss. He eyed the house, lit up by numerous sconces on the lower porch and upper balconies. She'd commented on it. He could have used it as a segue into a larger conversation. He could have used this moment to build a greater connection. It was evident she was hurting. *I could've comforted her.*

He didn't do any of these things. Instead, he backed away. He'd been so eager to get close, but without warning, he felt something new. Something he hadn't felt before. Her power?

It hadn't felt that way. It was something within him. Within her. Unknowns made him wary. He would need to get a handle on this quickly.

Blake shoved his hands into the pockets of his jeans, allowing his mind to wander as he continued to traipse up the drive. He saw her tears. It was yet another thing tonight on the long list of things he didn't like. The simple fact that he didn't like them was also on the list of things he didn't like. His head tilted, and his eyes narrowed as he tried to wrap his mind around that oddly revolving checklist.

Visibly shielded by a cloaking enchantment, he'd sat right beside her during her fight with that human frat paddle of a boyfriend. Taking Colin out of her life was part of the plan, but it appeared it wouldn't take much work. That part of the job was seemingly being done for him. Regardless, he didn't like the way he'd acted towards her.

His list was getting longer. *Fuck.*

The interaction at the pub when Colin had gripped the sides of the table while leaning in to hiss something at her set him off. He couldn't remember the words he spoke; he could only visualize the whites of Colin's knuckles from the strength in his grip. It was something Colin had done in anger to keep from lashing out. At that moment, he had felt an intense need to lash out himself. He shook his head at the memory as his hands flexed and fisted at his side. *Why? How?*

"I was wondering when you were going to head back this way. I thought maybe you'd decided to walk her home and tuck her in. Maybe read her a bedtime story about a magical, horny warlock."

Blake shook his head at his brother, Larz, who sat stretched out on the porch steps. "First . . . fuck you. And second . . . eavesdrop much?"

"First . . . not even in your dreams. And second . . . stalk much?" Larz countered, offering him a beer.

Blake took it, grateful for the distraction his brother offered. He took a seat next to him on the steps. His posture wasn't nearly as relaxed though, unable to shake the tension raging through him. With his forearms resting on his knees, he dropped his head forward as his thoughts still lingered on watching Kira in the pub.

Initially, he had planned to keep his distance and just observe, but the need to get close to her overruled any logical thought. Concealed in magic, he had sat in a chair right beside her. She was so close, only inches away. He could still smell the scent of her perfume, wild florals with oranges.

"Maybe if you find out what kind it is, I can buy you a bottle and spray it on your pillow," Larz teased, trying to hold together a passive expression before finally breaking into a smirk.

It took Blake a couple of seconds to comprehend his brother's words, and the fact that his mental walls were once again down. "Fuck!" He jumped to his feet, marching back down to the lawn, his hands in his hair, quickly putting his guards back in place.

Larz remained on the stairs, stretching out further, his arms lounging on the step behind his back, his beer dangling from one hand. He gave Blake a few seconds to pace the ground in front of him before he continued. "Is this going to be a problem?"

Blake stopped, his face deadpan. "No. It's not a problem."

Larz lifted his hands, his palms out, beer still dangling. "Hey man, I'm just asking. I'm here to help." He waited a few moments before easing back into a casual position on the steps. "I get it. Her energy is . . . bloody hell, I don't even know what to say. I could feel it all the way up here earlier."

Blake returned to pacing but said nothing.

"That's what you're worried about, right? Or is it something else?" Larz asked, his brows raised in question.

"Fuck. Of course, that's what it is." Blake made his way back up the stairs and took a seat one step above his brother, his arms again resting on his knees. "What else would it be?"

Larz shook his head, his lips threatening a smug smile. "I don't know. Maybe this centuries-old warlock thinks the *Supra Virtutem* is really pretty?" he mocked, trying to cover his own laughter with a swig of beer.

"Fuck off," he snapped, slapping Larz in the back of the head.

"Okay, seriously," he stated, pressing his palms to the air in front of him. "We've got you, man. We didn't expect this to be easy. That's why we chose you to lead us in this."

Blake glanced down, offering a slight nod, knowing what Larz meant. He was the oldest among them, born in 1602 in England. He was also an Iver, a warlock capable of inheriting the powers of all those who came before him. He'd descended from a long lineage rooted in power. But it hadn't mattered that he was an Iver. His father had been murdered, as well as his father's father. His lineage was gone. Their power hadn't been enough. He wouldn't allow that to be his own fate.

In the year 1621, Blake left England behind to journey to the New World. But it wasn't until 1626 that he discovered his ability to siphon the power from others with supernatural abilities. His given name, Lucem Ac Tenebras, meant both light and dark, but he used the name of Lucien Turner. He would change it again to his current name in the 20th century.

Without hesitation, he'd gravitated to the dark. He spent the next several years extracting the energy from witches and other warlocks alike. And as a gift, he shared that power with Khalida, the witch who had cared for him after the death of his parents. And in return, for every life offered, she granted him a year of immortality.

Perpetual life. Blake became obsessed with the idea, making it his mission to hunt every witch and supernatural being from every corner of the earth.

It was on this never-ending quest that he stumbled upon Larz when he returned to England in 1689. He was known as Larkin Durant, 'The Great Hunter' back then. It was the first time he had ever met another warlock with such a vast reserve of power. He soon learned it was because he had also acquired the skill of extracting energy from others. They formed a quick bond and set out together, maximizing their talents. More than three hundred years later, here they sat, making plans for their next big hunt

Blake blew out a ragged breath. "Her power is strong, but she has no clue of who or what she is. That will help, but it doesn't mean this is going to be a cakewalk."

"Agreed. We have a vast amount of time before she ascends. Her power is probably knocking on her door already. Who knows what she'll discover between now and then?"

"That's why we need to keep moving. Vincent did well, but he's not strong enough. Not by a long shot."

Larz finished his beer. "Bloody hell. Kid surprised me."

Blake shot him a questioning look. "You're surprised he did it?"

"No," Larz laughed. "He's one of us, man. I was surprised by the fact that he showed her the act of mercy," he explained as he leaned back, using his arm to pull another beer out of a small cooler.

Blake shook his head. "You're a fucking warlock, and you're walking around with a damn cooler. Want me to get you a koozie?" he chided, happily taking the new beer being handed in his direction.

Larz shrugged. "Dude, I like it ice cold."

They both sat in silence for a moment, enjoying their beers. Blake thought back to that moment in the cistern, making a quick check that all his mental guards were intact. He remembered the sensation he felt when he realized what it was Vincent was doing that night of his initiation. That he was gifting her mercy with a final prayer. He had shown humanity. In the four hundred years he'd been alive, he was sure that all of his humanity had been washed away.

"I wasn't sure you'd noticed . . . with Vincent, I mean."

Larz smirked, taking another drink: "He's a subtle motherfucker," he joked before shifting to a more serious tone. "But you're right. He's not strong enough to stand up against the *Supra Virtutem*."

"Then what are we waiting for?"

"Well, I'm glad you brought that up; we have a problem." Larz paused for a moment, gauging Blake's reaction before he moved on. "The covens are talking. Fucking technology, social media, and all that bullshit."

Blake shook his head, eyes narrowed. "What does that mean?"

"It means witches know something's up. They've gone into hiding." Larz chugged the remainder of his beer, punctuating his frustration. "The fucking word is out."

Blake dropped his head into his hands. That was the last thing he needed to hear. Vincent was young and unseasoned. They would need to carry out many more sacrifices in order for him to garner the energy he needed. Without it, he wouldn't be strong enough to execute the last order of the three.

The Third Order. Blake felt that unfamiliar feeling radiate through his senses. *Kira.* He made another silent check on his mental guards. "Do you have a plan?"

"Somewhat. It's in motion, but we haven't ironed out all the details."

"Care to elaborate?"

Larz stood, signaling Blake to follow him inside. They walked through the foyer, passing by the formal dining area on the left and the billiards room on the right. They continued into the rotunda, hanging a right just past the grand staircase. They paused briefly at a large carved door tucked under the archway of the stairs.

The door was made from one single massive piece of reclaimed wood. It was easily nine feet tall, half as wide, and nearly six inches thick. Its size alone was impressive, but the intricate handmade carvings woven throughout made this piece special. The carvings created the same unique symbols found on the gates of the garden's back wall, runes to keep those uninvited from entering.

Larz landed one courtesy knock before walking through. Armand and Vincent were in deep conversation, sitting on the spacious leather sofa against the wall and leaning over a list on the coffee table. The room was mostly simple. In addition to the sofa, two ample leather armchairs and a mid-century bar cart rested in the corner brimming with various libations in crystal cylinders. Glass tumblers sat on a floating shelf just above. The floors were made from thick planks of reclaimed wood, unlike any traditional flooring.

And then there were the walls. They were covered in an assortment of maps, markings, and various artifacts and magical symbols. There were no windows. The room was lit in a soft golden glow from the elaborate chandelier in the center. It was the only modern piece in the room.

"Fellas, share your thoughts with our fearless leader here."

Blake gave Larz another swipe to the head and took a seat in one of the chairs opposite Armand and Vincent.

Armand handed his phone over to Blake. An image of a pretty young dark-skinned girl with raven jet hair appeared on the screen. "Her name is Rayna Bennett. I came across her by pure accident in the coffeehouse."

Larz stifled a laugh, handing a low ball of whiskey to Blake.

"Pure accident, eh?" He inclined his chin to the disposable coffee cup on the table. "It's not an accident when you're there ten fucking times a day."

Blake and Vincent attempted to stifle their laughter with little success.

Armand, however, played it cool, letting it roll off his back. "What can I say? I like the coffee there," taking a deliberate sip from the disposable cup, smiling behind it, "plus the service is exceptional."

"Hear! Hear!" Larz raised his glass in salute to his brother's sexual pursuits.

They'd all watched him slowly make the moves on the pretty little barista, but none had yet called him out on it until now.

Vincent continued for Armand: "We believe there could be more, but these two members of her coven seem to be close to her." Vincent swiped the screen, showing Blake the other two witches. "The redhead is Akesha Karvana, and the blonde is Tatiana Duvall."

Blake looked through the pictures and then placed the phone back on the table before settling back into his chair. "How strong are they?"

"Enough so," Armand responded, leaning in across the table. "But it doesn't matter. That's not why we need them . . . we use them to lure out other witches."

Blake's eyes narrowed, glancing at Larz for counsel. He was intrigued. "How will that work?"

Vincent spoke up: "These witches are young but seem well connected. They're all local and will probably know if more witches are within the city, possibly even the entire southern area."

"How can you be sure of that?" Blake asked, his head tilted in question.

Vincent picked up the phone and lightly shook it in his hand. "Twitter, Instagram, Snapchat."

Larz's head rolled back. "Bloody hell . . . you're on fucking Snapchat." He couldn't contain the laughter that vibrated from his chest. "Fucking baby warlock over here."

Vincent nodded along. "That's right, grandpa. I'm twenty-four. What are you these days? Five hundred? Six, maybe? Was it A.D. or B.C. when you were born?"

Larz only laughed. "It's okay, man. You can say whatever you want, but you're on fucking Snapchat."

The jokes were a good source of distraction, and Blake was appreciative of them. It allowed him to process all the information as he took another sip of the whiskey. "Tell me more about what you would do. How do we know they'll lure them out?"

Armand and Vincent looked to Larz. Blake followed their eyes. "We make a deal."

Blake let that settle for a moment. That was why Armand and Vincent had let Larz take the lead on this one. He had a much better chance of convincing him this was a more viable option than the others. He turned up the rest of his whiskey. He let the thought mull around a little longer before leaning forward and placing the empty tumbler on the table.

He took a measured look at each of his brothers. "Do you think it's wise for us to make a deal with untested witches, especially with something as important as the *Supra Virtutem*?"

"We wouldn't share any details about her or our final plans," Larz offered.

The atmosphere in the room had shifted considerably.

Her. Even the mere mention of her had him careening into a headspace he couldn't afford to visit as her face flashed through his mind. He had to push that back quickly. "So, what is it we offer?"

"Protection," Vincent spoke up.

It was a straightforward answer.

Larz gave Blake another moment to absorb yet another detail.

"The covens are in hiding because they're scared. There is nothing about Rayna and these others that wouldn't make them any less scared. We promise them our protection." He grabbed the phone from the table, swiping through the images as a smug smile curved his lips. "And maybe as an added bonus, we offer some sexual favors."

Blake released a strained breath. Leave it to Larz to break the tension in the room. But it was a good idea. It would work. He simply hated the thought of relying on anyone outside of this room. "Okay."

Larz nodded. "Okay, but the blonde," he turned the phone screen towards Vincent and Armand. "Tatiana . . . I call dibs."

Blake raked a hand through his hair, laughing at his brother. "Bloody fucking hell."

Their house was a revolving door of beautiful women. He wouldn't be surprised if they each had a woman waiting in their beds at this very moment. Under normal circumstances, he would be no exception. But nothing about Blake's recent state was normal. Not now.

"While we're here." Vincent's face took on that curious display they'd all become so accustomed to seeing. "What more can you tell me about the *Supra*?"

They had only shared minimal information with Vincent. Though he'd joined their brotherhood two years prior, he'd only just finalized his initiation. He was now truly part of the Brethren. It was only fair to share all the details.

"She's the greatest source of power." Blake paused, her face flashing in his mind again. "The ultimate power. You know of Khalida. She helped my father care for me after my mother's death. She was also there for me after my father's murder. I'd always thought that she was a witch, but I began to realize she was more than that in time. Much more," Blake explained, staring blankly at the table. "We are somewhat human, but with special gifts."

"I've got your special gift right here," Larz joked, grabbing himself.

Blake shook his head, an esteemed smile on his face. Even in the most serious of moments, Larz had a way of lightening the mood. "Keep it in your pants, man. Nobody here wants to see your dick."

Larz threw his head back in laughter. "Your loss."

"I think I'm going to need another drink for this conversation." After four hundred years, you work up a major tolerance. He eyed the glass tumbler on the table. As he watched it, the warm brown liquid began slowly rising from the base towards the rim, stopping at the halfway mark. He picked up the glass and took a long but slow sip. "For as long as I had known Khalida, she'd spent her time searching for the fabled *Supra*. She claimed it would grant her a power unlike any other and give her the gift of eternal life."

"Fabled? You didn't think she was real?" Vincent asked.

Blake shrugged. "I don't think I thought much of it at the time. But then one day she claimed to have found the *Supra*. I personally never saw her, but I remember feeling that energy. Just an unequivocal raw power. It changed Khalida. She became something beyond her former self. Something beyond the supernatural . . . only I don't exactly know what that is." Blake watched that wash over Vincent. "But something went wrong in the transformation. She failed to fully absorb the *Supra Virtutem* of that time. It left her in limbo, so to speak. She had indeed become immortal, but in order to remain so, she had to continue to feed on the power of true and practicing witches."

"And this is where you stepped in?" Vincent asked. "You began hunting witches."

"Yes." He waited, seeing Vincent's mind churn with questions.

"You're an Iver. You already had so much power."

Though it wasn't phrased as a question, Blake knew what Vincent was asking. "You want to know why I helped her. Was it for her, or was it for me?"

Vincent only nodded. Armand and Larz remained quiet, listening intently.

"It was a long time ago. I'd say it was both. Khalida was a mother to me, so of course, I wanted to help her. But as you can imagine, I wanted something in return." Blake flashed a wicked smile. "And here I am, fucking fresh-faced over four hundred years later."

"But, why me? Why did you invite me into the Brethren?"

Blake took another long drink before continuing. "You're an Iver as well. That's why you're as strong as you are now. I sensed it when we found you. It's how I knew you would be our fourth." Blake's tone was soft, but clear. "Like me, you lost your father. And like me, you vowed you would grow strong enough to ensure his providence would not be your own."

Vincent stared back. His face was blank, but they all knew he was a master at controlling his outer emotions. He finally gave a nod in agreement. "So, this girl . . . she's a descendent of the *Supra Virtutem*?"

This girl. Blake worked his jaw. "Yes. We will finally be able to ascend to a higher level of immortality. Before we make our final offering to Khalida, we must enact the Order of Three."

"And what does the order entail?"

"One, she must willingly and physically give over her body. Two, she must willingly offer her blood. And three." Blake paused, his mouth going dry. Something buried deep down screamed with a vengeance at his senses. "Three, she must die."

NINE
DANGEROUS TERRITORY

The sun dipped behind the trees. The horizon was brushed in wide strokes of orange and pink, stretching far across the sky. Blake stood on the veranda, a beer bottle in his hand, soaking in the last few minutes of direct sun. He blocked out the loud music and voices, and instead, he fixated on the vivid shades that painted the sky. The streaks of pinks that danced on the clouds reminded him of the dress she wore a few nights ago.

He inhaled a deep breath and looked down at the ground, realizing his mind was drifting into dangerous territory. That was not what tonight was about. He needed to focus. He kept his gaze lowered for another moment before allowing himself to look back to the sky. He could spare another minute.

Watching those brilliant bands of color blend and slowly fade, he let his mind conjure up images of her. He smiled to himself, remembering the sight of her tossing a drink in Colin's face. *She's feisty.*

He had walked alongside her the entire time after she left the pub. He recalled that twinge in his gut as her anger had suddenly turned into sobs. He remembered his own unexpected desire to reach out as she hugged her arms around herself. He could hear her nervous laughter and see the startled expression on her face when he first spoke to her. That same twinge had echoed in his body when she finally flashed him a smile. It was the first time she had really smiled at him.

Blake took a long swig of his beer, an attempt at washing away the familiar ache trying to emerge from within. The light was quickly fading, and the bright colors of the sky were quietly being stripped away as his eyes drifted to the scene around him.

It was Memorial Day, and the Brethren were throwing their first party of the season. Being who and what they were, they didn't really have friends. They had each other. However, they were well-practiced in having fun and relishing in the perks their powers afforded them. A simple invocation of persuasion had attracted nearly two hundred guests, a mixture of locals and Tulane students, who were now partying at their home. It was still early, and more people were arriving by the hour.

"Hey, man!" Larz clasped a hand onto Blake's shoulder. "Nice, right."

Blake followed his brother's line of sight to a group of sorority girls clad in tiny bikinis lined up at the edge of the pool, their legs dangling in the water while sipping on brightly colored cocktails.

He nodded. "You never disappoint."

Upon reflex, Larz reached out in mid-air, grabbing a small white ball that had flown astray, inspecting it before tossing it up high and catching it again. "I'll school you in Beer Pong later," he called out, and then tossed it back over to the guys who had just lost it. "But we have work to do right now."

Blake raised a brow. "They're here?"

"Oh, yeah," he answered as he stepped away to a long table filled with an array of food and drinks. He grabbed two hot dogs and handed one to Blake, who shook his head in response. "Seriously? What's more American than a hot dog on Memorial Day?" Larz asked, around a mouthful.

"You're fucking British, dude."

"What's your point?" Larz responded with another large bite before giving Blake a nod, gesturing for him to follow.

They walked through one of the many opened French doors that lined the wall between the veranda and the main living space. People were not only socializing outside by the pool and the gardens, but many were inside, lounging on sofas or playing pool in the billiards room.

As they passed, Blake saw two girls dancing on top of the kitchen island while guys cheered them on. With the exception of the sitting-room beneath the stairs, which was heavily fortified with runes, keeping unwanted visitors out, the entire lower level was open for guests to wander. A set of runes disguised as an abstract painting at the top of the staircase served as a protection spell to ward off stray guests on the second floor. Blake continued to follow Larz past the rotunda, through the foyer, and out the front door.

There were at least thirty people on this side of the property, making up several small groupings. A distance away from the loud music, it was a much better atmosphere for deeper conversations. Several yards from the front steps on the lawn were a group of coeds passing around a joint. Not far from them, under one of the oaks, Blake could hear a couple in mid-argument. On the porch, a newly acquainted duo was becoming very comfortable with one another. And on one of the two spacious daybed swings were three young witches.

Blake and Larz took up a spot on the swing on the opposite end of the porch. From there, they had a great view of Vincent as he talked with them. He was relaxed, leaning against the railing on his elbows, his hands dangled casually with his ankles crossed. With a radiant smile, he nodded along in conversation. They were well out of earshot, but with their powers and abilities, they could easily listen in as if they were sitting no more than a foot away.

Blake made eye contact with Armand as he appeared from the front entrance, holding multiple beer bottles, three in each hand. "Here you go, ladies," he said, passing a bottle to each, allowing his finger to lightly graze their hands during the exchange. He pulled up a chair, straddling it, and rested his arms on the back. "So, what brought you guys out tonight?"

Larz laughed under his breath, watching how each of the witches' eyes lit up with recognition at Armand's touch. "Smooth, brother."

"I met Vincent at the bookstore this morning." It was Rayna who spoke. "We were both reaching for the same book."

As a group, the brothers had decided it best that Vincent take the lead in bringing the witches to the party. He was young, roughly the same age as the witches themselves. And although he possessed a significant amount of power, his aura did not exude it in the same way the others did. Armand himself, was having to carefully suppress his energy at that moment.

Blake and Larz, on the other hand, had immensely more power. They were well practiced in controlling it, but they didn't know these witches, and felt it was safer to keep their distance until the right time. They didn't want to spook them.

The plan was simple. Vincent staged an accidental run-in with Rayna. He purposefully touched her hand as they reached for the same book while opening his aura, allowing her to sense his magic. The move was calculated, giving her just enough of a taste to pique her interest.

The strategy had worked. He continued assaulting her with his own natural charm and good looks over coffee. During their conversation, unbeknownst to her, he slowly crafted a spell of persuasion. By the time he invited her to the party, it would have been impossible for her to say no.

"Vincent, you didn't tell me you knew a bunch of beautiful witches." He said it in such a nonchalant way as if he were merely commenting on something as simple as the weather.

Blake watched on, noticing the distinct change in their posture as the tension in their bodies rose. Their eyes darted back and forth between one another, having a silent conversation between themselves.

Vincent shook his head, laughing. "I wasn't sure," he lied, looking to Rayna apologetically. "I'm sorry. I suspected it this morning, but I thought it might just be me. I didn't say anything to my brother because, as you can see, he lacks proper decorum."

Rayna and her sisters were clearly taken aback and unsure of how to proceed. She was slow to respond. "It's okay. I sensed it in you as well. It's part of the reason why we came tonight. I wanted to know," she laughed, gesturing to Armand. "And now I guess I've gotten my answer."

Blake noticed the way Rayna held herself, the tone of her voice, how she seemed to take the lead. It was evident she was the head of this coven.

Armand raised his hands in mock surrender. "My apologies. Maybe if my brother had filled me in, I would put my foot in my mouth a little less often."

The witches smiled, still somewhat wary, but Blake could see their anxiety begin to fade as they grew more comfortable with their supernatural hosts. They continued to talk, exchanging in light banter.

The goal, at this point, was to see what information they might offer willingly.

More people were beginning to pour in. Blake's line of sight was constantly interrupted by the stream of new arrivals walking across the porch to the front door. He had stopped watching them altogether and focused on listening instead. The sound of a recognizable voice tore him from his concentration. It took several seconds for his brain to catch up to his eyes. Colin was on his front porch. "What the fuck is he doing here?"

Larz looked at Blake and then back to the guys who disappeared through the front doorway. "Who was that?"

Blake didn't respond with words as unfamiliar feelings overtook his senses. His jaw pained from clenched teeth.

"Oh," Larz responded flatly, reading his brother's mind. "That's interesting."

Blake cracked his neck to the side, uncomfortable with the way his body felt at the moment. The idea of jerking Colin back through the house and tossing him beyond the front gate gave him a sudden rush of adrenaline. He released a heavy breath, thinking better of it. Unfortunately, throwing Colin out would serve no purpose. If anything, it only had the potential to complicate matters further. Shaking it off, he focused his attention back on the witches.

"You know, I have to admit I was mostly surprised to bump into you because I haven't seen or heard from any witches in this area. I've always believed all the stories of how New Orleans was a Mecca of magic and supernatural voodoo," said Vincent.

"No, that's true. This area is home to a lot of witches, but," Tatiana's voice trailed off, looking to Rayna for counsel on how to proceed.

"But many have left," Rayna amended. "And many others are in hiding."

Vincent feigned an incredulous expression. "Why?"

Rayna stifled a laugh. "Many believe that there is something or someone here with the intention of causing harm to us," she answered, gesturing not only to her coven but to Vincent and Armand as well. "I wasn't sure I believed it myself, but a witch we know went missing only a few days ago. Her name is Nina. I don't know; maybe there's something to the rumors after all."

Blake's eyes shifted to Vincent to gauge his reaction. The girl Rayna spoke of was likely the tiny witch from their most recent ritual.

Vincent frowned. "I'm sorry. We haven't heard anything, but then again, we're kind of loners, so I guess it's not that surprising. Do you really think someone hurt your friend?"

The witches eyed each other. It was another unspoken conversation, considering how much to share. It didn't matter now, he could feel it.

They were scared.

"You know, I've got something we should show you. Maybe it can help," Armand suggested, standing from his chair. "It's just inside here."

Blake looked to Larz. This was it. They remained in their seats at the corner of the porch, watching Vincent and Armand lead the girls inside the house, who waited only momentarily before following.

Vincent led them to the rotunda, pausing at the archway's opening below the stairs to catch Blake's eye. "This way, ladies," he said, and opened the heavily runed door to the sitting room. He stood inside, continuing to hold the door open for them to enter.

Rayna took a cautious step, hesitating as she passed the door. She ran a hand along the etchings carved into the wood. Blake couldn't see her face, but he could sense her thoughts. Recognition. Survival instincts.

"No, I think we should go now," Rayna declared, turning on her heel before grabbing the other witches by their arms, ready to turn and sprint for the front door.

They only made it a step before Blake and Larz came up from behind, effectively blocking them from passing.

Rayna turned back to Vincent, who was still holding the door open, his arm stretched out in invitation with raised brows and a smug smile. Armand had already made himself comfortable inside, sprawled out in one of the leather chairs.

"This door was different earlier. I would've noticed it," she stated, working hard to maintain her composure and assert her position.

"You only see it now because I let you." Blake's voice was emphatic as he, too, made his position of authority clear. He could hear her heart rate increase, shielding the two other witches behind her with her body. "After you," he stated, gesturing to the door.

Wary, she led her coven inside, each taking a seat on the sofa. They kept close. "What do you want?" Rayna managed, her voice strained.

Vincent perched himself against the arm of Armand's chair and Larz took a seat in the open spot next to them.

Blake stood between them, his hands resting casually in his pockets. "You can relax. We didn't bring you ladies here to harm you. We simply need your help."

It took several seconds, but the witches visibly calmed, and released their grip on each other's hands.

The witch with the vibrant red hair and green eyes finally spoke up: "Help with what?"

"Akesha, right?" Blake waited for her nod before rounding the coffee table between them. He was no longer suppressing his power and he knew they felt it, watching them stiffen as he moved closer. He sat on the table directly in front of them, eye to eye. "I get it. You're all scared, and you very well should be, but I'm willing to make a deal so you don't have to be."

"A deal?" asked Rayna.

"As you said, witches have gone into hiding. I need your help to find them."

"Why would we do that?" Alarm tinged her voice.

"Because you're smart." Blake stood, walking to the bar cart. He poured several drinks as he continued. "You want to do what is best for your coven. You want to feel safe. But more than anything, you want power."

"I have power," she countered. "We all do."

Blake pressed his lips together, barely restraining his laugh. "That's cute." He passed out the drinks, taking his time before settling back on the coffee table. His stance was wide, resting his arms on his legs, holding his own drink. "You're amongst friends here, so there isn't any need to lie."

Blake watched Rayna's chest heave and her skin flush, but she remained silent, pressing her lips in a firm line. "What do you mean?" she asked.

"Okay, maybe it's not a lie. Maybe it's more like a last-ditch attempt at hope." He took another drink and glanced back at his brothers. "Or maybe it's more like a prayer. Like the one, your friend, Nina, spoke before Vincent here slit her throat." The sound created between their elevated breathing and the pounding of their hearts was like an orchestra to his ears. He loved it. "Most importantly, though, you have no power because you've gotten a sense of my own. And as you well know . . . that renders you null."

Rayna swallowed hard.

Blake leaned in closer. "The truth is . . . what you're feeling right now is merely just a tiny sampling of it."

"What do you plan to do with these witches?" Tatiana asked, her voice cracking with fear.

Blake's eyes narrowed, and his brows knitted together. "Nothing you need concern yourself with, but then again, I did just share with you the recent fate of someone you knew. So again, it seems you have gotten your answer."

"We wouldn't have to," Akesha spoke up again, her voice

faltering as she struggled to find the right words, "hurt them . . . would we?"

"No. We don't expect it, nor do we want your help with anything beyond telling us where to find them."

Their resistance was wearing thin. Blake knew they didn't want to do what he was asking. But they would, only because they each wanted to walk out of that room alive. He could see it in the shift of Rayna's posture, and the way her eyes roamed the empty space between them, searching the far corners of her mind for the right answers. In truth, he didn't require their consent or cooperation, but relying on sheer force ran the risk of defiance. There was also the added bonus of witnessing their fear and the overwhelming inner struggle before ultimately submitting. Something he liked.

Rayna lifted her chin, her back straightened; a final attempt at showing strength. "You need our help. You said you want to make a deal. Tell me what you will give us in return."

"Protection. It's the thing you need most." Blake smiled a wicked grin. "But it won't be the thing you crave most." He reached out, entwining his hand with hers. He locked eyes on her and conveyed something fervent and compelling before whispering, "Kunna."

Rayna inhaled sharply as her body fell back into the sofa, her arm outstretched with her hand still wrapped in his. Her head rolled back against the pillows, and her chest pitched high on another gasp of air.

Larz settled back in his seat, resting his ankle across a knee, hiding a proud smirk behind his glass. His brothers were in similar form, watching the witch writhe under Blake's touch, feeling the rise of anxiety from her sisters who sat helplessly beside her.

Rayna took several long seconds. Her breathing was labored before she finally rose back up to face him. "Again," she laughed, her eyes wide with wonder.

Blake released her hand. "My . . . my . . . aren't we the greedy little witch? We haven't even come to an agreement yet." He watched with a self-righteous smile as the witches exchanged glances amongst each other.

Rayna turned back to him, her smile even wider. "We have an agreement. Now please, do that again."

"Well, okay then!" Blake turned to his brothers with an egotistical grin. His brow cocked high. "I think it's time for some fun."

TEN
GIRLS' NIGHT

"You're going. I'll drag you out by your pretty little head if I have to." Nadia stared down at Kira, arms folded across her chest, giving her a playful but curt nod.

It had been three days since her fight with Colin. She had spent the majority of that time crying in her bed. They hadn't spoken. Between avoiding his calls, ignoring his texts, and having Kat turn him away at the front door, she wondered if this was it. Was it truly over? Did she want it to be over? Did she miss him? Yes.

Colin was a significant piece of the puzzle that made up her life. Almost all of her most cherished memories included him. How does a puzzle piece suddenly not fit when its shapes and curves and niches matched so perfectly for so long? If he were to suddenly become absent from her life, what kind of hole would be left in his wake? How would she survive if that hole were suddenly filled with pain, anger, loneliness, and regret? The chink in their relationship was only a fissure at the moment. And the hurt; it was already too much to bear.

Kira looked over to Kat for support, her shoulders slumped, and her voice was flat. "Please don't make me go. I'm not ready."

Kat reached out and gripped her hand with an affectionate squeeze. "I love you. I support you. I don't want you to do anything you're not ready for, but at the same time, I can't keep sitting here watching you spin your wheels and cry all night." She released a heavy breath. "I agree with Nadia. We haven't had a girls' night out in forever. I really think it will help take your mind off it. Even if only for an hour, it'll be worth it."

Kira rolled her eyes and dropped backward onto her bed. "Fine."

Nadia jumped up and down, clapping her hands. "Yay! Girls' night!"

Kira spent the next half hour watching Kat and Nadia bounce from room to room, wavering between clothing and shoe options while the music blared from downstairs. How great would it be if her greatest concern was a decision between casual chic with tattered jeans, or effortlessly classic in a little black dress? She looked on, envious of their happiness and casual indifference. She hated being this person.

Kira walked over to her mirror, looking hard at herself. Her small frame, even smaller now after not eating for three days, was swimming in the oversized sweats she wore. Her hair was flat, and her skin was still semi-splotchy from crying earlier. She looked as bad as she felt. This was not the person she wanted to be.

Kat paraded in, a towel wrapped around her body and head. She hooked arms with Kira, leaning her head on her shoulder. "It's okay, sweetie. You look like shit, but I'd still do you."

Kira cracked a smile, nudging her hip out to push Kat aside. It was what she needed to break out of the descent she was falling into. Kat was always there, a life raft in stormy seas, helping to keep her head above water.

"Pre-game, bitches!" Nadia pounced onto Kira's bed, a bottle of Patrón in one hand and three stacked shot glasses in the other. "I know you don't drink, baby girl, but just in case," she said, waving the third shot glass.

Kira bit her lip as she watched Nadia pour two shots before handing one over to Kat. She glanced over her shoulder at her reflection again. That sad girl staring back at her seemed to reach out, touching something within her, telling her to wake the hell up.

"Wait." She picked up the third shot glass and held it out for Nadia to fill.

Kat tilted her head, lips pursed. "Really?" She looked to Nadia, the same confused expression on her face. She shrugged her shoulders and watched her fill Kira's shot glass. "Okay. Cheers!"

The coolness of the glass on her lips, paired with the warmth of the tequila as it moved across her tongue and down her throat, sent a chill through her body, awakening something from within. She stretched an arm out to set the glass aside on the nightstand, but just as she was about to release it, that familiar ache in her palm lit up. Three delicate fingers still rested on the rim. She slowly rolled the tip of her finger along the edge, before gripping it again, holding it back out towards Nadia. "Hit me again."

Taken aback, Nadia looked to Kat for guidance. Kira didn't drink. It was never very clear if it was because of her parents' accident, or because she was a dancer who worked hard to maintain her body's condition. Maybe it was a mixture of both. Regardless, this wasn't normal behavior for their friend.

"Are you sure?"

"Hell, yes." She was quick to respond. She deserved a night free of the stress and the weight of the past year. She wanted a night where she wasn't burdened with all her own thoughts and inhibitions. Deserved it even. Tonight, she wouldn't be that sad girl in the mirror. She tossed the second drink back, rewarded once again with a light pulse that trickled from her palm up through her arm and out to the tips of her fingers. "I'm taking a shower."

It felt good. Amazing, actually. Standing under the warmth of the cascading water, all those negative feelings were seemingly being washed away in a mixture of hot water and tequila. With her fingers splayed in front of her on the tile, she rolled her shoulders, enjoying the sensation from the water pressure. For the first time in days, she realized she wasn't focused on her relationship with Colin, the fight, or even her dreams. She wasn't focused on anything. In the confines of her shower, none of that existed, her mind blank. It was freeing.

Kira basked in this new clarity as she tilted her chin to the spray of the water. She moved her hands across her face and head, down to her shoulders, and then felt that twinge in her palm again. She only smiled. It was no longer pulling her focus; instead, it further relaxed her. That tingle, once a surge of electricity to her body, was now a soothing force that made her feel safe. They were melodic and euphoric currents pulsing within her.

It was a drug. And she was more than happy to play the part of the addict.

Her fingers glided over the length of her neck before drifting down to her collarbone. She allowed them to linger for a moment. Her pulse raced as she mirrored the movement with her other hand, feeling the delicate angles and hollows of her décolletage. Her hand was singing to her now. A beautiful, honeyed song that melted into her flesh.

Kira stood, staring at the white tile in front of her as the water beat at her chest. Her hands slid farther down across her breast, feeling the hammering of her own heart. It was a strange sensation, the water, and her heart pounding on opposite sides of her skin.

One craving to seep in. The other desperate to get out.

Her soft touch grew slightly headier as she massaged her breast. Her hand responded with a high note, causing her body to flinch. She reached out with her other hand to brace herself against the tiled wall, taking a moment to recover from the spasm before continuing. Bending at the elbow, she leaned in, allowing the spray to rain down over her face. Kira wasn't sure if she was attempting to revive her own senses, or if she was hoping to drown in the moment and live there forever. The song that she felt beneath the touch of her hand urged her to move lower. She could hear it growing louder as her fingers mingled with the flowing streams of water across her stomach.

Her hands were at her hips now, sliding down the sides of her thighs. As her fingers made the trail across the front and edge higher, she paused. It had been so long since she touched herself. This was as much an emotional and mental act as it was physical. She eyed the tile, apprehensive of her own headspace. The heat and the steam enveloped her, providing an extra layer from everything outside of this moment. The ache in her palm sent another reassuring signal, giving her the push she needed to overcome her anxiety. Her fingers moved to the delicate space where the pelvic arch met her thighs.

A small shudder vibrated down her spine as her nails grazed the skin there. One more sweet note pulsed through her hand. She inhaled deeply, a steadying breath before leaping off a cliff. A single finger ventured to her center, slipping in between her slit. The contact against her overly sensitive skin was nearly her undoing, her knees giving way underneath her.

She moved closer to the wall for support, the water now beating against her back. She squeezed her thighs together in an attempt to alleviate this amazing ache. As her need grew wilder, her fingers explored further, a finger reaching inside before tracing back up to the spot that screamed for attention. She cupped herself, pressing her palm tight against her sex, trying her best to create more friction.

Faint moans escaped her lips as her movements intensified in speed and pressure. She suddenly felt hot as if she would suffocate in the steam, but her fingers would not relent. With her free hand, she fumbled with the shower nobs, dialing it down to cooler water. As the temperature slowly shifted, urgency took over. She turned her back to the tile; her legs no longer able to bear her weight and slid down to the wet shower floor. Her head lolled back, her knees bent and thighs open as she continued.

The water turned cold, hitting her shins. The sudden change in temperature did nothing to dull the flame that was building inside of her. She curled her toes, pressing the balls of her feet hard into the tile while her heels arched high. Her senses had abandoned her. She was blind. She could hear nothing. But she could feel one thing. Her thighs tensed; her knees were like magnets, pulling together from an unseen force. With the slight lift of her hips, the shock tore through her body. Her back pressed against the wet tile wall, her body quivering gently.

The moment was silent. She didn't utter a sound, but her insides were screaming. Her body went soft; her ass was again on the shower floor. Her arms dropped to the sides of her hips as she worked to catch her breath. Her other senses were slowly returning. The sound of water spraying against the floor was the first to return, followed by the realization that it was now cold. She reached a sluggish arm up high over her head to tinker with the knobs again, turning the heat back up. Her body was too spent to crawl from the floor just yet.

Kira remained there for several minutes before forcing herself up. Standing under the hot water, she let it sink into her already sedated body as she replayed everything in her mind. *It wasn't the tequila. It was him.*

She ran a finger across her palm, watching it as she waited for some reaction. Just before she was about to give up, it responded with a soft flutter as if to say, "Good job."

KIRA WALKED on unsteady feet alongside Kat and Nadia. They didn't know she had poured herself another shot while they were in the other room. Her body didn't want to let go of the feeling, but she needed something to help bring the boil down to a simmer. Otherwise, she wouldn't be able to function.

She wore jeans tattered at the knees, and a copper-toned top with a high neckline and open V down the back. The rusty hue highlighted the bronze tint of her complexion. Her hair was pulled back away from her face in a sleek ponytail. A few stray strands fell around the edges, framing her face, tickling the skin along her exposed back. Her brown leather peep-toe sandals gave her an extra few inches. She felt beautiful and sexy. Kira hadn't realized it until now just how long it had been since she'd had this feeling.

"Where are we going again?" she asked, focusing on her steps. *Damn, I should have eaten something earlier.*

"Um," Nadia hemmed and hawed around the words. "We're meeting up with Jade at a party."

They'd been walking for about ten minutes. Other large groupings of people walked along the sidewalk, and the street parking was completely packed. Maybe it was the tequila. Maybe it was her earth-shattering orgasm, but she was completely unaware of the direction they were headed. It was implausible that a neighborhood she walked through daily didn't register any familiarity. Either way, her inner thoughts were screaming at her the moment they rounded the corner, and the Calloway Estate came into view.

Kira stopped dead in her tracks as Nadia and Kat walked on for several feet before turning back for her. "Really?"

"What?" Nadia feigned innocence. "Come on. It'll be fun," she whined in a playful tone, tugging at Kira's arm.

Kira opened her mouth and closed it again. How could she justify her reasons for avoiding this place, her reasons for avoiding *him*? She shifted her stance, pressing her thighs closer together to smother the sudden sensation she felt between her legs. How did the mere thought of him make her feel like she was back in the shower? "We don't even know these guys. We can't just party crash."

"We're not. That one guy Jade's been going on about lives here. Remember? He invited her, and she asked us to meet her here. Plus," said Nadia, holding out a hand, gesturing to the house and the many people passing through the gates, "it kind of looks like a free for all."

"And you said that guy you met the other night was really nice," Kat added.

"Whoa! What? You met one of them?" Nadia's eyes lit up. "Which one?"

Kira shrugged, her eyes not meeting either of her friends. "It was nothing. I ran into one of them. Blake. I think he's the one who owns the house. We talked for like two minutes. It was nothing." She clamped her mouth shut at the realization she was repeating herself, which made nothing sound like something.

Nadia didn't waste a moment, grabbing onto her friends' arms, and dragging them across the street. "Sounds like an invitation to me!"

Kira eyed the gate as they approached it, suddenly wishing they'd brought along the bottle of tequila. Warmth filled her body as they passed under the gates. She flexed her hand but felt nothing. However, she continued to feel that flood of sensitivity between her legs, unsure if she loved it or hated it.

116

The driveway was long. Cars were lined up on both sides; the massive oaks hung above them. Ground lights pointed high to illuminate the trees and the moss that clung to them, providing a faintly lit path. A light breeze rustled the leaves and the branches, making the moss sway. Kira was in awe as she looked skyward. A break in the canopy above featured a blanket of stars against a velvety blackness. The stillness and quiet somehow managed to block out the noise of other guests hurrying past.

She paused midway, her eyes still locked on the sky. She felt something. It wasn't her hand. It wasn't the ache between her legs. It wasn't the alcohol. She tilted her head slightly, and closed her eyes, attempting to focus. It seemed oddly familiar, as if she'd sensed it before, something fluttering to life from deep inside of her.

"Let's go, weirdo! You need to introduce me to your friend."

Nadia's tug on her arm yanked her out of her stupor. She glanced over her shoulder at the space she was just standing in, half expecting to find evidence of the flutter she'd just felt. As she turned back, she caught Kat's eye who mouthed, *You okay?*

Kira gave her a less than believable smile. She had become so good at lying. Maybe the alcohol had thrown her off her game. She was grateful for the reassuring arm Kat tossed around her waist.

As they approached the front steps of the porch, the house seemed so much more grandiose than it had from the street. From afar, it was a palatial rampart of white stretching across the lush green lawn. Up close, she could see the many architectural details of the house, including the intricate patterns of the moldings and the ornate scroll and leaf designs along the friezes. The porch ceilings were painted a pale blue, like a summer sky, and boasted a large circular medallion that circled an openwork pendant lantern with an oiled bronze finish. Inviting daybed swings dressed with fluffy pillows flanked each side of the porch, and overhead fans offered a light breeze. Open to the flow of guests, the substantial double doors were surrounded by thick casings adorned with two bulky hand-carved corbels. Everything was a work of art, carefully crafted to be beautiful and comfortable.

"Wow. This place is amazing," said Kat as they made their way into the front foyer.

Kira and Nadia could only nod as they took in the scene.

The loudness of the music at the back of the home was invading the silence that her reverence had created. There was a peacefulness in that blissful ignorance, but she was suddenly crashing back into reality. *I'm in his house.*

She glanced around as they made their way to the back. To her left she caught sight of a large group of people shooting pool, and thought she heard the telltale clinking sounds of a pin-ball machine. An unexpected tug at her heartstrings made her think of Colin. She had purchased an old vintage machine for him on his last birthday. He hadn't gotten it up and running just yet, but he'd promised her the ceremonial first pull of the ball plunger.

As they passed through the rotunda, Kira had the same feeling she'd gotten when she walked up the drive. It fluttered to life, causing her to pause again. She turned to notice the massive door at the base of the staircase. She started for it, but from the corner of her eye, she spotted someone she knew. A girl from her modern dance class making out with a guy on the steps. Her skirt rode high on her thigh, her arms slightly limp. She appeared drunk.

Kira put a steadying hand on Kat and took in the sight for a moment before intervening. "Amy! Hey!" She smiled at the girl and made quick eye contact with the guy who seemed surprised and slightly annoyed. "Are you okay? Do you want to get some water?" She signaled to Kat and Nadia for help, lifting the girl from the stairs, and took her towards the kitchen before shooting the guy a look of disgust.

The kitchen was full of people, packed around a wide island

filled with plates of food, cocktails, and bottles of beer. Nadia found the fridge and retrieved a bottle of water for the girl just as her friend intercepted them.

"Thank you! I couldn't find her anywhere," she said, clearly relieved as she took the girl's weight off Kira's shoulders and walked her outside for some air.

"Good call. I got total date rapey vibes from that guy," Nadia stated, pulling out a couple of beers from the fridge, passing them over.

Kira eyed the bottle briefly before accepting it. She probably shouldn't have anything more tonight. She was past her limit already, but her nerves were still heavily present. She was appreciative that Kat didn't give her the uneasy look she'd been expecting. Kat wasn't judgmental, but she knew this was categorically uncommon behavior.

The three made their way through one of the many sets of French doors that opened out onto the veranda. As for where the front portion of the house was designed to elicit feelings of calm and nostalgia, this part of the house was created for function, entertainment, and visual appeal. It was just as beautiful. An aged, white-washed brick assembled in a herringbone pattern ran the length of the covered veranda. A step outside of it, a large yard of plush green surrounded a long pool, overflowing with half-naked coeds. Loungers and daybeds lined the stretch of water. Beyond it, masked in dim lights, Kira could make out rows of hedges and paths lined with trees and tiers of flower beds. Twinkle lights highlighted the oaks that flanked the main lawn's outer edges, and occasional ground lights and lanterns lit the paths through the gardens.

"Holy crap," Nadia exclaimed, taking a drink from her beer.

Kat followed her lead, taking a drink of her own. "Ditto."

They spent the next hour enjoying the night. It was indeed a great party. Fortunately, there were many people that they knew, keeping her busy, thus keeping her mind from straying into unwanted territory. It was nice living in the present, and not in a constant state of worry about all her issues. It was an unwanted weight off her shoulders.

Blake was still nowhere to be seen. *Maybe he isn't even here.* She absentmindedly sipped on a rum-filled cocktail after quickly downing the beer Nadia had stolen from the fridge. She was beginning to feel the alcohol take its toll on her faculties, but she was charmed by the liberation it offered as well as the warmth in her cheeks. Kira found herself back at the outdoor bar, asking for another drink. *Last one;* she told herself.

Looking back out over the lawn, she saw Nadia flirting shamelessly with a cute frat guy and Kat dipping her legs into the pool while chatting with Jade. It was the first time since they arrived that she was left alone with her thoughts, just her and Captain Morgan.

She turned and made her way back inside, taking the time to admire the interior. It was a beautiful blend of modern and old-world with rich woods, worn leathers, and clean lines. It wasn't what she expected from the outside, though she wasn't sure exactly what she expected. The rooms were stylish, but also warm and inviting.

It was later in the night now. The crowd was a mixture of loud and rowdy partiers, and mellow hookups in quiet corners. She made her way past the main living spaces with slow and careful steps, back to the rotunda where she had rescued Amy earlier. Kira eyed her drink, flooded with the ironic realization that she probably wasn't too far from the same state herself.

It was in that same moment when that little flutter stirred within again. It was much less pronounced this time, that she almost didn't notice it. Maybe the alcohol was drowning it out. She straightened her spine at the thought, realizing she actually wanted to seek it out. The door she'd noticed earlier in the night was now directly across from her. As she stood in the center of the rotunda, she stared it down. Guests brushed past her from multiple directions, but she never broke her gaze. The flutter grew stronger. It reminded her of nervous butterflies, but she didn't feel anxious.

It felt more like intuition.

Kira took a few steps and closed the space between herself and the door. She was within arms-length of it now. It was a massive piece of wood, towering high above her. It was a door, but it felt like so much more, a gateway into something entirely singular in the same breath. She inhaled, bracing herself as she lifted her palm towards it, her hand hovering only inches away.

Another sensation abruptly pulled her focus, one she was becoming more and more familiar with. She turned to find Blake rushing down the stairs, feet bare, as he pulled a black t-shirt over his head, catching a quick glimpse of the ripples down the lower front of his body. His eyes seemed feral and his hair handsomely disheveled. She lowered her hand, and forced a smile, pretending as if she hadn't just been caught about to sneak into a closed room of a stranger's home.

"Kira?" His voice was uneasy, appearing confounded and distressed as if he were the one about to break trust and enter through locked doors.

She gave a small wave, still embarrassed. "Hi." *Why are words so hard to form in his presence?* Those dreamy blue eyes locked onto hers. *That's why*; she suddenly remembered.

"Blake, what are you doing?"

Kira followed the sound of his name up the stairs, only six or seven steps above him. It was a beautiful dark-skinned girl in a similar state of undress that Blake himself was in just moments before. Her long dark hair was in disarray and spilled over her open blouse. The skirt she wore was still intact. Kira watched as she glided a manicured toe along the back line of her smooth leg. Her lips twitched, seeing that the girl's feet were also bare, before glancing back to Blake, only his eyes were still on her.

Blake ignored the gorgeous girl at his back as he took a small step towards her, his head tilted. "I wasn't expecting to see you."

Kira mirrored his step, moving slightly closer to him. "I'm sorry. My friends drug me here," she said, searching for a perfect explanation. "I think my friend, Jade, has a thing for one of your roommates."

Blake opened his mouth as if to say something, but then closed it again. Kira realized he seemed to be as nervous as she was. She couldn't fathom why. Her eyes broke from his as the girl moved down the stairs, folding herself into his side.

Kira forced another smile. *Of course, he has a girlfriend, you, idiot.*

"It's okay. I'm glad you came," he said, detaching his arm from the girl's grip, taking the final step off the staircase.

"Kira?"

Hearing her name again gave her a sudden sense of whiplash. She turned to find Colin standing a few feet away in the foyer. Her jaw slackened, and her eyes narrowed, unsure of how to respond. She was rooted to the spot, unable to look back at Blake, but also unable to maintain eye contact with Colin. Instead, she focused on the bottle of water in his hands.

"Hey," he said, taking a couple of cautious steps toward her, quickly shooting Blake a defensive glare before looking back to her. His eyes matched his softer tone. "Can we talk?"

All her emotions were betraying her right now. She felt everything and nothing at the same time. Unsure she could speak real words, she simply nodded. Kira turned back to Blake. Those blue eyes still as radiant as before pierced her all over again.

Talking with Colin had not been high on her priority list for tonight, especially after as many drinks as she'd had. But it felt safer than standing under the weight of Blake's stare.

"It was good to see you, but I need to," her voice trailed off as she gestured to Colin.

Kira followed him through the foyer and out onto the front porch. She hadn't looked back, but she sensed that Blake had watched her until she disappeared through the front doors. She was conflicted. A part of her felt a sense of shame, especially since this other girl boar witness to it, but at the same time, she felt a rush of electricity, one that ignited in her core and radiated outwards all the way to her toes.

Her hand wrapped in his felt foreign. She looked down at it as Colin led her to the far corner of the porch, setting his water bottle on a nearby table. She firmly held on to her cocktail.

Leaning against the railing, he avoided looking at her face. Like her, he heavily examined their fingers intertwined together. He stayed like this for a long time, as if there were no words to appropriately express his thoughts.

Outside, the noise from the party dampened, the air felt strange and flat, making her feel exposed. The silence between them was like a void with an urgent need to claw its way out to escape the bubble they were trapped in. The drink in her hand grew heavier by the minute. She wanted a sip, but even in her inebriated state, she knew it would be a slap in the face to Colin.

In an attempt to break their silent bubble, she stretched an arm out to the table to discard her drink, only to stumble on her heels. Colin grasped her by her waist, steadying her, and finally met her eyes.

She wished he hadn't done that. The thought of falling on her face and spilling her drink everywhere would have been a better fate than looking into those eyes. Kira looked away as tears spilled over before one word was ever spoken. Colin tucked a stray strand behind her ear before pulling her in close to his chest and rested his chin atop her head.

The water on the table stared back at her. *Stupid, judgmental water bottle.* "You're not drinking."

Colin created enough space between them so he could look down at her. He followed her line of sight to his water, realizing what she meant. "No. I haven't had a drink since that night," he confessed, searching her face for answers. "I messed up. I knew it the moment those words left my mouth. I didn't mean it. I was hurt."

Her eyes roamed over his briefly before turning away again. His face wasn't a safe place to rest, mostly because she could sense his sincerity. It would've been easier if he'd said all the wrong things and she could storm off in anger.

"I didn't want to be alone in that hurt, so I did the one thing I never wanted to do. I drug you down into that place with me," he stated, pressing his hands to the sides of her face, and tilted her head towards him. "And you don't deserve to live in that place. You are my light and my joy. You are everything good in my life. I love you."

She swayed in his arms. Captain Morgan was proving to be a terrible wingman. "I love you too. Let's go home." In her muddled mind and conflicted heart, it was all she could manage.

As they made their way off the front porch and down the stairs, she kept herself tightly folded into his side, using his strength to support her drunken weight. Once again, she couldn't bring herself to glance back across her shoulder as they made their way down the drive, because somehow, she knew Blake would be standing there.

AS HE BRUSHED HIS TEETH, Colin leaned in the door frame between the bathroom and Kira's bedroom. He watched her sleep, feeling a combination of relief that she had given him the time and space to apologize. But mostly, he was horrified to find her in the drunken state she was in. Kira didn't drink. *I did that. It's my fault.*

He was convinced more than ever that something was going on with her. She clearly didn't want to share it with him, but as he stood there watching her, thinking about the person she was and the relationship they had, it occurred to him she may not even know the issue herself. If he were honest with himself, he knew there was something he, too, was experiencing that he couldn't explain. His mind turned at the thought that maybe his actions were a result of hers.

Colin crawled into bed beside her. He sat up on his elbows and looked down at the woman he loved so much, wondering how everything had spun out of control so fast. He'd spent days trying to pinpoint the moment when everything had shifted but found it impossible.

"I love you," he whispered, leaning down to place a light kiss at her temple before falling back into the pillows.

It was late, and he was exhausted.

A couple of hours ticked away when Colin's sleep was interrupted by soft murmurs and gradual movement under the sheets. Yawning, he rolled onto his back, rubbing the remainders of sleep from his eyes. He looked Kira over, realizing she was in the midst of a dream. A good one, so it seemed.

"I sure hope it's me you're dreaming about," he muttered.

Colin didn't want to wake her, but he still felt the need to touch her. He rolled onto his side, pressing himself to her back, and placed a chaste hand at her hip under the covers. With his head buried in her hair, he inhaled deeply, remembering how much he loved these moments.

Surprising him, she quickly turned to face him, kissing him eagerly as she wrapped her hands into his hair and twined her legs with his. Caught off guard, he didn't immediately reciprocate, but her impassioned fervor awakened his own inner desire. He returned her kisses and matched her eagerness. His lips roamed down the length of her throat, his hands desperately pulling her closer and winding through her hair.

"I love you so much. I'm never going to let you go again," he panted into her ear between kisses.

Kira's moan was light, almost a laugh as she wrapped both hands around his head, pulling him close, her lips now at his ear. The sweetness in her voice evaporated, morphing into an almost vicious sounding growl, a sinister voice that was not her own: "She's no longer yours."

Colin's breath caught in his throat. He pulled back to put distance between them. Her eyes were closed as she laid motionless on the bed. *She's sleeping?*

He watched her for a moment as he gathered his composure. "Was I dreaming?" he whispered to himself. He ran a thumb over his mouth. His lips were slightly swollen, indicating that those kisses were real. He looked to her again, searching for answers, before finally laying back against the pillows. He rubbed his hands over his face, forcing out a heavy breath.

Convinced he'd dreamt it; he turned his head to find Kira staring back at him with blood-red eyes. He choked on a gasp, and fumbled backwards, his legs tangled in the sheets as he fought to move away. He hit the ground with a thud, but quickly wrestled his way to his feet.

His chest heaved as he paced backwards a few steps. The room was mostly dark, the streetlamps outside providing minimal light. Across the room, he could see that Kira was still curled up under the covers in bed. He took a few cautious steps towards her; his eyes narrowed. She was still sleeping. "What the fuck?"

He turned, looking around the room for answers. His breath still came hard and fast. He bent, bracing his hands against his knees for support. In the corner of his eye, he saw it, two bright red eyes staring back at him from the mirror.

"She's mine," the same sinister voice growled.

Colin fell backwards, hitting the ground – hard, before jolting straight up, finding himself in the bed again. He looked straight on; his hands clenched the sheets at his side as his lungs searched the space around him for oxygen. He jumped to the side at the sudden sensation of hands on him.

"Hey, are you okay?" Kira's voice was soft and laced with concern.

Colin stared at her, his brows furrowed in confusion, jaw slack. He flinched when she reached a comforting hand out.

"Hey. It's just me," she said, her tone even softer now as she cautiously tried to reach out again. Kira rubbed a hand along his shoulder and down his back, before scooting closer and wrapping him in a hug. "It's okay. It was just a nightmare."

He waited for several seconds before returning the hug, his breathing still heavy. Over her shoulder, he eyed the mirror across the room. "What do you see in that thing?"

Kira pulled away to look at him, following his gaze. "The mirror?"

Colin swallowed hard and nodded, still working to get his breathing under control.

Kira shrugged, running her hand along his arm. "I don't know. It just called out to me when I saw it."

Colin didn't know why, but he had an incredible urge to walk across the room and put a fist through the glass.

ELEVEN
DANCE STUDIO

With the quickest of reflexes, Larz dodged to his right, barely missing the lamp that flew past his head, crashing against the door frame he'd just walked through. His eyebrows drew together as he gave Blake a poignant look. A quick glance around the room was clear evidence his brother was beyond distressed. He didn't say anything and took up a spot in the far corner where there was little destruction. It seemed like a safe zone.

Blake paced now after having run out of breakable things to smash. "How the fuck did that happen?"

Larz's eyes followed him as he moved back and forth in front of the bed. He knew his brother well enough to know when, and when not to speak. It was best to let him get it all out first.

"How did none of us know she was there? How? She was in our damn house!" Blake bit out. He found an empty beer bottle at the foot of the bed, gripped it by the neck, and swung it towards the wall like a dagger. The glass shattered on impact. He spun around to look back at Larz. "She was at the fucking door. She saw it. Had I not sensed her when I did, she may have even gotten in." His eyes were wild, and his hands shook.

Larz leaned forward, resting his forearms across his knees. "She couldn't have gotten in. It's impossible." His voice was cool, but firm.

"You weren't there. You didn't see it," Blake shouted, shaking his head.

He couldn't be convinced, otherwise. His layers of control were peeling back again. Every shudder in his shaking palm was alien to him. He eyed it with disdain as he flexed his fingers in and out of a fist. An overwhelming pressure built in his chest with each failed attempt to get the shaking in check. Without warning, he took two quick steps towards the nearest wall, slamming his fist through the sheetrock.

Larz dropped his head. His long wavy hair hid the smirk on his face, but it wasn't enough to contain the laugh that slipped free. He looked back up, shaking his head as he watched Blake pull a battered and bleeding hand from the gaping hole.

"Oh, this is funny to you, is it? Every damn thing we've been working towards is at risk, and you're sitting there laughing."

"Bloody hell. Nothing is at risk. We are in the same place today that we were at this time yesterday. If anything, we've learned something. We know her magic is growing stronger. From where I sit, that's a good thing. She's the fucking *Supra*, brother. That's what we want."

Blake turned away, wrapping his mangled hand in a t-shirt.

Larz stood, his hands deep in his pockets. "But that's not really what this is about. Is it?" He waited for his brother to say something, but he remained silent, his back to him. "You can stack those bricks as high as you want around your thoughts, but I can still see it."

That blunt swell in his chest returned. Blake turned slowly to face his brother, using every passing second to gauge his expression, to weigh out how much he knew, and form a compatible response. Larz was typically easy to read, wearing his emotions on his sleeve, but he couldn't make heads or tails of what he should say right now.

He released a heavy breath, took a seat at the edge of the bed, and opted for another approach. "Then tell me what the hell it is, you see."

"It's simple. You like this girl."

"Bullshit!" Blake belted, his upper body falling back against the mattress.

"You just put a damn hole through the wall, not to mention the numerous antiques you demolished up here. Call me crazy, but that seems like something someone does when they're . . . *jealous.*"

Blake shot up straight, his head tilted, and eyes drawn together as his lips twitched. "What the fuck are you talking about? I don't do *jealous.*"

"I'm not sure that you're more upset about her being in our house without us sensing her, as much as you are about having to watch her leave with that walking, talking . . . what was it you called him? Oh yeah, that frat paddle of a boyfriend of hers," Larz remarked, light mockery lacing his tone.

He eyed his brother for a long time, allowing his words to sink in, before walking across the room. "I'm going out to get some air."

"Yeah . . . you go do that . . . and quit destroying shit."

———

BLAKE WAS STILL in the same jeans and t-shirt as the night before. He'd spent most of his night in mental turmoil, trying to overcome the feelings that were hammering his insides. In the bright light of the day, he realized how much he wished he'd showered. Rayna's perfume still lingered.

The thought had him pressing his hands tightly against his face, rubbing at his eyes and along his neck as if he could forcefully purge the memory from his mind. Larz was right when he'd said watching her leave with Colin bothered him more than him being caught off guard again. She had clearly been drinking, and seeing Colin be the one to take care of her made his fists coil.

It was late morning, but the New Orleans heat had already settled in for the day. Blake could feel the sweat bead on the back of his neck. He walked faster as if he could outrun his thoughts, but they were as stealthy as they were fast. He couldn't shake them easily.

Going nowhere in particular, he opted to cross the street to take a shadier path beneath the flowering dogwoods. They offered a minimal respite from the heat, but he was grateful for it. He carefully monitored his own footfalls as he stepped along the sidewalk, blanketed in fallen white blooms. It was almost like snow, but without the satisfying crunch beneath each step.

He liked the snow; he was highly accustomed to it, growing up in England, and then moving to Massachusetts. But this heat, on the other hand, he would be happy to do without.

"*Célnes*," Blake spoke the word softly under his breath, but the magic in that one word wrapped around him vibrantly. The coolness hit his face immediately and sent a satisfying smile to his lips. The breeze shook through the trees, allowing even more petals to float to the ground. *Almost as good as snow*.

He'd been walking for some time now. It was a much more pleasant practice with his own magical A/C unit following him around. It seemed the walk finally had the desired impact, clearing his thoughts. Kira was still there on the forefront, but his mind didn't feel as muddled.

Blake thought again to that one-word Larz had spoken: *Jealous.* He rolled his eyes. But fuck if Larz wasn't right. How could it be though? He'd given himself over to the darkness a long time ago. You have to care about something in order to feel jealousy, and he simply wasn't capable of that type of human emotion. That part of him didn't exist anymore.

Larz did, however, miss one thing. The one thing that was tearing at his insides more than anything was the moment when Kira looked up at him on the stairs, and then to Rayna at his side. Worse. A half-dressed Rayna. It barely registered on her face, but he saw it. Disappointment.

Blake pushed out a weighty breath. It was the reaction he should have been hoping for but seeing it behind those hues of honey and green stung him deep. What was eating at him today wasn't jealousy. It was shame.

Shame. He stopped in his tracks and flinched at the thought. As he stood there, he began to feel something else, something external. He spun on his heel as it wound around him. With his chin lifted, he inhaled deeply, recognizing it. *It's her magic.* Blake tuned out everything around him, the chatting of people on the sidewalk, the sounds of cars, the smell of the bakery next door, fixating only on the scent and feel of her power.

With his own, he locked on and walked a few further steps down the street, opening the door to a building without even looking to see where he was going. He made a beeline up the stairs, waving away the words of a woman, probably the receptionist, telling him he wasn't allowed to go up. "*Ungesewen,*" he whispered as he rounded a corner out of her sight, making himself unseen.

It was the same incantation he spoke the night he sat beside Kira as she and Colin fought. He continued the spell throughout the night, walking alongside her as she cried. Standing at a window along the wall of the long upstairs hallway, he now watched her as she sat on the floor, stretching out alone in a room full of mirrors.

The woman from downstairs was rounding the corner now. She breezed past him, peering through the various windows of the hall. Clearly confused about where Blake had disappeared to, she opened the door to Kira's studio, propping it open with her hip. "Hey! Did you by chance see a guy in a black t-shirt walk through here?"

She was far enough inside for him to slip in behind without touching her.

Kira shook her head. "Sorry, no." They both watched her disappear and walk through the hallway, continuing her search.

The small private studio was painted a stark white with floor to ceiling mirrors along two walls. The outer wall featured an expansive window to the city below, allowing the late morning sun to beam through. Standing here alone, in the bright light of day, was vastly different from walking alongside her in the dark, surrounded by others. The small space was quiet. So much so, he feared she might hear his heart pounding in his chest. As soundlessly as possible, he eased himself down against one of the mirrored walls.

Blake watched her intently. She still sat on the hardwoods, meticulously flexing her feet, and using her hands to stretch out her toes before sliding them into a pair of worn pink pointe shoes. With her foot placed firmly on the floor, she carefully made work of the ribbons, tying them tightly around her ankle. She stood, seemingly testing the fit, flexing her foot again as she held the wall for support.

He suddenly felt as if he was invading her space as if he were witnessing some special ritual meant for no one but herself. Maybe it was because she was under the guise she was completely alone. He'd invaded her space before, kept himself out of sight, placed himself in her dreams, made her feel things, but now in the bright white light, there were no shadows to conceal what he was feeling right now. It was a mixture of utter awe, outright fear, and an odd serenity. It reminded him of skydiving, the adrenaline of free-falling from ten thousand feet. The amazing sensation of flying, and the peace you get from seeing the world from that vantage point.

Yes, being here with her right now was like skydiving.

Without warning, she started walking towards him. Directly toward him. He pushed up with his hands and heels as if to flee just as she knelt beside him. He looked down at her duffle bag that rested only inches away. He looked back to her, watching her as she rummaged through it. He only had a short few seconds before she found what she was looking for, but in that moment, she was so close.

He'd been this close before, but this was different. The light changed everything. She wore no makeup, but her golden skin glowed. She wasn't wearing her normal perfume, but her hair smelled as if it were freshly washed, like strawberries. He watched her dip a single finger into a pallet of lip gloss and lightly rub it across her bottom lip, leaving a light sheen. An immediate need to wrap his fist around her fruit-scented hair, and kiss those newly softened lips surged through him.

She was better than skydiving.

Kira walked over to a small speaker in the corner, and thumbed through her phone, setting it down after a few moments. She quickly tied her hair back with an elastic from her wrist as she made her way to the middle of the floor, taking a statuesque stance with her feet pointed out at seemingly uncomfortable angles. One arm floated high above her head, and the other stretched out to her side. Despite the strength in her body, he noticed her hands and fingers appeared delicate, almost frail in comparison.

At the start of the music, she glided up onto her toes. It was a soft movement that matched the tempo in the melody. Her eyes followed the flow of her hands, never seeming to look down at her own feet, which perched precariously high over her toes. She made it look effortless.

This must be her own form of skydiving, he thought to himself as he quietly stood, and took a few steps closer, resisting the urge to grab her here and now. Her body was strong, but soft in all the right places. The strappy black leotard she wore silhouetted her form yet detailed the muscle tone in her thighs and calves. He imagined her wrapping those legs around him. On the hit of a note, she elevated into arabesque, balancing her entire body on the toes of her right foot, her left leg lifted high behind her, almost at shoulder height. Her right arm stretched delicately in front of her, her chin followed it gracefully as her left arm reached back. The move was as sexy as it was elegant. She moved like water, languid and easy, impossible to know where one part began and the next ended.

He backed up to the table holding the speaker, and her phone to take a glance at the song; *Tallisman Stallion*. It sounded to be purely piano. It wasn't something he would have personally chosen, but as he watched her, it was quickly becoming a favorite. At the end, she dropped to her flat feet. Even on pointed toes, she wasn't as tall as him, but the sudden height adjustment forced him to smile. *She's a tiny thing*.

Kira exhaled heavily, walking over to the table to grab her water. She pressed a dry towel to her neck while thumbing through her phone. His curiosity overcame him, leaning in closer than before to see what she was looking at. He knew right then he'd made a mistake.

The air shifted as he watched her muscles go rigid, and her breathing hitch. Her magic flared like a roman candle. With his hand to his chest, he took three slow, and steady steps backwards, trying to control his breathing, and remain as quiet as possible. He watched her stare down the space between them, almost as if she knew there was something there she couldn't see. She took a small step forward, closing the gap. Then another. She was less than three feet away, staring directly at him, but still not seeing him. Or was she? He almost wasn't sure.

Kira tilted her head; her eyes narrowed as if she could almost see it. Almost see him. Her breathing became heavier, as did his. His eyes widened as he watched her lift an unsteady hand in front of her, her fingers tracing the air between them. His mind and his heart were conflicted between the need to remain unseen and his desire to reach out and twine his fingers with hers.

The sudden roar of a Taylor Swift song jolted Kira out of her daze, dropping her phone to the ground. She placed a shaky hand on her chest. "Shit! What is my problem?" she chastised herself as she chased her vibrating phone across the floor.

Blake swallowed hard, taking this moment to walk to the far wall and slow his own thundering heart.

"Hey . . . yeah, I'm at the studio."

He slid back down the wall again. It was best to stay seated for now. He pressed his senses out, listening in on the other side of their conversation. *The roommate. At least it isn't the boyfriend.*

"I'm sorry you ducked out so early last night. I was so surprised to see Eric, I nearly fell in the pool. He told me you and Colin were talking."

"Yeah. We did."

"And?"

Blake watched her look around the room as if she were searching for the right words. "We . . . we talked. We made up. Things are not perfect, but," she trailed off, unable to finish her thought.

"But?"

"I don't know. I love him, but."

There was that 'but' again.

136

Kat finished for her: "But you don't know if it's enough anymore."

Kira slid down the wall on the opposite side of the room. Even with the expanse between them, he could feel the tear roll down her cheek.

"Maybe." She was lying. He could tell. Maybe she couldn't right now, but he knew it. "He was good to me last night. He wasn't drinking."

Kat laughed. "Well, that's a good thing. Except that you were a little less than sober."

"Um. Just a bit. It's a miracle I got out of bed this morning." She laughed dryly, pressing two fingers at her temple, massaging lightly.

"How are you feeling? I know that's not your thing. I wanted to say something, but I kind of felt like you deserved a pass. You're not pissed at me for letting you get wasted, are you?"

"No! Not even a little bit. Honestly, I'm kind of glad I did. Surprisingly, it helped me put some things in perspective."

Blake wondered if she meant him. Did she put him in perspective? He dropped his head in thought while still trying to listen in on their conversation.

"Huh? That's not usually tequila's strong suit, but if it worked, take your winnings, and run sweetie. You know, I did get to meet the guy Jade's been going on about. I think his name was Armand. Dude, he's hot! Did you get a chance to say hi to that other guy you met?"

Blake's head popped up again, staring across the space, eagerly waiting for her response. Kira was slow to speak. He knew her answer before it left her lips, watching her shake her head before the lie followed. "No. I don't think he was around. Listen, I've only got a little time left here. I'll see you at home later."

The sound of them saying their quick goodbyes was drowned

out by the lie she just spoke. He replayed it over and over in his mind, dropping his head down again as that nagging word loomed over him once more. Shame.

Blake had been so wrapped up in the idea of who and what Kira was to him. Consumed by these unnatural feelings, he had needed a palate cleanser; someone to take the edge off. Rayna was there. And after giving her a little taste of what she might experience, she didn't hesitate to follow him to his room. It had worked temporarily. Rayna had already sucked his dick, giving him a much-needed release. She was stretched out half-naked on his bed, his lips tracing up her inner thigh, prepared to return the favor when he felt Kira's power.

He'd run out of the room with no words, attempting to clothe himself as he made his way down the stairs. Her face was like a light. A beacon shining down to illuminate all his mistakes and missteps. The moment he saw her, he regretted what he'd just done with Rayna. He was a four-hundred-year-old warlock. He didn't do regret. But that ugly feeling would pale in comparison to the feeling that followed. The one when her face dropped at the sight of the girl who had clearly been in his bed.

Blake lifted his head again to see her sitting like a mirrored image across the room, their backs both against the walls, legs stretched out in front, and eyes forward. At least twenty feet apart, he felt like she was in his arms and a million miles away at the same time. He sat watching and waiting while the void between them filled up with this new guttural feeling.

Shame.

TWELVE
FEAR AND DESIRE

I t was dark as Kira made her way home after an evening in the park. It was a nice night. The moon was bright, illuminating the clouds that hung against the velvety backdrop. The heat, surprisingly, had subsided, leaving behind a mild breeze that toyed with the loose strands of her hair. She wrapped her arms around herself, clinging to the stillness.

Kira welcomed the light rain that began, pausing to allow her head to dip back and feel the cool mist on her face, each drop washing away everything bad - the nightmares, the fights with Colin, the girl who clung to Blake's side. Nature's baptism. She opened her eyes, blinking back the water that hung to her lashes. She watched the clouds move restlessly in the sky and felt the darkness grow heavier around her as they conspired to conceal the moon.

It wasn't until then she realized the streetlights were out. She wrapped her arms around herself a bit tighter now, the rain suddenly turning cold and piercing. She continued along the sidewalk, hurrying to get home, her chin tucked to her chest.

Several minutes passed, blankly watching the pavement beneath her feet, when she finally looked up. Her eyes narrowed, spinning around. It was as if she hadn't moved at all. She was still standing under broken streetlights. With the moon still hidden behind the clouds, she couldn't see far in any direction. She stood silently, grateful for the slight respite in the rain. Her temporary blindness, now granting her other senses a new acuity.

Kira managed to keep the rise and fall of her chest steady, despite her racing heart. She knew her eyes should be adjusting to the darkness, but it felt like the blackness was growing thicker. Like a deer out in the open, sensing danger, she froze, listening intently. It was so quiet. Too quiet. Seconds passed. Minutes. Then, footsteps.

Her heart rate doubled. Still unable to see anything, she remained fixed, her limbs unwilling to move. She thought about calling out, but her voice failed her, too scared to even utter a sound. The footsteps continued. They were slow, meandering. Her head pivoted on her shoulders, unsure from which direction they were coming from. Each footfall echoed, vibrating off the pavement, making it sound as if they were coming from every direction.

It wasn't until she heard the pace in those steps increase that she found the courage to move her own two feet. She started slowly, stretching her arms out into the black inkiness that surrounded her. After several successful steps without running into anything, her confidence grew, and her feet moved faster. The faster she moved, the tighter the fear gripped her, propelling her into a full out sprint. She couldn't hear the footsteps any longer, only the thundering of her heart and the whoosh of air being forced in and out of her lungs.

Kira only slowed when the clouds finally dissipated, giving the moon the allowance to light the way. Her mad dash was now a wearied slog. A twig crunching beneath her sneaker had her jumping out of her skin, frantically spinning in place as her fractured nerves took on a new concern.

She was in the middle of a cemetery.

The rain was picking up again.

"Fuck," she mumbled, unsure of how she got here or even where *here* was. There wasn't a cemetery anywhere near her block that she was aware of.

The wind rustling against branches and bouncing off stone markers made it hard to hear. Fortunately, she could see again. On full alert, she took slow steps, occasionally turning on her heel, walking backwards to ensure she covered all her blind spots. She ducked behind a tall headstone, taking a moment to gather her thoughts and her breath before moving on, desperate to get home.

Despite her caution, one misguided step and gravity was pulling her down into the earth. Only a small gasp left her lips before landing hard. Groping the ground beneath her, she felt something resembling wet, grainy silk. A glance from her peripheral vision confirmed her worst fear. She'd fallen into a coffin within a freshly dug grave. She rolled onto her back, the black sky staring back at her, when the lid suddenly snapped shut, locking her inside. The rain hammered against the wooden box as water began to pool inside.

"Let me out!" Kira screamed, banging with her hands, and kicking with her feet to no avail.

The lid would not budge. An entirely new degree of panic rooted within her. This was one of her worst fears; being buried alive.

With each thrash of her limbs, she could sense the box sliding deeper into the earth. She froze, inhaling deeply, trying to regain her composure. Kira pressed her hands firmly against the sides of the small space, hoping, praying that she might find a way to free herself. She could see nothing but blackness. An eerie silence filled the space. The only sounds were the rain and her breath. No . . . not her own breath. She could feel the warmth of it at the base of her neck.

I'm not alone.

Her heart thudded like tiny explosions in her ears. Before she could find her own scream, the lid was violently ripped away. The moon above granted her the absence of darkness. Kira remained still for only a moment, the rain soaking her face, before she clamored to her feet. Looking back down into the box, she saw that she was indeed alone. She glanced back up into the rain to assess her situation. She must have been six feet deep in the ground. Fighting to climb her way out of the hole, she gripped onto roots that were barred along the edge of the earth. But she slid back down, the dirt now all muck and slime.

Kira screamed, praying someone would hear her, "Help me, please!" Her frantic calls quickly shifted to weak whispers at the thought that the person behind those earlier footsteps might hear her. She needed to get out of this on her own.

Over and over, she tried to climb out as the casket continued to fill with water. Heaving for air, her muscles fatigued, she glared up at the wall of mud, feeling defeat. With one final push, she gripped firmly onto a root with one hand, her other clawing deep into the mud as she kicked off the side of the wooden box. *It's working.*

Her head was above the ground, her elbows just over the edges as her feet fought the gravity below them. As one foot found a firm grip against a rock lodged within the muddy wall, she could feel her freedom. One push, and she would be climbing out, but she put too much faith in the stone, allowing it to hold more of her weight than she should have. With one slip, she fell backwards, landing in a painful splash.

Kira laid there for several seconds, squinting from the rain, her chest heaving in exhaustion, before finding one more ounce of determination. But just as she began to crawl to her feet, she felt an invisible wall just above her. She pushed with her hands and felt the clear outline of a person. A man. Kira recoiled back, her eyes searching for something that was not there. She went still. A heartbeat passed. She could see it now. His breath. It hung in the air a mere inch from her face.

The rain was slowing. The clearing of clouds made way for the moon to shine brighter. Kira steadied her eyes upon the invisible force in front of her. She couldn't see him, but knew he was there. Raindrops hung and rolled down his invisible face, giving it a faint shape. Finding some boldness within, she straightened, slushing the pool of rainwater she sat in. She cautiously reached an unsteady hand out, her fingers pressing into the firmness of the man's chest. She felt his body shift under her touch, moving closer to her. She inhaled deeply, feeling the softness of fingers tracing the side of her cheek and tucking back strands of wet hair.

Kira was quiet; her eyes remaining on the only physical manifestation she could see, his breath that still lingered in the air. She wanted to say something. She wanted to know who he was. Why he was there. Could he help her? Just as she raised her eyes and parted her lips to speak, she felt strong hands grip the sides of her face and push her violently below the surface of the water. Her hands locked onto his arms, trying to push them away. Her eyes were closed tight, but she could still see darkness closing in. She opened them, desperate to find the light, to find oxygen; the surface of the water was a bare inch away.

Air. So close. She could feel herself fading. As the last puff of air bubbled from her lips, she saw him. His beautiful face leering down at her. The water distorted her view, but she could see his exquisite ocean blue eyes.

Kira bolted up out of bed, finding herself in the darkness of her room. Her breath was short and quick, her skin cold and damp with sweat. She leaned across the bed to flip on the lamp. As she pulled her hand away, she noticed the dark grime coating her fingers and nails. Biting her lip to stifle a cry, she glanced around her room, searching for an answer she knew she wouldn't find.

She stiffened at the sound of the knock outside of her door.

"Are you okay?" Kat asked with clear concern in her voice. "I thought I heard something, and I can see your light is on," she said, cracking the door open. "Can I come in?"

Still curled up with her knees to her chest, Kira blew out a sigh of defeat and tried brushing her hair and tears from her face. *How long can I continue to lie to her?* "Yeah, sure," she managed to croak out.

Kat darted to the side of the bed when she saw her. "Your face. It looks like you've seen a ghost. What happened?" she asked, crawling up beside her friend, taking her hand.

Kira risked a glance at the dirt that still soiled her nails and fingers. "Nothing. It was just another bad dream," she muttered, casually pulling her hand back, slipping both under the sheets. "I promise I'm fine."

"You are not brushing me off this time. You are tired all the time lately, and this isn't the first time I've heard you having a nightmare," she told her. "I am really worried about you."

Deep breath. Smile. Lie. New day, same routine. As good as she was at this now, she could see that it wasn't having the same effect. Kat knew her better than anyone. It took thirty minutes and as many lies before she hesitantly left the room.

Another several minutes passed before she found the courage to pull her hands from beneath her sheets. Kira glared at the dirt crammed under her nails, before jumping out of her bed to rush to the bathroom. She scrubbed hard, watching the blackness swirl in the sink before disappearing into the drain. Her hands still damp, she meekly made her way back into her room, catching her reflection in the mirror. She paused, squaring herself to the glass, taking a long deep look. Kira didn't recognize herself. It was clearly her, but she lacked something. Glancing down at her now clean hands, she wondered if what she was missing was left behind in that cold dark grave.

"I am so over this."

Throwing on a t-shirt and pair of shorts, she tiptoed past Kat's door and eased her way down the stairs, stopping to write a quick note on their shared dry erase board in the kitchen. *Going for a run and then to Colin's place.*

It was only 5 am and still somewhat dark outside. The moment she left the driveway and glanced back at her home in the rearview mirror, Kira let the tears flow freely. *Lies. More Lies.* She was cloaked in them.

"What is wrong with me?" she sobbed, slamming her fist into the steering wheel.

She didn't know where she was going as she drove aimlessly. This had not been the first time she'd used Colin as a ploy to distract Kat and avoid her questions. Kira slowed as she approached the turn that would take her to his apartment. A faint tug at her heartstrings willed her to make that turn. She sat in silence for a long moment before driving forward.

Minutes later, she found herself in the parking lot at the edge of Audubon Park. The sun was just starting to creep up and brighten the sky, tinging it with shades of pink. Kira made her way across the grass, still wet from the morning dew. She had a lot of amazing memories here. Picnics with her parents, school field trips, and play dates. She even had her first kiss under the big oak tree behind the pavilion.

Kira wrapped her hands around the cold chain links and settled into one of the many swings. She swayed lightly, dragging the toes of her sneakers into the ground. The air was crisp and fresh. She pushed her feet against the ground a little harder, allowing the wind to catch her hair. She shifted her weight, pumping her legs back and forth, picking up momentum. She felt that sense of freedom again. It was the same way she felt in her dance finals and again during her tequila laced shower. This place was anchoring her back to reality. She was alive.

After several minutes, she allowed herself to slow down and soak it in. "I'm okay," she told herself as if saying it out loud where her own ears and the sky itself could hear would make it true. Closing her eyes, she tilted her head, resting it against the chains, and let out a long-winded sigh, releasing everything that had been pent up deep inside. At that moment, she was herself again.

Opening her eyes, she took in the scene. The sky was growing brighter, and she could see squirrels rustling across the grass foraging for breakfast. Her own stomach growled in response. She stood, stretching her arms in salute of the day, but then she caught a glimpse of something she'd never noticed before. She made her way down the hill just beyond the swings. At the very edge of the park, surrounded by a short and aged wrought-iron fence, sat a cemetery.

Her legs carried her down the hill before she even had time to fully process it. Her eyes roamed the grounds. It was old and relatively small compared to the cemeteries she'd seen herself. Much smaller than the one where her parents were buried. There couldn't have been more than thirty or so graves. She glanced back over her shoulder up the hill towards the swings.

How is it I've I never seen this place before? She took a closer look, resting her hands against the rusted fencing. There in the center, she saw it; a tall Megalith headstone, aged and covered in ivy. *The same as in my dream.*

Her body automatically took several quick steps back, tripping over her own feet. She pushed herself up as quickly as she could manage and ran back up the hill. She turned one last time as she reached the top, looking down on the nightmare she thought she'd left in the dimness of her room.

Kira was prepared to bolt for her car when a familiar twinge fluttered through her body. *He's here.* She didn't know how, but she knew it with a deep-seated certainty. She froze, unclear of what to do. The image of those blue eyes staring down at her while she choked on her last breath raced through her mind. And in the very cemetery that sat before her now. She took another step back, rapidly shaking her head, a hushed denial on her lips.

That light twinge inside of her grew stronger. Her cheeks flushed as an aching heat wound in her core, spreading between her thighs. It was like being doused with kerosene on an already out-of-control fire. Her head and body battled between two conflicting emotions: fear and desire.

Glancing over her shoulder, she saw him. He was wearing a t-shirt, athletic shorts, and running shoes. The sweat on his skin glistened like shiny delicate crystal beads. Looking away, Kira squeezed her eyes shut before risking another peek. He was no more than thirty yards away, lunging into a park bench with his back to her.

As if on cue, he turned to catch her gawking eyes. He smiled and waved before removing his ear buds as he walked over.

Stop staring, you stupid girl. That fearful part of her had almost disappeared until he was directly in front of her. Now towering over her, his eyes served as a disturbing reminder of being held down in that casket. *It was just a dream. A stupid dream.*

"I think we can call it official."

Kira shook her head. *Use words, moron.* It wasn't the first time he'd rendered her speechless, although now, she couldn't decipher if it were because of his raw sex appeal or because she thought he might kill her. "What?"

"That I need to get that restraining order," he smirked, giving her a flirty wink. "But I won't."

A smile. It came naturally and quickly. It was a rarity for her these days, and she longed for someone or something that could make her feel like this. *God, please don't let him be a serial killer.* The sight of other runners eased some of her tension. "I watched the sun come up, so I'm pretty sure I was here first. I guess that means you're following, me." She casually took a few steps to the side, further from the cemetery and closer to her car.

"That's your story, and you're sticking to it, eh?" Blake eyed her, his brows drawing together. "I'll admit though, I kind of like you purposely popping up everywhere I go. Even in my own home. That was a bold move."

The fire and fear inside her melted as a mixture of humiliation and jealousy set in.

"I like bold, though."

"I'm sorry about that," she murmured, her embarrassment growing. Another runner breezed by, and in the distance more cars were pulling into the lot. *He definitely wouldn't kill me here.*

"No. Don't be. I'm glad you came. But I'm sorry you left so quickly." He paused, the features of his face twisting slightly. "So . . . was that the boyfriend, then?"

"Was that the girlfriend, then?" Kira countered quickly, a little surprised by her own brass.

He seemed to be as well, his eyes lighting up at the challenge. "Jealous?"

"Not even a little." Maybe her well-practiced lies were paying off.

Blake laughed, replacing one of his ear buds. "You just keep on telling yourself that, darling," he joked as he took a few steps backwards. "I'm going to finish my run now. Try not to stalk me while I do it."

Kira watched him for only a few seconds before turning away.

No, he was harmless. Devastatingly gorgeous with an ego for days, but he wasn't a psycho killer invading her nightmares.

Walking back to her car, she thought about what he said. It was true; only she wasn't ready to admit it.

THIRTEEN
PRESENT

I t was nearly two am when Larz came lumbering down the stairs, shirtless, wearing nothing but jeans, escorting a tall, brunette to the front door. The girl tiptoed across the hardwoods with bare feet, her strappy stilettos dangling in her right hand as she clung to his arm with the other.

Leaning against the pool table in the billiards room, Blake raised a brow, a cocky grin across his face as he watched them pass by in the foyer. The loud cracking of the cue ball striking its target filled the otherwise quiet space. He didn't need to look behind him to know that several solid balls were falling into the pockets. Armand was much more skilled at this game than he was.

"What, no spooning after?" Blake joked, holding out his cue stick.

Larz grabbed it as he waltzed into the room, a satisfied smile across his face. "You know I only snuggle with you." He paused assessing the situation on the table. "So what's up here, you pussing out, bro?"

"It wouldn't be a fair fight," Armand boasted, leaning into the table to line up a shot before expertly striking the cue ball. He gave Larz a patronizing grin as he waited for the thud of another ball falling into its intended pocket.

This wasn't his game either, but Larz never backed down from a challenge. "You're on, fucker."

"So, where did you find that one?" Blake asked with casual indifference.

"The party. I gave her my one and only panty-dropping smile, and she gave me her number. As on cue, pun intended," Larz laughed, coating the end of the cue stick with chalk, "she came over as soon as I called. What can I say, I'm a chick magnet. No magic required!" A proud smirk stretched across his face as he rubbed his free hand across his chest, completely unaware of Armand's methodical movements on the table behind him. "I should sell that as a slogan. Have that shit printed up on t-shirts."

Armand called his shot before his brother even had a moment to register what was happening. He landed the hit, watching multiple solid balls glide into position and into their intended pockets.

Larz clenched his jaw and pressed his lips into a firm line as he eyed the table. "This is why no one wants to play with you," he snapped, pointing an accusatory finger at him.

Grinning, Armand shrugged, sinking the eight-ball with quick precision. "Rematch?"

"Hell, no!" He grabbed a beer from behind the bar, taking a long chug as he glared at the table, still unable to resist the challenge. "Damn it! One game. And I'm breaking."

Blake relaxed back in a wide armed, oversized leather chair, watching the drama unfold. It was amusing, temporarily taking his mind off Kira. It'd been two days since his last encounter, doing the necessary work to insert himself into her dreams each night. The growing need to get close to her again was starting to pry at his sanity.

Blake looked to Vincent, who sat next to him, slowly enjoying a bourbon while engrossed in a book, secretly envying his quiet repose and transparency. Vincent was stoic and unflappable in almost everything he did. Blake, too, typically exercised that same control, but it didn't carry the same poise as Vincent. Even with nearly four hundred years on him, there was still something to be learned from his newest brother.

A streak of light shining through thin slits in the blinds pulled his attention. The crunch of pea gravel beneath tires had all four of them moving to the window.

"Witchy, witchy, witchy," Larz joked, recognizing Rayna's car before they each followed him out onto the front porch. "Hello, ladies . . . back for more already?" he asked, rubbing his chest as Rayna, Tatiana, and Akesha exited the vehicle.

Rayna stood casually, her hands in the pockets of her denim jacket, a brazen smile on her lips. "We brought you all a present."

Blake looked down at her, noticing how her smile widened, showing a row of gleaming white teeth. Whatever the surprise, she was clearly excited to give it to them. He hadn't seen her since the party when he'd handed her off to his brother. Larz hadn't complained, happily taking both her and Tatiana to his bed.

He looked to each of his brothers, raising his shoulders in a casual shrug, before making his way down the steps. "Well, who doesn't love a present?"

A proud laugh escaped Larz's lips as the scent of the magic hit him. "Oh what, oh what, could it be?" He walked around to the back, his palms rubbing together in anticipation before popping the hatch. An appreciative smile spread across his face. "Awe! It's like Christmas morning!"

Blake, Armand, and Vincent followed in behind him to inspect their unexpected gift. The witch was young and her magic, meagre. Despite that, they were impressed. It hadn't been pressed upon them to go this extra mile, but they did it, nonetheless. They were expressing their loyalty.

"My beautiful ladies," Larz wrapped an arm around Tatiana's waist and stretched his other across both Rayna and Akesha's shoulders, pulling them in tight, "how are we going to repay this kindness?"

"I have some ideas," Rayna responded, her eyes on Blake, full of expectation.

It didn't go unnoticed. He held her stare. She clearly wanted to finish what they had started. He was tempted, still feeling the need to purge his feelings for Kira from his system.
"Vincent . . . Armand, would you please take our friends inside for a drink? Make them feel at home."

Larz waited until they were inside before speaking, his tone flat: "I'm highly offended."

Blake raised a brow.

"I saw that look," Larz said, hoisting the tiny witch over his shoulder. "I gave that woman the best night of her life and she's still eyeballing you."

Blake laughed, shaking his head, following his brother down a path around the side of the house. "Maybe she doesn't like sharing."

"Oh, I do. The more, the fucking merrier."

"Sounds like you sent your brunette friend home too early tonight."

Larz stopped in his tracks, his jaw slackened. "Fuck."

Blake continued past him, making his way to the back. "Like I said earlier, you should have cuddled."

It was a clear night, and the moon offered enough light to navigate the gardens easily. They walked in silence for several minutes before reaching the back gates. It was darker on this side of the wall. As where the gardens were mostly open, the canopy of trees veiled this space. Only small fragments of moonlight sifted down through the branches.

Blake followed Larz up the stairway that led to their hidden cistern and ritual site. They each took their final step into the void, passing through the portal. Once inside, Larz pushed open the only door, carrying the unconscious witch down the stairs, and eased her onto the stone slab.

He inclined his head, examining her tattoo covered arms before looking back up to Blake, who perched on the balcony above. "Hmm . . . didn't realize goth chicks were hot."

"I'm not surprised. I don't think your tastes are all too discerning. Here," he called out, tossing a cream-colored linen shift down to his brother.

"What the hell are you rambling on about? You and I both know I have superior standards . . . Too bad she can't come out and play. She could have subbed in as my third," Larz said, ignoring his brother's insult as he unfolded the dress, laying it out neatly beside her.

"You're a somnophiliac now?" Blake accused, his brows knitted together, gesturing to the comatose girl.

"Hell, fucking no! It was a bloody damn joke!" he retorted, smacking his brother in the back of the head as they made their way out. "You really need to take it down a few notches, bro, or in your case, up! Walls, that is!"

"Fuck!" Blake belted back. His thoughts were slipping back to her without even realizing it. She had seemingly taken up residency in the chasms of his mind, materializing whenever his guard was down.

Larz paused at the base of stone staircase. "Seriously though, who's bed is Rayna going to be occupying tonight?"

He didn't dare look to his brother, keeping his eyes forward. He knew exactly what he was asking, and it wasn't a request for another threesome with their new witch hunters. Larz had already accused him of 'liking' Kira. Opting not to sleep with Rayna would be a nonverbal confirmation he was right. And he wasn't ready for that to happen. He gave his brother an arrogant smile. "Mine of course."

They entered the house through the back entrance of the veranda, where their brothers were entertaining the three witches in the kitchen. They seemed relaxed, drinks in hand and laughing at something Armand had just said.

"Armand, how many times have I bloody told you to stop telling that lie. Yours is not bigger," Larz mused, mocking his brother. "Don't make me prove it. There are ladies present."

"Don't mind him. I embarrassed him in a game of pool just before you all arrived, and I think his pride is still hurt."

"True story," Blake confirmed, pouring himself a bourbon before holding up his glass. "Ladies. My brothers and I want to thank you for your surprise visit. You've shown your loyalty. And as promised," he continued looking to Rayna, holding out a hand, "you shall be rewarded."

She paused for only a moment before accepting it, biting her lower lip to disguise her smile as he led her from the kitchen.

Larz followed suit, wrapping an arm around Tatiana, walking her towards the stairs. Vincent did the same with Akesha.

Tatiana looked over her shoulder, grinning with excitement for what was about to come. "What about you, Armand? We can't leave you down here all by your lonesome."

Larz brushed his lips against her temple. "Oh, don't you worry your pretty little witchy head about him. He's probably due for some coffee right about now. Aren't you, brother?"

Blake and Vincent burst into laughter, leaving Armand standing alone at the kitchen island, flipping them off. "Fuck all you guys!"

THE TINY FORGOTTEN forest encased by four stone walls was exceptionally quiet tonight. The four brothers were changing out of their regular clothing and into their ceremonial linens. No one spoke. Even the squirrels remained still, and the wind ceased to blow, creating a hushed silence through the branches.

They each moved soundlessly up the stone staircase, feeling the night's chill in the soft moss and coolness of the steps on their bare feet. This portion of the property was so well hidden in the shadows, that the sun never has the opportunity to create any real warmth there. It was a welcomed retreat from the stifling heat beyond these walls.

One by one, as they reached the summit, they stepped into the void, disappearing into nothing.

Inside the cistern, the brothers looked down over the balcony. It was just after midnight and the Rose Moon was at its peak, shining down through the structure's circular opening. The soft glow of the light on the pool below created a shimmering and inviting effect. Light could be deceiving that way. Just beyond the pool, they found their witch curled up on her side as if she were sleeping.

She wore the shift that Larz had provided the night before. Completely unbeknownst to the witches themselves, was that the granite slab from which they awake, was marked and carved with many runes, one of which instructs the witch to shed all of her earthly things, their clothing, shoes, jewelry, and even any makeup.

Many decades ago, Blake once secretly watched a witch go through the traumatic ritual of cleansing and preparing her own body for the ceremony that he was sure she knew would lead to her own death. They would wake with a heaviness, as if they had been drugged. That weight would then slip into something different and become more suggestive, telling them to change their clothing.

Confusion would overtake many of them, leading to compliance, but the stronger witches knew better.

With time, those light suggestions would become a scream, and the clothing they donned would begin to feel like fire and acid on their skin. By the time they were kneeling at the pool to wash their faces, most would be in tears. Some took longer than others, but no one was ever able to resist it. Slipping into the dress provided, and watching their belongings sink into the pool was a final goodbye. He wondered if any of these women would have ever dipped their feeble human hands into that pool if they knew what evil crept below the surface.

Larz and Armand took the stairs down the left side. Blake and Vincent mirrored them as they walked down the right side. The witch startled awake, lifting up and curling her feet further into herself. She wasn't strong. Blake mused at the thought that she likely knew little of witchcraft and only practiced it as a form of rebellion. Nevertheless, her magic existed. She just hadn't tapped into it thoroughly. It was a pity. Had she practiced more; she may not have found herself here today? It would have strengthened and grown her magic, in which case, she may have been more capable of eluding Rayna's coven. It also would've made a much more appeasing sacrifice to Khalida.

At the bottom, three of the brothers moved to form a semi-circle around the base of the pool. Vincent, though, paused, allowing his eyes to roam over the witch. Her breath was quick, and her heart raced, but she didn't speak.

Blake didn't say anything as he watched his brother. It was the first time Vincent had ever seen the before and after. She looked different now. Her dark hair was pushed back from her face, clean and free of makeup. The piercings were gone as well as the tattered black clothing. When you strip away all the excess, you are left with nothing but a flesh and blood human being.

Still standing in place, Vincent looked to Blake. The look in his eyes spoke to the anguish he felt. Blake knew he took no pleasure in this process. It was an unspoken request. He gave a slight nod, indicating his approval.

Vincent turned to the witch, waving his right hand in front of her face. *"Requiem."*

The word was soft and barely audible, but the effects were immediate. The young witch relaxed in her place. He quickly took his spot alongside his brothers at the pool.

Blake took a sobering breath, closed his eyes, and began chanting. His brothers followed along in unison: *"Omnes te invocamus . . . di immortatales inter omnes te Invocamus. Omnes te invocamus."*

With these words now spoken, each brother knelt, reaching below the surface of the water, their hands only reaching as low as their wrists. Mere seconds passed before they rose, their hands lifting from the water with their fists wrapped firmly around daggers. The hilts were crafted from gold and ornately designed to detail animals attacking one another. A dragon was delicately entwined, biting the back of a jaguar as it pounced upon a deer. It was an elaborate circle depicting the fight for survival. The blade was forged from iron with scalloped ridges through the center. The edges were like razors curving to an unforgiving point.

The four brothers spoke the same incantation once again, dragging the sharp edges of their knives across their palms. As blood swelled, they each held their hands out above the water, watching it seep into that eerie darkness below. They continued their chant. Their voices echoed throughout the room as their blood began to boil at the surface of the pool. Thunder rolled in, and the ominous black clouds combed the sky, darkening the room from the moonlight.

"*Leoht*," Blake said, causing two sconces on opposite walls to flicker to life, bathing the room in a dim torchlight.

A crash of thunder followed by a blinding bolt of lightning shot through the opening above, lashing at the water, engulfing the surface in heinous flames, and awakening the evil that lurked below.

The new light source made their shadows bounce and echo off the stone walls as they moved from the pool towards the witch. Her eyes didn't know what to focus on, the shadows that towered over her like giants or the deadly blades they held. Blake stood directly in the center, his eyes locked onto hers while Vincent and Armand took a stance to the side of him. Confusion settled on her face. He knew she was looking for the fourth, wondering where he was.

Blake stood over her, placing a gentle hand against her forehead. "I can feel your inner struggle, but it will do you no good." His voice was controlled, yet soft. "You cannot move. You cannot speak. You are a prisoner within your own body. The only thing you can now do is close your eyes, confess any sins you may have, and wait for your death." It was a kindness he had never offered in any of their rituals prior, but Vincent's presence and need for grace outweighed the indifference that he normally felt.

Armand and Vincent reached out, each taking one of her hands. Blake noted the gentleness in Vincent's grasp and reassuring squeeze, trying to console her. "You won't feel it. It will be quick. I promise."

"With this sacrifice, the blood will flow," Blake shouted as he watched a single tear escape before she closed her eyes. "With this sacrifice made, we will not grow old." His gaze shifted above her as Larz moved into position behind her. She was completely unaware of him or the dagger he fisted just above her shoulders.

Blake paused for a heartbeat, tightening his grip on the hilt of his weapon. "*Deao*."

All four brothers moved their blades in unison. Larz's dagger moved smoothly across the base of her throat, warm blood welling across the cold metal. Armand and Vincent sliced vertically along the artery that ran through her wrists while Blake held his blade horizontally, plunging the point directly into her heart.

Her body barely reacted, with only a small gasp of air leaving her lips. Her blood spilled quickly, covering the stone table and floor. Vincent stepped closer to take her weight and ease her back. In what few seconds the young girl had left, she managed to open her eyes to get one last glance at Vincent before the life faded away from them forever. "*Requience* in peace," he whispered, cupping his hands over her face to close her eyelids. She was gone.

Blake stepped up, lifting her into his arms. Her blood continued to spill, dripping to the ground as he carried her from the stone slab to the pool. He eased her into the water, being more careful than he normally would have been. He wasn't sure if he was doing it out of respect for Vincent, himself, or the girl. He only knew it felt different. He watched as pieces of her hair floated along the surface like inky tendrils.

He turned his attention to his newest brother now. His face was blank and impossible to read as he watched the girl slowly sink from existence. Blake reached out with his senses, desperate to know what he was feeling at the moment, only to be met with an invisible barrier. He could sense nothing. Vincent's control over his thoughts and emotions were like layers upon layers of concrete.

The hell? Blake couldn't remember being so engaged with his own humanity. Even in his earlier days when he was around the same age as Vincent, he didn't remember ever showing empathy or compassion for a stranger. He vaguely remembered a girl once, but that was before his twenty-first birthday when he'd inherited his power. Even then, though, he couldn't remember truly caring for her. Or did he? It was so long ago now that he was sure the memory only surfaced due to watching Vincent. Or was it, Kira? Was she making him remember and feel things?

Walls, brother; Larz silently reminded him.

Motherfucker! Blake rebuilt his walls, cursing himself, wondering why they were always down when Kira crept into his thoughts. *It's her. She's weakening me.*

It was an epiphany that nearly knocked the wind out of him. He placed his hand to his forehead, feeling a sticky coolness. Pulling it away, he realized it was blood, likely spray from one of the wrists. He sucked in a breath, remembering he still had work to do. This wasn't the place to analyze Kira's power over him.

The four each took a spot kneeling in front of the pool, where they waited for their offering to be accepted and to be granted their own reward. It was silent, and the coolness of the stone seeped through their thin linen pants. The floor was hard and brutal on their knees and shins, but they would wait this way for hours, even days if needed. The reward that would follow was better than any earthly drug.

The ground rumbled slightly, shaking the torches that lit the room. The water in the pool bubbled. Even in the dimness, Blake could see the water thickening and turning red. Blood. With another violent shake, the blood shot high like an explosive fountain. The brothers turned their heads to the sky, looking out through the opening in the cistern as the blood spray rained down upon them.

"Hostiam acceipit. Hostiam acceipit," they each chanted, their arms bent at the elbow with open palms. Their faces and chests were streaked with red. The linen pants were now soaked in the blood of their human sacrifice.

Blake could feel Vincent at his side. His breathing had increased. Out of the corner of his eye, he could see him looking down at himself. His blood-covered self. Blake started to reach out to see if there was a crack in his emotional exterior but thought better of it. He kept his walls up for a reason, and as brothers, they each worked to respect the other's space.

He felt his own breath hitch as the next portion of the ritual began. He closed his eyes, tilting his head back, soaking in the sensation. He could hear each of his brothers revel in it as well. It was as indulgent and delicious as the orgasmic release after an hour of foreplay, or a much-needed fix for a drug addict. It was sweet, relaxing, and energizing all at once.

Blake opened his eyes, watching as the remaining remnants of the blood soaked into his skin as if his body were a towel drawing in the moisture. There were still a few traces of blood along the stone floor. He watched as small red droplets were wicked into the air, floating like sinful bubbles until they met flesh. His veins dilated and pulsated in reaction to this foreign essence. They each could feel the magic seeping into their bones, mixing into their bloodstream, and forming new synapses throughout their nervous systems. It was becoming an innate part of their being.

"*Ave* Khalida," Blake stated, finally standing.

The others repeated him, thanking Khalida for her offering.

The entire process took only twenty minutes. Blake turned to Vincent once more to gauge his reaction. "How was it?"

Vincent took his time, his eyes still lingering on the pool. "Quick. Worthwhile."

Blake narrowed his eyes, glancing back to Larz and Armand. *Quick? Worthwhile?* He followed Vincent's gaze, which still rested on the pool.

"It's a short amount of time to completely erase a person from existence. But that's essentially what we did. She was here. A living, breathing person. Flesh and blood. And twenty minutes later, there isn't a trace of her left." Vincent's voice was calm and resolute, but not mournful. "Well, I guess that's not entirely true," he added, looking down at his own hands. "I can feel her inside of me."

FOURTEEN
THE CARNIVAL

"I'm so freaking excited!" Kat squealed, jumping up and down and clapping her hands with enthusiasm before clutching onto Kira's arm. "What should we do first?"

Per tradition, Kira and Kat donned their best red, white, and blue attire. Kira wore short denim shorts with frayed edges with a red, white, and blue tank knotted at her navel, showing just a hint of skin, while Kat looked classic and chic in a bright red tulle mini skirt with a white tee and blue headband. Her bright red lips set off the whole look.

Kira glanced out over the scene. The annual Fourth of July carnival was one of their favorite events. It wasn't yet dark, but the clouds hung low this evening, blocking out much of the sun. Neon lights spun wildly along rides. The Ferris Wheel featured a dazzling display of red, white, and blue lights that flashed and danced in intricate patterns. Rows of vibrantly colored booths housed a kaleidoscope of games and prizes. The air smelled like fresh-cut grass, funnel cakes, and candied apples. She soaked it in.

"I don't know," she said, listening to the screams of people as they revolved violently around the Ring of Fire. "Maybe we need to pace ourselves," glancing back as Eric and Colin approached, tickets in hand.

"No way! Let's get our ride on!" Kat whined.

"Slow down, baby," Eric said, passing over a fistful of tickets. "We have all night."

"Do we?" Kat eyed him. "Do we?"

Eric laughed, defending himself: "Last year was a fluke."

"Gravitron it is, then!" Kat spouted, clasping her hands to the side of his face, flashing her biggest smile.

"Hell, no!" Eric and Colin exclaimed in unison.

"Seriously? Let's take these babies to the carousel," Kira joked, linking arms with Colin, and rested her head into his arm. Easy. Familiar. Comforting. This was everything she needed right now.

Colin had been a stable presence over the past few weeks. He stayed with her often, curling up in bed together binging Netflix. He also gave her the space she needed, no longer smothering her with his presence or his needs. As a side effect, their sex life had dwindled even further. On nights that they were together, she found herself purposefully falling asleep early to avoid it. She still loved him and was happy to have him near her, but that carnal need just ceased to exist.

Unfortunately, her nightmares were still a regular occurrence. They had also been highlighted with occasional dreams of Blake. She hadn't seen him since their last run-in at the park four weeks ago. Then again, there hadn't been much of an opportunity for her to do so. Kira spent most of her days at home, attempting to avoid him. She'd heard through friends that he and his roommates had thrown several more parties. On one occasion, she even got dressed, tossed back a drink, prepared to go, but chickened out when she reached her own front door.

Standing there now, curled into Colin's arm, she knew she had made the right decision. This was where she should be. This was who she should be with. Together, they would find their way back to the couple they once were. She just needed time. She also needed to stay the hell away from Blake Michaelson.

Turning in slow circles under the dancing lights of the carousel, Kira and Kat perched themselves on a bejeweled unicorn, taking selfies and laughing over memories of past summers. As the ride slowed to a stop, she jumped over to Colin, phone in hand, and planted a big kiss on his cheek, snapping a shot of the action. She noticed the spark in his eyes and the dimple in his smile. That was his true happiness showing; her face turning sincere at the sight.

"We can get back there, you know," Kira said loud enough where he could hear over the music.

His face dropped for only a second, before returning back to a smile. "I know we will."

Stepping off the carousel, she felt as if she had left an enormous weight behind. As if she and Colin had sorted out a month's worth of therapy within a three-minute ride and a few short words.

They walked hand in hand through rows of booths, stopping several times to watch the guys and their failed attempts at winning the biggest prizes. Kira watched Eric secretly bribe a carnie with fifty bucks in exchange for a large stuffed animal. It was a total waste of money, but she could see that he got so much pleasure in watching Kat's face light up.

It was finally dark, and the fireworks were set to go off soon.

"Mmmm . . . I'm hungry and I smell funnel cakes!" Kat declared, clinging to Eric's chest as he carried her on his back.

They were rounding the end of the row at the edge of the carnival when they came across the funhouse. Kira slowed at the sight of it, clutching tighter to the stuffed bear she was holding for Kat. The entrance was the open mouth of a clown. Its cartoonishly large eyes were narrowed down the line of his nose as if he were staring down all those who entered.

"Awe, man, let's do this first!" Eric said, allowing Kat to slide down his back.

Colin turned back, realizing that Kira was no longer right behind him. "What's wrong, babe?" he asked, walking back to her.

She pursed her lips, shaking her head. "You guys go ahead. It's not my thing."

"Oh yeah. Clowns . . . I can wait with you while the guys go."

"No, no. It's not a big deal," Colin said, squeezing Kira's hand. "How about you girls go get one of those death traps out of your system, while Eric and I go get us some food."

"You sure?" Kira leaned in, kissing him on the cheek.

"Yeah. What do you guys want?"

"Deep-fried everything!" Kat called out, grabbing Kira by the hand. "And I mean everything!"

"And a diet Pepsi," Kira yelled.

"And some popcorn . . . oh, and cotton candy!"

"You know, carnival food is notoriously expensive!" Eric called back out to her, laughing.

Kat turned to her boyfriend, tossing her teddy bear back to him. "Then maybe you shouldn't spend so much bribing the carnies!" She laughed again, pretending to drop the mic as she strutted off in a mocking victory dance.

Even after the sun had gone down, the heat still lingered. Kat made a poor attempt at fanning herself with one hand, while trying to pin her hair up off her neck with the other while they stood in line for the Zipper. She gave Kira a poignant look before rolling her eyes and subtly gesturing to the two guys behind them who were ogling and whispering.

Kira moved forward, pulling Kat with her, trying to ignore the guys behind them who were becoming louder and more flagrant.

"We're not interested," she warned. She tried to sound as sweet as possible, but irritation vibrated through her tone.

One of the guys lifted his palms to the air, taking a small step back as an indication that her message was received.

Kira watched Kat's eyes widen with dissent as the two guys continued their hushed and lewd comments. It wasn't like Kat to keep her cool over situations like these. She was always very quick to speak her mind. Just as she expected her to snap, the line moved, and they were being led onto the ride. Perfect timing.

The ride was exhilarating as expected. Her body swayed ever so slightly once her feet were on solid ground again. She was somewhat relieved to have done this before eating. Linking arms, they made their way through the exit but were caught off guard as Kat abruptly turned and shoved the person behind her. "You, asshole!"

It took several seconds for Kira to comprehend what was happening. She gripped onto her friend as she began following after the two guys that were behind them earlier in line. They were backing away into the crowd, arrogant smiles written across their faces. Kat fought against her grasp. "Stop! What's wrong? What happened?"

Kat's chest was heaving. She took a moment to regain her composure, noting the passersby who stared at her. "That piece of shit put his hand up my skirt," she hissed through gritted teeth.

Kira's jaw dropped. "That bastard!" She started to make her way to find the guys herself, but her friend's grip on her arm stopped her.

"It's okay," Kat breathed, smoothing back her hair. "I mean, it's not okay, but they're gone now. Plus, I don't need Eric going to jail because he killed someone."

"I'm so sorry! I should have let you punch that guy in the face," she said, linking arms with her friend again as they walked. "You should definitely let me punch that guy in the face."

"Thank you. But we both know you don't know how to throw a punch."

Kira frowned, holding out her free hand, making a fist.

"Nope! See! You'll break your thumb that way," Kat chirped, her peppy demeanor returning as she held out her own hand to show her friend the correct way.

"Okay, fight club. Let's go find the boys."

As they walked, Kira felt her palm light up. Her body tensed, but she quickly rolled her shoulders back, attempting to stave off the mixture of anxiety and excitement that always followed. She flexed her fingers at her side, feeling a gentle tapping in the center. She allowed Kat to drag her along through the crowd as she focused her attention on her hand. It had been some time since she last felt it. She racked her brain, trying to remember it. Images of Blake popped into her mind.

"Are you listening to me?"

Kira popped out of her own reverie. "I'm sorry," she stammered. "I was still thinking about that jerk." *Believable lie,* she told herself, knowing that she probably would have been if her sexy palm twitch hadn't returned. She continued on, careful to listen to the words Kat spoke, responding when necessary, all the while feeling that gentle stroke.

As if on cue, her eyes zoned in across an open space. There he was, standing casually with his hands resting in the pockets of his jeans. He wore a black t-shirt that clung to his chest and bared his strong arms. She blinked, images of his smile flashing through her memory as a crowd of people passed between them. And just like that, he was gone. She blinked again, her head swiveling. *Where did he go?* She flexed her hand once more but felt nothing. It, too, was gone.

"There they are!"

Kira followed as Kat pulled her towards a grouping of tables. She sat beside Colin, putting on her fake smile, still feeling numb from the previous moment. "Yum," she said, grabbing a deep-fried Oreo, and shoved a large bite into her mouth. She continued this distraction for several minutes before she noticed the beer at Colin's side. She only eyed it for a second. *It's one beer.* Kira leaned into him, an attempt to reinforce her comfort. In her clutter of emotions, she wasn't sure who she was trying to convince; herself or Colin.

"Oh wow, do you guys know her?" Kat asked, pointing to a 'Missing Person' poster pinned to a post just off to the side. She stood, rounding the table to get a closer look. "It says she's a Tulane student. Nina Davenport?" She looked back to her friends. "She's been missing for over three weeks. None of you recognize her?"

"No, but I saw this morning there's been a total of like five girls gone missing in the area. No one has been found. It's crazy. Do me a favor and don't go walking the street at night by yourself," Eric said, reaching his hand out, and pulling Kat back into his lap. "Even if you're just walking over to the coffeehouse. That courtyard isn't well lit at night."

"You, too," Colin added, placing a kiss on Kira's forehead as he folded an arm around her.

Kira only nodded, staring over at the girl looking back at her in the poster. Something within her wanted to say something, recognizing that little fire that called out from somewhere deep inside. It wasn't the same as those little pulses in her hand. Where that sensation always felt as if someone was reaching out and touching her, this other felt like it originated from within, as if *she* was reaching out to touch someone. She'd felt it before, but it dwindled away as the sky erupted into a roar of colors.

Wrapped in Colin's arms, she looked on as streaks of gold rocketed into the sky before bursting into arcs of vermillion, emerald, and cobalt. The giddiness and awe that she felt as a child was replaced with a new sense of gratitude and nostalgia. It was a vivid and beautiful reminder she could still experience grace and joy. As if reading her thoughts, Kat reached out, grasping her hand, giving her a curt squeeze.

As the last sparks fell from the sky, Kat jumped up from her seat. "Okay, Ferris Wheel!"

Eric pulled her back to him, pursing his lips and shaking his head. "No, baby . . . let's just relax for a bit."

Kat snuggled against him, rubbing his back. "You poor baby, did you eat too much or are you just scared of a little wheel?"

"It's not a little wheel! Look at that thing. You can hear the metal grinding together," he stated, pointing incredulously.

Kira tugged at Colin's hand. "You aren't going to make me ride it alone, are you? I'll even let you give me a little kiss at the top."

Colin tucked a strand of hair behind her ear. "I would love that, but I just ate one of those massive turkey legs."

Kira dropped his hand and deadpanned to Kat. "Are they serious? Our boyfriends are big babies."

"Agreed," Kat said, jumping up to join her friend. "You babies can stay here and spoon each other. We are going to have fun!"

The line for the Ferris Wheel wasn't long since some of the crowd was dissipating. Parents with younger children began making their exits after the fireworks, but the area was still teeming with teenagers and adults. She and Kat took their seat, giggling like young schoolgirls as the bar latched across their laps. Despite giving Colin and Eric a hard time, she was grateful for this bonding time with her friend.

It was a slow ride to the top as the wheel consistently paused to exchange riders, jolting them with each stop. As they rose higher, Kira gained a better view of the ground below. From there, she watched as Colin and Eric grabbed another beer. As if by reflex, she looked away, biting her lip. She felt that familiar clench in her stomach and silently scolded herself. *It's not a big deal.*

Kat, ever the observer, noticed Kira's sudden shift, and looked down to where their boyfriends stood. "You guys have been good lately. He's trying."

Kira nodded, an unsure smile on her face. "He has. And I'm happy," she answered, not knowing if that was the truth, or if she'd become so good at lying that she no longer recognized it. She swallowed hard as that sinking feeling settled further into her body. *Pull it together;* she silently instructed. It was unfair that she could feel such joy and peace only to have it vanish into nothing in a matter of seconds.

Her gaze wandered out over the crowd as she worked to push aside the negativity. It was beginning to work until she caught sight of the two guys from earlier. They were talking to two young girls, most likely teenagers. As most girls do, they appeared to like the attention at first, but she could see that one of them was growing more uncomfortable. The guy who put his hands on Kat was leaning further into the girl's space, using an arm to effectively pin her against the picnic table where they were sitting. The girl pushed at his arm, but he didn't budge, using his free hand to touch her hair.

Kira focused all her attention there. Her blood boiled as images of her hands around his throat invaded her thoughts. She didn't feel the pain of her nails digging into the palms of her hands. She also didn't feel remorse as she watched him clasp his hands at his neck and stagger back before falling to his knees. She watched as his friend ran to his side, beating at his back, fearful he was choking. Others crowded around him trying to assist.

In the corner of her eye, she saw Blake again. She dropped her attention from the repulsive guy on the ground and focused solely on the beautiful man who still haunted her dreams. He was standing with his roommates and three stunningly beautiful women, observing the drama. She noticed the young woman on his arm was the same one from the party.

The small crowd began to disperse around them. Kira looked over to see the obnoxious guy standing, but bent forward, his hands braced against his knees as his friend nodded and laughed with the look of relief on his face. Kira's eyes moved back to Blake, who turned, looking up towards the Ferris Wheel, smiling, but not focusing on anything specific. Nevertheless, she had the sense that he was looking at her. Smiling at her.

The group moved on, and she lost sight of them in the crowd as Kat's bubbly voice broke into her consciousness. She seemed unaware of the entire event as she chattered on about something Jade had told her. As much as she hated admitting defeat, the heaviness had worked its way back into her body, and the contentment she tried so hard to hold on to was gone. They were stalled at the very top of the wheel now. Teetering at the top used to feel exciting and freeing. But now, looking out over everything, it made her feel small, and helpless as if the weight of it all would come crashing down at any moment. It was then that the awful thought of plummeting to the ground flashed through her mind. Along with drowning, it was one of her greatest fears.

Kat grabbed her hand, raising it in the air, waving it wildly. "Woohoo! I'm the queen of the world, bitches!"

Deep breath. Smile. Lie. Even if she couldn't enjoy the night, she would not disappoint Kat. After several rotations, they finally jumped off. "Tilt-a-Whirl?"

"Duh!"

They spent the next hour jumping from ride to ride. Bumper Cars. Ring of Fire. Pirate Ship.

Kira pulled at Kat's hand as they approached a new ride. "Wanna do it?" she asked, feeling that surprise sensation in her palm again.

Kat followed Kira's line of sight. "Um . . . No."

"I'm going to do it," she announced, running towards the caged compartment.

"No!" Kat called out, running after her, but Kira was already stepping inside.

The attendant closed the gate behind her. "Yes, I am!"

Real excitement found its way back into her body. Another lurid tap at her palm offered its approval and encouragement. She smiled down, giving a little wave as the crane hoisted her into the air.

Kira blocked out the wailing cries of Kat still calling out to her and focused on the breeze that wrapped around her. She soaked it in as the attendant tugged and adjusted her body while outfitting her in the harness. *You can do this.*

The sound of the gate opening raked through her, waking her back to reality. She took a timid step towards the opening, looking down. She didn't want to think about it. This was not the place to think. This was the place to exert her own will. She closed her eyes and surrendered herself to gravity. The rush of wind on her face was exhilarating. A roar of laughter escaped her at the sudden bounce as the cord fully extended. And then she was falling again. The second bounce was lighter giving her the confidence to open her eyes. She spotted Kat standing stiffly, hands covering her face. As they lowered her to the platform below, she was grateful to find that slice of excitement.

"Are you kidding me? I can't believe you just bungee jumped!" Kat scolded, smacking at her arm. "How was it?"

She only smiled, her face glowing from the aftermath.

"You are freaking nuts!"

Kira didn't think anything would pull her down from this high as they walked arm in arm, searching for the guys. She was wrong. They found them perched on the same picnic table from earlier. Eric held a beer, his face apologetic. Colin sat beside him, smiling and content, several beer cans at his side.

She was wary as she stepped into his embrace, not wanting to jump to any conclusions, but he reeked of alcohol. She stiffened under his clumsy kiss at her temple. *He's drunk.*

Looking over, she watched Kat and Eric's silent argument. She stood, not knowing what to do or say as Colin leaned his head into the crook of her neck, planting little kisses on her shoulder. Different emotions ricocheted throughout her body, paralyzing her. Exhaustion set in. Closing her eyes, she was ready to melt into Colin's kiss and forget it all.

The tapping in her palm once again snapped her awake. She calmly pushed Colin away, searching his face for several seconds. "You're drunk."

His eyebrows knitted together. "No . . . no, I'm not."

"Stop." Kira put a firm hand to his chest. "I don't have the energy."

"Kira." Colin stood, and took a small step to close the space between them. "I'm fine."

She shook her head, looking at the cans that littered the table. "You're not fine . . . *We* are not fine."

Colin looked back to Eric and Kat as if he hoped they would step in to defend him. He leaned in close, his voice low. "We are good. You said it earlier. Remember? We can get back there." His words were rife with panic.

Her emotions were so disoriented that the tears she expected to appear remained securely in place. "I need to go."

"I'll go with you."

"No," she countered, returning a firm hand to his chest. "We need some space."

He stepped closer, his words almost a whisper. "Please don't do this."

She looked back at him, not knowing if it was anger or sadness that was clenching at her heart. "*You* did this."

Walking away, she felt the sudden warmth of Kat's hands wrapping around her arm, her head leaning into her. "Are you okay?"

"Yes." It didn't feel like a lie, at least not on the surface. Her composure was still intact, but she could feel the ache winding in her stomach, deep down.

Kira ordered an Uber as they walked towards the parking area. Kat didn't say much as they waited, only offering a few apologies, and expressing her frustration that Eric should have put a stop to it.

"No, don't be mad at him. Colin is a grown man. He made that decision on his own. And I," Kira's words disappeared on her lips as her eyes caught sight of Blake a few feet away walking towards them.

"Hey, Kira! Long time, no stalk. I didn't know if I should be worried or insulted," he mused, a brilliant smile across his face before turning to Kat with an outstretched hand. "Hi, I'm Blake Michaelson. I'm sure whatever she's told you about me is the absolute truth . . . or an over exaggerated lie."

Kira felt Kat's eyes on her, and then felt the playful kick at her shins. "Hello. I'm Kat . . . Kira's roommate."

"Kat? And what is that short for?" another voice asked, stepping in, taking her hand.

Kira's eyes moved from Blake to the hulking man next to him. *How did I not see him?*

He was a couple of inches taller than Blake and with a much fuller build. His wavy blondish brown hair hung low to his shoulders, and his boyish dimples highlighted his smile. She flinched at the feel of another subtle kick to her shins from her friend.

"Katia," she gushed, the sound of her voice a pitch higher than normal.

"I'm Larz. It's very nice to meet you." He eyed her before leaning in to press a soft kiss to the back of her hand.

Kat turned to Kira, mouthing, *OMG,* before looking back at him. "And is Larz short for something?"

"Larson. Drake Larson, but *please . . .* call me Larz," he said smoothly, arching a brow.

She watched the flirtatious display with surprise. Kat was a sucker for an accent, but she'd never seen her fall prey to anyone's charm at this level.

"You'll have to forgive my brother. It's the English in him. He thinks he's Mr. Fucking Darcy when he's around beautiful women."

An audible giggle escaped Kat's lips, causing Kira's own laughter to bubble out. She tried to rein it in at the sight of Blake's smile. She'd seen him smile before, but it hadn't reached his eyes the way it did at that moment. It was genuine and magnetic. She swallowed hard, feeling her insides melt. Too much of a coward to look at his face again, she let her eyes roam over his shoulder where she saw his other friends, including the girl on his arm earlier in the night.

"So, that *is* the girlfriend," she asserted.

Blake turned, not truly looking over his shoulder. "And I suppose that was the boyfriend I saw earlier?" He paused to gauge her reaction, tilting his head slightly. "Or has something changed?"

Kira met his stare again, wondering if he'd witnessed their latest fight. She opened her mouth to respond but then closed it again, realizing she didn't know. *Did something change?* Grateful for the buzz of her phone, she pushed aside the thought. "That's my Uber."

"You're leaving?" he asked, disappointment laced his tone.

Still too scared to look directly at him, she turned to Kat. "Yeah, I'm heading home."

Kat gave her a comforting hug. "You going to be okay?"

"Of course. I promise. But maybe you should find Eric before you run away with that British non-construction worker," she added with a whisper in her ear.

Letting go, she looked back to the two insanely beautiful men standing in front of her. It was almost disorienting. She took a breath, giving herself a moment to recover before speaking when Blake took two steps toward her, taking her by the elbow and pulled her to the side.

"I'm sorry you're leaving."

Her eyes lingered where his hand touched her skin. His hand was no longer there, but she could still feel the heat of it. It took a lot of willpower to pull her attention to his face. She immediately wished she hadn't. That gorgeous smile was dangerous.

"When can I run into you again?"

Kira wasn't expecting that. She bit at her lip, gripping the phone in her hand even tighter. "I don't know," she replied, her gaze drifting back to the same pretty dark-haired girl, standing twenty feet away.

"She's just a friend." His words were soft but resolute. He didn't follow her glance, keeping his focus solely on her.

Risking another look, she saw how his eyes had softened just as much as his tone. The gentle expression he wore was at odds with the hard masculine lines of his face. She bit her lip again, fighting back the smile that threatened to appear. "So are we." It was all she said as she gave him a little pat on the chest, taking a step back. She looked back over to Kat, who was talking quietly with Larz. "Goodnight! See you at home later."

Kira offered one more smile in Blake's direction before she turned to walk to the car, feeling his eyes on her until she was gone.

FIFTEEN
THE FUNHOUSE

Deep breath in. Exhale out. Kira repeated the instructions in her mind over and over, fearful if she stopped the conscious act of telling herself, her lungs would betray her, forgetting their sole purpose. Breathing.

Deep breath in. Exhale out. Hearing the words in her head also helped to distract from the surrounding sounds around her. Even with her hands pressed firmly against her ears, the music still crept in. The high-pitched tones of the calliope echoed throughout the space.

Kira couldn't remember how she got here. Her focus was shot and her memory fuzzy. She opened her eyes for a brief second, only to regret it, closing them immediately. It was the same as before. A dark, bare room, with glowing florescent stripes painted along the walls and floor. Two long corridors stretched on opposite sides of the room. She had already tried multiple times, but the hallways always led back to this room.

Trapped. Alone. Terrified.

Sitting on the floor, she curled further into herself, bracing her elbows over her knees while keeping her palms pressed to her ears. It was getting colder.

Deep breath in. Exhale Out. She was wearing the silk camisole and matching shorts that she usually wore to bed in the summer months. The material was thin and scant. Chill bumps formed along her arms and her teeth began to clatter. *Colder.*

Kira nuzzled her face against her arm, seeking warmth wherever she could find it. Fatigue set into her muscles. Her arms felt heavier with each breath. She leaned back against the wall for support. The chill of it stabbed into her skin.

She could feel her judgement and ability to comprehend slipping away. It was like trying to count, but suddenly realizing you have no idea what number you were on. Desperate to grasp onto something, her mind foraged for images and memories. She saw Kat dancing in the kitchen, Colin pressing a kiss to her forehead, her first pair of pointe shoes hanging on the mirror in her room.

Kira heard waves crashing at the beach and felt the warm sand between her toes. She felt air rushing past her face, and the gentle push of strong hands at her back as her vision moved from blue skies to green grass, squealing to go higher. *Daddy.* They were at the park. She heard her mom's laughter as she ran a brush through her hair. Each memory faded as fast as it came.

Blake. His name sent a spark to her core. She reached out, looking for more. Blue eyes danced across her vision. The sound of his laugh and his stubbled jaw warmed her fingertips. She smiled, grateful for the reprieve, feeling his fingers against her skin. *Warmer.* This is what she needed to cling to.

Focusing all of her energy on thoughts of Blake, her visions shifted to the Calloway Estate. She saw herself walking barefoot in an ivory linen dress along a narrow path beneath a canopy of oak trees. Blake stood far in the distance. She squeezed her eyes tighter, searching for that warming spark, but found nothing. She felt her hand glide across the surface of something hard, yet smooth, her fingers tracing along dips and curves carved within it. A slight chill rippled through her body.

Her breath hitched as her mind raced. She was no longer able to recall what memory had brought her comfort. A sob escaped her lips as the cold crept back in. Pushing herself to focus once more, she saw herself standing somewhere new. Her brows furrowed as she looked down. She didn't know this place. It was a forest; green and overgrown, and in the center, stood the ruins of a stone staircase. She inhaled, taking one cautious step.

Kira choked on the cold as it raced back into her body. Her eyes popped open as she tried to get a grip on the sensation overtaking her. She no longer held her hands to her ears, and instead pressed them to her chest as she attempted to catch her breath. The room was the same, but her eyes couldn't focus past the sight of her breath escaping in a cloud as she exhaled. *So cold.*

The music still played, but the sounds had become muffled and distant. Her lids felt heavy as if she hadn't slept for days. They fluttered open and shut several times before she gave in. Her hands dropped to her sides before lowering her upper body to the floor, curling onto her side. She folded her hands together, tucking them under her chin. *This is it. I'm going to die.*

Time passed. Minutes? Hours? There was no way to know. There was only darkness and cold.

"Kira! Kira!"

The sound of her name broke into her consciousness, but she couldn't move. She couldn't speak. *Kat?*

"Hey . . . It's Kat, right? What's wrong?"

Another voice. A familiar voice. She listened. They had to be close, possibly just on the other side of the wall.

"Oh my goodness, Blake! I'm so glad you're still here. Have you seen Kira?"

Blake? Why is Kat talking with Blake? She heard the fear in her friend's voice. *She's worried.*

"No, not since she left earlier tonight. Everything is shutting down. We were just leaving. What's going on?"

"I went home, and she wasn't there," Kat stuttered, her voice shaky, "and a glass was broken on the floor in her room. I . . . I," her voice trailed off.

"Do you know for sure she went home?"

"Yes. Her phone was there. She had it earlier in the night." The panic in her tone was palpable. "Damn it, where is she?"

Kira wanted to scream, to crawl to the wall and bang her fist against it to alert them to her location, but she couldn't move. The cold had seeped into her bones and frozen her in this miserable, wretched place.

"Hey, it's okay. I'm sure she's fine. Do you think she's here?"

"I don't know. I thought that maybe she might have come back to find us, but her car was still at home. She would've needed her phone if she called an Uber, and she wouldn't walk here." Kat's voice was breaking. "I sent Eric to check the coffeehouse and Colin's apartment. What if something has happened to her?"

"Here, sit down. Take a breath, love."

Larz? That was his voice. Kira recognized it from earlier. They had to be close. She made another weak attempt to call out, but the sound cracked in her throat, dying before it even left her lips. She could feel the cold floor pressed against her cheek. *Deep breath in. Exhale out.*

She anchored herself back to this reality, flexing her fingers, feeling the same cold floor underneath her palms. Blinking back tears, she could only see darkness. With every ounce of energy she could muster, she tried to force herself up, but her muscles didn't budge.

She was paralyzed.

Kira closed her eyes, reaching out for something else. Anything else. In the blackness beneath closed lids, a small light flickered. That spark of warmth moved through her again at the sight of Blake's face. She channeled all of her strength there.

"It's going to be okay. We'll help you look for her," he said, kneeling, now eye level with Kat.

"You don't know that. You don't know that it will be okay." Kat shook her head vehemently, her tears falling faster. "All those missing girls . . . what if?" She looked away, unable to finish the sentence.

Blake swallowed hard, looking up at Larz. Uncertainty blanketed his features. "Don't think that way."

Kira's chest tightened, her breath quickening. Somehow, someway, behind closed eyes . . . behind solid walls, she could see them. It was as if she were sitting right there. They were close enough to touch. The fear in Kat's eyes broke her. She turned her focus to Blake. There was something entirely different in his eyes.

"We should split up. We'll cover more ground this way. Larz, go with Kat. You guys take the area past the Ferris Wheel, and I'll cover everything on this side."

Kira watched as they each moved, walking away from her vision, once again leaving her in darkness. She gasped for air as the chill of cold returned. Her body shook, and the heaviness of sleep threatened to overtake her again. Her mind reached out once more. *"Find me."* Her silent plea was barely a whisper on her lips. *"Please."*

Silence. It was all she could hear.

Darkness. It was all she could see.

Cold. It was all she could feel.

And then . . . warmth. Hands on her face; the masculine smell of spearmint, lavender, and dry woods. "Kira . . . Kira."

The sound of his voice broke through the cold. *Blake. He found me.* She wanted to reach out. To move. To speak. To open her eyes. But her body wouldn't respond to any of her commands.

"I found her. Meet me outside the funhouse." His words were anxious, but resolute.

Kira felt his hands wrapping around her. She welcomed the sudden heat of his body, and the thudding of his heart beneath his chest. The rocking motion of his steps lulled her senses even further as the sinister tones of the calliope faded. It was replaced by a stillness she couldn't quite recognize. The light breeze that carried the sweet smell of funnel cakes and popcorn told her she was outside now.

There was a sudden coolness against her back. *Grass?* She could feel the blades mingle between her fingers. An empty ache radiated in her stomach, spreading to her limbs. She could no longer feel his body heat, his touch, or his heart. The absence of him left her cold and desperate to pull him close.

"It's okay . . . Can you hear me?"

His voice sounded disquieted and uncertain. She was still trapped in darkness, her eyes refusing to open. She felt his hands again. They moved cautiously across her shoulder and down the length of her right arm as consecutive loud clicks rang in her ear, like the snapping of fingers.

"Oh my gosh, Kira! Kira, sweetie!" Kat's voice was uncertain, a mix of anxiety and relief.

"Whoa, hold on," Blake said. "Give her a minute."

"Kira, sweetie?" Kat's tone suddenly softer and drenched with confusion and worry. "What's wrong with her? Why isn't she responding?"

"I don't know. She looks like she's in a hypnotic state or maybe having a seizure of some kind."

"A seizure?"

"Yeah. Sometimes you can have them with no movement. It's called an aura. There were a lot of crazy lights in the funhouse. Has she ever had any sensitivity to lights before?"

"Not that I'm aware of. Wait . . . What? The funhouse? You found her in there?"

"Yes."

"Why was she there? She hates those things. There's no way she would go there on her own. Is she bleeding? What happened?" Kat asked, the panic in her voice returning in full as she took note of the fabric wrapped around her arm. A tinge of red seeped through.

"It was just some superficial cuts. Nothing bad."

"I shouldn't have let her go home on her own. Kira, sweetie, I'm so sorry," she said, leaning down to brush a strand of hair away from her face.

Kira felt fingertips graze against her skin.

"She's so cold . . . Aaah shit!" Kat's scream was sudden and loud as she pushed her heels into the ground, backing away.

"Bloody hell, are you okay?" Larz asked, reaching out to her.

"Something shocked me. Fuck, that hurt!"

There was silence between both Blake and Larz. But Kira was desperate for them to say something. To reassure her they were still with her. That she wasn't alone. *Blake?*

"Kira?" He spoke her name as a question, cautiously placing the back of his hand to her cheek.

Blake. She felt his hands on her again, lifting her. He pulled her close into his chest. She was grateful for the return of his warmth, and nuzzled into it, her fingers tightly clutching at his shirt.

"Kira? Can you hear me now?"

Kira blinked several times, her eyes adjusting to the darkness of the sky above her, and the bright fluorescent lights of the carnival.

A weak smile curved her lips at the sight of those circles of ocean blue staring down at her. She was still too weak, too exhausted to speak. *You found me.*

His features shifted. Confusion and surprise morphed into something else. She was unsure, but she thought she saw a hint of excitement reflecting in his eyes.

"Yes. I found you."

Kira's smile faded as her brows knitted together. She hadn't spoken.

He *heard* her thoughts.

SIXTEEN
SHADOW MAN

The moon was her companion. Kira didn't dare pull her stare away as they drove from the carnival. It floated like a bright beacon, enveloped in darkness. It was her safety net, believing if she somehow kept her focus there, she wouldn't fade back into the blackness.

Kira watched it through the window, grateful that it seemingly followed her home as if it were just as keen on protecting her. She was stretched across the backseat of Kat's car, her cheek pressed against Blake's torso. Her fingers still fisted the material of his t-shirt. She hadn't let go since the moment he pulled her back into his arms.

Exhaustion racked her body and her mind, but she couldn't help but think that Blake was somehow her 'moon' tonight. He'd been that bright spot, keeping her warm even in the darkest and coldest of places. It was why she couldn't let go.

The fear she'd developed before, due to her dreams, faded tonight when he carried her out of that horrid nightmare. Lying there in his arms now, an entirely different type of fear seeped into her heart. In some cosmic and completely implausible way, they were connected.

In the darkest of places, she'd somehow heard him. Saw him. And in return, he'd somehow found her. Heard her.

It was impossible. He was a stranger, but she felt the connection. It was keen and brilliant, and at the same time, somehow blurred and broken.

It left her feeling lost and tired. Between the car's rhythmic vibrations and the continuous gentle stroke of Blake's thumb across her shoulder, sleep overcame her need to stay within the light. Without that constant glow, the shadows and the bleakness were free to wander back into her mind, invading her dreams and baring all the secrets that her waking mind wanted to forget. She may have been physically free from her cold prison in the funhouse, but the memory of her ordeal could still haunt her dreams.

And it did.

THE HALL of mirrors seemed to span forever, trapping her in an inexplicable maze. Her reflection was chased by the shadows cast by the dimly lit space. The calliope's eerie whistle was loud here as the sound bounced off the hard surface of the mirrors. She wanted to cover her ears, but needed her hands to navigate the space, pressing her palms along the path as she worked to find a way out. Kira called out for help several times, but the music drowned out any attempts she made.

"This is impossible." Her tone was strained and defeated. Kira leaned into one of the mirrored walls and slid down it to rest on the floor. She tucked her knees in tight to her chest, wrapping her arms around them, and dropped her head. "I can't do this."

For several minutes, she remained there, afraid of what lurked ahead. The music continued its relentless assault on her ears and psyche, feeling a dull throb forming at the base of her skull. Desperate to escape it, she raised her head, prepared to try again. Across the space, only feet away, she caught her reflection in a mirror opposite her. She was still sitting with her hair draped across her shoulder, her bare feet pressed into the floor. Confused about how she got here, she stared back at herself, silently searching her memory.

I was at the carnival. I saw the funhouse, but I didn't go in. Kira bit her lip. She was sure of it. *I went home early. I went to bed.* She squeezed her eyes shut, concentrating. *No. I didn't make it to bed. I was walking across the room to turn out the light and I saw something.* Kira opened her eyes, slowly raising her gaze to meet her reflection. *I saw something in the mirror.* She swallowed hard as that something came into view. Staring across the space, she watched as a shadowy figure approached her from behind. It moved slowly, towering over her. She could hear its breath, the sound of the calliope now suddenly silent. It walked like a man. Her chest tightened, her muscles went rigid, locking her in place.

The figure stopped.

She didn't move.

It didn't move.

Time didn't move.

Certain her heart would explode from her chest; she remained as still as possible. The only movement was the rise and fall of her own strained breaths. The minutes seemed to stretch forever. *Does it see me?* She wasn't sure.

The figure took one relaxed step, but it was more than enough to set her panic into overdrive. Kira pushed herself to her feet, making a frantic effort to navigate through the maze as the music of the calliope roared back to life. She focused her efforts on paving her way through the path, occasionally glancing at her reflection to see the figure moving behind her. Her movements were rushed and desperate, but the shadow moved with ease and indifference. The cavalier nature of it only amplified her fear.

Like before, she found the maze impossible to escape. Trapped in a dead-end and unable to backtrack, she pounded at the mirror in front of her, hoping to smash it, but her fists only bounced off. She took a small step back, sucked in a breath, and rammed her shoulder into it. The glass shattered, falling in large fragments to the ground.

Her heart soared when she found it led to a new passageway, one that did not include mirrors. She stepped through it, breaking into a full out sprint. The halls were short, splitting into numerous paths with quick turns and forks. Flashing strobes broke up her vision, causing her to miscalculate the distance in some hallways and collide into walls.

Between the flashes and the raging music, she was beginning to miss the hall of mirrors. At least then, she could continuously keep track of the shadow chasing her. It was disorienting and impossible to discern how these halls twisted and weaved, making her unsure if she would crash directly into the figure. She risked a glance behind her shoulder, grateful she didn't see anything, but as she turned, her face slammed into a wall, nearly knocking her to the floor. Staggering back, she took a moment to catch her breath and rest her eyes against the onslaught of the strobes.

And then the music stopped. Her head snapped up, her eyes adjusting to her surroundings. The dimly lit hall no longer flashed wildly. She pushed away from the wall cautiously, holding her breath as she listened. It started light. So much so, that she wasn't sure she heard anything at all. But as the seconds passed, the sound grew.

Footsteps.

Fortunately, her feet were bare, making little noise as they hit the ground. Kira was careful but swift, moving down the hall on the balls of her feet. She paused in her tracks as she rounded a corner and found a narrow, but brightly lit corridor. The walls, ceiling, and floor were painted in an array of vivid colors. Every few feet, a niche was cut into the wall displaying various life-size characters. Their faces were animated and striking, featuring the same vibrant colors of the space.

The first one just to her left was a fox, and a little further down on the right was a tiger in a top hat. These were innocent enough, but it was the third one down that gave her pause, a clown with large bulging eyes and a wide smile showing two rows of boxy square teeth. The hall wasn't terribly long. She could see a door at the end, only thirty yards away. *A way out?*

Kira took off, only to trip a few feet in, falling to her knees as a wretched screech pierced her ears. She turned to see the fox leaning forward from the wall, mechanically moving its arms and twisting its head towards her. Kira kicked away, scooting backward until she felt the tiger at her back, the motion setting off the animatronic character. The tiger babbled, "hello" as it tipped its hat, leaning into a bow. She pushed herself to her feet quickly. Her heart caught in her throat, unable to find the scream that burned inside.

Kira twisted her body, pushing it against the opposite wall as she moved past the clown, too frightened to look away as a shrill laugh broke free. Its mechanical arm waved, and its eyes rocked from left to right. Now passed it, she turned to make a similar move along the opposite wall, avoiding the next character, but a new sound assaulted her ears, rooting her to the spot. Her skin prickled and her chest tightened so fiercely she thought she would pass out.

"Kiiiira . . . Kiiiira."

She turned slowly, knowing what she would find, but her heart and mind were not prepared even then. The clown still stood in place, its head pivoted on its shoulders, looking straight at her, its large eyes ticking within those circles. She waited.

"Kiiiira - I've – been – waiting – for - you." The eerie, high-pitched sound gritted out her name from behind those boxy teeth.

"Hell, no!"

Kira didn't wait; she ran as fast as her feet would allow her, setting off each of the animatronics as she passed by them. A girl in pigtails and a red dress singing 'Ring Around the Rosy' spun in circles. Another clown jumped out of a jack- in-the-box. A monkey with rosy cheeks and a Shriners' hat clanged symbols as it jumped and wailed. Thirty yards suddenly felt like a marathon.

The sound of her name again screeched loudly, "Kiiiira - Kiiiira," following her as she made her way to the end of the hall.

Kira reached the door. Moving through it, she closed it swiftly behind her before bracing herself against it, fearful something would try to push past her. With her hand to her chest, she took a moment to analyze this new room. It wasn't the door to her freedom, but it looked far less scary than the previous few.

It was the size of her bedroom. It was bare and dimly lit. Black lights highlighted the florescent neon stripes painted along the floor and walls. And on opposite ends, two long corridors stretched. She had three options at this point. Go right, go left, or turn back the way she came. She looked back and forth between the two halls. They seemed similar with no distinct indication to take one over the other. She took a breath and headed to the right.

Kira moved quickly, keeping her eyes peeled, running her hands along the sides to be sure she didn't miss any dips or doors that may be camouflaged along the wall. She walked for about five minutes before finding herself back in the same room. She looked back over her shoulder, confused. She'd initially taken the right hall, but she re-entered the room from the left.

It's a circle. "No. I'm missing something," she grumbled, immediately moving back through the right hall. She took it slower this time, taking careful measures to search for anything that would indicate another door or exit. She released a frustrated sigh as she stepped back into the same room again. "It's a damn circle. There is no fucking way," her voice broke, terrified she would need to go back through the door and possibly work her way back.

Kira sucked in several reassuring breaths before moving towards the door, stopping in her tracks when she met the blank wall. She circled in place, searching all four walls of the room. *There's no door.* "No," her voice was firm but tinged in panic. "No."

Kira moved to the walls, pressing her body close, allowing her arms and hands to roam across every inch. *No door.* She was in an empty room with a single long corridor that snaked into a circle. *There's no way out.*

She gave herself time to process it, sitting in the center of the room where the glowing neon stripes spiraled in forming a tight circle. It was getting colder. Her thin pajamas were meant for summer weather. *It shouldn't be this cold. Why is it so cold?*

Kira rubbed her hands over her arms to create some friction and keep warm, realizing then she was bleeding. She inspected her arm, pulling out a two-inch piece of glass. She desperately needed to get out of there. Another deep breath, and she was running the corridor again. And again. And again.

Sliding down a wall, she curled into herself. She was getting tired and needed a break. The temperature continued to grow colder. She closed her eyes and searched her mind for anything that may help, grappling over any detail she may have missed.

"There you are. I've been looking for *you*."

Kira's head whipped around at the sound of a familiar male voice. The shadow had found her. He was crouched down directly in front of her, dressed in a dark cloak that veiled his face with the exception of his jaw where she could make out a deep scar. She was terrified, but it wasn't his presence alone that caused her heart to race. His body was surrounded by inky black tendrils that billowed out, floating on the air like smoke.

"I like to move within the shadows," he answered, reading her thoughts. "This helps."

"Why am I here?"

She couldn't see his face, but his jawline told her he was smiling.

"To have fun, of course! After all, this is the funhouse, Kira. I thought that was obvious." His tone was light-hearted but dripping with arrogance.

"This isn't fun." Kira's words were barely a whisper.

"Oh, don't you worry." He rose, standing over her. "We're going to have lots of fun . . . *soon*," he promised.

She watched him as he walked away, disappearing down the hall.

He's leaving. There is a way out. She didn't want to follow too closely, out of fear he may turn back for her. Kira took her time, even more careful to search for the exit as she made her way down the hall. She cringed with a curse as the sound of the calliope returned, but grateful that it was low.

Circling back into the room with no success was crushing, but she was still cold, and it was best if she kept moving. She took another turn; the music seemed to grow slightly louder, spurring her on to move faster. Another turn quickly turned into another. With each circle of the corridor, the volume of the calliope increased.

Kira couldn't stand it anymore; she was tired, and the cold was starting to permeate deeper into her bones while the deafening sounds threatened to drive her mad. She leaned into the wall and slid back down to the floor. She would try again soon, but for now, she just needed to focus on her sanity.

SEVENTEEN
IT'S THE SAME PERSON

H er lids felt heavy, falling shut, even as she protested against it. *Deep breath in. Exhale out.*

"Soon."

His breath was at her ear and the sound of the shadow's voice vibrated through her body.

"No!" Kira thrashed. Her hands fought, and her feet kicked wildly, trying to push him away. "No!" she shouted.

"Whoa, whoa! It's okay. You're safe now."

The sound of Blake's voice bore into her senses, waking her from the nightmare. Her breath came heavy and quick as her eyes adjusted to her new surroundings, moving slowly, processing one thing at a time. *I'm in my room.*

Strips of light painted the hardwood floors from the faint light breaking through the blinds. *Morning?* Looking down, she found herself in the same silk camisole and shorts from her dream, and her legs tangled in a mess of sheets. The sudden feel of warm hands at her shoulder had her scattering towards the edge of the bed. Her heart raced once again, and her eyes narrowed as she pulled the sheets to her chest. "Blake?"

He smiled that delicious smile. The one she both loathed and loved. "I'm sorry. I didn't mean to scare you."

"Why are you here?" Kira asked, pulling the sheet even higher to her chin as she moved back to stand at the edge of the bed.

Blake remained still with his back leaning against the center of the headboard, his legs stretched out comfortably. His features softened as he tilted his head, measuring his words. "What do you remember from last night?"

Kira searched the space between them. *He's in my bed. Oh, no. Did I? Did we?* Her mind was spinning, but she worked to keep her expression passive. "I . . . I don't know."

"Oh, Kira, sweetie! You're awake!" Kat beamed, rushing through the open door, two coffees in hand with Eric at her back, also holding coffees. "How are you feeling?"

Kira's mouth was slack as her eyes roamed from Kat to Eric and then back to Blake again. She watched, her brows knitting tightly across her forehead as Eric passed a coffee over to Blake.

"Thanks, man," he said, standing from the bed with his eyes still fixated on her.

"No problem. I feel like we owe you so much more than a coffee. Larz as well. Please tell him thank you for me. Kat said he was the only reason she didn't completely fall apart."

"Oh, I don't know. She kind of freaked out a bit. Let's not give him too much credit," Blake joked, breaking his gaze from Kira for a brief moment before he returned to his vigilant watch.

"You know, I think I held it together pretty well, considering," Kat laughed before looking back to her friend, her tone softening. "But seriously, are you okay? I got you a mocha. Jade added two extra pumps of chocolate."

Kira reached out for the drink, noticing the bandage wrapped at her arm. She ran a finger over it, turning back to Kat. "What happened last night?"

"You don't remember?"

Kira frowned, shaking her head.

Kat glanced over her shoulder at Eric and Blake, looking to them for guidance on what to say.

"Kat!" She looked to her friend with wide, expectant eyes. "Tell me."

Even with Kira's forceful eyes boring holes into her, Kat stood, unable to find the words. "Let's sit," she insisted, placing a reassuring hand on Kira's elbow, and led her back to the bed. "You went missing last night after the carnival. I went back thinking I might find you there. I ran into Blake and Larz and they helped me look for you."

Kira swallowed. "I was at the carnival?"

Kat's tone was soft and supportive. "Yeah. Blake found you."

She risked a glance at him under her lashes, looking away quickly. He stood like a statue in the door frame with his arms crossed over his broad chest, staring her down.

"Was I in the funhouse?"

"Yes. You remember it?"

She blew out a breath and shook her head. "Not really. It's vague. I thought I dreamt it."

"Do you remember how you got there?"

Kira pressed her lips together in a tight line. The dream she'd just woken from replayed through her mind. Every vivid detail screamed out at her. Her eyes wandered to the mirror. That familiar cold settled into her bones.

She took a deep breath and exhaled out. "No."

AFTER SENDING EVERYONE AWAY, Kira sat alone in her room, desperate for her own space. Sitting crisscrossed on her bed with her journal in her lap, she stared over at the mirror. The beautiful antique piece called out to her the moment she saw it. Even now, she felt a connection. Stepping away from her bed, she approached it, observing her reflection.

Kira looked tired and pale with blueish gray circles under her eyes. Her hair was flat and dull. She still wore the same silk pajamas, the ivory color now appearing dingy. Her heart clenched a little at the thought of lying on the grimy floor of the funhouse. Glancing further down, she noticed a speckling of small dark bruises along her knees and a larger one on her upper thigh that ran up to her hip. Her mind flashed to the hallway with the animatronics.

It had to have been a dream. She closed her eyes, willing it so.

Kira could accept that she somehow got lost in the funhouse, but everything her mind had recounted could not have been real. "It was just a dream," she whispered. "Just another dream."

As always, she wrote everything down. Her journal had become a roadmap depicting the vicious journey her mind had been on over the past several months. Like she often did when writing something new, she took time, pouring over the pages that came before it, reliving all of those moments. Some were mind-blowing with carnal sexual experiences, where others were terrifying to her very core.

Kira re-read her latest entry. It started from the moment she woke in the hall of mirrors, to the moment she heard the man whisper that one word to her. *Soon.*

She felt that same tightness squeeze around her heart, the rise and fall of her chest quickening. That one word—*soon*—replayed over and over as if he was in the very room right now whispering it in her ear.

Her fingers furiously sifted through the pages. The dream she'd had right before her ballet exam floated into her mind. She danced in front of a man surrounded by blackness. His hands had been on her and then again during her exam. She remembered it so vividly. It wasn't necessary to look; she knew it was there. But looking down confirmed it. In her own handwriting, the word 'soon' stared back at her from the paper. She scanned more pages, finding the entry recounting the night in the parking lot. It was the first time she'd met him.

He said I wasn't ready . . . but I will be . . . soon.

Kira slammed her journal shut, her eyes aimlessly scouring over her duvet as she internalized everything. That darkened face that sat behind the table in that club while she danced was the same. It was the same figure who came to her in the funhouse.

"He moves in the shadows," she whispered as she looked down at her palm, flexing her hand in and out of a fist, flipping it over to fully examine it. Her memory twisted and turned every detail she could recall. "It's the same person."

The Shadow Man.

Blake.

The sudden thought sent a wave of nausea through her, sending her running for the bathroom. She retched as if she needed to expel those very thoughts from her body. Free it of those visions. After emptying her stomach of what little was there, she pushed herself back to rest against the wall, her chest heaving.

"I'm wrong."

Her heart needed her to be wrong.

"Hey, you."

Kira didn't realize Kat was in the room with her until she was already in the door frame, her voice soft and comforting. She looked over at her, happy she'd been able to hold back the tears that wanted to rip through her.

"Hi."

"What can I do?"

Kira looked at her blankly.

"I mean . . . you wanted your space earlier. I . . . I want to do that for you, but I also can't sit by and watch you go through this pain on your own." Kat was stammering. It was unlike her.

Kira wanted to put on a brave face and convince her friend that everything was fine, but she was far too exhausted to attempt it. "I'm confused," she confessed. The words just spilled out, but as the truth left her lips, she felt a minuscule amount of weight slip away.

"Confused about what?" Kat asked as she settled herself onto the bathroom floor, mirroring Kira's position with her head resting against the wall, legs stretched out.

A light laugh escaped her. "Everything. I don't know how I ended up in the funhouse. I had a dream that someone was chasing me inside it," she admitted, and then paused, taking a moment to decide how much to share. "I dreamt that it was Blake . . . or at least I think it was him."

Kat's brows arched high. "Really? Is that why you acted so strange when you saw him this morning?"

Kira sat up straight, turning her body completely towards Kat. "I acted that way because there was a man other than my boyfriend in my bed. A man I barely know."

Kat nodded, her face solemn. "I understand. But are you worried or scared that Blake did this?" She waited for a response, but Kira said nothing. "If so, I don't think that's something you should worry about."

"Why do you say that?" she asked, her tone rising an octave.

A slight smile curved at Kat's lips. "Because I was there. Blake was the one who found you. I saw his face. He was just as worried as I was. Of course, that makes me wonder what is going on with you guys?"

Kira shrunk back a bit. "What do you mean?"

Kat's brows arched again, her smile spreading further across her face. "I don't know. I guess I saw something there. A spark, maybe?"

Kira sat in silence again, careful not to give anything away. Well, not that there was anything to give away. She was as confused about him today as she was that very first night.

"Okay . . . Maybe I'm wrong. Which I never really am about things like that, but I will tell you this," she said, that knowing smile still clinging to her lips. "The reason Blake was in your bed last night is because you wouldn't let him leave. Once he had you in his arms, you held him tight. Even when he tried to put you in your bed last night and leave, you refused to let go. Your little grabby hands were fisted into his shirt . . . Sweetie, he stayed for you."

That familiar flutter somersaulted in her stomach, and she knew the light in her eyes probably wasn't going unnoticed by Kat.

"You had a horrible experience, and I can't even begin to know what that was like or even how it came to be, but I do know I've never seen you cling to Colin the way you did Blake last night." Kat paused, giving Kira a moment to soak those words in. "And if you dreamt about him afterward, it's probably because you sensed his presence. After all, he was in your bed with you."

Kira heaved out a weighty breath.

She wanted to be wrong about Blake.

Her heart wanted her to be wrong.

And now, with Kat's words, she was certain that she was.

EIGHTEEN
THERE IS NO US

T he next morning, Kira rolled over in her bed, her eyes greeting the ceiling. She didn't want to move. The heavy weight of the day was already pressing into her. She felt lighter after her conversation with Kat last night, but it was short-lived. Looking at her phone, she saw that Colin had called five times yesterday and sent three times as many texts. It was only 10 am, and he'd already sent her one this morning. The simple, "I miss you" on her screen only added to the weight.

Kira planned to talk to him today, still unsure of how to approach it. Fortunately, he wasn't entirely aware of the circumstances surrounding the night of the carnival. Eric had gone to Colin's apartment that night, but he was too drunk to remember any of the details. Otherwise, she was sure Colin would be banging down her door to ensure she was okay. Another wave of guilt laced nausea rolled through her at the thought.

Guilt. She searched herself, examining all the emotions that racked her mind and heart. Kira felt guilt at the memory of Blake in her bed and the warmth it brought her. She felt it because she knew her behavior was likely the cause of Colin's actions. Mostly, she felt guilt, because he no longer occupied her thoughts as much as he once did. Someone else resided there now.

Kira moved slowly as she crawled from her bed. A once over in the mirror reminded her of how bad yesterday had been. She never managed to find the energy to change or take a shower, leaving her in the same dingy pajamas from her night in the funhouse. She took in a deep breath, determined to push that memory deep down somewhere it would never again see the light of day. She ripped off the pajamas and tossed them in the trash.

A hot shower went a long way to wash away much of the negativity and guilt, but the confusion she felt about Colin was still latched to her heart. Even now, as she drove to his apartment, she could feel it growing. Was it time to give up? Did she still love him the way she once did? Did he still love her the same way? Was love enough to get past their issues? Was it unfair of her to leave him when he clearly had a problem? A problem she'd possibly created. There were so many unanswered questions. It seemed almost impossible.

Pulling into a space outside of his apartment, she noticed his truck. Her stomach sank a little further. She pressed her back into the seat, unable to open the door. Closing her eyes, she pictured his face. That wonderfully boyishly handsome face that until recently had done nothing but make her smile. She held tight to the vision, remembering what it felt like to be happy in his presence, to feel his hand wrapped around hers, to kiss him.

Blake.

Her mind shifted imperceptibly, and before she could process it, visions of Blakes's mouth on hers flooded her thoughts. Warmth filled her core, spreading out through her body like a small ember igniting the flame.

"Damn it," she scolded herself, dropping her head forward only to jolt backward at the sound of the horn. With her hand plastered at her chest, she choked out a nervous laugh. "OMG, Kira, get your shit together."

She took a couple of deep breaths to center herself, glancing around the empty parking lot. Her knees locked together as she fought against the sensation that was still coiling between her thighs. The more she resisted, the stronger the feeling grew. It was like an itch you couldn't scratch.

Her head fell back against the headrest, eyes closed, mouth slack. Her left hand rested along the lines of her collarbone as her mind drifted. The heel of her right hand rubbed against the skin of her thigh just below the cuff of her shorts. The delicate touch of her fingers burned her skin. She was fearful the action would put her over the edge. Her knees rose as her feet arched, curling up on her toes, feeling it over every inch of her body.

It was hot. It was cold.

It made her burn. It made her shiver.

It was like magic.

"Stop it. Stop it," she commanded in a whisper, her eyes still closed. Her hand was hastily working the button of her shorts when her eyes popped open, her chest heaving. With her free hand, she flipped down the mirror, eyeing herself with disdain as she took note of the flush in her cheeks. "What the fuck is wrong with you?" she asked herself, her voice breathless and uneven. She flipped it back up quickly, ashamed to even look herself in the eye. The idea that she nearly got off in the car as she thought of another man moments before visiting her boyfriend was too much to accept.

She smoothed back her hair and tucked it behind her ears before taking a deep breath and exiting the car. It was hot outside. The heat from high noon instantly zapped away the remaining traces of the flame burning inside her. She kept her focus on the ground and made her way across the parking lot, diverting her eyes from the sun as her mind processed through the conversation she was about to have.

Standing at his door, she hesitated, taking several long seconds to take it in. Kira didn't come with the expectations of ending things with Colin. More than anything she wanted to make everything right again, to feel the way she once did. But standing there now, the plain blue door she'd walked through hundreds of times before seemed like an undefeatable obstacle.

She knocked lightly, waiting, running her finger along the teeth of the key he gave her on the same day he moved in. Another light knock, but there was still no response. Kira let herself in, calling out Colin's name as she entered.

He emerged from his room, stumbling as he secured the buttons of his jeans. His eyes went wide at the sight of her. "Hey, babe!" He went to her immediately and hugged her tight.

Kira let him, relaxing into it for a moment before pushing back to look at him. She could smell the alcohol. A glance around the room littered with empty bottles confirmed it. She steeled herself, prepared to do what was necessary to make it work. This wasn't the time to argue, place blame, or criticize.

"I think we should talk," she said, stepping away to find a place on the sofa. Looking up at him, she couldn't place the look on his face. He appeared distracted, or maybe even nervous.

"Um . . . I really do want to talk, but I . . . I think we should do it somewhere else. Maybe get some air. Go for a walk," he rambled as he rounded the coffee table, sitting down in front of her, grasping her hands. "We can walk to the park."

Kira shook her head. "No. It's really hot out there today." She looked around the room, biting at her lower lip. "You look like you just rolled out of bed. Maybe you can get a shower and I can clean up a bit. We can drive over to that diner you like and get some ice cream. And then we can talk."

Colin looked down at the ground, fidgeting with her hands still wrapped up in his. "I . . . I think that sounds good." He looked around the room. "I'm sorry you had to see it this way."

Kira shook her head. "Me too, but I know this isn't you."

Colin pressed a kiss to her forehead before heading back to his room, closing the door behind him. The sound of the shower followed by music came quickly after.

Kira briefly dropped her head into her hands, swallowing back the frustration and pain before pushing herself up, and grabbing an empty trash bag from the kitchen. Walking through the living room, she collected empty bottles, trash, and pizza boxes. Colin lived like most college bachelors, so this wasn't the first time she'd cleaned his apartment, but the state it was currently in was excessive. As she scanned the room for anything else to grab, her eyes caught sight of something she wasn't prepared to see. Something she never expected.

Dropping the bag to the floor, she crossed the space to the small corner dining room. Her eyes grew wide as she lifted a lacy red bra draped across the back of the chair. She felt her chest tighten and her stomach roll. Kira made a move towards his room just as he rushed out, pulling the door closed behind him, but it was too late. She saw her through the crack just as it closed.

Her feelings morphed from hurt, to confusion, to anger in a matter of seconds, hurling the lacy fabric in his face as she backed away. "You have a girl in your room! Are you fucking kidding me?" Kira turned away, pacing towards the kitchen. He took two quick steps towards her, his words escaping him, but Kira shook her head forcefully, backing away another step. She eyed the bra now on the floor behind his feet, feeling the world crumble down around her.

It was quiet for several long seconds. The creak of the bedroom door had her turning away, unable to watch the girl make her exit. It was only then from the corner of her eye she saw something that had her craning her head up. Her jaw dropped even further. She waited for the door to close again before she directed her gaze back to him.

Colin said nothing, dropping his head even lower, his hands laced behind his neck, bracing the tension in his body. He looked tired. He looked broken. Ashamed.

The explosive ache that sliced through her felt like nothing she had ever experienced before. It was a betrayal that ripped at the very fabric of their relationship, and she knew without any doubt it was something that couldn't be repaired. Without words, her arms wrapped around herself as she made a move towards the door.

"Please don't . . . please," Colin pleaded, stepping in front of her. His face was solemn.

Kira looked up, her eyes meeting his as a tear broke free. "Two? Two girls?" Her voice cracked. "It wasn't enough to cheat on me with just one. How could you do that to me? How could you do that to us?"

Colin shook his head, his hands cautiously reaching out to her. "I don't know. I don't even remember it happening . . . Babe, I'm so sorry."

She retreated another step.

Colin rubbed his hands over his face as if he were trying to wipe away a bad memory. "That night . . . that night at the carnival. You said something, and I wanted so badly for it to be real, but I got nervous. I was so scared I would mess it up again," his voice faltered, his strong demeanor fraying. "So . . . I had a beer to take the edge off. I don't even remember how one turned to two. It just happened."

Kira stood like stone with her arms wrapped tightly around herself. The tears paused for the moment. The vision of her cleaning his apartment while two girls laid in his bed played like a silent movie in the background of her thoughts as she listened to him speak. Her sadness faded as anger took a more prominent position in her heart.

"I tried reaching out so many times yesterday, but you wouldn't respond. I guess . . . I got scared again . . . so, I had a drink. And then another." He paused, looking down at his feet. "And I guess you know by now lately, that once I start, it can be hard to stop." He looked at her again, his face softer now. "I didn't even realize I'd done what I did until you knocked on my door and I woke up with them in my bed."

Silence permeated the space. Kira didn't know how to respond. She could feel something flickering within her that she couldn't place.

"Tell me how I can fix this."

More silence. She kept her attention focused on the blue door, remembering how she felt no more than twenty minutes before when she stood on the other side of it. She wanted to go back there, to the other side, to a world where the person she loved and trusted the most in this world hadn't betrayed her.

"This isn't fixable." Her words were soft but resolute as she stepped around him to leave.

Colin quickly moved, blocking the door. "Don't say that. Please don't leave. This is us."

Kira looked right past him, her eyes still resting firmly on the door. She needed to get to the other side. The flicker was growing stronger, winding in the depths of her stomach. "There is no us."

Her words unraveled everything that had been building inside, and Colin's sudden touch at her elbow sent it bursting free. Without warning, they both jerked at the loud sound that erupted within the room. To her right, she could see debris from the TV shattering and falling to the floor. She steadied herself, her hands folded at her chest. Colin stood to the side, his eyes wide and his breath heavy and quick, but he no longer held her arm, nor did he block the door.

Kira took a long look at him, his face pale and defeated, and then back to the door, knowing when she stepped across the threshold it would be the last time.

"Goodbye, Colin."

NINETEEN
GAME TIME

I t wasn't the first time Blake had done this, and he knew it
would likely not be the last. With each encounter, he learned
something new, gaining more insight into who Kira was. What she
thought, and the density of the unexplored magic that idled below
the surface. Sitting across from her at a table on the patio of some
obscure bar; he was also learning more about how she made him
feel.

And he didn't like it.

She couldn't see him, of course, once again cloaked by his
magic. He sat back relaxed in an iron patio chair, his left ankle
resting across his knee, examining her every move. Kira sat alone,
quietly sipping a bright red fruity concoction. The tears were gone
now, but the telltale pale streaks below her eyes indicated she was
recently crying.

It was that thought, that caused the slight pang in his chest. He
didn't like it. Knowing he was the reason behind those tears only
sharpened that pain. He really didn't like that.

Blake had felt a sense of joy as he watched her emerge from the boyfriend's apartment. After the carnival and the subsequent incident at the funhouse, he thought it was high time he put an end to that relationship. Not that it was hard. Colin had already done most of the work for him but adding two girls to the mix would surely spell the end. Kira didn't seem the type to be okay with infidelity.

But as she made her way to the car, the somber expression on her face gave him pause. He'd watched as she sat there for several minutes looking blankly past the windshield. Minutes passed and nothing changed. He anticipated a shift to anger, but instead, he saw her resolve dissipate into anguish. It wasn't just simple tears; it was the breaking of everything inside of her. It wasn't quiet or soft. He watched her struggle for breaths between sobs and how her body shook. It was a violent storm ripping at the shreds of her very being.

And he did that.

Blake was responsible for that pain. For those tears. He'd seen her cry before, but this was different.

From the moment Blake turned twenty-one and he fully ascended into his power, he gravitated to the dark. Nothing had changed over the past four hundred years. He didn't know empathy. He could barely identify with the feeling when it came over him. Being close to someone else's pain can change a person. And he didn't want that. It has the nagging ability to bring a person's own pain to the surface. But then he wasn't a person. Not really.

Paying careful attention to not make any noise, he leaned forward in his chair, observing her more closely. She was beautiful by any standard. Even behind her tear-streaked face, she glowed. Her neck was long and elegant. His eyes rested there for several heartbeats, watching the fallen wisps of her hair as they caught on the breeze and brushed against her skin. The lines of her collarbone and shoulders were delicate, almost fragile in appearance. It was hard to reconcile that fragility with the strength of the magic he could feel vibrating in the space between them. His eyes drifted over her petite frame, and though her legs were currently hidden beneath the table, he remembered how strong and graceful they appeared while watching her dance. There was so much power packed into such a tiny person.

Small. Fragile. Vulnerable.

These were all characteristics that implied weakness and inferiority, yet she wielded something over him he could not place. Kira was the *Supra Virtutem*, but she was also a twenty-year-old ballerina with zero knowledge of her growing power. He was a four-hundred-year-old warlock who'd spent centuries siphoning the power from thousands of witches, and other supernatural beings. There shouldn't be any contest, but then there he was, feeling things.

He didn't want to *feel* anything.

Magic. It has to be her magic. It was the only answer that made sense to him. Magic can sometimes be intuitive and prolific on its own, teaching the witch or warlock who claims it how to employ it. The idea her power was manipulating him as a means to protect her was a reasonable possibility.

Kira stared past him, her expression blank, her eyes not resting on anything in particular. At first glance he thought she was deep in thought, but the more he watched her, he began to realize the warmth that usually reflected in those hues of honey had evaporated. Her expression was simply hollow. Empty.

He'd seen this before; outside the funhouse. In those moments before she woke, her eyes were void of any light. It was as if she had retreated somewhere deep down inside of herself. He wondered if that were what she was doing right now, compartmentalizing, and tucking away the pain somewhere she, nor anyone else, could never find it.

Her phone rang and vibrated on the iron table. Her continuous blank stare across the parking lot remained unbroken for several seconds before she finally acknowledged it. She picked it up, watching as it continued to ring, and returned it to the table once it stopped. He didn't need to look to know it was the boyfriend. It was written across her face.

As much as he enjoyed these observations, he knew it was time to do more. It was obvious the boyfriend wasn't going to disappear. And countless women did stay with unfaithful men all the time. And after seeing how distraught she was, he began to understand how much she cared about the insignificant human. Would Kira be one of those women? He didn't sense that within her, but he also wasn't prepared to wait and find out.

Careful to not scrape the iron against the concrete, he stood from his seat and walked back inside the bar, uncloaking himself before he ordered a bourbon. It was still midday, so it was relatively empty overall. Kira was the only person outside on the patio.

Game time.

He casually strode out the side door leading to the patio, one hand in his pocket, the other firmly wrapped around the lowball glass. Averting his gaze towards the parking area to ensure she saw him first, he stood silently, taking a long drink before turning back.

He inclined his head, eyes narrowed. "Well, hello there." It was a perfectly crafted accidental run-in.

Her face mirrored his own, head inclined, and eyes narrowed in confusion. As usual, she didn't say anything.

Blake took a couple of steps towards her table, glancing at the drink she was now wrapping both of her hands around. *She's nervous. Good.* He liked that. More so, he wanted her. He probably wanted her more than any woman he'd ever met, but he also wanted her to fear him on some level. It was counterproductive to the objective, but just like she exerted some type of power over him, he felt the need to do the same to her. "Day drinking? Alone?"

Kira tugged on her bottom lip, looking down at her drink before looking to his. "Kettle, meet pot."

A tentative grin played at his lips as he looked out over the railing. She had a unique ability to surprise him sometimes. Women were often assertive and always willing, but it was rare to speak to one who challenged him the way she did. "Touché," he replied, sitting down in the seat opposite her; the same one he'd occupied only minutes earlier. "Do you want to talk about it?"

Kira fidgeted with her hands as she continued to nervously bite at her lip, maintaining eye contact. "Talk about what?"

"People don't typically drink alone in the middle of the day unless something's wrong."

"Maybe I'm not drinking."

Blake leaned forward, resting his forearms on the table, his glass still in his hand. He scrunched his brows, pursing his lips as he eyed her drink. "Hmm . . . I am new here. But do cocktails not count in the South? Kind of like there is no such thing as non-sweet tea."

The corners of her mouth curved slightly before she unfurled her hands from the glass. "It's a Shirley Temple."

A tiny laugh escaped him. *So many surprises.* "Seriously? I didn't know they put those in big kid cups. Maybe that's also a southern thing."

Kira shook her head, her smile much more prominent now. "No. I think it's more the fact that we are in a bar. So, no baby cups were available," she said, taking a sip. "I don't really drink."

"And yet, you're in a bar?"

She was silent for several seconds, seemingly contemplating how much to share. "I was upset earlier and wanted a drink. A real one. But when I got here, I remembered that I'm not twenty-one yet."

"I see. Well, let's remedy that, shall we? What's your pleasure?"

He grinned at the confusion and crinkle in her forehead. "What can I get you to drink?"

"I can't."

She's a good girl. Her magic was still in its raw form. It didn't live in the light or the dark. He had never taken magic that dwelled in the Aether. Most humans live in the dark. They are selfish, lustful, calculating, untrustworthy. It was rare to find a human who lived in the light. He could see it in her.

"Of course, you can. This doesn't really look like the kind of place that cares," he remarked as he stood. "I'll surprise you." *She wouldn't be the first woman I've enticed out of the light and into the darkness;* Blake smirked to himself as he walked away.

As he watched the bartender make the drink, he felt that same pang from earlier. He squashed it quickly and headed back to the table. "You look like a gin and tonic girl," he said, handing over the drink as he took his seat. "Cheers."

Kira took a small sip, quickly followed by another.

"So, tell me," he continued, relaxing back in his chair, "what was it that brought you here today?"

Kira took a deep breath and smiled before shaking her head. He saw the shift in her eyes. She was steeling herself against the emotions that threatened to burst free. That deep dark place she shoved everything into earlier wasn't as secure as she wanted it to be, but her recovery was impressive. "It's nothing."

"It couldn't be nothing. Otherwise, we wouldn't be here right now. I'm a great listener."

Her lips pressed into a thin line before scrunching her face. "You know, it's really not worth talking about. What about you?"

"What about me?" Blake asked, his smile wide and vibrant.

"What's wrong with you?"

His brow arched high, taken aback by the reversal of the

question. "What makes you think there is anything wrong with me?"

"A wise man once told me people don't typically drink alone in the middle of the day unless something is wrong."

He laughed. Truly laughed. "A wise man, eh? Hell, I don't think that moniker has ever been assigned to me."

She leaned in and braced her elbow against the table with her chin resting on the back of her hand. "No? You just kind of seem like the kind of guy who has it all figured out."

Blake realized he was reeling her in. At the same time, he felt her doing the same to him. "Interesting. May I ask what would make you think that?"

Kira pushed off the table, relaxing back into her seat as she took another sip. "You're deflecting," she challenged, pointing a finger. "So, tell me. What's wrong? I'm also a great listener."

Blake laughed again, inhaling deeply as he steadied himself against the sudden realization that a woman had never made him laugh before. "What's wrong with me? Let me think." He paused for a moment, his gaze resting on hers. "I don't know . . . maybe it's because I keep running into this really beautiful woman," he said, leaning in even further. "I want to believe it's fate, but then there's also the chance that she's stalking me."

Kira looked down, smiling as a blush heated her cheeks, but quickly looked back, meeting his eyes.

"Either way though, I think I'll take my chances," he added before glancing at her drink. A third of it was gone. He ran a single finger vertically along the outer edge of his own glass, watching as the clear liquid rose in hers.

"Once again, I was here first," she countered.

"Ahh. Then it's definitely fate."

"Maybe," she giggled, her eyes flicking back out over the parking lot again while she gathered her words. "I didn't get a chance to say thank you the other day." She looked back to him. Her expression was soft but serious.

That obnoxious pang was back. It was like a needle piercing his chest, not deadly, but sharp and annoying as hell. "You're welcome. I'm happy I was there to help." He paused to see if she would say more. "Do you remember anything?"

She was quick to say no. Too quick, which made him immediately believe she did indeed have some memory of that night. His memory, on the other hand, was quite clear. He could still hear the sound of his name reaching out through her own thoughts. He remembered her hands gripping his shirt and her refusal to let go. And the absence of her weight pressed against his chest as he slept was all he thought about since he woke yesterday morning.

"So, what brought you and your friends to New Orleans?"

That's a loaded question. "That's an easy one to answer. I came here to claim something very valuable," he admitted, internally laughing at the truth in his words. "I inherited the estate. It's been in my family for generations. It belonged to my great grandparents, though they never actually lived there to my knowledge. I honestly don't know much about the property myself, but I was intrigued and thought it would be a good investment."

"And your friends?"

"They're all very married," he joked, smirking behind his glass. "I'm sorry, but I'm the only one available."

Kira scrunched her nose. "That's so weird. It seems like *your* very married friend was kind of flirting with *my* practically married friend the other night."

"You know, I didn't notice. *I* was too busy trying to flirt with *you*." Another one of her blushing smiles equaled another pang in his chest.

"All while your girlfriend stared us down?"

He felt a different kind of pang this time. "I told you, she's just a friend," he insisted, hands raised in the air in defense mode. "Besides, do you think I could get away flirting with someone in front of my girlfriend without her knocking me down a peg?" *I could totally get away with it.* "But then I guess I keep forgetting about the boyfriend."

Kira tipped back her drink, almost emptying it. He waited for her to divert her eyes, before giving her another enchanted refill.

"I don't know," she admitted, her expression changing into something that resembled exhaustion. "I think that may have ended today."

"I see . . . and that's why I found you drinking alone in a bar."

Kira nodded before taking another drink. "Exactly! So let's not talk about that. It will completely kill my buzz," she said, looking at her drink now. "Geez. I've barely touched this thing, and I already feel it."

That's because you've had two, already. "Okay, it's my turn. Tell me something about you that would surprise me." He was starting to enjoy this more than he wanted to admit to himself.

"Hmmm," she smiled, tapping a finger against her lips. "I used to drag race with my dad."

He arched a brow, eyes widening. *So many surprises.* "Really? That's amazing. You'll have to show me sometime."

She shrugged a shoulder. "I don't really do it anymore."

"Why not?"

"Um," she searched for her words. "It was something I only did with my dad. My parents died a few years ago. And now I guess I'm just really busy with school and dance."

"I see. I'm sorry to hear about your parents. I lost my mother when I was a young lad, then my father some years later," he said, his voice soft and apologetic. Of course, he knew about her parents already. He'd thoroughly researched everything about Kira since the moment he found her. However, the drag racing hadn't made it on his radar.

"Thank you. I'm also sorry to hear about yours."

"Don't be. It was so long ago I don't really remember much. You mentioned dance."

"Yes! I study ballet and modern."

Blake loved the way her face lit up when she spoke about dance almost as much as he did watching her do it. "Wow! You're a drag racing ballerina. Who knew?" he mused, smiling wide. "That's not a combination you see very often."

"I guess not," she laughed. "Okay, it's my turn. Tell me something you would never tell a girl on a first date."

"Oh, I'm sorry, is this a first date? I had no idea. I mean, I would have brought flowers had I known."

"No, it's not a date. It's a hype . . . hypo . . . ," she closed her eyes, focusing on her words, "hyp-o-thet-i-cal question."

The gin's taking effect; he thought to himself behind a smug grin. "I don't know . . . it kind of feels like a date."

"Do you really want to be on a date with a girl who just broke up with her boyfriend an hour ago?"

"That's a fair statement. We should probably give it a twenty-four-hour waiting period and call tomorrow the first date," he joked. Watching her press her lips tight to contain her laughter was everything at this moment. How he felt watching her cry and mourn the loss of someone she loved was drastically different from seeing her happy. "No, you're right. We'll give it forty-eight hours."

"You're deflecting again. I'm still waiting on my answer."

"Man, I hope you're not this bossy on our date," he said, standing from his chair. "I'll be right back."

Waiting at the bar, he realized he was still smiling. He pushed out a heavy breath and closed his eyes in an attempt to try and reestablish his focus. *It's only her magic. And there are no rules that say you can't enjoy this part of the mission.*

"Okay, darling," he said, returning to the table, two drinks in hand. "You want me to tell you something I've never shared on a first date. Well, here it is. I am *magic*."

Kira's brows knitted together as she readily sipped on her new drink.

"Observe," he said, pulling a cherry from his glass.

"Oh no, are you seriously going to try and impress me by tying that thing in a knot with your tongue? I really expected so much more from you."

She is fiery. "That is not my plan, but if you are curious about how skilled my tongue is, I'd be more than happy to oblige," he boasted with flirty wink. He watched with satisfaction as pink tinged her cheeks. "I am, however, going to tie this stem in a knot." He held the cherry in the center of his palm, the stem long and straight. "Watch carefully," he insisted as he quickly tossed the small red circle high into the air and caught it with the same hand.

Kira's eyes widened expectantly, leaning across the table on her elbows as his fingers unfolded from his palm. Her mouth dropped open. The cherry rested in the same spot in the palm of his hand, its stem tied in a neat knot.

"How did you do that?"

"A true magician never reveals his secrets."

"Seriously, how did you do that?"

"One more time," he said, pulling a second cherry from his glass.

Like before, he held it out in his palm before tossing it in the air, but this time he leaned forward, catching it with his mouth. A wide smile revealed the plump cherry resting between his bared teeth. He winked again, before ripping the stem away and swallowing the fruit.

Kira looked down at the knotted stem resting on the table in front of him, her expression dumbfounded. "Any other magic tricks up your sleeve?"

She's hitting all the right buttons. "So, so many . . . But they're not up my sleeve." The flush in her cheeks returned in full. The innuendo and the images that flooded his thoughts caused his own blood to surge, however, his traveled much further south. "My turn. Tell me something you've only ever told your best friend. And I'm guessing that's Kat, right?"

"Oh geez, there is so much to choose from." Kira pulled her knees to her chest, the heels of her sandals resting on the edge of her seat. She continued sipping her drink as she mulled over the answer. "I had a dream about you."

"Well, now . . . . things are getting interesting. Do tell."

"I'm sorry. That was a poor choice of words. I suppose it was more like a nightmare."

Blake shifted in his seat, his hand braced against his chest. "You wound me. Are you trying to kill my ego over here?"

She took another long sip, still unaware of her magical bartender. "I'm not sure that's possible."

"With me, anything is possible," he confessed, waggling his brows.

"Case in point," she joked, gesturing to him.

Blake finished off his drink, setting it aside before relaxing back. "Tell me about this dream. Was I as handsome and charming as I am now?" He was making light of the moment. But overall, he was truly very curious after spending so much time crafting the thoughts and dreams he'd placed in her subconscious.

"Hmm . . . charming is not the word for it. You were more like a creeper chasing me through a never-ending maze in the funhouse. But, on a positive note, you were not as creepy as the clown."

Blake swallowed, biting back the reaction he felt inside, and

220

instead pursed his lips as he nodded. "Not as creepy as the clown . . . Huh, I'm not sure if that's going to win me any dates. Do you think I should leave that off my dating profile?"

"Something tells me you don't have any issues with your dating pool."

He gestured to her. "Clearly, you are overestimating my abilities."

Kira laughed behind her raised glass, not realizing she was well on her way to finishing her fourth gin and tonic. It hadn't been his intention to get her drunk. The goal was simply to put her at ease so she would open up more. He hadn't expected it to work quite so well. They continued to talk, sharing stories about their past and plans for the future. He had to make some allowances and deviate from the truth when necessary. He became so engaged in their conversation and its rhythm, that he'd become unaware of how long they'd been sitting together until other patrons began filling the surrounding tables. The five o'clock happy hour was just beginning, and Kira was well ahead of the crowd.

"I hate to say it. But I think I need to get you home," he said, suddenly regretting his decision to feed her so many drinks.

Kira opened her mouth and closed it again. He could see that she wanted to protest, but it was clear her inability to focus on anything put the thought in check. Instead, she only nodded before slowly standing. Two steps from the table and the true weight of the alcohol slammed into her, causing her to stagger briefly. Blake quickly sidled next to her with his hand braced around her back as he walked her out.

The car ride home was quick. She sat quietly in the seat next to him, her head limply rolled to the side, asleep. His eyes lingered over her face as they idled at a red light. Watching her now, he noticed something. There wasn't much of a difference between all the times before when he cloaked himself in magic. But somehow, this moment was as distinct and unique as if he were laying eyes on her for the first time.

Another deep pang sliced into his chest. He swallowed hard before driving forward. He didn't look at her again until he was sitting in her driveway. Even then, he stared ahead for several long seconds before exiting the driver's side and rounding the car.

"Kira." Blake spoke her name softly, running his thumb along the line of her jaw and curling his hand at her neck. "Let's get you inside."

Her chest rose as she inhaled deeply, reacting to his touch. Her eyes opened, smiling back at him before accepting his hand to help her out of the car. She almost immediately wobbled on her feet, gripping his arms for support. Once she had a moment, Kira was able to steady herself, walking to her front door on her own, but with Blake's hand lightly resting against her lower back, prepared to help if she stumbled.

Blake steeled himself as she turned her key in the lock, preparing himself for the goodbye that came too fast. Turning towards him in the door frame, her expression came across as confused, but he also recognized something else, an emotion he, himself was feeling. *She doesn't want me to leave.*

Kira leaned in closer, her hands reaching out to his. "Do you want to come in?"

Without hesitation, he had one foot in her door, their bodies even closer together now, his hands wrapped around hers. *Yes.* It was exactly what he wanted. He could hear the uptick in her heart. Leaning his head down, he took an audible breath, his forehead resting against hers.

"I can't . . . I . . . I have to go," he said, still holding her close for several seconds, before pulling back and lifting her hands to his lips. He backed away, still smiling. That prick in his chest inched deeper with every step. "I'll see you again. Soon."

TWENTY
THE TWINS

The three witches had so far proven themselves to be not only loyal, but also surprisingly efficient. After taking the initiative to locate and hand-deliver the first witch, they had since been able to assist the brethren with six others. How they acquired the witches varied. True to their word, the Brethren never requested anything more than a location. After the first, the girls stood back, allowing them to seek and find them on their own, but they soon realized the rewards were never quite as sweet as that first night. And they wanted that again. Craved it.

The power the warlocks shared was unlike anything they had experienced. It was electricity and serenity wrapped together, creating a sensation that was both relaxing and bone tingling at the same time. The energy that flowed through them was a full sensory experience. Upon opening their eyes, everything was more acute, brighter even. It was honey on their lips, sweet and satisfying.

More than anything, the feeling left upon their skin in the wake of receiving the power, was what they loved most. It was tactile, both smooth and hot as if they'd spent a long day lounging on a beach. Beneath their fingertips, their skin felt freshly polished by millions of granules of sand and feverishly warmed from the sun. It was an unparalleled high. And like any drug addict, they were willing to get their hands dirty to get their next fix.

By the time they were working to locate the fifth witch, they were in agreement, consigning themselves to become full-service witch hunters. It had worked. After another surprise gift, Rayna enjoyed another mind-bending night in Blake's bed, relishing in not only the magic, but his divine skills beneath the sheets. It was only one night later at the carnival that she realized something was changing.

He'd left her once before, turning her away to Larz's bed after some no-name human girl showed up at his party. She remembered the look upon his face that night on the stairs. She saw it again when he spoke to that same girl at the carnival. Afterwards, he and Larz had instructed the others to take the three of them home. Rayna wasn't sure how she knew it, but she was certain the bond she was forging with Blake was slipping away, and her nights with him between her legs were numbered.

"Would someone please remind me why we're doing this?" Akesha moaned, slinging her hand to remove some gunk that stuck to her fingertips as she continued to use her hands to clear a path through the murky bog.

"Because two is better than one. Plus, it's only been a couple of days since we each received some of their power. We're stronger now, and we should take advantage of it," Rayna answered, certain her words were true.

The three witches were deep in the bayou of St. Charles parish. They were currently working their way through the murky swamplands that surrounded Lake Salvador. The brush was thick with groves of cypress and decaying trees that rose from the water's surface like stalagmites. Duck weed blanketed the swamp in a mush of green that clung to the witches' thighs and anything else that touched it. The bacteria-laden water produced high doses of methane and sulfide, giving the air a rancid smell.

For anyone else, this was a fool's errand. Humans wouldn't dare wade into such dangerous waters, but then they were not regular humans, nor were the duo they were currently hunting.

Serena and Savannah St. Claire were twin sisters. Both were powerful witches in their own right. Like Blake and Vincent, they were Ivers, inheriting their magic from their mother, but because there were two of them, that power was split between them. Together, they were formidable, but separated, they were potentially at risk.

After much research, Rayna and the others learned that the twins owned a small plot of land deep in the swamp where a small fishing shack was located. It was a great hiding spot, far from the reach of most magic. With a little old-fashioned detective work, they were certain they would find them here.

"I think the smell might kill me before we get there," Tatiana complained, holding her arms up high above her torso to avoid the water.

"Stop whining, both of you," Rayna ordered, gripping onto a cottonmouth snake slithering towards her. She held it firmly eye to eye, her fingers wrapped around its head to keep it from lashing out, hissing at it mockingly before slinging it out across the swamp. "Just imagine the reward when we show up with the twins."

"Umm," Tatiana closed her eyes, bringing her hands to her chest. "I can still feel it."

Akesha rolled her eyes. "Can't we just use our magic to get us there already? This is insanity."

"No. We need to conserve our power. Serena and Savannah are strong. Plus, they knew something was coming for them. Otherwise, they wouldn't be hiding." Rayna paused, giving her sisters a poignant look before continuing to trudge forward. "We stick to the plan."

They continued through the bog for nearly another hour. Sunset had come and gone, and the swamp was now black. Witches or not, the atmosphere put them on edge. The bayou came to life at night. Crickets and frogs created a melody of sounds echoing off the cypress. In the moonlight, they could see the telltale rings of water expanding out as alligators dropped in off the banks. Sounds made by other critters drew their attention to the trees.

Rayna stopped in her tracks and put an arm out to brace her sisters from moving forward. Up ahead, they could make out the faint outline of the fishing shack. It was small, likely only one room in total. A rickety dock jutted out from the narrow porch with a small fishing boat tied at the edge. It would have looked long abandoned if not for the small glow of a lantern that permeated through the gaps and cracks in the wooden walls.

"Honey, I'm home," Rayna said sweetly, smiling at her sisters. "Let's go and get our gifts."

Tatiana and Akesha waited for Rayna's approving nod before moving towards the water's outer edges, pulling themselves onto the grassy banks. They walked slowly towards the shack as they watched their sister move to the deep sections of the river, the water now at her chest. Rayna continued on, swimming for the dock.

Tatiana split from Akesha, leaving her in position at one corner of the back of the shack, finding her own spot at the other corner. Each was no more than thirty yards away. By now, they knew Rayna would be quietly pulling herself out of the water upon the edge of the dock, taking up her own position. They each stood quietly, waiting, their arms lowered with their palms facing out.

Blake had shared something incredible with Rayna on that first night before they were interrupted, and she was subsequently cast out of his bed. He showed her just how strong the bond between her coven was and how much more it could be. He taught her how magic existed on a wavelength, and that with practice, it could be stretched further and farther out, connecting, and merging into other frequencies. With his help, she dropped the walls around her mind, walls she didn't even realize existed. She had reached out and connected to her sisters, hearing their inner thoughts, though they were each in differing rooms down the hall. It was an exciting experience, and one she was eager to teach and to use again.

Standing at the edge of the dock, slimy water dripping down, she closed her eyes, dropping her barriers and reached out for her sisters. *Ready?* She waited for her sisters' mental responses before she began speaking the silent incantation: *Adiuro vos. Tribus et obligantes devine potestatem.* Forming a circle around the shack, the witches continued with their binding spell, further protecting themselves from the twins' magic.

Seconds passed. Then minutes. Everything remained steady and quiet. Rayna paused their incantation, listening closely. The only sound she could hear was the melody of the crickets and the occasional rustle of the branches. She focused her eyes on the slit of light that peeked through the crack between the porch floor and the tilted door. There was no movement inside. She took a step closer, reaching out with her mind to warn her sisters to be on alert.

Rayna stepped cautiously along the dock. The boards creaked beneath her weight. Even the telltale signs of an impending intruder didn't startle the twins into moving or giving up their location. Rayna stretched out an arm, her palm flat, facing the shack. She pushed her energy out, prying and exploring, but she felt nothing. She dropped her arm. The twins were not there. She opened her mouth to call out to her sisters, but a noise at her back caused her to jump. Rayna took several quick steps backward, searching the blackness that hung over the swamp. Without intention, she backed herself directly into the now open door of the shack, tripping and falling hard onto the wooden planked floor.

The entire sequence alarmed her, and it took a few moments to adjust her gaze. A chilling scream broke through the humid night air as her eyes settled on the object that caused her to stumble. The gory remains of one of the twins laid at her feet. Rayna quickly kicked her legs, moving herself along the boards, pushing her body back. Now frozen in place, the only sound she could hear came from the thundering in her chest as she sat and stared back at the hollow orifices where Serena's eyes should be.

An unexpected shriek from outside drew her attention. Rayna clumsily stumbled to her feet, hesitating for only a second to avert her gaze, but the sound she heard was from Akesha and that was far more important. She pried away a decaying board from the back wall and slipped through it, immediately searching for her sisters who should be standing by. *Akesha! Tatiana!* She waited for a few moments, stretching out her senses, reaching out for them.

Akesha's scream sounded in the near distance. It was all Rayna needed before she was running through the blackness. Branches and vines whipped at her face. They were on land, but the ground here was still wet and murky, making it harder to run. Her lungs burned, but she pushed through. A minor break in the canopy above allowed the moonlight to seep through. It was then that Rayna caught sight of Akesha, and directly behind her was Savannah. Chasing her.

Rayna stopped in her tracks, holding a firm hand out and shouted, "*Subsisto!*"

It seemed to have worked. Savannah halted, standing in place, saying nothing with her head facing down. Rayna's steps towards her were deliberate, but cautious as she eyed both the witch they came to kidnap and her sister.

Akesha stood ten yards in front of the witch as she watched Rayna approach from the opposite direction. Savannah's face was still pointed to the ground, making it impossible to gauge her reaction. The violent thunder that rolled in the distance distracted them both, bringing their eyes to the sky. Just as a dark cloud passed over the moon, it blanketed the swamp grounds in darkness, giving the witch the opportunity to run once more. She was moving again before either of them could even register it, nearly crashing into Akesha as she ran past.

Akesha screamed, gripping her left arm.

Rayna was there now, holding her. "Are you okay?" Her head pivoted on her shoulders looking in all directions. "Where did she go?"

"I don't know, but my arm, it's bleeding," Akesha whimpered, shaking her head as she held her hand tightly over the scrapes along it. "Where is Tatiana?"

"Was she not with you before?"

"No. We heard you scream, and then all of a sudden, the twins were chasing us. They separated us somehow."

"The twins? Both of them?" Rayna asked, her eyes incredulous. "That's not possible. Serena was dead inside the shack . . . Never mind, it doesn't matter. We need to find Tatiana and get the hell out of here. Now!"

The girls held tightly to each other, moving slowly through the swamp. Rayna reached out with her mind, searching for her sister. If they weren't in close enough range, this would never work. She considered yelling for her but was fearful of what danger it would create. They were not deliberate in their direction as they roamed, yet they found themselves behind the shack again, the faint glow showing from inside. She had no intention of returning there as she and Akesha kept a strong distance, huddling together in the safety of the trees.

Rayna tried reaching out again. *Tatiana? Where are you?* There was silence for several moments, but then she saw movement from inside.

I'm inside the shack guys. It's okay; Tatiana's voice was calm but anguished. She went to the back and stuck her head out through the same missing plank Rayna had removed. "Are you guys, okay?" she asked, motioning for her sisters to come in with her.

Once inside, a hushed gasp broke from Akesha's lips, but Rayna was there pulling her back, and calming her down. She'd already seen the cause of her sister's scream, or at least half of it. There on the floor next to Serena's lifeless body laid Savannah, a knife in her hand and blood pooling beneath her neck. Serena's body was seemingly deflated as if she were nothing more than a husk.

"We need to get out of here," Rayna's words were crisp and anxious, grabbing the hands of both sisters, leading them past the dead girls on the ground, and through the front door to the dock.

They boarded the small fishing boat; grateful they wouldn't need to trudge back through the swamp. They rowed quietly; none of them spoke of what just happened. Partly because they didn't fully understand it, and partly because they were still fearful that something else was out there with them. Possibly watching them from the grassy riverbanks.

The moon hanging high above, casting tinges of light on the water below did grant them some comfort. As they continued down the river, Rayna couldn't help but realize they were escaping on the very boat the twins likely used to get here. The same boat that ultimately resulted in their violent deaths.

TWENTY-ONE
FINGER ON THE TRIGGER

K ira jolted up, her heart racing wildly beneath her chest. With a hand planted to her beating heart, her eyes roamed the space, taking in the comforting sights of her room. Exhaling heavily, she fell back onto her pillow. *Another nightmare.* A dull ache swayed in the back of her skull, wrapped in a heavy fog. *And a hangover.*

Yesterday's events played at the edges of her mind. *Colin. The breakup. Blake. Drinking with Blake.* It was all there, but like most of her dreams, the images were never fully clear or intact. *Throwing myself at Blake.* She rolled over, moaning into her pillow, mortification seeping into every bone in her body. At this point, she was grateful not to have her full memory.

As she laid there, her mind drifted to other things. *A swamp. Running. An old shack.* She rolled back, eyes to the ceiling, concentrating hard, trying to pull the pieces back together, but the fog in her mind made it impossible. She leaned up on her elbows and caught sight of the glass of water and the two pills on the nightstand.

"Thank you, Kat," she whispered, downing it all, not realizing just how thirsty she was.

Kira stood up and walked to the bathroom to retrieve more water when she felt the wetness beneath her feet. Looking down, she didn't see anything, at least not well. She reached over to her nightstand, flipping on the light. On the area rug, she noticed the faint outline of a footprint. Instinctively, she placed her foot over it. *A perfect match.*

Her foot sunk into the rug as moisture seeped out from the sides under her weight. She did the same with the next foot, matching it to the wet marks on the rug. She followed it along, reaching the edge, but stopped there, not continuing any further. Instead, her eyes followed the footstep shaped puddles atop the hardwood that continued beyond the edge of the rug. It was where they stopped that got her attention. *The mirror.*

Everything went still. Her breathing. Her heart. She was sure she was dreaming again. Taking one step back and hearing the sound of the waterlogged rug gushing beneath her feet made her pause only for a moment before she slammed the glass down on the nightstand and ran for her bathroom. Grabbing a towel, she immediately fell to her knees, trying to wipe away the evidence. Once the hardwoods were dry, she crawled to the rug, and pressed the towel down, soaking up as much moisture as she could.

"Hey, sweetie. Whatcha doing down there?" Kat asked as she watched her friend furiously cleaning the rug.

Kira averted her gaze, concentrating on the towel in her hands. "I um . . . spilled some water."

"Oh. How are you feeling? I see you took the Tylenol I left for you."

Kira exhaled, resting back on her heels, content she'd done enough. "Yeah, thank you for that. How did you know?"

Kat curled up on her bed just above her, looking down. "Blake called yesterday evening. He said he dropped you off, but he didn't think you should be alone." She paused, clearly trying to gauge Kira's reaction. "He didn't say why. He just said that I should talk to you."

"He must've told you I was drunk," Kira replied, pointing to the now empty glass.

"Oh no," Kat smiled, swatting a dismissive hand. "I figured that out on my own. Do you not remember the really awkward crawl we made last night up to your room?"

Kira searched her mind, but last night was a big blur. "I broke up with Colin," she finally managed, the words slipping out of her mouth without any warning. She looked up at her friend, confident in the choice she made.

Kat's forehead wrinkled, her eyes seemed worried. "Oh, sweetie, are you okay? Is it because of the carnival?"

The carnival? Wow, that night felt like a million miles away. She quickly did the math in her mind. No, it was only a few days ago, but somehow it felt like an eternity. She shook her head. "No," she finally answered, pausing as she decided whether or not to share any additional details. She would later, but her head was still too cloudy to wander down that path.

"Well, I guess I should tell you that Colin is hell-bent on talking to Blake."

Kira's head snapped up, looking wildly at Kat. "What? Why?"

"I don't know. Eric just called a few minutes ago to let me know that Colin is freaking out. It's weird he didn't mention you two broke up," Kat said, pressing her lips in a firm line as she prepped herself to say the next part. "Eric may have mentioned that Blake helped find you that night after the carnival, and then I suppose someone saw you guys together yesterday. It sounds like he's jealous and wants to pick a fight."

Kira stood as anger coursed through her, throwing the towel

down. It was the last thing she wanted to deal with at this moment. She massaged her temples and closed her eyes as she fell flat on the bed. "I really don't want to deal with this right now."

Kat stretched out beside her. "I'm so sorry, but I don't think you're going to get off so easily. From what Eric thinks, he's planning on confronting Blake today."

One eye popped open, the other firmly held shut as she looked at Kat, her face only a few inches from hers. The dull ache in the base of her skull pulsed. All she wanted in the world was to crawl beneath her covers, but this was a mess of her own making. From what little she could remember from yesterday; Blake had already dealt with her issues far more than he should have. She was still unsure of what he was to her, if anything at all, but a confrontation with an ex would likely go a long way to ensuring Blake moved on. Oddly enough, she realized she didn't want that to happen.

"I need to go see him."

Kat arched a brow. "Go see Blake? Is something going on between you guys?"

"No." Kira inhaled deeply, turning her gaze back to the ceiling. It wasn't a lie, but strangely so, it felt like it was. Her brain was still too sluggish to analyze the thought. "I promise I would tell you if there was, but I do find him interesting. And he's been really nice to me."

A wide smile spread across Kat's face. "Plus, he's super-hot," she added, playfully nudging her elbow at Kira's side. "But seriously though, breaking up with Colin is a really big deal. You have to be feeling something."

Should I? Kira wondered. Beyond the stress of what she just learned from Kat; she was numb to it all. "I'm fine right now. I think I just still need to process through it all." Truth? She wasn't completely sure.

An hour later, after finally saying enough to appease her friend,

234

she found herself at the gate of the Calloway Estate. She stood there for a long moment; her eyes resting on the sidewalk beneath her feet. Something stirred inside of her, not butterflies, but something stronger. It was here in this very spot that she spoke to Blake for the first time. She vividly remembered the surge of energy she felt when their hands touched, and how quickly it evaporated when he stepped away. Kira lifted her chin, peering down the long oak-lined drive, her fingers entwined together over her stomach.

"I do feel something," she whispered to herself, answering Kat's earlier question. "I just don't know what it is or why."

She'd walked beneath these oaks before, her arms linked with Kat and Nadia's, tequila coursing through her system. It was dark then, the path lit by the moon. Looking up, Kira noticed the gap in the canopy, remembering how the stars peeked through. Now, it was just a large swath of clear blue sky.

Everything looked different in daylight. The numerous cars that lined each side of the drive were gone, allowing her to see the massive tree trunks and how the branches waywardly grew and stretched, the Spanish moss ornately clinging to them. The crunch of the pea gravel beneath her sandals was soothing, easing her nerves as she made her way to the house.

It was much like she remembered it, ornate but still delicate and tasteful. Beautiful. She knocked on the door, stepping back to wait. She glanced to the side, noticing the large daybed swing stacked with fluffy pillows, a soft throw draped over the side. *Bachelors do not live like this.*

"Well, hello! This is a pleasant surprise," Larz greeted her with a smile, opening the door wide, encouraging her to enter.

At her hesitation, he reached out, pressing a chaste kiss to the back of her hand. It made her wonder how they were raised. *Guys today don't do that, or even open a car door anymore. It's nice.*

"Hi. Thank you . . . um," she stuttered, her nerves suddenly returning, "is Blake around?"

"Yeah, I think he's upstairs sleeping. Let me . . . "

"No," Kira reached out to him, softly grasping at Larz's arm. "No. Please don't. I shouldn't wake him."

She was already turning on her heel and heading back towards the door when she heard Blake's voice from atop the stairs. "Now what kind of man sleeps when a beautiful woman calls on him?" Blake said as he padded down the stairs wearing only a pair of ripped, faded jeans. They hung low at his hips, portions of his sexy v-lines peeking out at the top.

For a brief moment, she allowed her eyes the opportunity to explore his divine physique. Warmth flooded her cheeks, forcing her to put that in check and focus on his face. It didn't help. His hair was tousled, a lock hanging low over his forehead across his left eye, and his angular jaw was covered in more stubble than she'd seen before. Images of the last time she saw him on those stairs surfaced at the back of her mind. Involuntarily, her eyes flicked up a few steps behind him, wondering if another half-dressed girl would follow in his wake.

She silently scolded herself for it and smiled sweetly. "Hi! I'm so sorry. I didn't want to wake you," she said, maintaining her stance near the door.

Blake's smile was casual as he made his way across the foyer, taking her hand and leading her into the billiards room off to the side. "You didn't. I was just upstairs reading," he said, pulling her down beside him on a leather sofa. "And even if I was, I would insist that you personally be the one to wake me up."

Kira swallowed, trying to pull herself together. *Why am I here again?* His half-naked body was clouding her ability to think.

"Where are my manners?" Blake jumped up and rounded the

236

sofa to head for the bar. "No worries, darling. It's just water . . . sans the gin."

Her eyes raked over the corded muscles of his stomach as he stepped past her, taking his seat again. She happily accepted the water, sipping it as a distraction, taking a moment to fully take in the tattoo that covered his entire right peck. She'd glimpsed a fraction of it before. The end of a tail of what she now saw was a dragon. It was what had peeked out from the sleeve of his shirt yesterday. She was curious at the time, but never asked about it. The inked dragon clawed over the edge of a large shield featuring some sort of insignia or crest. Its tail ascended upward across his shoulder before bending down and wrapping around his bicep.

"Admiring the view?" he asked, flexing his ink-covered pectoral in jest.

Kira averted her gaze to the ground for a few brief seconds to recover before meeting his eyes again. What should have embarrassed her, had instead, made her laugh. "I guess I am." She jutted her chin, gesturing to the tattoo. "Any special story behind that?"

"Not really. Just college and poor decisions," he remarked, playfully rubbing his bare foot along her leg. "So, tell me, what brought you to my humble abode this morning?"

Kira's eyes glanced around the room. There was absolutely nothing humble about the room she was in. She took another sip of her water to cool herself down from the flames erupting in her belly from his touch.

"I think my ex-boyfriend is planning on confronting you. I don't know why, exactly. I think Eric told him about that night at the carnival, and then somehow, he found out about us having drinks yesterday. I'm not sure, but I think he's," Her words trailed off at the feel of Blake's hand on her arm. Her need to take a breath was a reminder that she was rambling without pause.

Blake nodded, smiling. "He's jealous. I get it. I can't say I blame him. I would be hella jealous too, if my girlfriend were stalking and flirting with some other guy. Especially if that guy was as handsome and charming as me."

Kira raised a brow. "He doesn't have anything to be jealous of. One, I'm not his girlfriend anymore. Two, I'm not stalking or flirting. And three, you're not as charming as you think you are."

She tried her best to sound confident, but it lacked conviction. The flame she was still trying to douse roared back to life at the sight of his wicked grin. It was different from his soft smile. This expression was one she was becoming more and more familiar with. It was arrogant and all knowing.

"You keep telling yourself that . . . And just to be clear, you didn't argue with the handsome part." He inched a little closer, his jovial demeanor shifting with the movement. The features of his face softened.

Her heart rate kicked up a notch. He was so close. Her body was all too aware of the hand that still rested on her arm. *This would be so much easier if he didn't look like that. If he didn't have that stupidly perfect face.*

"If I had a woman half as beautiful as you, devoted only to me, like you so obviously were to him, I wouldn't want anyone else." His free hand traced the line along her cheek, his thumb grazing her lower lip. "Ever."

Her lips parted. Whether it was to protest his words or fall into the kiss she felt was coming, she wasn't sure, but the sound of pounding at the front door pulled her attention. The knocks were loud and frantic, causing her body to go rigid. The wide doors of the billiards room were open to the foyer, but the front door was out of her line of sight. Though she couldn't see him, every fiber in her body told her Colin was standing on that front porch.

"Blake Michaelson! Get your ass out here now!"

Kira's heart leapt into her throat as her worst fear was confirmed with the sound of his voice. She reached for Blake's arm as he stood. "No. Just ignore it," she pleaded, trying to pull him back.

Despite what Kat had told her, she didn't truly believe he would show up unannounced at his door. And the fact she was there only further complicated this issue.

Blake took her hand, gently prying it from his arm, and kissed the back of her knuckles before releasing it. "It's okay. We're all adults. We'll talk, and then he'll leave."

Frozen in place, she watched as he disappeared around the corner. Her eyes darted to a small area on the hardwoods as her body battled the decision to interfere. She listened closely, hearing the front door open and close. Blake's voice was muffled and low, but Colin's was much louder. She tore her gaze from the floor at the sight of Larz. He stopped short of going outside, opting to wait in the center of the foyer. A wink and a smile in her direction gave her legs the encouragement she needed to move and join him.

Through the glass frames of the door, she could see Blake standing tall, but his stance was still calm and casual with his hands in his pockets. She couldn't see Colin, but she could hear him clearly. His voice, his anger, his words. None of this was the Colin she knew. Then again, she never believed him capable of infidelity either.

Standing there now, watching everything unfold felt like an out-of-body experience. She stopped hearing the words as her mind retreated somewhere else. Something from within tugged at an invisible string, causing her to look over her shoulder, but she saw nothing. Turning back, she felt that twinge at her palm again. Without looking, she flexed her fingers, her arm still hanging down beside her.

"I'm about to beat the hell out of you . . . you sorry piece of shit!"

Colin's threat broke through the fog. Still, she couldn't bring herself to move as she watched Larz move hastily to the door, his body blocking her view as he filled the doorframe.

"What the hell is your problem? And you show up here on my property uninvited."

Now that the door was open, she could hear Blake. His tone was still equal and measured.

"I heard the story about the funhouse. What were you doing there? Did you hurt her?" Colin interjected.

Kira felt her chest tighten as the emptiness in the pit of her stomach increased as her nails dug into the palm of her hand. She wrestled with the sensation that started as a light stroke but was quickly growing into an achy throb.

"Of course not. I helped her. Took her home."

"Yeah, fuck you. She went through something, and then you take advantage of her and crawl in her damn bed. You're a fucking joke."

"I stayed with her because she wanted me to." Blake paused. The pleasure behind his words was evident in his tone. "She wouldn't let me go."

It all happened so quickly; she almost didn't recognize what was happening. Larz and Blake's bodies shielded her from seeing Colin, but not enough to keep her from seeing his arm swing back and his elbow extend out as his fist moved forward in a rapid motion. Larz immediately moved out onto the porch, allowing her to see Blake's profile, his hand rubbing against his jaw.

Her eyes widened, but she still couldn't bring herself to move. Colin had clearly just landed a severe punch to Blake's face that would likely flatten most guys, but he continued to stand firm. From what she could see, his expression was almost amused.

"Is that all you came here for?"

"Fuck you!" Colin spat, throwing another punch.

This time, Blake responded in kind, one arm grasping at Colin's shoulder, the other flexing wildly as it moved quick and low, connecting his clenched fist into his stomach. Colin began to double over on impact, but Blake's grip on his shoulder kept him upright. Just as he was about to land a second punch, he stopped at the sound of Kira's voice.

"Stop!"

Blake instantaneously released his hold on Colin, his eyes wide as he stepped to the side, his hands held out. "Kira? What are you doing?"

"Kira?" Colin's voice was strained and incredulous. He hadn't even realized she was there. "Wait. What are you doing here, babe? Come here. It's okay."

Kira shook her head. Her nerve endings were on fire, making it impossible to process through her emotions. More so, she had no recollection of how the gun she currently held got into her hands. It was weighty and the steel was cold to the touch. Her arms stretched out far from her body, both hands gripping it, finger on the trigger. Everyone's eyes were on her, but she couldn't take hers off the gun as it shook violently in her hands.

"Hey. It's okay. It's over. We're done. No more fighting," Blake said in an assuring tone, inclining his head, attempting to meet her eyes.

All three men took cautious moves toward her, each hoping to disarm her. Out of fear that one may get to it before the other, they all closed the last few feet quickly, working to pry it from her hands.

The noise rang out deep, reverberating through her body. It was a brutal shout in her ears, deafening her from the words that left everyone's lips. She looked at their faces, their expressions were the same, but the stories behind them were so distinct. Larz's face revealed shock and disappointment. Colin's face was filled with sadness and shame.

And then there was Blake.

She looked back at those beautiful shades of blue. So much was hidden there, but she saw the anguish and the guilt. Her eyes drifted away from his. That's when she realized she was lying on her back, the porch ceiling stretched out across her vision. She smiled, happy they had painted it blue, and that the last thing she saw before she died reminded her of his eyes.

TWENTY-TWO
IT'S THE SAME

K ira gasped, her eyes popping open. Up above, her own ceiling stared down at her. She pressed a hand to her heart, attempting to calm the rapid rise and fall of her chest. "Son of a bitch," she mumbled, attempting to get up, but the swimming in her head had her falling back against her pillow.

Slowly, she shifted to check the time. Her brows knitted together at the sight of two pills and a glass of water with a note from Kat. Kira read it: *Eat me. Drink me.*

She rolled backward, momentarily looking to the ceiling again. Boring. White. Not blue. Not the color of his eyes. Her eyes scanned the room as she tried to mentally configure the puzzle that presented itself.

Images of yesterday fell into place. Kira remembered the breakup with Colin, running into Blake, and then drinking heavily with him. She cringed as the memory of asking him to come inside and his polite decline played in her thoughts like a bad 80's movie. She pulled the duvet over her head, content to die there in her shame and humiliation. Eventually the headache and dry mouth forced her to confront the daylight again.

Kira pushed herself up, achy but grateful for Kat's gift, quickly taking both pills. Reaching out to set the glass aside, she missed the nightstand, dropping it to the ground, water splashing everywhere. "Shit!" Kira jumped up, grabbing a towel from the bathroom before dropping to her knees to dry up the water from the area rug.

The feel of the cold water absorbing through the towel sent a chill down her spine. Kira stiffened; her hands still splayed across the dampness. She looked back over her shoulder, checking the hardwoods before glancing up at the mirror. No watery footprints lurked behind her. The stone forming in her stomach eased, but the general sense of foreboding still hung over her like a dark ominous cloud.

"Hey, sweetie!" Kat chirped, jumping up on the bed. "Whatcha doing down there?"

Kira frowned, her eyes narrowing as she rocked back on her heels, looking down at the towel and then back up at her friend. She took a long moment before responding: "I um . . . spilled my water."

Kat angled her head, her expression showing concern before checking the nightstand to see that the pills were gone. "You, okay? Still, hungover?"

Kira pressed her hand to her forehead, her eyes blindly scanning the floor as she tried to find her center. She felt clammy, and her chest tightened as she worked to maintain a passive face. "A little. How did you know I got drunk last night?"

A laugh broke free from Kat. "OMG! How could you forget our very awkward crawl up the stairs last night? Honestly, I think it might go down as one of my favorite memories ever. You, my friend, are not always a graceful ballerina." She paused, smiling

244

down at her. "But seriously, what was going on yesterday that caused you to go out drinking?"

Kira pressed her lips in a straight line as she examined her memory, comparing the present to her most recent dream. Kat hadn't yet mentioned anything about Blake. *This isn't the same. You're freaking yourself out for no reason.* "I broke up with Colin," she blurted.

Kat shot up, her eyes wide. "What? Seriously? Kira, I'm so sorry. What happened?"

It was unfair to live this moment over again. Leaving Colin was one of the hardest things she'd ever done. Kira only shook her head, still unable to find the words. Saying that he cheated out loud wouldn't feel real. Seeing it with her own eyes hadn't felt real. It didn't feel real when she walked out of his apartment. She would share the truth with Kat soon, but for now, she wanted to live in a different reality.

"I just need some time to process."

Kat only nodded, her expression grim.

"What?"

Lying was not in Kat's skill set. "I guess I understand more now about what Eric just told me."

The stone in Kira's stomach came rolling back, causing her breath to hitch a bit. She looked back down at the wet towel on the rug, too scared to look her friend in the eye. "What did Eric say?"

"That Colin's freaking out over Blake. Apparently, he let it slip that Blake helped us out that night at the funhouse, and then I think someone saw you guys together yesterday."

All the oxygen in the room felt like it was evaporating. She closed her eyes to control the spinning.

"I promise it wasn't me. I hadn't even told Eric that Blake brought you home last night."

Kira opened her eyes, and finally looked up at her friend,

knowing the answer, but she needed to hear it. "How do you know Blake brought me home?"

"He called me yesterday and told me that I should come home and check on you."

It was all she needed to hear. Kira was on her feet, running down the stairs before Kat could finish her sentence. Her friend's concerned words were drowned out as she frantically searched for her keys before racing out the door, leaving Kat stunned and standing on the staircase alone.

Kira's mind raced frantically as she drove to the Calloway Estate. *It's not the same. It's not the same.* Her fingers gripped the steering wheel hard, remembering that she walked to Blake's house in her dream. *It's not the same.* She looked down at the pajamas she was wearing, shaking her head. "And I was definitely not wearing this."

Driving down the path, she heard the crunch of the gravel beneath the tires, reminding her of how the same sound underneath her sandals made her feel in the dream version of these events. She stopped in the circle drive just below the front stairs, pausing momentarily to revisit the dream in her mind. *Am I really doing this? It's not the same.* She pulled the mirror down to glance at her appearance. "Well, if this doesn't scare him away, nothing will."

Kira made her way up the stairs, hesitantly looking up at the porch ceiling. Its pale blue color loomed over her as if it knew her fate. The ten feet between the steps and the door felt like a mile. Her fisted hand hovered in the air for several seconds, her head telling her to run back to the car while her heart screamed at her to knock.

For once, she listened to her heart.

Blake's face lit up at the sight of her, but quickly dropped as he registered the distress in her expression. "Come in," he insisted, ushering her inside, his hand at her back.

Kira released a heavy breath as she entered the foyer. Larz had opened the door in her dream, not Blake. With his hand still pressed in the small of her back, she followed his lead into the billiards room. Sitting beside him on the same sofa, her eyes roamed his body. Beyond his bare feet, he was fully clothed. *Not the same.*

"I'm flattered that you rushed out of bed this morning to come and check me out. I knew you would come around."

Kira dropped her head into her hands as her brain finally caught up to the urgency and emotion spurred on by her heart. "I'm sorry. I'm so embarrassed. I probably shouldn't have come here," she mumbled, her words muffled by her hands and the curtain of hair that shielded her from his view.

Blake wrapped his fingers around her wrists and pulled her hands away from her face. "No. Don't be," he said, lifting her chin, holding it with his thumb and forefinger so they were eye to eye.

The gesture was soft and far more intimate than she expected he meant it to be. For a moment, she forgot why she was there. The tension she felt earlier faded as his hand softened, moving from her chin to her cheek. Her eyes closed, sinking into the sensation of his thumb grazing against her skin.

His touch felt so familiar. This moment felt so familiar. He'd said something before. He'd told her she was beautiful. Yes, she remembered those words.

She could feel his body shift closer, glancing briefly to catch his eyes fall to her lips. After so much denial, she was ready to welcome it, but then she saw it. The tip of his tattoo peeking out just beyond the sleeve of his shirt.

Kira straightened, breaking the connection before his lips met hers. "A dragon," she whispered.

Confusion registered across his face. He didn't protest as she pressed him back against the sofa, rising to her knees, pushing the hem of his shirt up past his chest. "Hey, hey there," he laughed, clearly excited by the sudden onslaught.

She swallowed hard at the sight of the dragon inked across his chest staring back at her. She'd only ever seen it in the dream. Shaking her head, she fell back, her hand over her mouth. "It's the same."

Blake's expression faltered, looking down to his own chest. "What's the same?"

Her eyes met his, but a sudden crashing sound sent her heart colliding into oblivion. A lump formed in her throat, making it hard to speak. She knew that sound, knew what waited on the other end of it. She reached for Blake as he stood, shaking her head frantically.

He furrowed his brow, cupping his hands under her chin. "What's wrong?"

Kira tried to swallow down that lump in her throat, her breath coming faster now. "It's Colin. That's why I came here."

"Kira!" Colin shouted, pounding at the door again.

She looked over her shoulder, remembering her car was parked outside. *Shit! He knows I'm here.*

"Your ex? Why is he here?"

Kira opened her mouth, but the panic rising within kept words from forming.

"Blake Michaelson, get your ass out here now!"

"It's okay," he promised, taking her hand, and pressed a kiss at the back of her knuckles. "We're adults. We'll talk and then he'll leave."

Blake left her standing in the billiards room; her eyes chasing after him, but her feet were unable to move. She heard the door open, giving her the encouragement she needed to step out into the foyer. She locked eyes with Colin on the other side of the door.

The look on his face struck her hard. He stepped back, shaking his head in denial as his eyes glanced down the length of her, seeing her in nothing but her skimpy pajamas. His glare lingered on the bruises. Kira's eyes followed his to the splotches of yellow, blue, and gray that covered her knees and thigh, a result of her night in the funhouse. She saw his chest expanding, forcing air into his lungs before turning to Blake as rage blazed behind his eyes.

"You motherfucker!"

Kira flexed her fingers, looking down, wondering if her hand would respond in the same way it had before. Would another gun materialize out of thin air again? The sound of the gunshot reverberated down her spine, the memory all too vivid for her comfort.

Suddenly everything was moving in slow motion.

"Blake!"

Larz's voice pulled her from the far depths of her mind, watching as he raced past her. Her eyes followed to see him catch Blake as he fell backward through the door frame. She took a cautious step forward before crumpling to the ground at the sight of blood pooling onto the white oak floors. Her eyes floated up to where Colin stood, gun still pointed in midair.

It felt like an eternity. Larz's muffled voice sounded so far away as he called 911. One minute. Two. Three. She just kept staring at Colin until he lowered the gun, turned, and walked calmly down the stairs. It wasn't until he was completely out of her sight that the sounds of everything around her came rushing back in a whoosh. Kira crawled over to where Larz sat, his hands pressed tightly against Blake's torso, using his own shirt to try to stop the bleeding.

Tears blinded her vision, but she tried her best to assist, blood covering her hands now. "I'm so sorry," she whispered. "Stay with me. Please." She wanted nothing more than for him to open his eyes, to see those pools of blue again.

Minutes later, she followed medics as they carried him out. Kira stood on the porch; her arms wrapped tightly around herself as they loaded him into the ambulance. The tightness in her chest felt like it would suffocate her as she watched it drive away. Her eyes flicked upward. That same blue ceiling loomed over her just as it did in her dream, because right now she felt utterly dead inside.

WAITING IS THE WORST PART. Every second stretches into eternity. The "not knowing" eats away at your sanity while the "what ifs" play over and over in your mind. You prep yourself for the worst-case scenarios while outsiders hold your hand and tell you to stay positive.

The waiting room hadn't changed much. The benign images of abstract art in cheap frames on the stark white walls did little to warm the space. It was just as cold and impersonal as she remembered. The air was dry with the faint sterile scent of bleach wafting in from the ER. It was loud. The sounds of staff bustling around the front desk and the opening and shutting of automatic doors, but she shut all of that out, listening to the soothing buzz of the vending machine against the wall behind her.

Kira kept her eyes focused on her feet. The small smear of red on her sneakers was a harsh contrast to the white-tiled floors. The blue scrubs, given to her by one of the hospital volunteers, were clean and free of any such stains. She'd spent at least ten minutes in the bathroom scrubbing away the blood from her hands, watching it disappear down into the drain. She thought she had freed herself of that sight, but there it was, staring back at her, a small reminder of what she'd caused.

"Hey, he's going to be just fine. Don't worry," Larz assured, giving her hand a squeeze.

Kira forced a smile, remembering she was the outsider right now. Larz was Blake's best friend, his brother. She needed to be positive for him. "You're right," she replied, returning his reassuring squeeze.

"There is something we need to talk about though, and I need you to listen to me very carefully. Kira, it's important," he stated, his expression and tone turned grave. "The police are going to show up and start asking questions. Let me talk, and no matter what I say, no matter what you hear, do not say anything to alter the story." He paused, looking toward the entrance as two officers walked through. "Because you were not there."

Kira stared back at him unsure of what to say.

"I know my brother, and I know he wouldn't want Colin arrested."

Colin. From the moment he disappeared from the porch steps, she hadn't thought of anything apart from Blake. *Colin would be arrested. He would be in jail.* She hadn't even begun to contend with her feelings. What he'd just done or the consequences of his actions. It was an impossible task. *He isn't a killer.* The person on that porch was not the person she loved. "What are you going to tell them?" Kira asked, her voice shaky as she watched the officers speak with a nurse at the front desk.

"Nothing more than they need to know."

Her eyes searched him for answers.

"Love makes people do crazy things," he added softly as the officers approached.

"Hello, you two came in with Mr. Michaelson?"

"Yes, sir, I'm Drake Larson, and this is Kira Lockwood, his girlfriend," Larz answered, shaking hands with both of them.

Girlfriend? She wondered if that was part of Larz's story or if he really thought of her that way. She'd only met him once before.

The officers took a seat. "We got a report that your friend suffered from a gunshot wound. Do you know what happened?"

"Yes. I'm Blake's roommate. I was at home with him when it

happened. Kira," he said, gesturing to her, "thank God, wasn't there at the time, but she did arrive just a couple of minutes later."

Kira kept her face passive, focusing on the officer's hands as he took notes of Larz's account of what took place.

"We were playing pool. There was a knock at the door and Blake answered it. I heard some guy asking him for drugs . . . I'll be honest, we throw a lot of parties and have a lot of random people over. There probably have been drugs in the house at some point, but neither Blake, nor I, or any of our other roommates use them." Larz rubbed his hands over his face, his expression distraught. "I just remember rounding the corner, coming into the hall to see the guy pointing a gun. I think . . . I think maybe he saw me, panicked, and accidentally shot Blake."

Larz was an excellent liar. For Kira, his accounting of the story was more believable and real than the truth itself. She continued to listen to the exchange between him and the officers. He attempted to describe the man he saw, admitting that it happened so fast that he didn't get the best look at him.

"How about you, Miss Lockwood? You weren't there at the time of the shooting. But did you possibly see anything unusual or anyone as you arrived?"

Kira slowly shook her head, making only brief eye contact. "No. I don't think so," she answered, her heart leaping into her throat as a doctor approached.

"Mr. Larson?"

"Yes, that's me," Larz responded, standing with anticipation.

The officer interjected, standing up themselves. "We'll let you handle this and will get back to you later with any more questions."

The doctor gave the officers a moment to leave before continuing: "I'm Dr. Rottner. Your brother is conscious. He's stable, but it's critical that we get him into surgery right away."

"Okay."

"His medical history shows he's AB negative, which is very rare. And unfortunately, we are experiencing a critical shortage of the universal type O. He told us you were type O and would be willing to donate."

Larz shook his head, his expression grim. "I don't think I can. I'm . . ." He paused, looking to Kira. "I'm three years in remission from Leukemia. I don't think Blake realizes that makes me ineligible."

The doctor pressed her lips into a straight line, clearly disappointed but still apologetic. "I'm sorry, that does render you ineligible."

"I don't understand. This is a hospital! How do you not have O?"

"We had two major traumas last night that utilized most of our reserve. We have more being flown in as we speak, but we need to get him into surgery right now."

"I'll do it," Kira said, jumping to her feet. "I can donate. I'm O negative."

Larz looked to her, the tension receding from his body, before enveloping her in an enormous hug. He held her tight for several long seconds. "Thank you."

Kira had never donated blood before. Three years ago, after waiting for hours in this very hospital, she listened as doctors explained they had done everything they could. Death wasn't kind. It took her parents, but it also robbed her of so much. She didn't know Larz that well, or even Blake, for that matter, but everything within her told her she couldn't let her experience be the same for them.

She smiled, looking over her shoulder to Larz as she followed the doctor through the automatic doors, confident the outcome would be different this time.

TWENTY-THREE
YOU HAVE HER BLOOD INSIDE YOU

The room was as stark and sterile as he imagined it would be. The incessant beeping of the monitor was beyond annoying. Four hundred years and he'd never seen the inside of a hospital room. Fortunately for him, he never planned to see one again.

He considered ripping all the wires away and walking out, but he knew Kira would be there soon, or at least he hoped she would be. Laying on the floor, bleeding out, he could hear her crying beside him. He felt her hands press against his chest, whispering to him to stay with her. Blake dropped his head back against the thing this place called a pillow.

He was *feeling* things again.

"Hey, brother!" Larz called out, entering the room, clasping hands before leaning in for a bro hug. "Bloody hell, you look like shit."

"Well, I did just almost die. What's your excuse?" Blake shot back, pausing as he caught sight of Kira standing in the door, her face downcast on the brink of tears. He pushed up, sitting straight. Yeah, he was definitely *feeling* things. "Hey, you, come here."

Kira was hesitant, walking slowly to his bedside, biting at her lip, a clear attempt to hold back her emotions. With her hands weaved together under her chin, she looked him over, unable to meet his eyes. Shaking her head, she forced a tight-lipped smile before her tears broke free. "I'm so sorry."

"Hey, no," Blake said, his tone firm but soft, taking her hands and pulling her down onto the bed beside him. "This is not your fault. Look at me." He shifted to meet her eyes. "This is not in any way whatsoever your fault."

"No, it's that stupid fuck's fault!" Larz cut in.

Blake cut him off, reading the guilt on Kira's face. "It's fine, brother. It's over. I'm okay. He must have been more upset than anyone knew."

Kira ran her hand along the edges of the bandage that covered his torso. "This is not okay," she whispered.

He inhaled, steadying himself. *She's never touched me like that before.* It was soft, compassionate. Intimate. *She cares.* "I promise, you, it is. Look at me. I feel fine."

Larz dropped himself into the chair at the corner of the room. "Bloody hell, they gave you the good shit, didn't they?"

"Indeed, they did," he said, flashing his wicked smile and cocking his brow high before reaching out to brush away another tear that escaped down her cheek. "I'm perfectly okay. Scouts honor."

Larz stifled a laugh. "Brother, I must say, I always thought of you as a virtuoso of talking to beautiful women, but seeing you now in action, you bloody suck at it."

He ignored his brother, his attention fixed on her. "Can I not say anything to make you feel better about this?"

"Well, you can bloody well start by thanking her. You probably wouldn't be alive otherwise."

Blake narrowed his eyes at his brother and pulled back slightly to look at her. "What do you mean?"

Larz waited, looking at Kira for several long seconds. "You forgot about the Leukemia. I couldn't donate."

Blake was quiet for a moment before he pulled her hands to his lips, pressing an appreciative kiss against the back of her knuckles. "You donated?"

Kira only nodded, but finally held his gaze.

He was quiet as he watched her. "Do you mind giving us a moment?"

"Okay, brother but hey," he said pointing a finger at Kira, "don't let him talk you into his hospital bed. The dude just had surgery."

Blake fought the laughter as his brother flipped him off. "Dude . . . get out."

Larz stopped midway to the door, his hand over his chest. "Oh wait, I forgot, you don't have any game when it comes to her."

Kira's lips tipped up at the edges, a smile tempting to break loose as Blake grasped the pillow from behind his head, flinging it at his brother. He felt her stiffen as the door shut. Larz may have briefly broken the tension, but she was clearly nervous about being alone with him. He reached out, gripping her legs behind her knees, pulling her completely onto the bed with him.

"Stop, you're going to hurt yourself."

Blake shook his head, pulling her against his chest. "Nope. I told you, I'm completely fine," he assured as his gaze met hers again, his expression softer. "Thank you for that."

She relaxed into his shoulder, staring back at him.

What is she thinking? Sometimes he felt like he knew her every thought, could predict her every move. But other times, like now, she was an enigma.

"Larz lied to the police. He never mentioned Colin. He said that a stranger shot you."

Her face still gave nothing away. She may have spoken words, but he still couldn't get any sense of what she felt. "My brother knows me well."

Her eyes narrowed as she waited for him to explain. The little crinkle in her forehead was cute.

"Clearly, I would have much preferred a different outcome, but honestly, I don't blame Colin at all for what happened," he explained. "It appears he's hurting enough already. Having him go to jail seems like adding insult to injury."

Kira looked back at him distraught and confused. "I don't understand. He . . . he shot you. You almost died!"

"But I didn't," he corrected, his thumb working small strokes along her forearm. "Let's be honest here. I've been hitting on you since the moment we first met. I won't flatter myself and say I had anything to do with your breakup, but I know I probably didn't make things easy. I don't really care about him, but for some reason unbeknownst to me, I care about you. And I know you care about what happens to him."

"That's . . . ," she bit at her lower lip as another tear broke free. "but, I don't even . . . thank you."

"Hey, you gotta stop with these tears," he said, brushing them away with his thumb. He didn't pull his hand away, allowing it to linger on her face. She was so close, her body pressed against his own. It wasn't her magic he felt. *It's her.* Without any hesitation, he shifted, pulling her closer, his lips falling softly against hers. He felt the tension in her body, causing him to pull back. "I'm sorry. I saw an opportunity, and with the drugs they're pumping into me, I got brave . . . Sue me."

Kira blinked as she processed his words . . . his kiss. She shook her head, brows drawn together. "Shut up." Her response was breathless, wrapping her hands around the back of his head as she pulled herself closer to return his kiss.

Though he fully embraced it, he wasn't prepared for this. Her lips were delicate and sweet, but the power behind the kiss was eager and unyielding. He'd spent hours watching her, learning every feature and detail of her face. He knew every line, every angle. He thought he knew her lips.

Blake thought he knew what it would be like to kiss her, but never in his wildest imagination did he think he would feel this. And the best part, he knew she felt it, too. Any tension she'd had before was gone. She completely eased into his touch. Her hands explored the lines of his shoulders and her fingers sifted through his hair.

Pulling apart, but still close, Blake rested his forehead gently against hers. Silently, he studied her face, attempting to gauge her emotions. The smile beaming through her eyes told him everything he needed to know. He continued holding her face between his hands, his thumb stroking along her jawline.

"Boom! Looks like a bullet can't keep a good man down!" Armand raised a celebratory fist as he entered the room with Vincent and Larz following behind, breaking the bliss their sudden passion-filled kiss had created.

"Seriously, Kira?" Larz asked, his tone mocking. "It's only been ten minutes. I expect this shit from him, but I clearly told *you* not to let him talk you into his bed. I'm thoroughly disappointed."

Kira melted back into the nook of Blake's shoulder, eyeing Larz. "It seems you were wrong. He has more game than you thought."

Blake, Vincent, and Armand all erupted into shocked laughter, their eyes wide with surprise, jaws dropped. Larz stood alone, a mild grin on his face as he absorbed it all.

"How you, feeling man?" Vincent asked, setting aside a large bouquet of balloons.

"Awe, you guys do care," Blake joked, gesturing to the gift.

"Well, I suggested the finest bottle of Macallan, but this one," Armand said, finger aimed at Vincent, "thought it would be in bad form."

Vincent moved towards the bed: "Yeah, I didn't think a $12,000 bottle of scotch is something you enjoy while loaded up on morphine . . . Hi, Kira. I'm Vincent St. John," he said, smiling as he reached out to shake her hand.

"Nice to meet you."

"Oh, sorry!" Armand jumped up from his place and stretched out his hand. "How rude of me. I'm Armand Moreau."

Kira inclined her head, lips pursed as she took in the length and sheen of his hair. "Armand?" She smiled. "Like . . . the *vampire*?"

Blake, Vincent, and Larz all moaned with mocking animation as Armand grinned at each of them, nodding emphatically. "Exactly! I'm just like Antonio fucking Banderas!"

"Bloody hell, were you even alive when that movie came out?" Larz erupted with laughter.

Kira pursed her lips, hiding a smile. "I don't know. But my mom had a thing for Brad Pitt, so I may have seen it a few times."

A true smile broke out across Blake's face, seeing hers. He squeezed her a little tighter into his chest, pressing a kiss on her forehead. Listening to her share small insights into her life, learning more about who she was, brought him an odd sense of joy. Glancing over, he caught Larz's gaze. It was a silent reminder to rebuild his mental walls. Blake swallowed, resting his head back into the mattress as he silently restored that barrier.

"Well, I think I should go and let you visit with your friends," Kira said, pushing herself up. "You also need to rest."

Blake reached for her hands, not ready for her to leave. "You don't have to go."

Kira glanced up at the clock on the wall. "I'm sure Kat is freaked out wondering what's going on. I kind of ran out and

259

abandoned her this morning. Plus, like I said, you need to rest," she amended, sliding off the bed, adjusting his blanket.

"Okay," Blake replied, placing another kiss on her hand. He could already feel the ache from the absence of her body against his own. "I'll see you, soon."

THE CLICK of the hospital room door closing behind her shouldn't have hurt, but the sound sliced through her. She stared at it for a moment before turning her attention to Larz who had followed her out.

"Are you okay?"

His question surprised her. She wondered how much her face gave away. Was her expression as grim as she felt? Could he see how hard it was for her to leave? "I don't think I'm the one you should worry about."

"Pshh . . . I'm not worried about Blake," he responded, shoving his hands into the pockets of his jeans. "I've known him for a really long time. Dude's got nine lives."

She didn't know Larz . . . not really. She hadn't spent any significant time with him outside of the events of today, but his words did bring her a measure of comfort.

"Remember now, you weren't there. You know nothing about it."

That sinking feeling settled into her stomach again. She bit at her lip but finally nodded. She'd grown accustomed to withholding the truth . . . to the lies over the past year, but this felt wrong. She didn't know what else to say to him as they walked silently along the hospital corridor. A person she loved shot and nearly killed his brother . . . *because* of her. He should be furious with her.

"I know it seems like an impossible task, but you're going to need to let it go. It's not your fault. You can't carry this around. It'll make you crazy."

She kept her eyes forward. "I think we both know that's much easier said than done."

"That doesn't make it any less true."

She slowed as they neared the exit, turning to him. "You're a really good friend . . . To Blake, I mean. Thank you for what you did." She couldn't decipher his expression. He appeared conflicted, but the smile he offered felt genuine.

"You know we're friends now, too." He hooked up a thumb in the direction that they came from. "Along with those other two assholes. Blake kind of comes as a package deal."

She nodded, returning his smile in full. "I have one of those."

"Ahh, yes. Miss *Katia*."

Kira closed her eyes, pressing her fingers to her temples. She hadn't spoken to Kat since she ran out early that morning. "I don't know how I'm going to explain this to her."

"You can't."

She glanced up under her lashes, the tips of her fingers still working to soothe the headache that was threatening to take root. "She's my best friend."

"That's exactly my point. You don't want to drag Kat into this mess. To lie would be granting her a kindness. Trust me." He paused, pushing out a heavy breath as if he were carrying the weight for everyone involved. "Love can make or break you, and sometimes in life, we have to do things that seem wrong . . . things we would never consider in order to protect the people we love."

Kira forced a tight-lipped smile. "It sounds like you're speaking from experience."

He glanced to the outside doors, the lines of his forehead creasing as if he were intensely considering her words. "Maybe I am."

IT WAS silent for a long time. Blake just stared at the door, fully aware that each of his brothers were watching him. Even when Larz returned to the room, he continued to watch the door. It was almost as if he expected to her to walk back through it. He finally turned his head and acknowledged them.

"It's so weird. It's like she's still here," Armand stated with a shrug of his shoulders.

Blake narrowed his eyes, unsure of what he meant.

"He means her magic," Larz explained. His expression was passive, but Blake detected the apprehension behind it. "You have her blood inside of you."

Blake lifted his arms, flipping them over, inspecting his own flesh. He traced his hand over the bluish tinged veins that ran the length of his forearm. *Fuck. It's her magic.* Holding her close, kissing her; it had all felt so real. He hadn't sensed her magic then. He only felt her light, her goodness, and for a moment, he felt his own black heart worthy of it.

He released the breath he didn't even realize he was holding and ripped the IV from his arm along with the wires that were connected to the patches stuck along his chest. The alarms from the monitors wailed, causing him to groan. *I really hate that sound.*

A nurse rushed in, shocked to see him standing. "Sir, you can't do that."

"*Subsisto. Audi me,*" Larz spoke the incantation swiftly, cutting her off. "Mr. Michaelson has healed quite nicely. Will you please prepare his discharge paperwork?" He smiled, watching her nod, her eyes wide. "Thank you. Hurry along now."

Vincent reached into the duffle bag they'd brought with them, pulling out jeans and a t-shirt, tossing them to Blake. He slipped on the jeans and began to peel at the tape that held his bandage in place.

"Wait. Don't do that," Larz ordered, his hand held up, palm in the air.

"Why?" Blake asked, looking to each of them. "We all know I'm perfectly fine."

"Of course you are, dumb-ass, but Kira doesn't know that. She's already going to wonder how you were discharged so early, but if she catches you without any bandages . . . shall I go on?"

Blake gave a curt nod but didn't say anything. He was too busy attempting to process the emotions that were coursing through him. Unfamiliar emotions.

"I spoke with the cops while you were in *surgery*," Larz said, gesturing with air quotes on that last word. "No one will ask any further questions."

He sucked in a breath. "Good." He knew his brothers would have made all the arrangements to make this incident all but disappear from public knowledge. There would be no questions from neighbors, doctors, or police. They had even taken the necessary steps to compel Colin, inhibiting him from speaking the truth about what had transpired.

They were officially one step closer to their end goal. The magic he'd spent a lifetime searching for was literally pulsing through his veins. But there was a persistent and uneasy sensation that shrouded the satisfaction Blake knew he should be experiencing. It eclipsed the light and joy he felt only minutes before when he was with her.

Was it her?

No. It couldn't be. It had to be her magic.

THE SUN HAD JUST SET as they arrived home. Blake tossed the duffle bag on the pool table as they walked in, immediately heading behind the bar and pulled out the scotch Armand had purchased. He took a long slow drink, enjoying the richness of the clove and orange, even the slight burn in his throat. Setting his drink aside, he once again studied his hand, turning it over, trying to understand the connection he still felt to Kira.

The others followed suit, pouring their own drinks, falling onto the sofa and chairs. Blake still stood at the bar; his nerves were too frayed to sit. He ran a hand over his face, trying to scrub the sensation away before tilting his glass back and downing the remainder of the amber liquid.

"I'm taking a shower." He left the room without saying another word.

Upstairs, he stared at his reflection in the bathroom mirror and pulled away the bandages. He could get more before he saw Kira again. *Kira.* Just thinking her name sent his emotions into overdrive, unable to pin down any one specific thought or sensation. Her blood inside him was as richly exhilarating and arousing as anything he'd ever experienced, but at the same time, he needed it to be gone. Her blood was intoxicating to him. The magic laced within it was blinding him of everything he knew.

He stepped into the shower, turning on both the body jets and the overhead rain feature, hoping this would wash away at least some of his anxiety. Standing under the spray, he leaned forward, his fingers splayed, bracing himself against the tiled wall. He dropped his head, allowing the water to beat down on his neck and shoulders.

Behind closed lids, he saw her. Her own eyes were closed, her hands tracing the lines of her shoulders as the spray of the water fell to her chest. Blake jerked, his eyes flashing open, spinning in place, half expecting Kira to be standing behind him. His head pivoted, scanning the area as his chest heaved. He looked down to his hands again, turning them over, eyeing the veins and the blood that he knew currently flowed through them.

Blake steadied himself, closing his eyes again. And there she was, her chin pointed high, her mouth open to the spray, her hand roaming lower over her breast.

He sucked in a breath, his eyes opening once more. "What the fuck?"

He rubbed his hand over his face, water pouring down. He pressed his hands to the wall to support his weight, trying to analyze what he saw, what he was experiencing. *Her blood? Is this a memory? Her memory?*

He swallowed hard, allowing his lids to fall once again, and there she was. She was beautiful. Her skin glowed, hot, and wet, her cheeks flushed with color. The smell of coconuts and strawberries from her shampoo invaded his nostrils. Each of these things alone sent his heart pounding, but it was the faint sounds that he heard escaping her lips that made his body quake and his cock harden. He squeezed his eyes tighter, blocking out everything around him to focus solely on those tiny moans.

Blake watched as the water cascaded down the curve of her body, her hands chasing it lower and lower. From her stomach to her hips, and over her thighs, her fingers traipsed along her bare flesh. Blake pushed himself off the tile wall, freeing himself to grab his erection, his hand moving slowly at first, his eyes still closed, eagerly clinging to this memory. He wanted to see her body, but he didn't want to tear himself away from the expression on her face. She bit at her lower lip as she slid down the wall to the shower floor. As the speed and pressure of her movements increased, so did his own.

He leaned forward against the wall, holding himself up with his free hand as his other worked feverishly to match her pace. He felt the tension building within himself, a dire need taking hold over him. Blackness started to creep into the corners of his eyes, but he fought to hold on to the vision. He saw her feet arch, her hips lifting off the shower floor. Just as he heard the whimper of her own release, the energy that had coiled within him unleashed like an explosion.

His shoulder pressed into the tile as he rounded onto his back, attempting to catch his breath. Darkness took over, encouraging him to open his eyes again.

Pulse thrumming, and heart racing, he dragged a hand across his face, still stunned by the whole encounter. "Bloody hell."

An abrupt pounding at the door pulled him back to reality. "Blake! We need you downstairs, man."

He rocked his back against the wall. "Fuck," he spat out, not prepared or even willing to leave this moment behind. "Not now!"

"It's important, man."

His brother's tone was serious. *Damn it!*

TWENTY-FOUR
THE BLOOD OATH

Blake felt the presence of the witches' halfway down the stairs. Larz was waiting for him at the runed door to the sitting room; his expression indicated trouble. He walked in to find them huddled together on the sofa. Armand was making himself a drink. Vincent had taken a stance against the wall, arms folded across his chest, his face a mask of imperceptibility as always.

"What the fuck is going on? Last I checked, I didn't actually die today."

Larz came in from behind him, slapping him on the shoulder. "Yeah, the girls don't know about that story," he said, looking at the witches with a casual shake of his head. "He's fine."

Rayna looked to Larz as if she expected him to explain further, but his silence told her otherwise. "The girls and I attempted to track and capture the St. Claire sisters last night. They were hiding out in a shack in the swamp."

Blake inclined his head. "The Iver twins? Why would you do that?"

Rayna swallowed, looking to her sisters for moral support. "We thought we could handle it. We could still feel the power you shared with us a few days before . . . and from the research we did, the twins only inherited power from their mother. Their grandmother died when their mother was young, far before she ascended. And because they were twins, the power they inherited was split. We thought we could take them," she explained, finally meeting his glare.

"And now you're here to tell me you didn't? And that we now have two witches out there who know our intentions?" Blake hissed, his voice growing harsher. "And that *you* led them straight to *us*?"

Rayna shook her head. "No." Her response was tight-lipped.

Blake glanced to his brothers. "Then what the hell is our issue?"

Larz made his way to one of the chairs opposite the sofa, encouraging him to follow. "It seems the twins are dead."

Blake looked back at him, eyes wide. "What? How?"

Larz didn't respond. Instead, he looked to Tatiana.

"I watched Savannah take her own life. She said they knew something terrible was coming for them, and that Serena sacrificed herself so their power would no longer be divided. She gave it to Savannah. Serena thought her sister had more of a chance of beating it . . . surviving it if she held all of their power."

Blake dropped back into his seat, his fingers rubbing across his chin. "And you're saying you saw Savannah take her own life."

Tatiana's face was pale as she nodded her confirmation.

"So, Savannah killed herself because she didn't want to be without her sister." It wasn't a question. He knew exactly why the witch had taken her own life. It hadn't mattered to her that she held all of her sisters power. If she didn't have the one person she loved, it wasn't worth it. Blake swiftly checked that his walls were intact as his mind took note of the unnerving parallels between their current conversation and his feelings for Kira.

"Maybe . . . but things are a little more complicated." Vincent chimed in, still blending into the wall. "When the girls found the shack, they circled it with the intention of using a binding spell."

"I was on the dock, and the girls were at the back of the shack. I heard," Rayna strained, trying to find her words, "I *felt* something behind me. I don't remember everything clearly. I just remember backing up, and then I was inside the shack tripping over Serena's body."

"You didn't see anything?"

"No. I screamed, and moments later I heard both of them scream, so I ran out. I couldn't find either of them at first, but I finally spotted Akesha. Savannah was chasing her. I used a spell to stop her, but then we somehow lost her in the dark. We finally found Tatiana back at the shack. Savannah was also there . . . dead."

Blake rubbed his hands across his face, trying to make sense of their story.

"I think the more interesting detail here is that Akesha claims she heard Rayna scream, and immediately both twins appeared outside of the shack chasing her and Tatiana in opposite directions," Armand stated, still clutching the drink tight in his hand.

"But that couldn't be possible if Rayna had just tripped over Serena's dead body," Larz amended. "Which begs the question, who was the second person chasing these two?"

Rayna jumped in, her words swift and unsure. "I'm sorry. We made a mistake. Last night, we each experienced something separate from each other, and no matter how hard we try to piece together the puzzle, something doesn't fit."

Blake leaned forward, resting his forearms on his knees, taking several moments to collect his thoughts. "First off, we appreciate your loyalty, but no more hunting. It's too dangerous. Second, I think it's important that you understand something very fundamental about the power we share with you. It's . . . it's not *true* power. You can feel it. You can sense it. It's more like a drug so to speak. Like a high that makes you feel like you can fly," he stated, watching their faces as his words sunk in. "But you can't fly."

Rayna shook her head. "But you taught me things. Things I couldn't do before."

"Yes, you could," Blake said, cutting her off. "The things I taught you were already within your own power. You just didn't know how to utilize it."

We need to wrap this up. It's almost time.

Blake looked to Larz, acknowledging the silent message he just heard. "Go home, ladies. My brothers and I have some other work to attend to."

BEHIND THE GATES of the back wall, each of the brothers were changing out of their clothes and donning their white linen pants. It was silent, even though there was so much to say. Between the time Kira arrived at his door that morning to this very moment, so much had happened. So much had gone right. Yet, so much had gone wrong.

Inside the cistern, Armand and Vincent worked to maneuver the harness in place, securing it in sections along the rim of the opening in the ceiling. Blake watched, mentally preparing himself for the ritual, for the Blood Oath. He glanced down at his arms, happy to rid himself of her blood. He wanted to once again feel like himself, but he was also fearful of losing the connection to her. She was his drug, and he wasn't sure he was ready to give it up.

"Okay, you ready, brother?"

Blake stifled a laugh. "To be drowned in a dark pit full of blood. I can't wait. Let's do this."

"It's just like any other Thursday night," Larz joked, helping his brother into the links.

Vincent worked the crank, lifting Blake high into the air, positioning him directly over the pool. Leather cuffs wrapped at his ankles, suspending him upside down, his arms hanging.

Larz pointed, his smile wide. "When this is over, I want to install this contraption in my room. There's a lot of fun to be had here."

Blake flipped him off.

"Okay, my brothers. Let's do it," Armand shouted, clearly pumped, taking his place at the base of the stairs on the left and Larz taking his on the opposite side.

Vincent knelt at the pool just below Blake, his hand moving into the water as he spoke the incantation. "*Vocamus super omnes deos . . . immortatales. Vocamus vobis,* Khalida*."*

Lifting his hand from the water, he gripped one of the sacred daggers, depicting the circle of animals and the fight for survival.

The dragon, forged in iron was the same as the tattoo inked across Blake's chest. The dragon, like him, was the ultimate predator. There was nothing stronger. Blake reached out, accepting the dagger from his brother. He paused for a moment, holding the blade to his own wrist. She was with him right now, coursing through his very veins and within minutes she would be gone.

Images of her curled up next to him in the hospital bed flashed through his memory. He felt her fingers glide across his stomach. He saw the worry and the pain in her face. Closing his eyes, he relived the moment he kissed her. *That kiss was everything.* This ritual would get him one step closer to immortality, but right now, he wondered what eternity would be like without those lips on his. *It's not real. It's just the magic.*

Blake pressed the sharp edge along his wrist, moving the blade vertically, slicing through the artery. Blood flowed out, dripping down into his palms to the tips of his fingers into the pool below. He grabbed the dagger with his blood-soaked hand, dragging the blade across the other arm, before dropping it down into the water below.

He hung this way for several minutes, allowing every drop of her blood to leave his system. His body wrenched at the absence of her. It wanted her magic, but his soul wanted her.

Standing at the base of the pool, Vincent, Armand, and Larz began their incantation. *"Immortalem nostrorum, sanguis, juramento . . . Immortalem nostrorum, sanguis, juramento . . . Immortalem nostrorum, sanguis, juramento . . ."*

The explosive crash of thunder reverberated through the room. Lightening streaked through the sky, illuminating the scene with blinding flashes of light. Rain poured through the opening in the ceiling, the drops bouncing off the pool. The rain soaked into Blake's skin, mixing with the blood that continued to flow from his wrists.

There was movement within the pit, causing the surface of the blood and water to bubble. They felt the vibrations beneath their feet as the cistern itself began to shake. Delicate fingers breached the surface, coated in the blood that dripped from Blake's body. They reached higher, fully exposing the arms of a woman before her hands grabbed Blake's wrists, violently ripping him from the shackles and pulling him deep within the pit below.

Vincent's sudden intake of breath was audible and uncharacteristic from his usual demeanor. Armand's expression was equally disturbed, but Larz remained calm, giving them a reassuring nod. Several seconds passed. Then minutes. The silence filled the space like a heavy fog, thick and disorienting. Even the rain that continued to fall seemed to possess no sound. Finally, they heard faint echoes. They each edged closer to the pool, looking, and waiting. They watched the blood-red liquid dissipate, returning to its usual inky blue hue.

Seconds later, Blake burst from the surface, his lungs screaming for oxygen, forcibly sucking in air. His brothers grasped his hands and arms, pulling him out, dragging him onto the stone floor. He laid there for a long time; the quick rise and fall of his chest slowly became more controlled. His self-inflicted wounds were no longer visible.

Larz knelt at his side, holding out a hand, pulling him up to his feet. "You okay, bro?"

Blake took another steadying breath, brushing back his wet hair. "Yeah . . . let's finish this."

They each kneeled at the base of the pool, their hands resting on their knees, palms facing up. A low growl echoed through the cistern, bouncing off the stones. And then, in the starkest of contrast, a silky soft voice spoke. Her tone was melodic and beautiful, wrapping around their very souls. *"Nomen dudium."*

The Blood Oath had been accepted.

THE SUN WAS RISING, but the sky was still bleak and gray. The clouds and the rain persisted long after they'd completed the ritual. On the front porch, Blake lounged on the daybed swing with one knee pulled up, his arm resting across it. His other leg draped over the edge, his foot planted to the ground, pushing the swing in a lazy glide. He kept his gaze steady on the rain hitting and bouncing at the edge of the porch, hoping the steady patter would calm his nerves.

It wasn't working.

He couldn't feel her anymore. That light was gone. Khalida had taken every last drop. What replaced it was hollow and dim. He drowned in that pit, and whatever emotions he'd developed for her died along with him. He was reborn into something darker than before, leaving him to struggle with the memory of her light.

Larz stepped out, two low ball tumblers of scotch in hand. "You never slept."

"I had a lot on my mind."

"Like what? Almost dying? I mean, you kind of did that twice yesterday. So yeah, I guess you can say you had an eventful day," he joked, taking a seat at the opposite end, lounging back far, one arm stretched back behind his head.

"It wasn't supposed to happen like that."

Larz took a slow drink from his glass. "You mean with Colin?"

"I wasn't ready."

"Bloody hell! I don't think any of us were ready for that."

"The Blood Oath is the Second Order. I should have made her mine first. What was he doing there?"

Larz pursed his lips, shaking his head casually. "I'm not sure. Outside of the timing, everything went as planned. The details may have been all wrong, but the broad strokes of it overall were right. She was there. Check. Colin shot you. Double-check. She believed that I had leukemia, felt really guilty about her boyfriend shooting you, and donated her super witchy blood. Triple check," he said, holding out his hand, counting each check with the flip of a finger.

Blake finally took a sip from his glass, his eyes roaming, trying to piece together the events of yesterday morning. "She showed up in her pajamas."

Larz narrowed his eyes, looking to his brother, unsure of what he was getting at. "Okay, and?"

"It was like she rushed over here straight out of bed. Why would she do that?" Blake turned to his brother, who only shrugged his shoulders. He looked back to the rain, searching further into his memory, relaxing back into the pillows.

"I don't know. I hadn't even thought about it," Larz confessed as a smile crept over his features, holding back a laugh. "Maybe she was dreaming about you, woke up, and just couldn't wait for the real thing."

"No . . . I wasn't in her dreams that night."

"Just because you weren't magically invading her dreams that particular night, doesn't mean she wasn't dreaming about you," Larz informed, kicking back the rest of his drink. "Trust me."

Blake mulled the thought over, suddenly straightening. "My dragon," he blurted out, looking back at his brother, his hand resting across his chest. "Shortly after she arrived, she jumped on me, pulling up my shirt-"

"Aha!" Larz snickered, cutting him off. "Called it!"

Blake shook his head. "No, she was looking for my tattoo. She said," he narrowed his eyes trying to remember, "she said it was the same."

"*The same?*" Larz rolled the words around on his tongue, trying to make sense of them. "What does that mean?"

"I have no idea," he answered, dragging a hand across his face, pushing out a heavy whoosh of air. "I swear, the more time I spend with her, the more confused I feel."

Larz went quiet, his expression becoming unusually passive.

"What?"

"Nothing."

"You're a fucking bad liar."

Larz took a moment, working his jaw as he got up from the swing. He leaned back against the porch railing to face his brother straight on as he contemplated his words. "I've had to tell you quite a few times lately to keep those walls up," he explained, watching for Blake's reaction. "I didn't realize how much she had gotten to you until yesterday."

Blake took in a sobering breath, knowing exactly what Larz had seen. "You don't have to worry about that anymore. It was just her magic."

"Are you sure about that? Because I'm not."

"I'm sure. Her magic sensed me. It tried to protect her by making me care."

"What if it wasn't her magic? What if it's just you?"

Blake killed his drink and stood up, facing his brother head-on. "For a moment there, I thought the same damn thing, but last night Khalida reminded me why I always gravitated to the dark. Why I've done so many unforgivable things in my life." He paused, looking back out to the rain. "It's because my heart is black."

"You may gravitate to the dark, but it doesn't mean your heart is. People with black hearts don't know how to love. I know what I saw, and I think you love this girl."

Blake placed his hands on Larz's shoulders and grinned. "First, I don't even know her, to love her. Second, I don't know how to love her. And third, . . . that's a good thing, because I'm going to kill her."

TWENTY-FIVE

YOU KILLED ME

"I'm gonna die. Seriously, I think this heatwave is going to kill me," Nadia whined, dramatically falling back onto Kira's bed. She wasn't wrong. New Orleans was experiencing the hottest day so far this summer. "Fortunately, I brought this!"

Kira caught the scant piece of fabric Nadia tossed in her direction. She pursed her lips as she eyed the tiny red bikini before tossing it back to her friend. "You do you, babe."

"So, what are you going to wear?" Kat asked, her wide smile plastered across her face as she crawled onto the bed next to Nadia. "This will be the first time you've seen him since the hospital . . . and you know."

Kira felt the tug at the corners of her own mouth, but fought back her grin, pressing her lips into a tight smile. It had been four days since she'd seen Blake. She'd planned on returning to the hospital the very next day, but Larz had insisted that he was too tired for visitors. However, he did text her several times, assuring her he was fine and that he was excited to see her this weekend. In her mind, she envisioned bringing him soup and fluffing his pillows while they talked or watched a movie. Instead, she would be attending his celebratory 'I'm Alive' party.

Nadia noticed the innuendo in Kat's comment. Sitting up, always eager to hear gossip. "*And you know what?* What else do you know, Miss Lockwood?"

Kira shrugged her shoulders; her smile finally breaking free.

Kat hugged Nadia's shoulders from behind. "I hate to disappoint you, sweet girl, but our good friend Kira here, donated a bit more than her blood," she teased, dodging the pillow that Kira slung at her head.

"What! Did you sleep with Blake?"

"No! I did not!" Kira asserted, pulling another pillow into her lap, hugging her arms around it. "Geez, guys. He's been in the hospital recovering from a gunshot wound."

Nadia eyed her expectantly, waiting for the details.

She looked down, scrolling through the handful of texts he'd sent. The flutter in her stomach and chest was just as strong now as it was the moment their lips met. It still took her breath away. "He kissed me." It was all she could say.

The evening after the shooting, she arrived home in scrubs, her blood-soaked pajamas trashed in the hospital bathroom. Kat met her at the door, furious because she'd run out so abruptly that morning, and then refused to answer any of her calls throughout the day. After leaving Blake's bedside, the memory of the shooting crawled back into her thoughts, unleashing a torrent of guilt and anger. She was unable to convey anything to Kat. No one was supposed to know the truth.

Her emotional state was fractured and frayed, making it impossible to lie. Instead, she brushed Kat off, insisting that she was fine and that they would talk the next day. It was by far the worst fight the two had ever had.

The next morning wasn't any easier. Kat was still angry while

Kira was still experiencing a host of emotions. Eventually, she was able to get the basics of the story out, excluding Colin from any part of it. Considering the magnitude of it all, Kat was quick to forgive her, still unaware of the truth. Another day had passed entirely before she could bring herself to tell her about the kiss they shared. Even then, she held back, too scared to admit to anyone how it made her feel.

"Seriously!" Nadia squealed, unable to contain her excitement. "Are you serious? His eyes are so dreamy. How was it?"

Kira rocked back on the window seat, leaning her head against the wall. Despite Kat's demands, she struggled to explain it then. Sitting there now, she still grappled with it. Words alone simply lacked the capacity to sum up the experience.

"I got this," Kat declared, pulling Nadia to face her before proceeding to act out the scene as she perceived it. "He held his hand here at her cheek, leaning in, kissing her ever so lightly."

Nadia pretended to swoon, releasing an animated sigh. "But you know, Kira. She's in her head far too much, so of course, she kind of pulls back. And then, being the gentlemen that he is, he apologizes," Kat said in a mockingly severe tone. "And then," Kat pounced onto Nadia, wrapping her hands around her head and body, rolling with her onto the bed, laughing hysterically.

After several seconds of uncontrolled laughter, Nadia finally rolled over to face her friend. "No way! You jumped his bones. I had no idea you had it in you, girl! So, let's see, Jade has pretty much called dibs on Armand, and now you are lip-locking with Blake. What's a girl gotta do around here?"

"Well, if this doesn't work," Kat said, holding the red bikini top to her own chest, "you'll probably have to donate some blood."

Kira launched another pillow at her friends. "You guys really do suck."

APPROACHING THE HOUSE, Kira saw the large 'I'm Alive' banner strung across the top balcony. As happy as she was that he survived the shooting, the joke banner stung a bit. Her friends only knew the version of the story that Larz had come up with, and as promised, she never deviated from that account. Stepping onto the front porch, her eyes automatically tipped up, taking in the ceiling's blue hue. They were stopped there by a couple of girls they knew from school. As Nadia and Kat happily chatted, she couldn't help but turn her attention to the floor a few feet away.

Just over the threshold of the front door was the spot where Blake had fallen. It was where his blood pooled to the ground. It was where she cried and pleaded for him to survive. It was where her world changed forever. Her eyes were so focused there, she didn't even see him approach until his hands were linking into her own.

"Hey, darling."

"Hi," her words were breathless, surprising her. She recovered quickly, finding her normal voice. "How are you?"

Blake pulled her in close, placing a kiss at her temple. "I'm great. Kat, you've been taking care of my girl these past few days, I assume. I know she's been worried."

My girl. The thought swam through her mind.

"Of course. You know, I wouldn't have had to if you would've just let her come visit," she said, arms folded across her chest.

"That's my fault," Larz corrected, stepping in from behind. "I told her to stay away. See, I know my brother, and he wouldn't rest if she was around. Seriously, ten minutes out of surgery and these two were already snogging in the damn hospital bed. So, I um . . . I doubled up on his meds for a couple of days."

Blake looked to Larz, his expression incredulous. "I wondered why I was so fucking exhausted."

"Bloody hell, I did you a favor," he joked before turning to Kat, inclining his head. "*Katia.*"

Kat arched a brow, lips pursed. "*Drake.*"

Larz's lazy smile was genuine and didn't go unnoticed by Kira. Her friend's deliberate chiding was something she'd never seen before, but she chose not to point it out. "It's okay. I'm just happy he's feeling better," she said, running a reassuring hand across Blake's bicep. "Oh, and this is my friend, Nadia. She was here with me at your last party, but I don't think she had the chance to meet either of you."

Larz drug his attention from Kat, slightly narrowing his eyes as if he were studying her intently. "Hmmm . . . Hello, witchy, witchy."

Nadia's brow creased, her smile hesitant, clearly unsure of what to say.

"You're obviously here to put a spell on all the men . . . with all your charms," Larz said, his gaze resting on her tiny red bikini top paired with even tinier shorts. He took her hand along with Kat's, leading them away. "Let's get both you ladies, a drink."

Nadia turned back to Kira, mouthing the words, *OMG*, fanning herself with her free hand.

"He's certainly a charmer," Kira said, relaxing into Blake's arms, somewhat surprised by how easy it came.

"You have no idea. Come on now, let's get you your own drink."

Stepping outside onto the back veranda, she noticed there wasn't much difference between this and the first party she attended here. It was packed, loud, and everyone seemed to be having the time of their lives. The heat had driven many into the pool while others lounged nearby, drinking, and talking. Many others danced in an area just on the other side of the water beneath an array of twinkle lights. Looking around, she recognized a few faces, but it was weeks into summer and most Tulane students were back home. Most of the people there must have been local, but she realized she didn't know anyone outside of the girls they ran into when they first arrived.

"How do you know all of these people?" Kira asked, accepting the drink Blake handed over, the volume of her voice louder than usual so he could hear her over the music.

Blake pulled her in close, his mouth next to her ear. "I don't, really. These things tend to take on a life of their own. You put the word out of a party, and poof, it's like magic."

Kira frowned. The idea that a party to celebrate his life was filled with strangers did not settle well with her. But then this thing between them was very new. She wasn't even sure what to call it. Were they dating? He called her his girl earlier. Was this casual? It didn't feel casual. It felt personal and intimate, but then she did watch her boyfriend shoot him and later donated her own blood to save his life. It didn't get more personal than that.

Blake must have sensed her sudden tension. "Are you okay?"

She quickly nodded, taking another drink of her gin and tonic, unsure if it was the truth. The past year had been nothing but complicated, and she yearned for something easy and simple. Blake, on the other hand, was anything but easy and simple. He was complicated. Together, they were complicated, but the way she felt beneath his touch trumped any negative emotion or thought.

Taking her hand, he led her back inside. "Follow me."

She glanced back out over the party once more, hoping to catch Kat's eye, but it was impossible to spot one individual amongst the sea of bodies. Just as Kira lowered her head, she locked eyes with a dark-skinned raven-haired beauty. She swallowed, and averted her gaze, realizing she was the same half-naked girl from the last party. With her eyes cast down to the floor, she blindly followed Blake. It wasn't until they were at the staircase that she realized he was taking her upstairs.

Suddenly, she was sixteen again.

Butterflies fluttered in her stomach as she bit at her lower lip. She started to protest, but then thought better of it, realizing she wanted this alone time. The scene downstairs wasn't conducive to any form of real communication. Walking into his room, she released the breath she'd been holding onto.

Blake watched her eyes roam around the room. "What?" he asked, noting her expression.

Kira pursed her lips, shrugging. "Oh nothing . . . Your room seems totally normal."

"Oh yeah? What were you expecting?"

Kira took a few steps, circling the space. Compared to any other twenty-something male she knew, it was far from normal, but it still fell short of where her imagination had led her.

"Oh, I don't know. Red silk sheets. A lot of mirrors," she remarked, gliding a hand along a row of books, surveying the titles. "Maybe a coffin."

Blake's laughter filled the room. "So, I'm a narcissistic vampire with bad taste?"

"If the shoe fits," she smirked, still making her way around the room, taking in the sight of it all.

It had more of an industrial vibe than the rest of the house. The outer walls were the original raw brick, and despite the outside darkness, she could tell that the large windows gave grand views of the gardens below. The large platform bed was covered in a mixture of black, white, and grey linens with several fluffy pillows, a faux fur throw draped across the bottom. It looked warm and inviting. She stayed clear of it as remnants of jealousy threatened to worm their way into her thoughts.

She skimmed her hands across a handful of vinyl album covers resting on a table next to a vintage record player. "I didn't peg you for a hipster."

He fell into one of the two leather chairs at the foot of the bed. "I think the word you are looking for is nostalgic."

Kira glanced in his direction, noticing where he perched. *Chair, not the bed. Maybe he really does just want to talk.* "Hmm," she pondered, staring him down. "Maybe you are an old soul."

He flashed her his best devilish smile, teeth gleaming. "The oldest."

She turned back to the record player and lifted the needle before gently placing it on the vinyl. "Let's see what kind of music you've been listening to."

The static electricity popped and crackled during the first few rotations, but then a familiar sound filled the space, causing her to do a double-take from the record back to Blake.

He inclined his head, a questioning expression on his face. "What's wrong?"

She looked at him for a long moment, almost as if she were looking past him, searching for someone. It was an eerie version of déjà vu. She hesitated, stumbling over her words. "This . . . this song. It's Talisman Stallion," she said, turning back to the record player. "I didn't even know they made this on vinyl."

"You know it?"

Kira stifled a slight laugh, still processing through the odd sensation that pulsed through her body. "Yeah, I've been working on a piece with it."

"A piece?"

She looked back, noticing the question in his eyes. He was leaning forward, his forearms resting on his knees. "For dance, I mean. It's a contemporary piece."

Blake nodded, smiling. "That's right. You're a dancer. It's weird," he said, walking over, taking her hand, spinning her in one rotation before pulling her back to him, "you told me about dancing before, but the truth is, we really don't know a lot about one another. I haven't even seen you dance," he lied.

He was so close. As close as he was days before while they were in the hospital. It clouded her senses and her ability to form thoughts and words. Those earlier butterflies were fluttering to life again, but she finally found the courage to meet his eyes. "No, we don't," she said. His soul-searching blue eyes brought something out from within her, a flicker of something bold and bright, making her braver than she had ever been before. "Let's remedy that."

Kira pushed him back in his chair and kicked off the leather sandals at her feet. The olive-green romper she wore was strappy, but flowy enough to allow plenty of movement. Lifting the needle once more, she set the record to replay before flashing him a smile and finding her beginning stance.

At the sound of the music, she rose onto her toes. Without point shoes, she lacked some of her height, but the movements still flowed seamlessly. She moved into an arabesque; her elevated leg rising high into the air, holding the position for several seconds, illustrating her strength and poise.

Kira wasn't sure if it was the darkened room, the intimate nature of the space she was in, or the feeling of his eyes on her that propelled the confidence that coursed through her in this moment. She moved across the floor in pas de bourrée before rotating into a piqué attitude derrière. It was something new that she hadn't originally put into the piece, but she latched onto the inspiration of the moment.

As the last notes floated on the air, she finished, falling into fourth position. Looking at Blake, she saw his smile was soft, but approving. He motioned for her to come to him with the crook of his finger. Her own hands reflexively arched at the sight. Memories of her ballet exam drifted into the corners of her mind. For so long, she felt like it was him; that he was the man from her dreams, the one who held her attention with a simple graze against her palm. She even wondered at one point that he might be the same man from her nightmares. Those nightmares were still all too fresh and real. But in this moment, she didn't care.

Her heart didn't care. Her stupid, stupid heart.

Blake pulled her down into his lap, his hands wrapping into her hair as he rested his forehead against hers. "That was amazing," he said before he kissed her, pulling her closer into his body.

Just like before, it started slow, but the intensity picked up quickly. The confines of the chair suddenly had her wishing he'd chosen to sit on the bed. She maneuvered her body, angling herself into him, pleased at the low groan he made in response and the urgency behind his kiss. It took a couple of minutes before her logical senses kicked in.

She immediately jumped back, standing over him, one hand over her heart, the other over her mouth. "I'm so sorry. Are you okay?" His expression confused her. "I thought I hurt you . . . your . . . your *injury*," she said, pointing. She almost said gunshot wound, but that description left a bitter taste in her mouth before it could leave her lips.

His smile was brilliant and honest, making her heart do things it shouldn't. "No . . . I'm fine. I promise," he assured, pulling her back down into his lap.

Kira was semi grateful that he hadn't pulled her into another kiss. It was like drowning but having forgotten the concept of air or its necessity. What he'd said earlier was right, they didn't know each other, and neither a single dance, nor a soul-searing kiss would change that. From the corner of her eye, she could see he was studying her face. She needed to focus elsewhere; his face was distracting. That stupidly gorgeous face was capable of making her think and feel things she shouldn't.

The wall behind his bed was painted a matte black. A large, framed poster hung, centered above it. The image was stark white, depicting bold black letters that spelled out the word *Kairos*. "What is that?"

Blake shifted, looking over his shoulder before easing her out of his lap. His hand twined with hers, pulling her along with him for a closer look.

"Kairos. It's just a word that I like," he answered, placing a kiss to the back of her hand. "I mean, it's kind of fitting, right? With you. With me."

Kira took a step closer, reading the fine print written below defining the word: "The perfect, delicate, crucial moment, the fleeting rightness of time and place that creates the opportune atmosphere for action, words, or movement." She stood there, unsure of what to say. He was right. There were never any words to describe how she felt or what he was to her. But, in an odd twist of fate, the right word had been there the whole time. "I like it, too."

"Come on. We need another drink."

Emerging from the dim quiet of Blake's room, confronted with the party's chaos downstairs shocked her senses. She didn't realize how far she had retreated into that moment until it was gone. The drink Blake brought her was well-received. She drank deeply as they stepped back out onto the veranda, her eyes roaming for her friends, but part of her couldn't help but notice the sudden shift in Blake.

Her gaze dropped, but she watched him in her peripheral vision. He stood beside her; his hand wrapped around hers as he looked out over the grounds. She watched as he took a long drink from his glass, noticing the tightness in his jaw.

Something was off.

"Hey, I see someone I need to say hi to," he said, giving her hand a light squeeze, before walking away.

Kira only nodded. He was already on his way before she could say anything. She took another contemplative drink while she flexed her free hand. It felt cold without his own wrapped around it. She suddenly realized what was different. His grip on her hand had been soft and firm as it always was, but it lacked something. Usually, he would always stroke his thumb across her knuckles, as if it pained him to not be actively touching her. It was a simple touch, but he somehow spoke a million words with that gesture.

What she'd just felt was empty in comparison. And he was clenching his jaw, almost as if he were upset. *Why would he be upset? Did I do something?* She racked her memory, but everything was good upstairs. She was disappointed when he suggested they come back down.

"There you are!" Kat's voice beamed beside her.

Kira almost choked on the drink at her lips. "Hey," she replied, glancing behind her friend. "Where's Nadia?"

"Oh, you know her. She found some hot frat boy. Apparently, they met here at the last party we were at. I think they picked things up just where they left off."

Kira scrunched her nose. "Oh, I'm sorry. Have you been wandering around down here by yourself? I should be a better wingman."

"I don't need a wingman. I have Eric," she affirmed, smiling. "And my new British friend."

Kira tilted her head, a curious smile played at her lips. "Oh? Have you been hanging out with Larz?"

"A little. I found Jade, but I think she's disappeared again with her new boy toy after she and I teamed up to take on Larz and Armand at Beer Pong."

"Are you still undefeated?"

"You know it!" Kat exclaimed, high fiving her friend. "Larz was kind of a big baby about losing though. It's sort of surprising.

He's got that big, sexy, British Tom Hardy thing happening, but then he's kind of like . . ." She bit at her lip as she searched for the words.

"Umm . . . or a Tom Ellis?" Kira added with a playful grin before her friend's words had the chance to settle. "Wait! Sexy? Did you just call him sexy?"

"No! That's," Kat grumbled, swatting at her friend, "that's not what I meant."

"Okay, if you say so," she placated, her eyes blinking as she observed her glass. "I swear, these are bottomless drinks."

Kat rubbed a comforting hand behind her back. "How many have you had?"

She shook her head. "This is just my second, but I'm definitely feeling it."

"Sweetie, you have to pace yourself," Kat said, pursing her lips, glancing out over the party, before looking back to her. "Look, there's absolutely nothing wrong with you enjoying yourself. I'm happy that you are, but we both know it's out of character for you . . . so I wouldn't be a good friend if I didn't ask if everything was okay?"

That's a loaded question; Kira thought to herself as she took another short sip. Everything was weird. Then everything was great. Now everything was weird again. She wanted nothing more than to settle onto a path of normalcy, happiness, and calm. *Breathe. Smile. Lie. Drink. That's another new one.* "I promise I'm fine. Maybe, I'm still working through some things." She thought of how much of an understatement that was as she pulled together a reassuring smile. "But I think I'm pretty happy."

Minutes later, Kat was searching for a bathroom, and Blake still hadn't come back, leaving Kira to roam the party on her own. After searching for him out by the pool, she finally made her way back inside. Her intentions were to head to the front porch, hoping she might catch him there, but she stopped mid-step as her eyes locked in on that spot just beyond the front doors.

Kira took two steps closer, looking down at the white oak floors, almost as if she were inspecting it to see if any traces of blood were left behind. She could see everything again. He was there, bleeding.

Panic and fear swelled within her as she searched the room, silently pleading for help. No one seemed to notice what she was witnessing. She turned back to the floor, seeing how her own body was draped across his, feverishly trying to help him. Her hands shook as she knelt beside the vision of herself, paying no mind to the numerous partygoers that stepped around her. She watched herself cry, reaching out tentatively with shaky hands to help, but pulled them back to her chest. She held them there, fisted under her trembling chin.

Blake wasn't just bleeding. He was dead.

Kira shook her head as a knot formed in her stomach. *That's not right. That didn't happen. Where's Larz?* She glanced around the room but saw no one; even the partiers were gone. The foyer was empty. The sound of a door opening drew her attention. It was Blake. He was exiting the odd door from under the stairs. She'd seen that door before. Behind his shoulder, she saw the pretty raven-haired girl leave the same room. *Have they been together all this time?*

He approached her, his hands casually shoved into his pockets. "What's wrong?" he asked, his tone riddled with confusion as the girl turned the opposite direction, disappearing down the empty hallway.

Her lids fell shut, feeling the rush of tears roll out onto her cheeks. *It's just a dream . . . just a dream.* The knot in her stomach had seemingly worked its way up into her throat. She swallowed hard before opening her eyes. Blake's lifeless body was still splayed out beneath her. Risking a glance to the side, she saw no one else.

The vision of herself was gone. The Blake that had just strolled across the foyer was gone, but the one bleeding on the floor remained. It was just the two of them now.

Well, not really. Blake was dead.

She was alone.

The room was mostly quiet. A muffled white noise wrapped around her, but it wasn't enough to drown out the thundering of her heart or the shakiness of her breathing.

She looked down at her hands, soaked in blood. His blood. Not only could she see it; she felt it. Lifting her palm, she watched it smear back and forth across her skin, the red stain baring that once invisible touch. She fisted her hand, willing it away.

Kira hovered even closer now, desperate to reach out for him. To help him. To fix him. With a hesitant hand she stroked his cheek, marring it red. Anguish and regret tore through her. Her breath was ragged between sobs. "I'm so sorry," she whispered.

Blake's eyes opened before the final syllable fell from her lips, his hand shooting up to her neck, gripping it tightly. "You killed me. It's only fair that I kill you."

"Kira . . . Kira."

The same muffled white noise that had clouded her grew louder. And the sound of her name and the feel of a hand touching her face pulled her back to reality. She blinked away the blur, focusing on Blake's eyes. His expression was worried. It was then that she realized she was kneeling, practically blocking the entrance. The sudden loudness of the music and the crowd shook her senses. Her eyes searched that space on the floor once again. He wasn't lying there. There was no blood.

She blinked back tears as Blake's other hand wrapped around the other side of her face, along her jawline, pulling her attention back to him. His hands were soft but firm.

He shook his head. "Hey. It's okay. Stay with me, right here, okay." Her eyes attempted to drift back to the floor, but he gently tugged her chin, locking his gaze on hers. "Right here," he whispered.

"What happened?" she finally asked, her breath still not entirely calmed.

Kira didn't follow his line of sight, but she knew he was looking at the same spot on the floor. He looked as pained as she felt, but then watched as his demeanor shifted before her own eyes.

He shook his head, a forced smile on his face. "I think I need to stop making your drinks so strong," he said, helping her to stand. "Stay here. I'll get you some water."

She didn't know what to say. Instead, she only nodded, watching him walk back through the foyer. As he walked away, she saw her. It was the pretty girl from the stairs, from the carnival, and from her very vision only moments ago. She was watching Blake from the alcove under the stairs by the odd door with all the carvings.

Kira bit her lip. *Were they together? In that room?* Her eyes dropped to the floor, trying to remember what she had just seen. Clearly parts of it were a hallucination brought on by a combination of the trauma of what she had witnessed a few days prior coupled with one too many drinks. But the girl who currently stood below the stairs was very real. *Was that a dream?* She didn't want to risk another glance in that direction, and she couldn't bear the humiliation if she was wrong. Instead, she took one sobering breath and ran out the front door without looking back.

TWENTY-SIX
HANGOVER

The soft light of morning crept through Kira's window, silently wishing she'd remembered to pull the blinds down last night as she hid beneath her duvet. Upon awakening, her mouth was dry, and her head pounded. She risked a peek at her nightstand to see if Kat was as gracious last night as she was a week ago.

Kira smiled, seeing that her friend never failed. Two orange pills and a glass of water sat at the edge of her table. Her head throbbed as she pushed onto her elbows to retrieve them. She chugged the water and settled back into her pillow. Thoughts of last night were far from her mind; however, she was painfully aware of the forming pattern.

She attempted to count the days, but her head was too fuzzy. It didn't matter; she knew that this was the second time within a matter of days that she'd rolled over in her bed, a hangover weighing her down. Clearly, Kat was aware.

Colin. Her guilt was immeasurable. In a weak attempt to protect her own heart, she'd pushed him far from her mind during the days that followed the shooting. She wondered how he was, how he was coping. *Was he drinking? Was he with those girls?* Her mind sifted through all the possibilities. She had pushed him away as she dealt with her own neurosis, blind to what he may have been battling. Alcohol wasn't the problem, but it was a factor. A pit formed in her stomach as the irony sunk in.

Kira mindlessly turned to her phone, scrolling to the last text he sent; *I'm sorry. I love you.*

It was from the night of the carnival. There were no more after that. The situation had escalated so much, and so quickly. Her fingers hovered over the screen as her heart and brain battled over what to say, typing out several things before immediately deleting them. It made her wonder if he'd done the same. Had he attempted to reach out, only to decide that there were no words? If so, she understood. There were none.

She took a deep breath, pushing herself up before curling her legs in tight to her body, trying to remember the last words she spoke to him. Tried to remember their last kiss. Tried to remember the last time she heard him laugh. Colin had owned her heart for three years, yet nothing came to mind. Her heart ached at the thought, knowing they both deserved some semblance of closure.

She typed the words; *Are you okay?*

Hitting the send button released everything that was bottled up inside. Her face twisted, a silent scream burning in her throat. Her chin trembled as she waited, staring at the phone, praying for a reply. With her knees tucked to her chest, she rocked back and forth, trying to soothe her own sobs.

Minutes passed. Then an hour. She was lying on her side now, fingers still clutching the phone. The crying had passed, but the emptiness inside remained. The chime of her phone sent an immediate pang to her heart.

I'm okay. I'm so sorry. I know you are going through something, and I hate that I can't be the person who helps you now. I just want you to be happy. I will always love you, no matter what happens from here. From whatever you decide to do.

Kira smiled as another tear rolled down her face. *Thank you. And I forgive you.*

She waited for only a few seconds, knowing he would not respond again. Closing her eyes, she soaked in the feeling. Was this closure? Even though nothing about what happened with Blake was mentioned, the hurt clawed at every piece of her emotions. In the same breath, she felt a heavy weight lift from her chest. She laid there motionless for a long time, silently mourning the loss of her first love.

The pills were beginning to dull the ache she felt since she first woke. Kira pushed herself out of bed; her hunger finally forcing her to abandon the sanctuary of her room. She abruptly halted halfway down the stairs, almost causing herself to stumble down the remaining steps. Her eyes roamed the living room, searching for Kat.

The only person she saw was Blake.

He was resting on the sofa. His long legs stretched out across the floor; his ankles crossed. His arms were draped across his torso with an elbow propped on a small pillow, his head lolled to the side. His eyes were closed. She took a quiet step, watching the gentle rise and fall of his chest. *He's sleeping.*

All the thoughts from last night, the ones she had successfully ignored this morning, came rushing back, attacking all of her senses. She glanced down at the bottle on the coffee table. *Tequila?* The memory of coming home and grabbing Nadia's Patrón from the freezer came to the forefront.

Kira looked back to Blake, replaying the horrible vision she had at the party, as well as the flashback of the pretty girl he'd been with while she hallucinated in the middle of the floor. She took a few more steps, sitting down on the table in front of him. She'd never seen him this way.

His eyes were always so enthralling. It often distracted her from any of his other features. Before, she always saw the raw magnetism first, his sex appeal dominating all of his physical traits. But here, in the quiet of the room, she saw a gentleness she hadn't before. His dark brows sloped down as he slept. His lips were soft and relaxed.

She glanced down at his hands. They were large and robust, but he always handled her with such care. Looking at them now, the memory of him holding her in the backseat of Kat's car played in her mind. Her breath caught in her chest. It was a piece of time she had lost from that night. She remembered the feel of his thumb moving in reassuring strokes across her shoulder as if he wanted to remind her he was there. More importantly, she remembered how she felt, how she wouldn't let go. He'd been her bright spot when everything else went dark.

Kairos. He had been that perfect, delicate, crucial moment—a fleeting rightness of time.

Blake moved slightly, turning his head. His eyes drifted open slightly, catching sight of her, jarring him awake. He sat up, alert, but also seemingly cautious, nervous even. "Hi."

"Hi," she replied, her face and tone were listless.

"How are you? Are you okay?"

Her gaze drifted down, noticing how his fingers barely grazed the skin at her knees as if he were wary of touching her. "I'm okay," she answered, meeting his eyes again. "Why are you here?"

Blake scooted closer to her, his hands now firmly resting at the sides of her legs. "You disappeared on me last night. I looked for you and finally got worried enough to ask Kat. She came with me here. And." He paused, glancing at the bottle, "She found you upstairs asleep . . . so I stayed. I wanted to be here when you woke up."

"You slept here all night?" She swallowed hard as he nodded, wrapping her arms around herself, still too nervous to touch him. "Where's Kat?"

"She left earlier with Eric. I hope you don't mind, but she was worried, so I told her what happened."

Kira shook her head. "What do you mean?" Memories of her vision last night filled her thoughts. She hadn't told him what she'd seen, but he wasn't stupid. He'd understood.

He averted his gaze, seemingly searching for the right words. "I'm sorry. I should've handled things differently last night. You were looking at the floor, you know . . . where it happened. You had that same blank expression on your face. Almost like you were somewhere else. It was the same that night at the funhouse."

Another gamut of haunting images ran through her mind, but she remained silent.

"I don't think I ever even considered how you were taking it," he said, running a hand across his stubbled jaw. "At least not until last night. I never gave you any time to process it. Instead, I just pretended as if Colin never existed, and I pulled you into something . . . ," his voice trailed off, shaking his head before grabbing both of her hands, wrapping them within his own. "I don't know what this is, but I do know that it is something."

Something. She mentally absorbed his words. It *was* something. More than something. Sometimes it felt like everything. As she looked down, watching his thumb rub those small circles across her skin, she knew what they were feeling was the same. Emotions, too many to process, were seeping in at every corner of her heart. Her stupid, stupid heart.

She jumped up, turning away as a single tear broke free, quickly running the back of her hand across her cheek. "Oh my gosh," she said, her voice cracking with nervous laughter, "you say everything right, but for some reason, I'm always crying."

"It's okay. I told you once before, I'm a good listener. I'm also a good shoulder to cry on."

She smiled, but kept her gaze lowered as she worked on composing herself. Looking at him always came with the risk of distraction. Those eyes had a way of making her fumble for words and articulate thought. "Thank you," she said finally, taking a few more deep breaths before she curled up on the sofa beside him, deliberately keeping some distance.

Blake clearly noticed the space she'd put between them but didn't make any effort to invade it. Instead, he leaned back, his head turned toward her with his hands fisted together in his lap. "Please . . . say something."

Kira searched his face, wondering why it was so hard. Was she scared to be hurt again? Was it too soon? Or was she simply terrified of her own feelings? Maybe it was everything. "It is *something*, but I also don't know what that *something* is," she confessed, pressing her lips in a firm line. "And honestly, that scares me."

"It scares me, too." His expression was earnest.

She stifled a laugh. "I can't imagine that anything scares you."

He worked his jaw, masking his own laugh. "I didn't think so either. And then I met you."

Kira turned her head. His hands were still in his lap, but his words were melting away every bit of her resistance. She needed to keep her focus and looking at him made it difficult. "I saw you with that girl last night."

"Rayna."

He didn't say her name as a question, as if he knew exactly who she meant.

She met his eyes again. Putting a name to the pretty girl's face did nothing to calm the unrest she felt in the pit of her stomach.

"She was with me just before I found you last night, but I promise you nothing is going on between us."

No, that part wasn't a dream. He confirmed it. He didn't hide it. "But there was . . . before, I mean?"

Blake turned and looked down at his hands, nodding. "There was," he admitted, twisting in his seat to face her, "but it wasn't anything at all like this. And like you said, that was before. We're just friends now . . . And she works for me."

Works for him? Kira sat silently for several long seconds, those words playing on repeat in her mind. She dropped her head, shaking it as a discomfited laugh broke free.

"What?" he asked, reaching out to smooth the hair back from her face.

Kira looked up, her laughter nearly bringing tears to her eyes. "There is so much intensity and . . . so much drama," she explained, her hands moving back and forth between them as she spoke. "I feel like we've gone through so much, and yet I don't even know what you do for a living "

Blake dropped his head back, laughing himself. "You're right. You are so right. I think we need to start over," he paused for a short moment before straightening himself, his hand held out. "Hello, I'm Blake . . . and you are?"

She smiled at the novelty of his gesture and took his hand. "Kira."

"Kira," he repeated, pressing a kiss to the back of her knuckles.

The sound of her name on his lips was sweet and soft, warming her from the inside. She believed him. Her heart was gravely wrong once before, but looking back at those oceans of blue, she saw nothing but sincerity. "What do you do, Blake?"

"Investments mostly."

"What do you invest in?" The normalcy of this new

conversation felt odd. It was such a contradiction, but she welcomed it.

"It varies—stocks, property, art, antiquities. Anything of value, really." He paused, glancing down to her hand that still rested within his own. "Rayna helps me acquire rare items."

Hearing her name again didn't thoroughly wash away the moment, but the sting was still present. *Jealousy doesn't look good on anyone,* she silently reminded herself. "What kind of items?"

"Precious things. She was actually giving me some bad news last night. One of my recent deals fell through. It was a centuries-old painting of twin sisters."

"I'm sorry about your deal," she said, sighing deeply. "I'm also sorry about . . . about everything else. It isn't my place to be jealous of women you've been with."

"Hey, stop," he said, pulling her into him, erasing the distance she'd created earlier. "We're not doing that. We started over, remember. In fact, I'm pretty sure we just met."

Kira could feel the tension fade as she leaned into his chest, his thumb softly stroking her arm. "Hmm . . . I don't usually snuggle so close to strangers."

She couldn't see his smile, but she could hear it in his words. "Well, I am quite charming. And exceedingly handsome. Plus, you don't know this about me yet, but I'm excellent in the kitchen."

An audible gasp escaped her lips. "It's like you are reading my mind. I'm so hungry."

"In that case." He jumped up and made his way to her kitchen.

Kira followed, perching herself onto one of the bar stools at the island and silently watched as he sorted through her fridge before giving her a pained look. "What?"

"You have the fridge of a college student."

"I am a college student."

"Touché. Unfortunately, there isn't much I can do with a bottle of wine, cheese, and a box of Chinese leftovers," he teased, pulling out his phone. "I guess we're ordering pizza."

"Ummm . . . ham and pineapple, please."

"Oh, really? You're one of those," he said, wrinkling his nose.

She narrowed her eyes. "One of those, what?"

"If I took you to Italy tomorrow, I promise you would never see pineapple on a pizza. It simply isn't done. But for you, I'll survive it."

Thirty minutes later, she was curled up on the sofa; her legs draped across his lap, exchanging stories while eating pizza straight from the box. It felt right. Her mind still had a million questions, but her heart was content with what it knew. She pushed the dreams, the nightmares, the break-up, the shooting . . . everything deep down.

"In the spirit of us getting to know one another, ask me anything," Blake suggested.

"Okay . . . favorite food?"

"Definitely not this." Blake held up a slice of pizza, before dropping it back into the box. "I grew up in Massachusetts, so I love a great New England clam chowder. And you?"

"Cheese fries."

He laughed, shaking his head. "That explains your fridge."

Kira snuggled further into the sofa, enjoying the feel of his hands against her knees. "Where did you go to school?"

"Oxford."

"Oh wow. That's very impressive. What did you study?"

"History."

Kira pursed her lips. "Is that what got you interested in antiquities?"

He nodded. "I'd say so . . . amongst other things. I had this professor who, over a lifetime, had amassed this phenomenal collection of relics. I eventually became his TA, and we formed a great relationship. Then one day, he asked me to help him sell one of his pieces. It was this Corinthian figurine of a sea serpent dating back to the sixth century BC. It was this tiny thing, but it sold for $150,000.00," he explained. "Unfortunately, I soon learned he was under investigation, and the remaining artifacts were all seized."

"Were you in any trouble?"

"Fortunately, no. But it was a great learning experience. There's a lot of interest and even more money in that particular industry. I do my due diligence when I'm acquiring an item to ensure I'm steering clear of the black market."

"So, Oxford . . . is that where you met Larz?"

"Yes."

"And what about Armand and Vincent?"

"Same."

"You all have been together since college . . . you call them your brothers. Were you guys in a fraternity together?"

"No, not exactly. We'd all lost our parents. So, by default, we were a part of a club that no one wants to be in . . . I'm sure you can relate," he said, gesturing to her. "None of us had any siblings, and somewhere along the way, we became one another's family."

Kira nodded, an empathetic smile on her face, knowing the feeling all too well.

"My turn," he said, as he continued to glide his thumb in lazy strokes across her knee. "Why dancing?"

"Oh wow, I," she trailed off, searching her thoughts for an answer. The tension in her body grew slightly. She could tell Blake sensed it with the change of how his hands moved across her, but he didn't say anything, giving her the time and space she needed. "My mom always said I started dancing before I ever learned to walk. That I went through this phase where I was always wearing a tutu and walking on my tiptoes."

Blake ran his hand over the top of her feet. "Watching you last night was . . . sublime."

"Thank you." She only allowed herself a moment to think back on their private moment in his room last night as heat threatened to wash across her cheeks. "After my parents died, I actually stopped for like six months. They were always my biggest cheerleaders. They spent years chauffeuring me back and forth to classes, private lessons, clinics, competitions. They were there for every performance. I couldn't bear to do it without them."

"What changed your mind?"

Kira took an audible breath. "Kat and Colin. They were the ones who really took care of me afterward, reminding me that my parents wouldn't want me to quit," she said, releasing another heavy breath. "So now, I guess I dance for them, hoping on some level that they're watching over me and are proud."

"I'm sure they are. I didn't realize though, how long Colin had been in your life." His words were genuine, but she felt his hesitance. "Are you okay?"

The shift in their conversation made her mouth go dry. He wasn't asking if she was okay with the breakup. He was referring to the shooting. Kira nodded as she contemplated furthering that line of discussion. "I actually texted him this morning. I wanted to know if he was okay."

"And?"

Kira noticed how his jaw clenched, but as a whole, his expression remained neutral. "He didn't say much other than to say he was okay and that he was sorry," she said, pulling her legs away from his lap so she could move closer to him. "Thank you for what you did. I don't expect this to be any form of solace for you, but the Colin you met is not the same one I knew."

Blake looked down at her, studying her face before leaning in to kiss her. His lips were gentle and generous, but also wholly unwavering as if his only goal were to leave her with the memory of this single moment in time. He pulled back slightly, wrapping his hand at her jawline, and tucking back a strand of her hair.

"New question. If you could go anywhere in the world, where would you go?"

She bit her lip as she mulled it over. She always dreamt of traveling, but she hadn't seen much of the world outside of the occasional family vacation. "At first thought, I would say somewhere tropical. Lying on a beach somewhere with a good book and a glass of wine. But then the other part of me would like to do something more adventurous, like going to the mountains and learning to snowboard."

Blake's lips curved into a wicked grin. "Seriously? I can teach you."

"Why does it not surprise me you know how to snowboard?"

"I have a place in Lake Tahoe. I'll take you there this winter and show you how it's done."

Kira couldn't hold back the huge smile plastered across her face. "Oh my gosh! Really?" she squealed, playfully slapping his arm. "You know, I've never even seen snow."

His brows arched high. "No way! You've never seen snow?"

Kira shook her head, shrugging her shoulders. "I grew up in New Orleans. It's basically a sauna for two-thirds of the year."

"Yeah, I've become brutally aware of this."

She watched as his face scrunched in deep thought. Even then, he was the most excruciatingly beautiful man she'd ever seen. "What?"

"I have an idea. You know, some bad weather is expected here next week if that hurricane stays on the same path. Maybe we should getaway for a few days. Lake Tahoe is just as beautiful in the summer. You and me," he said, leaning in for another kiss, pressing them lightly across her forehead, her lips, and down the side of her neck to her shoulder. "I would love to have you to myself, but you could also invite Kat and Eric if you like."

His kisses ignited something deep within her. She angled her body, giving him more access as he trailed his lips across her skin. The idea of spending a few days alone with him was exciting, but this thing between them was still new, and so far unlike anything she'd ever experienced.

She pushed him back. "I really like this idea, but I don't know if I trust myself alone with you."

He winced, placing a hand over his heart. "My lady, you wound me. I am a complete gentleman."

"One who is also quite charming, and how did you put it? Oh yeah, exceedingly handsome, and excellent in the kitchen. So how could a girl resist? But I think I'll bring Kat along as my backup, just in case."

He pulled her in close, nuzzling into the crook of her shoulder. "Sounds good to me, but you know, I'm pretty good in other rooms, too," he joked, tickling her ribs, and nipping at her neck.

Kira squealed in laughter, before slapping at his arm. "Case in point!"

TWENTY-SEVEN
THE GET AWAY

New beginnings are not for the faint of heart. They are rife with twists and turns, confusion, and heartaches. But the adventurous path that lies between an ending and a beginning can also be rewarding, leading to new friendships, love, and personal growth. In the chasms of such a rocky road, you can find happiness, strength, and forgiveness.

After a year filled with such stress and strife, Kira was ready to embrace something new. She was no longer willing to idle in the chaos. With her hand firmly wrapped in Blake's, she searched the approaching earth outside the window of the plane, feeling that adventurous spark igniting within her. Certainties didn't disillusion her, but the moment her feet left the ground, a new hope wedged its way into her heart.

In the days following their conversation, Blake had gone the distance to show how much he cared. In the periphery of her vision, she watched his thumb make those small, but infinitely delicious strokes across her arm. It was surprising how much someone could convey with even the most imperceptible touch. Colin had always been attentive and kind. She tried to remember if she had ever been as fully aware of his hands and her body's response to them. Not even in the early months of the relationship could she recall ever craving him so much.

As if he could sense her very thoughts, he lifted her hand to his lips, pressing a kiss to the back of her knuckles. "Thank you for coming with me."

"Thank you for bringing me," she said, biting at her lower lip. "I mean, the private plane feels a bit much."

"Speak for yourself, girl," Kat called out from the seat behind her.

"Same, girl. I don't think I can ever go back to commercial," Nadia added, lounging further into her seat. "I mean, if he's going to spoil all of your friends this way, I can't imagine how generous he's going to be with you this weekend."

"Very generous," he informed, that devilish smile she was growing to love, plastered across his face.

Kira blushed. "Stop it."

"No, don't stop!" Nadia spouted, pressing her lips together to contain her own laughter.

Unable to resist, Kat joined her, laughing and calling out breathlessly, "Don't stop! Don't stop!" as their feet lightly kicked at the back of Kira and Blake's seats.

"Seriously, if I'd known my friends would be so embarrassing, I would've left them at home."

"Oh, you shouldn't worry, they'll fit right in with Larz and Armand."

"And what about Vincent?"

"No worries there. He's the mature one of the group."

Kira leaned over, her elbow resting on the console between them, her head propped on her fist. "And what about you?"

His devilish smile grew even wider as he met her lips. "I thought we covered that already. I'm the generous one."

STEPPING OUT OF THE UBER, Kira inhaled deeply. The air felt clean, and the scent of pine clung to the air. The stuffiness of humid summer days was gone. The sky was blue with wispy streaks of white. This was a sanctuary. Any tension she was unintentionally harboring evaporated within seconds of her feet being on the ground.

"OMG. I thought you said he had a cabin," Nadia whispered, Kat and Jade at her side.

The large three-story house was modern, rustic, with clean lines and framed in metal with an abundance of glass and warm, rich woods. Massive boulders, smoothed and weathered with age, dotted the grounds mixed within the landscaping. The house wrapped along the edges of the circular drive. From her viewpoint, she could see an expanse of tree-covered mountains stretching out from behind.

"Ladies," Larz said, gesturing for the girls to follow him inside.

Kira couldn't help the wide smile plastered across her face as Blake rounded the car, their bags in hand. "This place is amazing. I mean, the house in New Orleans is beautiful, but this place is," her words trailed off as her eyes continued to roam the surrounding space.

"I'm glad you're here. And you haven't even seen the best part."

Inside, she noticed the same rich woods that highlighted the exterior were also utilized throughout the interior, creating beautiful ceiling scapes. Despite looking like a work of art, the main living space was inviting and warm. The back wall along the kitchen and dining area featured vast floor to ceiling sliding glass doors, creating a seamless transition between indoors and out.

The guys and her friends were already outside on that very balcony, taking in the views.

"Come on."

Kira sucked in a breath as Blake wrapped his arm around her side, pulling her along with him. With every step they took, she could feel the flutter in her stomach increase as more of the scene fell into her view. The sweeping vistas of crystal-clear emerald and turquoise turned a deeper azure hue as it stretched into the distance. The balcony extended over the water, granting them a clear view of the boulders and rocks covering the lake floor.

"It's so pretty here!" Kat squealed. "I don't think I can go back. Kira, I'm afraid you'll need to put out a search for a new roommate. I live here now."

"I'll be your roommate," Blake chimed in, pressing a kiss into her hair.

"No . . . I think I'll still be here with Kat." She was in utter awe.

He laughed, pulling her back into his chest.

"So, there are five bedrooms," Larz said, pointing down the halls on opposite ends of the space. "Jade, Armand will show you guys to your room. Blake and Kira, of course, have the top floor suite. Vincent, you know where to go. And then that leaves you two. The fifth room has two doubles, but there's always room in my king if either of you gets lonely. Katia?" His smile was almost as devilish as Blake's, waggling his brows.

Kat gripped Nadia's hand, pulling her along. "No, thank you, *Drake.* I think we're good. And if you'll excuse me, I promised Eric I would call him when we arrived."

"Isn't he busy saving ducks and fish from drowning, or something?"

"No. He stayed behind because he had to work. He's protecting the animals at the aquarium during the hurricane."

Larz tilted his head, and chuckled. "So, yeah . . . ducks and fish."

Kat stood silently, her eyes staring him down, her jaw tight.

"Forgive my brother. He can be an overly egotistical ass sometimes. Let me help you with those," Vincent said, taking Kat and Nadia's bags, leading them down the hall,

Kira suppressed the laughter that wanted to bubble up as she watched Kat and Larz fight, teasing each other. She was somewhat surprised to see it. Kat had mentioned they'd spent some time together at the party, but she failed to mention the flirtation that laced the edges of every conversation between them since the moment the guys picked them up that morning.

Everyone had separated off, each to their respective rooms. It was just the two of them standing outside on the balcony now. Blake still held her tight from behind, his chin resting on the top of her head as they both looked out over the water. She was more than use to her heart and mind being at war with one another. But the sudden onset of two emotions, seemingly born from her heart, were now at odds. A form of serenity she'd never experienced before overcame her.

She was happy. But being here alone in his arms made it all the more real. With every passing second that he held onto her; she fell a little deeper into something she knew she would never climb her way out of.

Love.

Kira internally groaned as he pulled her back inside. She wasn't finished soaking it in. She followed him up another flight of stairs. It was the only bedroom on the top floor of the house, allowing them plenty of privacy. It was spacious, with many of the same architectural and design elements downstairs. She immediately headed for the glass door that walked out onto their own private balcony.

"I'm never going to get you inside, am I?" Blake called out from the room.

"Why would you want to be inside?"

"Oh, I can think of a few reasons."

Kira turned, leaning against the railing to see Blake stretched out across the bed with his arms behind his head, ankles crossed. "Oh, are you sleepy? Need a nap?" she teased, her smile widening as she approached him.

"There will be no napping," he said, reaching out and grabbing her before she could retreat, pulling her onto the bed.

Laughter between the two filled the space as they wrestled before he finally tackled and pinned her beneath him. She tried to gain control of her breathing as she looked up at him, but the sensation that rose within only made her heart accelerate more. His kiss was masterful. It was softer and slower than his previous kisses, but the passion behind it remained, almost as if he were savoring the moment.

Maybe his restraint lay in the fact that six of their closest friends were likely waiting for them in the other room. Or perhaps it was because he wanted to take things slow and respect her space. Either way, it did little to curb the need rising within her. Her fingers fisted in the material of his t-shirt, feeling the rigidness of the hard muscles beneath. His hands twined into her hair, his thumb delicately tracing the line of her jaw. The softer his touch, the more she wanted him.

The sound of voices and laughter floated from below up into their room. They broke their kiss, their heads tilting to the open door leading to the balcony which hovered above the main level. Blake released a heavy sigh, dropping his head into the nook of her neck. He stayed there for several long seconds before pressing a kiss into her shoulder and lifting himself back to his feet, pulling her along with him.

"I suppose we should join our friends."

Kira scrunched her nose. "I was kind of enjoying being your friend in here."

"Ha! Well, I'm happy to let them all starve for you."

"Oh, were you planning to flex your excellent cooking skills? Trying to impress me?" She hooked her thumb to the balcony doors. "Because I think that boat has sailed."

"Hmm . . . really?"

Kira watched as he tipped his head as if he were mulling something over. "What?"

Blake smiled, taking her hand and pulling her behind him down the stairs, but he continued, passing the hall back to the central part of the house. He turned past the landing to descend into another short flight of stairs that led to a single door.

"I have something you might like." He flipped on the lights as they entered. Her mouth slackened as her eyes roamed the space. It was a large garage filled with several cars. Expensive cars. At first glance, she wondered if he was showing off. Boasting didn't exactly match Blake's style, but as she rounded an exceptionally sleek Aston Martin, she suddenly realized why he brought her here.

"This is a 1963 Shelby Cobra, Mark III. This is the car that Ford and Carroll Shelby made to beat Enzo Ferrari at Le Mans. One of only 56 made," he informed, enthusiasm radiating throughout as he smoothed a hand over the frame. He stood admiring it for several seconds, before turning to another. "And this one is a 1973 De Tomaso Pantera. It's not as iconic but, it's wicked fast."

Kira swallowed hard, suddenly missing her dad, knowing he would've loved to have seen these. "Wow! I didn't know you were into cars?"

"A little. Cars kind of fall under the umbrella of valuable items, and somewhere along the way, I had the opportunity to acquire one. It was only after I had it that I realized I didn't want to give it up. Plus, Armand is really good with old cars, and he's been teaching me a lot. We have an original 1976 Pontiac Firebird Trans Am back at the Calloway Estate. He's working on adding a 1977 front end."

"Wait," she pursed her lips together in deep thought as she traced a finger along the shiny blue paint of the Cobra. "The car from Smokey and the Bandit?"

He smirked, folding his arms across his chest. "I'm impressed. You know your cars."

She shrugged. "Not really. But it was one of my dad's favorite movies. Gosh, we must have watched it a thousand times together." She didn't say anything else as she walked, studying each of them, in awe of how beautiful and unique they were.

It hadn't gone unnoticed to her how he referred to his house in New Orleans by its name, as if he were detached from it. Like he didn't consider it as his home. And if it wasn't home, how long did he plan on staying?

"I know you said you used to race with your dad. Wanna go for a spin? I promise not to break the speed limit . . . *too much*."

There was no way to hide the excitement. She jumped up and down, clapping as she hurried to the driver's seat of the Cobra. "Please," she said, gripping the steering wheel, batting her lashes.

He took several long seconds, eyeing her as he retrieved the keys from a plaque bolstering several sets on the wall. "Are you sure you can handle this?"

"Do not insult me, sir . . . Just call me Dominic Toretto. It's time to unleash the beast."

"The Fast and the Furious? Really?" Blake laughed, pushing a button on the wall that lifted the garage door before he climbed in beside her. "Easy now . . . she's a classic."

Kira was slow as they pulled out of the drive, but once she was on the road, she made quick work of the gears, expertly navigating through the turns along the road. "A classic made for racing." She pressed harder on the gas, smiling as she noticed Blake's tight grip on the console before he finally eased back into his seat, an approving grin on his face.

They drove for a while, with Blake guiding her on the turns, leading them to a scenic lookout with views over Emerald Bay. Standing on that balcony earlier, she couldn't imagine anything more beautiful, but he was able to surprise her again. From here, the sun bounced off the water, creating a delicate shimmer.

She pulled into a spot. They sat for a moment in silence, staring out over the water.

Blake shifted in his seat to face her. "So, why don't you race anymore? It doesn't seem like you lost your skill . . . or your nerve."

"Hmm . . . that was fun. I guess it never occurred to me to do it anymore. I think my dad was a little jealous that my mom and I bonded over my dancing. Don't get me wrong, he was always there cheering me on at my recitals, but I think he wanted something that was just ours. It started out as just a fun thing to do while he was teaching me to drive. I don't think he ever told my mom exactly how fast we were going at the track."

"Do you miss it?"

Kira thought for a moment. "It's weird. I didn't realize I did until today."

"Is that a good thing or a bad thing?"

Kira's smile beamed brighter. "It's a great thing."

They sat there, continuing to talk as they watched the sunset together.

"It's so beautiful." From the corner of her eye, she could see him watching her. She could feel the intensity of his gaze, as if she were the only thing he could see.

"I agree. So damn beautiful."

"SO, what exactly did you do yesterday when you guys disappeared?" Kat asked as she worked on maintaining her balance.

She, Kira, and Jade were paddle boarding while Nadia and the guys hung out on the balcony above, grilling, and preparing lunch for everyone.

"We went for a drive, and watched the sun set over the bay. It was breathtaking."

"Yeah, we know that much," Jade said, skillfully gliding across the water like a pro.

"He showed me his car collection and let me take one of them out for a spin."

"OMG. He has a car collection, too? How rich is your boyfriend?" Kat asked as she unsteadily lowered herself, finally opting to paddle the board from her knees. "This is easier, right?"

Kira was much sturdier than her friend, but still winced as her board bobbled on the water after small ripples caused by the wake of distant jet skiers moved beneath her. "You know I don't care about that stuff."

"I know you don't, but the perks definitely don't suck."

"They definitely do not," Jade added, happily soaking in the sun.

"And what about Armand? What kind of perks does he have?" Kat joked, animatedly waggling her brows.

"My goodness, I think you've been hanging out with Nadia too much!"

"It's not my fault. Larz was feeding me mimosas all morning . . . I blame him," Kat protested.

"Hmm . . . that's interesting," Kira mused, crawling down to sit on her own board next to Kat. "You just called him Larz, but when you're around him, you call him, Drake."

Jade laughed, paddling up close to join in. "Wow. You're right. I hadn't noticed it before."

"Hadn't noticed what?"

"You are totally flirting with Larz," Kira giggled, pointing playfully. "And he calls you Katia. Ahh! He's flirting with you."

Kat shook her head. All the amusement vanquished from her face as she tipped her sunglasses down the slope of her nose. "No. No . . . just no."

"Oh, don't pout. I don't think it means anything. You love Eric. I love Eric. Everyone loves Eric."

Kat only smiled, pushing her sunglasses back up.

They continued to float out on the water, using their boards more for sunbathing than paddle boarding. They discussed the guys and their relationships. Kat talked about how much she missed Eric. Jade spoke more about her growing feelings for Armand, but admitted he kept up a wall. Surprisingly, neither of them mentioned her recent breakup with Colin. She sometimes worried about what her friends thought after she seemingly moved on so quickly.

Colin had been a part of her life for so long. It wasn't that she'd completely forgotten him and written him off. And it wasn't that she didn't still care about him either. She did. But there was something about Blake she couldn't shake. It had been there since the first time she saw him. The first time he'd touched her. The first time he smiled at her. The first time he'd kissed her. He was everything she couldn't explain.

"You know, you're doing it wrong!"

The girls all glanced up to see Larz standing at the balcony, his hands in the air, mocking them. The others stood alongside him, each holding cocktails in their hands. Kat resumed her position, lying flat on her back, and held her hand high, flipping him off.

"Don't make me come down there, Katia."

Kat raised her second hand, mirroring the first.

"Okay, girls. I'm roasting. I'm going to head back," Jade said, pushing herself back up into a standing position. "You two coming, or staying?"

Kat peered up at her through her sunglasses. "I live here now."

"Go ahead without us. We'll be back up soon."

Another few minutes of silence passed before Kat finally spoke again: "So . . . you didn't flinch when I called him your boyfriend."

Kira scanned her memory of their earlier conversation before turning her head to look at her friend. "So?"

"Is that what he is now?"

She thought about it for several seconds. "We haven't put a label on it yet, but yeah, I . . . I think so."

"You look happy. Happier than I've seen in a while."

"Thank you. I am," she admitted.

Kat's expression softened. "I lied to you before."

Kira lifted herself onto her elbow. Kat never lied.

"Eric didn't have to stay behind and work at the aquarium. I mean, he is volunteering, but he could've come. He was worried about how Colin would feel, knowing he was here with you and Blake."

"Oh my gosh, Kat, I'm such an idiot. I didn't even think about that." Colin and Eric had become close friends over the past year. It was incomprehensible that she hadn't considered it. She felt some guilt in the oversight. More so, she felt the guilt of her friend's honesty. Kat never lied, but her reasoning behind it was entirely selfless, and in the end, she still managed to share the truth. She, on the other hand, was still living within a lie. "Has he said anything to you?"

"Not a lot. But he did say he was dealing. Apparently, he's been much better the past couple of days. I partially think that's why he decided to stay. He didn't want to give him any reason to fall off the wagon again."

"See! That's why everyone loves Eric," Kira said, placing her hand against her heart.

"Yeah, I think I'll keep him."

Kira straddled her board, dangling her legs into the cold water. The cove was somewhat shallow here, with her feet sometimes drifting over the smooth boulders that rested just below the surface. The water sheened a stunning emerald tone and was crystal clear, allowing her to see straight to the bottom, even in deeper areas. She ran a finger over her palm as a familiar sensation pulsed at the center. It had been some time since she last felt it.

Instinctively, she glanced up, searching for Blake. He was standing at the balcony railing, talking with the others. He was too far, at least thirty yards away and twenty feet higher, but she could still feel his smile.

"Okay, I think I'm going to give this another shot," Kira said as she carefully maneuvered into a standing position.

"Maybe you can tow me in."

"I'm sure Larz will come out and give you a lift."

Kat gave her the same one-finger salute.

"Well, aren't you a saucy one today?"

Kira paddled out a little further. There was a peace out there on the water she didn't believe she could ever find anywhere else. It surprised her, given the way her parents died.

The thought of them pierced at her heart a bit. "Dad, you would have loved that car, and mom, you would not have believed this view. I wish you were here to see it all. And I wish you could have met Blake," she whispered, her chin to the sky, closing her eyes in a silent prayer to them.

Out of nowhere, a precipitous cold enveloped her body, sending her heart rate skyrocketing. She opened her eyes, seeing the blur of daylight above her, partially blocked by her board. *I'm in the water.* She swam, kicking her feet as her hands reached high, but the light only seemed to grow farther away. The urgency for oxygen increased with every passing second as the pressure in her chest intensified.

She could no longer concentrate on the light above; her own thoughts unraveling with the currents. The cold seeped deeper into her body, but it didn't hurt as it did on impact. Tendrils of her dark hair floated across her vision as the last remnant of air left her lips, bubbling to the light she could no longer see.

"Kira? Earth to Kira!"

Her sight suddenly snapped back at the sound of Kat's voice. She squinted against the glare of the sun, holding her arm out to shield it. The brightness blinded her as if she'd been sleeping in a dark room, only to be awakened by the pull of the curtains. Her eyes drifted up at the sound of birds overhead, watching them fly amongst the clouds. She turned to see Kat sitting on her board about twenty yards away.

"I'm getting hungry. Wanna head back?"

Kira looked down, steadying herself. The sound of the water lapping beneath her sent her heart racing again. "Yeah . . . just a second."

She looked around, seeing nothing out of the ordinary. Blake and the others were still on the balcony, but their backs were turned. *Another dream?* Her eyes roamed the length of her arm. An icy chill prickled her sun-warmed skin. It felt so real. In the distance, she saw one of the jet skiers come closer into the cove, turning quickly, and speeding away, churning the water in its wake.

Time is an indistinct concept, as shapeless as water, yet somehow as constant as the stars. Time is trustworthy. It will come and go, no matter the circumstances. But time betrayed her as she watched the ripples glide across the water. They moved in a slow motion, bewitching her as the circle expanded, moving closer and closer. She never averted her gaze, even as the first swell moved beneath her board. And then the second.

The familiar feel of cold water took over her senses. Pain shot through her skull and then . . . blackness.

TWENTY-EIGHT
SO VULNERABLE

I t was warmer today than he expected, but he was grateful for it. It gave him an excuse to send Kira and her friends out on the paddle boards. He needed the separation. Having her so close to him all night was difficult.

Blake had come out of the Blood Oath ritual with a reaffirmed sense of who and what he was. His mission made it all the more evident. But time was betraying him. Each second of each minute he spent with her since then was beginning to weigh on him once more. Her magic was like a drug, peeling away at every piece of his resistance.

He watched Kira as she slept last night. It reminded him of when she fell asleep in his car the day he drove her home from the bar. It was different than observing her while cloaked in magic. Just like then, this was a distinctively singular experience. She'd slept in the crook of his arm, her head resting on his chest. He could smell the sweet scent of her magic swirling beneath her skin. She was so vulnerable.

The abrupt sound of jet skis pulled his attention, watching one come closer into the cove. It was dangerous for them to come so close out of risk of hitting the boulders. It appeared he realized his error as he spun the vehicle 180 degrees back.

"Dude, that guy was cutting it close," Larz said, raising his glass in salute to the ballsiness of the move.

"Kira! Kira!"

Blake turned his attention to Kat, watching as she scrambled off her board into the water screaming Kira's name. He scanned the surrounding area, spotting Kira's board bobble on the dissipating swells created by the jet skier's wake.

"Kira!" His eyes continued to search, finally finding her a few feet away, slowly sinking below the surface.

He didn't think. With one breath, he leaped onto the railing, launching himself forward into the shallow water below. His hands reached the rocky bottom, but he was able to easily maneuver and straighten his body, propelling himself closer to where he saw her moments before.

Blake only breached the surface once to gather his bearings. He heard Larz directly behind him, not surprised that his brother would also jump, but didn't spare any time to look before diving below again. Swimming beneath the water, he spotted her; a red cloud danced above her head. *She's bleeding.*

The water was relatively shallow here, around 8 feet deep, allowing him to wrap one arm around her and push off against the lake floor up to the surface. A trio of large boulders formed a small island nearby. He headed to it, only having to swim a couple of yards before his feet touched the bottom. He climbed onto the rocks, pulling her with him.

Blake sucked in a nervous breath at the sight of her lifeless body draped across the rock. Kat's screams in the distance let him know that Larz was keeping her at bay. It didn't matter; magic wasn't going to help him if she was dead. His hands shook as he struggled to find her pulse, his own heart thundering in his ears.

"Stay with me," he whispered as he leaned over, trembling hands on her face, opening her mouth before blowing a single breath into it. Blake watched as her chest rose slightly. He waited a few seconds, and blew again before pressing down on her chest, repeating the motion several times. "Please, Kira," he whispered again, closing his eyes for a moment between breaths and compressions.

He tried once more. His heart sank further and further. Those few seconds in between each attempt were in slow motion. The sudden onset of her choking for air released most of his tension.

"Hey . . . hey, you're okay," he said, looking down, smoothing wet hair away from her face. His thumb traced along the edge of the small contusion at her temple.

Kira continued to cough, her lungs yearning, desperate for air. But it was the look in her eyes that concerned him most. He saw fear. Not the fear of nearly drowning. It was something else entirely. He could feel the magic within her flaring, sending her senses on high alert.

"Kira! Sweetie! You're okay!" Kat cried out, clamoring up onto the rocks with Larz right behind her.

She still didn't speak but nodded to reassure her friend. Her breathing was starting to normalize as he watched her expertly push back the emotions and force a small smile. The confusion, the fear; she swallowed it back, replacing it with a false veneer. *She's a good liar.*

"We should get her upstairs. Get that cut taken care of," Larz stated, reaching out for Kat to help her off the rock.

"Yeah." Blake found himself preoccupied with the expression he'd just witnessed to think clearly. He was also contending with the conflict of his own emotions. "Come on. I got you." He wrapped

Kira in his arms and carried her through the water. Ahead, he saw Armand and Vincent standing at the shoreline comforting a crying Jade and what appeared to be a concerned Nadia.

Kira shifted in his arms once they reached the edge of the lake. "I'm okay. I can walk."

Blake was reluctant to put her down, walking several more feet to the balcony stairs. She squirmed in his grasp. "Let me carry you up."

She pushed against him again. "Put me down, Blake."

"No. You hit your head. You shouldn't be walking up these wet stairs."

He heard the girls behind him, encouraging her to listen, but she continued to fight against the hold he had on her.

Halfway inside the living space, she jerked hard enough to pull her legs from his hand, her request now bordering on a scream. "Put me down!"

Blake was resistant, but he eased her down to her feet. His eyes narrowed in confusion. *She's angry.*

For the first time, she didn't want his hands on her. The room was dead silent as they stared each other down. The others were behind them, but they each remained quiet, clearly as stunned as he was. Not knowing what to say, he dragged a hand across his face as he stood there and watched her disappear into their room.

A FEW HOURS had passed since he last saw her. He'd followed her to their room but found that she'd locked herself in the bathroom. He attempted to talk through the door, but she kept insisting she was fine. The anger of that moment seemed to subside, her tone much softer. Eventually, he gave her the space she wanted, asking Kat, Nadia, and Jade to check on her.

The sun was setting, dipping down below the mountains behind them, but the sky itself was still awash with vibrant streaks of orange and purple. He hoped she was in their room, seeing it through the balcony doors. She'd been taken aback by the views last night overlooking the bay, but the colors tonight were even more dynamic. He swallowed hard, clenching his jaw at the realization that he didn't want her to miss it. That he cared.

His brothers were quite as they all sat together on the balcony. They were showing respect, waiting for him. He took a long drink from his bourbon. "I don't know what happened." He knew that was the question burning in each of their thoughts.

Larz took several seconds, leaning forward in his seat, his own drink resting between both hands. "Her magic . . . it was screaming out there on that rock."

"Yeah, I could feel it all the way up here," Armand affirmed as Vincent nodded in silent agreement.

"Whatever it was she was feeling, I'm sure that was the reason behind the outburst. She still doesn't know what she is, plus she has no control over the power inside her. It's like a," Larz's words trailed off.

"Like PMS times a million," Armand finished for him.

"Exactly!"

Blake didn't say anything. They were probably right on some level, but they didn't see her face. There was something else.

"Hey guys, do you mind giving me a minute alone with our brother?"

Blake watched as Armand and Vincent disappeared inside before turning back to Larz. He didn't meet his eyes, afraid of what his brother would see. "All my walls are intact. So what do we need to talk about that you don't want to say in front of them?" His tone was insolent and sharp.

Larz, ever the casual one, leaned back in his seat, smiling. "Wow, someone else is PMSing. It's not contagious, is it?"

"Fuck you," Blake shot back, standing and walking over to the balcony railing. His eyes scanned the water, still searching for an answer.

"What do you want to do?"

"I want to find that fucker on the jet ski."

"Hmph." Larz stood, joining him. "And what would that accomplish? It was an accident."

"You didn't see her face when she regained consciousness. There was . . . something. I don't know what, but something stirred up her magic."

"Almost drowning?" Larz mused. "Her magic was probably thinking, oh, shit, we almost died. Bloody hell, I'm sure it didn't like it any more than we did."

Blake downed the remainder of his drink before taking a step back and chucking the glass tumbler as far as possible into the lake. He gripped the railing, dropping his head low as he braced his weight against it. "She almost fucking died! Fuck!" he screamed, beating at the rails, blood rushing to his face.

Larz gave his brother a moment to vent. "You said I didn't see her face, but you also didn't see yours . . . I did."

Blake paused, turning to glare at him. "What do you mean?"

"You know exactly what I mean. I've told you before, it doesn't matter how high you build your walls. I know you."

He shook his head. "You're wrong."

"Am I?"

"Blake?"

The sound of Kira's voice had him reeling around. He started to rush towards her but slowed at the memory of their last encounter. "Hey. How are you feeling?" he asked, watching as the girls crept past them into the kitchen.

Kira swallowed, seemingly nervous. "Can we talk?"

"Of course," he replied, taking her hand, and walking with her to their room.

Her magic had simmered down, but like a faint electrical current, he could still feel the pulse of it thrumming through her skin.

Once inside the room, he pulled her close, wrapping his arms around her completely. When she didn't resist, he held her even tighter, moving his hands against the back of her head, twining his fingers into her hair. "You scared me," he finally whispered and sucked in a breath, realizing his words were true. It did scare him. *That was what Larz had seen.*

Kira pulled back, pressing her hands against his chest. "I'm sorry about earlier. I . . . I was freaked out. When you were holding me, I started to feel . . . I felt a little claustrophobic. Like I." Her voice trailed off.

"Like you couldn't breathe."

Kira nodded weakly, her eyes cast down, guilt shining behind her expression.

"Hey, no. It's okay. That makes sense. It was my fault," Blake said, bending slightly at the knees to see her eyes, holding her head between his hands. It did make sense, but he still knew there was more. She was well-practiced in hiding the truth.

"You're not mad?"

Blake pulled her down to the bed. "No. Of course not. Come here."

They laid there for a long time, saying nothing. She rested on his forearm, her back pressed against his chest as he lazily rolled his thumb in small circles at her side. His eyes roamed past the opened glass doors, noticing the colors in the sky had faded into near darkness. He couldn't help but notice the quiet contentment that filled him. The doors were open. She must have seen the sky. She hadn't missed it.

It was silent. Her magic finally receding somewhere deep within. Instead, he focused on the sound of her breathing. He almost thought she had fallen asleep when she suddenly rolled over to face him.

Her smile was weak but sincere. "Thank you."

"For what?"

"You saved me, right?"

He returned her smile. "Well, I guess I owed you one."

The reflection in her eyes changed. It was a small shift, but he saw it. He didn't know what to make of it until her lips were on his. He felt it then. The passion behind the kiss was heady and adamant, pushing him back against the pillows before climbing onto his body. She wanted him, but he needed to see it once more. He moved his hand to her chin, pulling away from her kiss as he re-oriented her face, holding her gaze for several seconds. The fierceness of their stare only blazoned the fire building between them even more.

Blake sat up quickly, returning her kiss as he rolled her onto her back, pinning her beneath him. There was an urgency behind it as if his own breath lived upon her lips. It was a primal and raw exchange, a promise of something tangible and absolute. Everything beyond this moment, in this bed, blurred from his vision and thoughts. He lowered himself closer at the feel of her hand in his hair, the other wrapping along his shoulder.

He reached up and pulled her hand from his body, lacing his fingers with hers and pressing them into the pillow above her head. Her magic was alive again. Beautiful currents surged from her palm into his, traveling up his arm. Her power was delicious. He rocked against her, lightly squeezing her hand, pleading for more.

Blake's lips traipsed across her face, planting kisses along her jawline, and down her neck before gravitating back up to find her mouth once more. His hand raked down her side, finding the hem of her shirt, his fingers grazing across her delicate skin. Her body gave him the response he wanted. He pressed his palm flat as he slid it beneath her, wrapping an arm behind her back. He sat up, bringing her with him, tugging the shirt over her head. He reached one arm behind his back, grasping the fabric of his own t-shirt before ripping it up and over his head.

They moved together again, both eager to continue their kiss. The feel of her bare skin against his own sent his heart racing. He was crossing the Rubicon and the bridge was burning behind him. He couldn't turn back if he tried.

His lips broke away to graze against her shoulder. "I need you to tell me now if you don't want this," his voice was raspy and laden with want as he continued to press kisses along her collarbone.

Kira didn't speak, tightening her arms, pulling him closer to her.

But just like he needed to see it in her eyes, he wanted to hear her say it. "I need you to tell me now if you don't want this. Kira, I need you to tell me." His words were barely a whisper now; his mouth too focused on exploring her body than in the words he spoke.

"I don't want you to stop," she managed, her head dropping back, giving his lips more access to her neck.

It was all he needed to hear. "Thank fuck!"

With one hand behind her back, the other beneath her, he swiftly lifted her against him as he stood. His erection grew headier as she wrapped her legs around his waist. The hand he held at her head moved around, his thumb gently tracing the line of her face. He had been with so many women. Countless. But none were this beautiful. None made him feel this way.

Blake looked at her for a long moment, wishing he could read her thoughts. With their chests pressed together, skin to skin, breath to breath, he eased her back down onto the bed. He reached out, his fingers hooking at the fabric of her shorts, pulling them away, dropping them to the ground.

He stood looking down at her in the dimness of the room. He unbuttoned his jeans, stepping out of them and bent down, one knee at her side, the other between her legs. His hands roamed as he slowly crawled atop her, planting kisses along the way, starting at her thighs, and then her stomach, across her breasts, to her neck. He wanted to explore every contour of her body.

"I've wanted this since the first moment I saw you," he murmured against her ear before finding her lips again. "So fucking much."

He groaned low in his throat at the feel of her nails gently scraping against the coiled muscles at his side, igniting his vigor even more. He was more than supernatural in the bedroom, he was a beast. His hand slid down the length of her arm, taking a few seconds to relish in the sensation of the power pulsing from her palm. He reached lower, brushing his fingers across the thin lace that separated them, moving them in slow circles. A small whimper escaped her as she dug her heels into the mattress, pushing her hips closer into him.

Blake pulled the fabric to the side before rubbing his length against her. It glided across her sex, causing her to lift her hips once again. He dropped to his elbows, his head now in the crook of her neck at the feel of her hands wrapping around his cock. They were soft, but still firm and confident. She held it against her there, writhing beneath him, controlling her own pleasure. He nearly came undone.

"I want you." Her words floated breathlessly on the air.

But he wanted her more. More than a human should ever want another human. Maybe it was because he wasn't really human. Neither was she.

He entered her gently, feeling her tense beneath him. Her nails drug across his skin again as her thighs squeezed together against him. He moved slowly at first, reveling in the feel of her wrapped around his length. Her teeth grazing against his shoulder spurred him further, his movement increasing, thrusting into her to the hilt.

In one fluid motion, Blake rolled, pulling her atop him, her legs straddling at his sides. He sat up, his palms against her back, supporting her weight, allowing her to fall back. Her upper body stretched out over his legs as he rocked beneath her. The tiny moans that escaped her lips continued to fuel him. He needed more.

He pulled her back to his chest, her legs wrapped around him, still straddling his lap. His fingers deftly maneuvered around the clasps of the lacy black bra she still wore, unhooking it. His teeth grazed her shoulders, planting kisses in the wake of the straps that fell down the length of her arm.

Blake's hand slid from her back, across her breasts, his mouth tipping down to explore her newly exposed skin. Her back arched in response, her hips shifting against him, driving him deeper.

The motion must have hit that perfect spot as she continued to roll her hips, undulating against him, her legs wrapping tighter around his waist. He pulled her closer, his kiss more eager than ever before, his lips crashing against her wildly. They moved against each other, their bodies melding together in unison. The magic within her was blinding. He could only see white and feel the heat blazing from it. He didn't care.

Rolling her to her back, he splayed his body completely over hers, pinning her hands above her head, holding them there with one hand, his other braced against the bed. Burying his head into her shoulder, he moved his hips faster and harder. He could feel the orgasm coiling inside of her before she finally cried out. The contracting of her muscles around him was his culmination.

Blake rolled to the side of her, pulling her hands to his chest as he gathered his breath. Her light was invading all of his senses.

Suddenly, he was Icarus. He flew too close to the sun, and she had now forever scorched his heart.

THE SKY WAS CLEAR, and the moon hung over the lake, shedding light on everything it touched. The air was cool and crisp against his skin as he rushed down the balcony stairs. Blake paid no matter to the rocks against his bare feet, but he did wince against the bite of the cold water he waded in. One foot, two, three. Once he was thigh deep, he dropped to his knees, the water lapping against his chest now.

It wasn't enough to wash away the images in his mind. He ducked his head under the surface. Her light was creeping into the darkest hollows of his being, illuminating pieces of him that had been long covered up. It scratched away at an old and forgotten scar. One he didn't even know existed. One that centuries worth of memories had successfully buried deep in the recesses of his mind.

Blake turned, looking up at the bedroom balcony. She was still asleep behind those doors. He'd held her for the past several hours, soaking in the feel of her skin against his own. Making love to her was the pinnacle of his four hundred years on this earth. The moment that feeling truly sunk in was the same when it wholly shattered, when he realized the significance of the mark on her skin.

It was more than an hour later when they were stretched out on the bed, her bare legs draped across his waist, both enjoying their post sexual bliss. He was still savoring the high of her magic that swirled within his senses when he saw it.

It was small. Insignificant. He'd spent the past few months learning everything about Kira, studying her every movement, memorizing every feature of her face, every contour of her body. *How did I miss it? Did her magic conceal it?* It didn't matter. It was there. The letter N was marked in the smallest of scripts at the base of the inside of her ankle. He replayed the moment he saw it in his mind.

"What is that? You have a tattoo? Is that an N?"

Her laugh was slight. "Yeah."

The smile she wore was different than anything he'd seen her express before. She was happy, but there was also a sadness behind it. There was something bittersweet lingering in her eyes.

"I was adopted. It was a closed adoption, so my parents never had any real details about my birth parents. Except for one thing . . . at least that's what they told me. They had a letter from my birth mother, written right before she died, the same day I was born. It was short, she didn't say much. She just wanted to be sure I knew she loved me," she told him, running her finger across the black ink. "And she signed it. Her name was Natalia."

The name left Kira's lips and invaded something deep within Blake's mind. It was a tiny bomb exploding in his heart. Only he didn't know why.

"I know it sounds silly, but her name is the only piece of her I knew. I wanted some way to always carry her with me. When I was sixteen, Kat and I secretly went out to get tattoos. Well, I did, anyway. She chickened out. Obviously, I needed to keep it small and well-hidden so my parents would never see it . . . so, I settled on her initial."

Blake had listened to every word she spoke, working hard to manage a passive expression. He rolled the name over and over in his mind, trying to peel back the edges of a memory that refused to come forth. There was nothing. Eventually, he pushed it to the side, unwilling to allow it to dampen the other feelings that were coursing through him.

It was hours later when Kira was sleeping, her back tucked tightly into his chest and he was drifting into a satisfied and quiet sleep when the image of her face flashed across his vision. It was as if she were in the room with him. His heart began to race, and his breathing labored. Quietly, he slipped from the sheets, left the room, and fled outside into the night air.

Sitting in the coldness of the lake, he ran his hand over his face and through his hair. Her features were slightly different than Kira's. Her frame wasn't as petite. Her skin was fairer, almost alabaster against her dark hair. But they shared the same soft elements in their faces, the curve in their lips, the straight line of their noses. But it was the same, amber-colored eyes that he couldn't shake from his vision. The small flecks of green in Kira's eyes were the only thing that set them apart. Without it, he feared he wouldn't know the difference.

"Natalia Rose," he whispered her name to himself, his call falling deaf in the listless night.

It was a name he hadn't spoken in more than four hundred years. Saying it now felt like a betrayal to the woman in his bed. He shook his head, silently willing the thoughts from his mind. How had he forgotten her? It seemed an unimaginable possibility.

His heart clenched as he looked up at the balcony once more. The First and Second Orders were complete. Within a few months, he and his brothers would complete the Third Order. And then, like Natalia, Kira would be dead.

Blake was unaware of how long he sat in the still and bitter water, but the glow of light peeking out from behind the mountains told him it was time to go. He didn't want to be gone when Kira woke. But the memory of Natalia was like shards of glass. The more he traced back through his thoughts, the more they sliced through him. Climbing back up to the balcony, he worked to push those piercing thoughts to the back of his mind.

"Early morning swim?"

He jumped, gripping the railing at the top of the stairs to turn and see Nadia curled up in one of the plush outdoor chairs, a coffee cup wrapped in her hand. The only person to ever catch him off guard was Kira. He felt immeasurably off balance.

"Yeah," he finally managed.

Nadia smiled wide, her eyes falling below his waist. "In your pajama pants?"

Blake glanced down at the water that dripped from his body. The thin linen pants he wore clung to him, leaving little to the imagination. He swallowed hard, too unfocused to think of an excuse and too unhinged to care. Saying nothing in return, he left a trail of water in his wake, and continued back to his room, certain of absolutely nothing.

TWENTY-NINE
UNSPOKEN CONNECTION

Kira blankly stared at the open window of her room. She could hear the sounds of birds trilling, and the wind rustling the leaves of the large magnolia just outside. She watched the breeze carry through the window, gently blowing the shears in her room. Her head rested against his chest. He pressed a kiss into her hair as he continued lazily rolling his fingers across her arm.

Lying next to him was the greatest contradiction she'd ever known. His skin against hers set her aflame, erupting inside, ready to ignite every sense. She could feel it in her bones. And yet, at the same time, she'd never been so at peace. There was always an unspoken connection between them, but their night together in Tahoe cemented it even further.

She was happy. She felt safe.

It was the first day back to school. She was grateful to get back into a new rhythm, but the past couple of weeks with him had been nothing short of amazing. It would be hard to break away.

"I think I have to go," Kira muttered, snuggling deeper into the crook of his arms, her eyes closed.

Blake nuzzled at her ear, murmuring softly, "Really? You don't appear to be going anywhere."

"I know. I think you're going to have to push me out of this bed."

He did the opposite, clinging to her even more tightly as he trailed light kisses down her shoulder.

"You are not helping."

"We have a few minutes. Keep those eyes closed."

Kira's breath hitched at the feel of hands brushing across her body. His mouth grazed the skin at her collarbone, teasing her but never going lower. Instinctively, her hands reached out, desperate to touch him, but he gripped them tight, pulling them above her head.

"Just relax." His words were merely a whisper. "Let me take care of you."

Her mouth parted, attempting to form words, but none came. Maybe it was because she couldn't decide whether to protest, or to cry out for more. The room was painstakingly quiet as he continued his rapturous assault on her body. She could only make out the sounds of the clock ticking away on her nightstand.

One. Two. Three.

Her hands were still resting above her head. He stroked a single finger across the center of her palm, guiding that beautiful twinge back to life. It pulsed in her hand, sending a surge of energy from her fingertips to her core. Her toes curled as she dug her heels into the mattress. Everything disappeared. It was just them. His hands. His lips. They moved generously across every inch.

They were everywhere. At the same time.

She felt his finger trace across her cheek while also gripping at her waist and sliding down her inner thigh. His mouth was on her neck while simultaneously pressing kisses along her hip bone. *How is he doing that?*

Her body writhed under his impossible touch. Her heart raced.

The sound of it mixed with the ticking of the clock. She felt him inch further down. He hadn't touched her yet, but the orgasm was already winding deep within her.

His mouth was just where she wanted it, his lips trailing across her inner thigh. Another surge in her palm caused her to reach out with a need to twine her fingers into his hair and urge him on, but her hand met nothing but open air. She opened her eyes, pushing up on her elbows.

He wasn't there.

Kira was alone.

She was cautious as she lifted herself up, her eyes scanning the room. The sun still shined through the open windows. The birds continued to chirp. Her curtains continued to sway slightly in the breeze. The ticking of the clock on her nightstand still echoed in her ear. She glanced down at it, watching the hand steadily tick away. One. Two. Three. *Another dream?*

Her heart sank a little. More ticking. Four. Five. Six. And then it stopped. The silence in the room was piercing.

Kira turned her head, tentatively reaching out for the alarm clock. Without warning, she felt the pull of hands at her shoulders. Her eyes widened as she caught a glimpse of another pair of hands bursting free from the mattress, stretching over her waist. Her scream caught in her throat as the hands on her shoulders pinned her down. She reached up, attempting to claw them away just as a third set appeared, clamping down across her mouth, pulling her deep into the mattress.

She fought against the pull, her legs kicking and her hands prying. She was sinking deeper, the material of the mattress enveloping around her.

A soft voice sounded in her ear, "Soon."

A loud thud caused her to jump in her seat, and her eyes popped open in astonishment. Hushed laughter floated across the quiet room. Kira worked to regain her composure, righting herself in her chair. She swallowed hard as her professor knelt to the ground, picking up the textbook she'd just elbowed onto the floor.

"Good morning, Miss Lockwood. We are so glad to have you join us," he announced to her and the entire class, eyeing her with little patience as he placed the book back on Kira's desk. "If you plan to stay in this class, I hope you will grant us all the courtesy of staying awake in the future."

"Yes, of course, Dr. Brown. I'm so sorry."

Kira was mortified. It was far out of her character to fall asleep in class. It was even rarer for her to be in trouble with a professor. She sat through the rest of the class, working hard to maintain her focus on the lecture, but the dream she had just experienced continued to creep into her thoughts.

It was the first nightmare she'd had in weeks. She almost thought she was on the other side of it. Sitting in that room, faces all around her, murmurs of theory and history floating past her ears, she realized she was wrong. Blake was her buffer. He'd kept her mind, her body, and her heart occupied. There wasn't any room for nightmares.

After class, she wandered across the quad, her textbook cradled in her arms. She needed to spend this spare time in the studio, training, but she couldn't bring herself to do it. Apathy settled into her bones. The sudden realization that no matter what she did, no matter how happy she was in one moment, it could be struck down in the next. She wasn't escaping the torment of her nightmares. Instead, they were following her outside of the confines of her bedroom walls.

Kira curled up on a bench under a shady tree. She silently debated skipping her classes for the rest of the day but quickly decided it would be a huge mistake. She had successfully auditioned to enter the BFA program in the spring, which meant a more stringent training and technique schedule. Skipping out on the first day would not earn her any praise from her instructors.

"Hey, you!"

Kira glanced up to see Kat walking in her direction. They rarely had classes together, but since Kat was a theater major, they were often in the same area or building on campus.

"Hi!"

"I thought you didn't have any downtime today. Aren't you supposed to be prepping yourself for your Brazilian Dance class," Kat asked, attempting her best Portuguese accent as she animatedly danced the last few feet to the bench before collapsing onto it.

"Yeah . . . I should be. I'm just really exhausted. I actually fell asleep in my morning class and got scolded in front of everyone."

Kat stifled a laugh. "Oh, sweetie, you're just going to have to tell Blake to cool it off a bit. A girl needs her beauty sleep."

Despite the dream she'd had, she smiled inwardly at the thought of Blake in her bed.

"Please remind me why you're even taking that class. Is it just for fun?"

"No, it's a requirement. Remember, I auditioned for my BFA last semester."

"That's right, I forgot. But sweetie, you took on such a heavy load in the spring. I was hoping you were going to cut yourself some slack this go-around."

"Why? Because I'm in a new relationship?"

"No, of course not. I would never suggest that. I want you to do what feels right to you, not to dictate your life around some guy." Kat inclined her head, tugging her bottom lip in. "No matter how hot that guy might be. Or how good he is in bed . . . or if he has a gorgeous lake house in a place, I can only assume to be Heaven on earth. I want you to be happy."

Kat really was a bright spot in a world of gray.

"Thank you. I really needed to hear that this morning. But out of curiosity, how do you know he's good in bed? I didn't tell you we slept together."

"Oh, I'm totally aware you haven't told me. I've been biting my tongue for weeks, wondering when my best friend was going to spill the bloody tea."

Kira narrowed her eyes, grinning. "Bloody hell, I think Larz is rubbing off on you."

"Ewe, no. And don't change the subject."

Kira averted her gaze, staring out across the quad as she considered her friend's question. "I'm not sure, really. I think I just wanted to hold on to it myself for a while. I've only ever been with Colin. And we haven't been apart for very long."

"Please tell me you don't think I would judge you for jumping in bed with Hottie McHot because of Colin." Kat paused, her tone more serious now. "Or are you worried that I would tell Eric? And then Colin would find out."

Kira bit her lip. *Is that why I didn't tell her?* "Maybe. I'm sorry. I know you wouldn't say anything if I asked you not to, but I also don't want to put you in that position."

Kat playfully slapped at her friend's leg. "Stop it. We do not keep secrets from each other. I've known about you and Blake since Tahoe, and I haven't said a word to Eric. It's none of his business anyway. With that said, I'm pretty sure he just assumes it since you guys went on a trip together. Hell, I think Eric would have sex with Blake if I was into that kind of thing."

Yeah, she was definitely Kira's brightest spot. She always knew the right things to say to make her laugh. "So, how did you know about Tahoe?"

"Are you kidding? Everyone who was in Tahoe knows about Tahoe."

Kira shook her head in question, brows knitting.

Kat pressed her lips together, holding back her laughter. "Do you remember us opening the balcony doors when Nadia, Jade, and I were in the bedroom with you?" she asked, waiting for the realization to fall on Kira's face. "Yeah, sweetie, you guys forgot to close that back."

"Oh, no. You can't be serious," Kira murmured, dropping her head into her hands. "You guys really heard us?"

"The fish at the bottom of the lake heard you, sweetie."

"No! Why didn't you do something?"

"What would you have had me do? Knock on the door and say, 'hey, guys, can you enjoy yourselves a little more quietly' or would you prefer that I whip out some ninja parkour moves, and jump from the main balcony to yours and casually close the door for you?"

Kira dropped her head back into her hands again. Her cheeks flushed with embarrassment.

"Don't worry. You guys sounded great! He seems like he's got a really good rhythm," Kat continued to tease, smacking at Kira's arm. "We only heard a little bit. Larz was actually the one who made all of us come inside. But then the walls were a little too thin for the likes of you guys."

She groaned, her humiliation growing by the second.

"So then he made everyone retreat to his room at the far end of the house."

Kira peeked her head out from behind her hands, surprised. "Seriously? That's so sweet of him."

"I know . . . total buzzkill."

"No, I'm serious. I told you Larz was a good guy, but I think you already knew that."

"Yeah, yeah. He's alright. I've just never met someone as arrogant in my entire life."

"I won't argue that point," she agreed, pulling the strap of her dance bag over her shoulder.

"Where are you off to now?"

Kira pushed out a heavy breath before forcing a smile. "To the studio. I should go and get stretched out. Thank you for giving me some perspective. I've wanted to get into the BFA program since freshman year. I might be tired, but what I want hasn't changed. I can't slack off now."

"Awe! Look at you, making good choices! Okay then, go dance your ass off!" Kat called out, backing away. "Your Brazilian ass off! Love ya! See you at home!"

Kira smiled to herself as she walked away. Everyone should have a little Kat in their pocket. Her dream wasn't entirely out of mind, but she was able to push it aside for the time being and focus on the current task. As she rounded a hedge along the sidewalk, she stopped dead in her tracks. *Colin.*

He was walking down the sidewalk from the opposite direction, his head down and a backpack slung over his shoulder. Her chest tightened and her mouth went dry, forming a huge lump in her throat. She thought about fleeing, but her feet were cemented to the ground. Texting with him a few weeks prior had been hard enough. She hadn't allowed herself to think about what it would be like to see him again.

What she should have been preparing for, was what she would do at the moment he saw her. Because that was far worse. The world simply stopped turning for several minutes. Standing several feet away from one another, they just stared at each other. She suddenly realized there wasn't much one could do or say to a person you once loved who recently tried to kill the person you are currently falling for.

It must not have been any more comfortable to be in his position.

Without saying a word, he turned, and walked in the opposite direction, leaving her to watch him disappear.

Take a deep breath, bite back the tears, and smile.

Even with months upon months of practice, she couldn't keep the tears from breaking free this time.

THIRTY
FEAR AND FASCINATION

The summer heat was finally waning, allowing autumn and all that it entails to creep into the air, through the trees, and into hand-warming mugs of pumpkin spice lattes. Like most southern cities, New Orleans was always slow to embrace this season, hanging onto its humid summer nights until the bitter end. The leaves still clung green to the branches. Still, fall blooms of chrysanthemums, marigolds, and celosia adorned planter boxes and flower gardens throughout the city, preparing to turn it into a pallet of rich golds, ambers, and reds.

It may have been a cliché, but Kira loved Fall. She had fond memories of her dad spending the afternoon raking leaves in the yard so she could later run through them. They would carve pumpkins together while her mom baked toffee cookies and bread. To this day, the scent of banana bread caused her stomach to flutter. And the cooling temps were the best excuse to curl up with a good book under the quilt her mom had made from an array of t-shirts from her dance competitions. Each was a small image that filled the chapters of her life. She often kept those thoughts on a shelf, but on occasion, she felt the need to dust them off and soak it all in.

It was mid-October now. Her schedule at school was rigorous and wearing on her, but she persevered. The BFA program was even more arduous than the heavy load she took on during the previous spring semester, but surprisingly, she found it more tolerable. With Blake's support, she was getting things done. She was finding her stride again.

It wasn't without some hurdles and anguish. The dreams and nightmares still lingered. Fortunately, the bad dreams were less frequent. But they were, however, shifting, becoming more menacing, more vivid.

More real.

There were incidents where she questioned whether or not she'd even been asleep; questioned if her dreams were possibly something more. Something deeper. Something beyond her own reality she couldn't explain.

Sitting on the window seat of her room, she thumbed through the pages of her journal. She traced a finger across a smudge of ink, a painful testament of former tears. Several tear-streaked pages reminded her how often she'd cried this past year.

Kira walked over to her mirror and settled down on the rug in front of it. Last night's dream had jarred her, converging between her fear and fascination. She opened the journal to a new page, recounting her memory.

I've been spending most of my nights at Blake's house. His bed is bigger, and he has jets in the shower. We've taken advantage of both. He even gifted me with my own toothbrush to keep there. There are occasions when I don't stay, usually when he's working late, or if I know Rayna is in his office. He doesn't tell me to go, but I always make an excuse. It feels odd to be there with her.

I slept in my bed last night. It felt strange not to have him next to me. It's like he owns a part of me now, and when I leave him, my body protests the absence of that missing piece. I would say it's my heart, but it's more than that. It's different. I loved Colin with my whole heart. I loved my parents more than anything in this world. My heart broke with their loss. That's how I know this is different. This is something deeper.

When I sleep next to him, the scary dreams always seem to stay at bay, so I was apprehensive when I went to sleep last night. I don't even remember when it started. I just remember being here in front of the mirror.

Kira paused, her eyes studying the mirror that loomed over her. There was something romantic and compelling about the piece. She fell in love with it the moment she saw it.

Breathing in and out, I placed my hands against the glass. I could feel it matching my breath. The glass moved beneath my hands. As my breath quickened, so did the movements of the mirror. I could hear its heart beating. It was like we were connected. I could only see my reflection, but there was something more, something past it. Something deeper.

Kira hesitated, halting the pen on the page. She scanned the words she'd written, finding a passage that echoed the one she had not only written, but just thought. *Something deeper.* And then she felt it, that little piece she'd described. It was a faint flicker.

347

She dropped both her journal and pen, pulling her knees to her chest. She was spiraling. Her memories made no sense. What she felt made no sense. She gazed back at her reflection. Despite her outward denial, she knew she was looking at something beyond herself, even if she wasn't willing to commit to that thought on paper.

So, she just sat there . . . staring.

It was unclear what occurred first. Did she hear the lilting music? Did she feel the brush of others as they floated past her? Did she smell the mix of lilacs and citrus? No . . . She saw it first. She was so raptly focused on her reflection, focused on her own eyes, that everything else almost went unnoticed.

The Kira who sat silent and unmoving on her bedroom floor, journal resting at her feet, was not the Kira staring back. She slowly crawled to her knees, reaching a hesitant hand out. She watched as this *other* version of her mimicked the motion, the tips of their fingers seemingly touching from opposite sides of the glass. She ran her other hand along her jaw, curling it under her chin, observing as her counterpart echoed every movement.

It was her. But it wasn't. This other Kira wore a velvety black mask trimmed in crimson. Soft black feathers adorned the outer edges. Her complexion was pale against the obsidian veneer draped across her face. Her lips were a matte red, another deep contrast, causing her skin to look like marble. But it was her eyes that held her attention for so long. Those amber eyes were the same and though they lacked her small flecks of green, she still recognized them as her own.

She held that gaze for so long.

And then her *other* winked.

Kira rocked backwards off her knees, using her feet to push farther away until she felt the frame of her bed at her back. It wasn't just a wink. The gesture was meant for her. Even now, she watched as this beautiful doppelgänger smiled *at* her, white teeth gleaming against the red of her lips.

And then she was being pulled away. Kira watched as the view within the mirror widened, revealing a scene as if it were playing out like a movie. It was an opulently impressive room with white porcelain tile floors. The white walls were adorned with panels featuring gilded moldings. The ceiling boasted an ornate crystal chandelier that cast the entirety of the room in gleaming light. Soft instrumental music enveloped her senses. The sweet sounds of a cello and violin working in harmony together eased some of her tension.

Kira continued to watch as this otherworldly version of herself danced in the arms of a masked man. They flitted through the movements quickly, spinning amongst a sea of other masked couples. And even though she still sat on the floor of her bedroom, she could feel the rustle of air against her skin as dancers dashed past.

She was utterly enthralled.

The women were dressed in elaborate ball gowns, full and fitted. Jewels gleamed around their necks, wrists, and ears. Diamonds. Emeralds. Sapphires. It was as if she were bearing witness to a 17th century Met-Gala. They all wore intricate masks, embellished with exquisite textiles, feathers, and gemstones.

While the theme for the women seemed to be sumptuous abundance, their companions' fashions were more minimal and modern. The men were uniform, wearing tailored black tailcoats with white waistcoats. Their masks were less ostentatious but equally stunning, featuring intricate detailing and shapes.

She wasn't sure what she was witnessing, but she relaxed enough to edge closer. Resting on her knees, only an arm's length away, she watched this beautiful symphony of sounds, colors, and movement manifest itself in the most extraordinary way.

And then she felt him. That lovely pulse in the heart of her palm was the only thing that could have pulled her attention in that moment. She looked down for only a brief second, but the sudden yet gentle tug at her chin forced her eyes back up.

Kira sucked in a breath; her lungs desperate to find air. Even behind a mask, she knew those ocean blue eyes.

Blake.

His mask was black, simple, but with some baroque details at the outer edges. That wicked grin was even more sinful when half of his face was concealed, highlighting the strength of his jaw and the square of his chin.

She felt his hands, one wrapped around her own and the other firmly set at her waist as he guided her through a series of steps and turns. She never studied ballroom dancing, but she recognized the movement as a Viennese waltz. Kira wasn't on the floor of her bedroom anymore. She was in that ballroom. In his arms. Dancing.

She peeled her gaze from his to fully take in the sights around her as other dancers spun in their wake. She could hear their laughter. She could feel the fabric of their dresses rustling against her own as their gowns billowed outward on a turn. It felt as real as the stone beneath her feet.

A shift in the tempo of the music had her spinning, and before she could process it, she was eye to eye with another masked man. The stranger held her steadfast as he led her through several steps before spinning her out once more.

Another handsome, masked face stranger held her now.

Kira peered over both shoulders, searching. Every man looked the same. They moved and spun so quickly she couldn't focus on any one face for more than a few seconds. While switching partners again, she caught sight of him. She held his gaze for as long as she could before he twirled his partner, breaking their line of sight.

She almost missed it. It was quick. But she saw her. The *other*

her. The more radiant and regal version of herself was dancing with Blake. The smile she wore felt every bit of grim and dire. And within a blink, as a stream of other dancers moved between them, she was gone.

Nausea threatened Kira as her head reeled. Heat flooded her cheeks. Her vision blurred. With each new spin, she lost another fraction of physical control. The ground felt unsteady beneath her feet. She winced as her current dance partner released her, knowing she would fall. She could feel her legs crumpling beneath her. She waited for the crash, for the blow of the hard stone floor. It never came.

Instead, she felt his strong arms wrap around her, holding her steady. The softness of his wool suit pressed into her cheek. She was limp in his arms, but he carried her weight, swaying slightly.

He rested his chin atop her head. "Shh . . .," he consoled. "it's just us."

His voice was soothing. She listened to the steady thrum of his heart to try and balance out the thundering within her own, matching her breaths to the rise and fall of his chest. She was a skilled dancer, but she'd been so frantic in her attempts to find him in the crowd that she hadn't found her center. It was a technique she always used during turns and pirouettes.

But it didn't matter now. He was here. He was her center.

"I love watching you dance . . ., but dancing *with* you is," he pressed a kiss to her neck just below her ear, "bewitching."

Kira inhaled deeply, euphoria seeping into every fiber of her being. *We're dancing?* She was certain she wasn't moving her feet. Her head was swimming as he continued to trail kisses down the length of her neck and across her bare shoulder. It was a painful bliss against her skin. A torturous rapture. It intoxicated her. She was drowning in him.

"Do you remember the first time you danced for me?"

Remember? No. She couldn't remember anything. There was only right now. This moment. This heartbeat.

"Do you recognize this song? It's ours."

She listened. The melody was background noise against the hammering of her chest. She stilled, concentrating to hear the sounds outside of herself. She did know the song.

"You were barely wearing anything then."

A vision of herself spinning with wild abandon around a steel pole flashed in her mind's eye. And the song . . . It was the same. Tallisman Stallion. That was how he had the record. Why he had it.

But the memory of those moments faded from her thoughts as quickly as they came, her body too focused on how his hands explored her now. They stretched across her back, pressing her deeper into his chest, his fingers curling into the fabric, tugging at the strings of her corset.

"And yet, somehow, you look as equally stunning in this dress. It makes me want to do sinful things to you."

Sinful things? The excitement and need within sharpened at the thought of what those wicked things would entail. Her lips parted, gasping at the feel of his teeth raking gently across her neck. She clutched the lapels of his jacket even tighter now, a silent plea for more. Close would not be close enough until their bodies were melding together.

"You were magnificent then. It's a miracle I was able to control myself . . . that I didn't take you right then. But you were not ready."

I'm ready. She desperately wanted to say the words. Scream them. But she was incapable of doing anything other than feel. Feel his hands. Feel his warmth. Feel his heartbeat. She wanted to feel him inside of her.

"And unfortunately, despite every inch of my body telling me otherwise, I know we have more to do. You are not yet ready," he whispered against her ear, pressing a chaste kiss to her hair. "But you will be . . . soon."

She clung to him, her fingers twining further around the fabric of his jacket, unwilling to let the moment go. *Not soon. Now.*

Despite her efforts, she felt him disappear from her grasp. She opened her eyes finding herself where she'd started, sitting on the floor of her room. The absence of his warmth hurt. Physically hurt. She squeezed her hand, searching for him, for some proof that what just happened was real. Kira scanned the room, blowing out a ragged breath as she willed the aching heat that throbbed within to subside. She stood, overwhelmed by its intensity and desperate to rid her body of the coiling tension. Her arms hung at her sides as her fingers pressed and kneaded the skin just below the hem of her shorts. God help her, she still wanted him. Her hands were moving to the buttons at her waist, preparing to satisfy that ache when she saw her.

Kira stilled. The throbbing heat that was coursing through her was doused by what she saw.

It was her. The *other* her. And she was smiling back from the other side of the mirror.

"Hey, you!"

The sound of Kat's voice sent her reeling, an audible shriek tore through her. "Shit!" She bent forward bracing her hands against her knees. She risked a glance back at the mirror. The only thing she saw was the stunned expression of her friend.

"Geez, sorry. Are you okay? I didn't mean to scare you . . . . What's going on?" she asked, a mixture of concern and humor clung to her words as she eased back onto Kira's bed.

She gave her friend a tight-lipped smile, quelling all the emotions her body had just endured. Confusion. Desire. Disappointment. Shock. Everything that had come before was replaced with exhaustion. "I must have been daydreaming?" she managed as she eased herself back down to the floor, knees folding beneath her.

"Sorry I interrupted. I hope it was something good," Kat giggled, "I'd let you get back to it, but I need some help. Are you free for a couple of hours?"

Kira would have laughed if she had the energy. *It was better than good. At least until . . .* She swallowed as she checked the reflection once more. Still normal. "With what?"

"My Halloween costume."

"Oh? You and Eric aren't planning something epic like last year?" Her ability to shift gears so quickly almost bothered her. But then again, she was happy to forget about her eerie clone.

"Um . . . no," Kat hesitated for a few moments before continuing: "Eric won't be here the weekend of the party."

Kira's faux smile faltered. "Why? What's going on?"

"He . . . he's road-tripping to Tennessee with Colin."

"What? Why are they going to Tennessee?"

Kat slipped off the bed down onto the rug with Kira. "Colin's moving. He's transferring to the University of Tennessee next semester." She paused, allowing her friend a moment to digest what she'd just been told. "Eric's going to drive up with him right after mid-terms, help him get moved in, and then he'll fly back home."

Kira pressed her lips in a thin line, nodding as she processed the information. "That's where he wanted to go before," her voice trailed off.

"Before he decided to stay in New Orleans with you . . . You know, you still never told me what made you end things."

Her brows knitted together as she searched her memories. *Have I really not told her?* The realization that Kat was right hit her hard. So much happened directly after the breakup. And Kat wasn't one to pry. "Oh my gosh, how have we not talked about this before? And

354

how did we go to Tahoe without Nadia bombarding me with questions?"

"Because I warned her specifically not to ask. It was a condition of her invitation." Kat's tone was jovial, but there was a seriousness behind it.

She laughed, sliding over next to Kat, leaning against the side of the bed frame. "I don't deserve you."

"That's probably true."

Kira took a deep breath, mentally preparing herself. "Colin cheated on me."

She watched Kat's eyes widen and her mouth drop. She shared all the details, somehow managing to keep her tears in check throughout. Speaking of Colin in the past tense was both odd and sad.

"I'm . . . I'm stunned. That is definitely not something I could ever see Colin doing."

"I kind of thought Eric would have told you."

"Oh, trust me, Eric does not know. He's asked, but Colin always told him it was private and for the best. I told him to drop it, that you guys would tell us when you were ready."

Kira looked back at her friend, tears threatening at the back of her lids. Even when she was completely unaware of it, Kat had her back. There was no one she trusted more. She stood, slowly pacing the room. From the corner of her eye, she could see Kat watching her from the floor. She opened her mouth several times, but quickly closed it again.

"OMG! Would you please just tell me what it is you're wanting to tell me already. Nothing could be as bad as what you just told me. You're making me dizzy."

She felt her stomach tighten. Her friend had no idea how bad it could get. She dropped back to the floor, her fingernails digging into the palms of her hand. The words rested at the edge of her lips.

Once it was done, it could never be undone. She wouldn't be able to take the words back. Ever.

"Colin shot Blake." Her words were like a quiet bomb exploding in her ears.

This secret had been a heavy weight on her shoulders, and she expected to feel some relief after sharing it, but the respite never came. She held Kat's gaze, giving her the time to process the damage she'd just inflicted.

"I'm sorry, what? I don't understand." Kat's face was blank.

"Colin is the one who shot Blake. I was there. I saw it myself," Kira said, surprisingly keeping her composure. The events of that day had played over and over in her mind so many times, making her almost numb to it. "Blake and Larz lied to the police. They said they didn't know who it was, that it was a random stranger looking for drugs."

Kat's expression remained unreadable. "Why . . . why would they do that? Colin? I still don't understand. Are you sure?"

"For me . . . Blake lied for me," Kira explained, sucking in a deep breath as she recalled the conversation with him that day in the hospital. "He didn't want Colin to go to jail. He believed he was hurting enough already. But mostly, he was worried it would hurt me."

Emotions finally began to register on Kat's face. A lot of emotions. She pushed herself to her feet and began pacing the room just as Kira had done minutes before. "What the fuck, Kira! Why didn't you tell me this?"

The shock and awe in her friend's voice sliced through her. "I wanted to, but I was scared. Ashamed, maybe? I'm not sure." She glanced around the room, searching for the right words. It was the truth. She hadn't known how or what to feel during those first several days following the shooting. "I also didn't want to pull you into this lie." The memory of her conversation with Larz burned in her ears.

"Fuck! Colin? Really?" Kat ranted as she settled back down beside Kira. "I can't picture him with a gun in his hand, let alone, actually shooting someone."

Kat wasn't alone in those thoughts. It wasn't something she ever imagined him capable of doing. It was still as surreal today as it was the moment she heard the shot ring out and watched Blake fall to the floor.

"You can't say anything to anyone. Not even Eric. Promise me."

"Of course," she finally managed after several seconds. "Who else knows?"

"Larz was there. He knows. I," she hesitated as she considered her words. Larz told her to protect Kat from the truth. Had he and Blake done the same with their brothers? Was that what she saw in his expression that day? The pain of lying to his brothers. Or was it something else? "I'm not sure if Armand and Vincent know."

"What did Colin say? Have you talked to him at all?"

She shook her head, omitting both the texts they'd shared and their run-in on campus, deciding she wanted to hold on to their final goodbyes for herself. Kira was grateful that she was no longer keeping her best friend in the dark on something so important but couldn't shake the feeling she had just reopened a wound that was finally beginning to heal.

"What's wrong?" she asked, watching Kat's expression grow even more confused.

"That morning . . . you ran out of here so fast. I had just told you about Colin flipping out about Blake. I don't think I even finished what I was going to say. You were just gone. Almost as if you knew something."

Kira's mind flashed back to that morning, to the dream. And then she felt it again. It was faint, but it was there.

Her head swiveled towards the mirror, her eyes dropping to the journal just below it. In those moments before she ran out, she'd felt it, something deep within herself. She could remember it so clearly now. It wasn't a voice per say, but she could sense it speaking to her. It didn't make any more sense to her now than it did at that time, but at least she had something she could point to with some certainty.

There were clear variances in how things ultimately occurred that morning, but the overall message remained the same. She thought of Blake's tattoo. She'd given herself many excuses over the past week as to how she'd known about it, but none of them held water. And now she knew why. The dream she had was more than a dream.

It was a premonition.

Kira swallowed hard at the thought. The dreams and nightmares of the past year flashed through her vision. The most recent one from only minutes before was still fresh in her mind. Kat's hand on her knee brought her back to earth.

"I'm sorry. I was just replaying that day in my head." *Deep breath. Smile. Lie.* She didn't want to lie to Kat anymore, but how do you explain that you might suddenly be psychic? "It's all kind of a blur."

"Sweetie, you literally ran out of here in your pajamas."

Kira pressed her lips in a thin line, nodding at the memory. "It wasn't my finest hour."

Kat scooted closer, placing both hands on Kira's face, smiling. "I love you, but it kind of made you look like a crazy person. "

She couldn't help but laugh.

Without knowing, Kat had just hit the nail on the head.

———

IT TOOK SOME TIME, but hours later, she finally began to feel good about her decision to talk to Kat. Of course, she had more questions, and Kira answered them all as honestly as she could without sharing any details about the dream that proceeded the events of that morning. But eventually, she started to feel the way she had expected it to, like a burden lifted from her shoulders. The weight of one less lie was the reprieve she desperately needed.

"What about this?"

Kira turned to her friend, who held up a plastic-lined package portraying a skimpy nurse costume. She wrinkled her nose.

"This one?" Kat's voice was more exuberant when she held up the sexy cop costume. "Ugh. I'm about to call it quits on this and go as Mrs. Potato Head."

"I'm sure there's a sexy Mrs. Potato Head around here somewhere," Kira teased, only to turn and see Kat flipping her off with a cheeky grin. She let out a giggle and scratched her head as a thought entered her mind. "Doesn't this place rent costumes for the theater department?"

Kat's face lit up. "Yes, they do!"

In the back, there were racks upon racks of high-end stage costumes. Wigs, detailed rubber masks, hats, and an array of other accessories lined the walls. Kira traced her fingers across the fur of an impressive and realistic Chewbacca costume.

"Yeah, I don't think that one's for you, sweetie."

"No, you don't think I can pull this off," she asked, pulling the large headpiece on before attempting her best impression of a Wookie.

"You've proven me wrong. I think this look would totally turn Blake on. I would ask if that's the sound you make when you guys are having sex, but then I realize I already know the answer to that."

Kira returned the piece to the shelf, cutting her eyes at Kat, and returned the gesture with the middle finger. "You are so hilarious."

Kat ignored the foul gesture as she held a gold masquerade mask to her face. "Oh, I could do one of those big ball gowns with one of these."

A nervous laugh escaped her at the sight of her friend. *You were daydreaming.* She silently willed herself to believe it. *Take a deep breath. Smile. Lie.* "Look. This one is pretty," Kira said, holding up a lacy black mask. "It's very Yennifer of Vengerberg."

"Oh! Gimme, gimme."

"That looks great on you." Yes, she could still do this. No one had to see the crazy that lived inside her head.

"I agree! Eat your heart out, Geralt."

Kira made her way over to the gowns, looking for something that would work with the mask, flipping through several dark dresses, none of which seemed right.

"You know, I think I have the perfect dress at home. I'll just have to whip up some lacey sleeves and neckline to add to it. I'll bust out my sewing skills." Kat paused, her expression bemused as she watched Kira holding a dress against her frame, admiring it in the mirror. "That doesn't seem very angelic?"

It was a period gown reminiscent of the 17th century. "Yeah, I know . . . it's just so beautiful."

Kira had intended to attend Blake's Halloween party as an angel. He was planning to portray the Devil, and though they hadn't coordinated anything, she thought an angel would be the perfect anthesis. But then this dress . . . it seemed to call out to her. Kira glanced back to the rack where she found it, seeking an explanation for a question she knew she already had the answer to. She recognized it from the dream. *It's the same.*

"Oh! You could go as one of the Salem witches! That's where he's from, right?"

Kira paused for a moment, mulling over the idea. Nothing about the dress itself screamed witch. Especially when all she could visualize was a lavish affair filled with chandeliers, ballgowns, and sexy men in masks. She rolled her eyes at the sudden warmth that bloomed between her thighs. "Wouldn't I need a pointy hat to pull that look off?"

"No! Now go try it on, Goody Proctor!"

Kira knitted her brows together as she ducked behind the dressing curtain, multitasking as she mentally processed what she was feeling while carrying on a normal conversation. "What's a Goody Proctor?"

Kat clutched a hand to her chest, feigning shock. "I'm horribly offended that you don't remember my epic portrayal of Abigail Williams, the young woman who accused John Proctor's wife of witchcraft during our school's rendition of The Crucible."

"Oh. That was that witch hunt play, right?"

"Yeah, yeah. Way to dumb it down . . . you know, you are far too hot for Goody Proctor. You are much more suited as a Mary Sibly."

Kira pulled back the drape, turning to seek help with the closure. "Who?"

"Oh—my—gosh! You look amazing! Yep, definitely a Mary Sibly."

Kira looked back at her reflection. She felt beautiful in this gown. It was long and somewhat voluminous. The fitted bodice and swooping neckline that hung just at the fall of her shoulders made her feel sexy. The dress was deep black and made from a rich velvet brocade woven and edged with a metallic crimson stitch. The front panel of the corset featured a jacquard fabric in the same dark and crimson hues. It looked worldly and opulent.

"Do you think I can pull something like this off? It feels a little extravagant for a Halloween costume."

"Yes! And it doesn't matter. Halloween doesn't have any rules."

She ran her hands along her side, admiring the way the material clung to her body. It was as if it had been tailored specifically for her. And then she felt it again. Like the twinge she often felt in her palm, the flicker of light in her core came at unpredictable and nondescript moments.

That little flutter deep inside was like second sight, an unexplainable awareness. If she could only pull back the curtain a little further, she knew she would see something. Maybe she would have some answers. Her eyes roamed the cheap wall mirror again, mentally trying to pry past the layers of glass and silver.

Whatever the answers were, they didn't exist here.

THIRTY-ONE
HALLOWEEN PARTY

The leaves were finally beginning to fade into a rich array of crimson, russet, and gold. Only a few had fallen from the branches, but the occasional crunch beneath Kira's feet as she walked along the sidewalk was a sign that fall was truly here. The new autumn air was brisk, but it was warmed by the earthy notes of sandalwood that hung in the air.

The sun had disappeared from the sky, leaving behind brilliant streaks of pinks and blues. The street-lamps flickered on, glowing orbs to light the way for the legion of trick-or-treaters that wandered the neighborhood.

Kira made a quick maneuver to dodge a rambunctious alien just as she turned onto the stone path to her front door. She held her hands high in the air, saving the two cups she carried. "Woah, little dude!"

She and Jade had just returned with coffee and pastries while Kat and Nadia manned the front porch candy bowl.

"Thank you," Kat said, eagerly taking her cup from Kira, wrapping her hands around it.

"Okay, so you need to go finish getting ready. Shouldn't we be heading over soon?" Nadia asked, whipping the golden lasso that accompanied the tiny and tight Wonder Woman costume she wore.

"Yeah, I just need to get my dress on, but there is something I wanted to grab. Kat, can you come help me?"

Kat followed Kira upstairs, furrowing her brow as she watched her drag a chair into the hall before climbing it to reach the pull-down of the attic door. "What the hell are you doing? I didn't even know you had anything up there."

"Yeah, there isn't much. I have a few boxes of my parents' things," she said, unfolding the stairs. She shook off the waft of cooler air that floated down.

"I've never been up there. It's not one of those super creepy attics with spiders and rats, right?"

"No rats. I would be more worried about the ghost, but it's only on 'All Hallows Eve' when they can hurt you." Climbing up, she looked down with a mock gasp. "Oh, no! That's today!"

"I hate you."

Kira laughed as she stepped into the attic, surveying the room. The space was somewhat dim, but the light stretched enough to illuminate every corner. There were more boxes than she remembered. "Liar. You love me," she said, kneeling by a group of boxes, twisting, and turning them to note the markings on each. *Photos. Dad's Books. Dad's Office.* She shoved them aside until she found one that was marked as *Mom*.

"What are we looking for?"

"A really ugly necklace."

Kat frowned. "We're looking for an ugly necklace?"

"Okay, it's not ugly. I just remember it being really." She paused, trying to find the right words. The image in her head was faint. "It's really ornate."

Kat didn't say anything; she just kneeled alongside her and

watched as Kira carefully sorted through her mother's belongings. Things that she and her mother helped her friend pack away a few months after the accident. There were several boxes, but in the grand scheme of a lifetime, even one cut short, it didn't seem like much.

Kira moved on to a second box, sliding it over to Kat. "Check this one."

Several minutes passed as they both sat quietly, examining the contents. Occasionally, she would come across an item that took her back to a time when her parents' lives weren't tucked away in cardboard boxes.

"Oh, my gosh! I remember this!" Kat beamed, pulling out a camel-colored wide-brimmed hat, and placed it on her head before striking a pose. "Remember, your mom let me borrow it for one of my theater auditions."

A gentle flutter settled low in her stomach. It was a peacefulness, something she hadn't expected to find up here. "It looks good on you . . . you should keep it."

Kat looked at her friend, her smile soft and appreciative. "Are you sure? Maybe you should keep it."

Kira shook her head, a tear breaking free without warning, causing her to laugh. "Oh, my goodness! I didn't see that coming?"

"Oh, sweetie! It's okay!" Kat said, rushing over to her side, giving her a quick hug before taking her head firmly into her hands, wiping away a smudge. "It's okay to cry."

"No. I don't want to."

"Okay then, let's knock it off. You're going to ruin all the hard work I put into your makeup," Kat teased, bringing a smile back to Kira's face.

"Thank you." She took a deep breath, sobering herself from the onslaught of emotions this process was tossing at her. She missed them . . . so, so much. "I'm okay. But seriously. I want you to keep the hat. It doesn't deserve to be shoved back in a box."

"You are welcome and thank you. And thank you, Mrs. Lockwood, for having superior taste in fashion!"

Kira stood, searching the room once more, spotting a large trunk tucked against the back wall where the ceiling sloped down. She pulled it out to allow enough room to lift the lid. Her hands froze at the sudden flutter of light deep within her. She swallowed, looking over her shoulder to Kat, who was focusing on another box. She didn't know what this feeling meant, but she was confident that it was significant and attempting to tell her something.

Various items were inside, a neatly folded scarf, a couple of framed photos, including one of her mom and herself when she was a toddler. Some antique perfume bottles were nestled in a small box. Underneath it, she found another box filled with old notes, ticket stubs, and photos of her parents when they were younger. She pulled out a woven throw blanket, recognizing it as the one that sat across the edge of her parents' bed. An image of her mom curled up with it while reading flashed in her memory. Kira held it tightly, breathing it in. It no longer smelled like her mom, causing a small pang in her chest.

Kira folded the blanket over the edge, continuing her search. Beneath a few more scarves, she found it, her mom's jewelry box. She carefully lifted it out, closed the trunk's lid, and placed the glass box on top. Most of her mom's jewelry was put away downstairs. It was one of the few things that she sorted through herself, but there were a handful of pieces she knew she would never wear, which were ultimately packed away.

Kira's chest tightened, and her breath hitched as she reached for the necklace. She could feel that inner flame burning a little brighter as she traced her finger across the stone. It wasn't entirely what she remembered from her dream. The chain was old and slightly tarnished, and the attached pendant was weighty but fit nicely within her palm. The brushed bronze setting included elaborate ornamentation with scrolling foliate details. A faint patina along the edges showed its age. In the center, it bore a sizeable amber-hued stone. She held it closer to the light, noticing how it reflected undertones of gold and saffron. It wasn't the ugly clunky necklace that she recalled. It was distinctive and striking.

More importantly, that little piece of her from within recognized it as something of importance. She hadn't ever thought of the necklace, or remembered it to her knowledge, but last night the memory of it suddenly floated into her mind. She couldn't help but wonder if this unexplainable thing she was now feeling was responsible for it.

"Cool, you found it!" Kat said, peering over her shoulder. "I have to say that doesn't seem like something your mom would own, much less, ever wear."

"I know, right. I don't think she ever did. It must have belonged to my grandmother or something."

"Okay, can we get out of the creepy attic now?"

Kira pushed out a deep breath, glancing around the room one last time. She needed to come up here again. Sort through it all and bring some memories back to the world of the living. Her parents' past didn't belong up here, collecting dust. She gripped the necklace in one hand, grabbed her mother's throw and draped it across her arm. It belonged downstairs on her window seat. Even if her mother's scent was no longer there, she knew she could wrap herself in it while she read and feel her presence.

"HAPPY HALLOWEEN! I love your tutu! And that is a really cool light saber. May the force be with you," Jade said, kneeling low to

367

talk to the kids, handing out her last few pieces of candy to the ballerina and Jedi.

"Oh, my goodness!" Kira exclaimed as she and Kat walked out, both fully dressed in their costumes. She knelt down, smiling brightly at the young trick-or-treater. "You know, I'm actually a ballerina also. Do you want to dance with me?"

"Really?" The little girl was beaming.

"Yep!" Her dress wasn't made for dancing, but she attempted her best pirouette. "Okay, do you know 1st position?" She waited and watched as the little girl quickly placed her heels together with toes pointed out, her arms bowed at her side. Kira continued to walk her through the other four positions and a simple pirouette. "Very good! You are a fine ballerina."

The pang in her chest as she watched the two kids run back to their mother who waited at the sidewalk surprised her. She instinctively put a hand to the pendant resting on her chest.

"Awe! That was cute! But we are officially out of candy now . . . so I guess we should head over."

"Hmm . . . sounds like someone is eager to see Armand. Is he the Kylo to your Rey tonight?" Kat teased, swinging her friend's toy light-saber playfully.

Jade's smile widened, her cheeks flushing. "Yes, he is."

Her friend's conversation was enough to pull her back from that somber edge. Now wasn't the time to visit memory lane. "How is that going? Are you guys official?"

"Um . . . I honestly don't know. He isn't really the type of guy who gets caught up in the labels, but I'm also certain he isn't seeing anyone else."

Kira opened her mouth to ask Jade another question but closed it as Nadia approached her, her head dipping low to her chest to examine the necklace.

"Where did you get that?"

Kira's hand still rested at her chest, her fingers absently tracing along the side of the stone. "It was my mom's."

Nadia pursed her lips together as if in deep thought, before quickly straightening and flashing her best smile. "It's absolutely beautiful, and so is this dress. It matches it perfectly."

"Thank you," Kira replied, her tone soft, her hand still lingering on the stone. Nadia was one of her closest friends, and there wasn't anything unusual about what she said. Nevertheless, the exchange left her feeling wary and unnerved. She said nothing, however, doing her best to dismiss it.

The sky was no longer graced with pink and blue streaks but was now a deep velvety black. The moon and stars still burnished brightly despite the few clouds that still hung in the air. Trick or treaters were slowly beginning to disperse as the girls made their way to the Calloway Estate.

Still, a block away, they could smell the smokiness of the bonfire that was expected to be in the back. Cars were lined up and down the street as they usually were for any of their parties. Even before they rounded the corner, they could see pulsing flashes of strobes and hear a steady stream of squeals and screams.

Blake had warned Kira in advance how he and his brothers were relatively well known for throwing epic Halloween parties each year. Of course, this would be the very first at the Calloway Estate. The girls linked arms tightly as they turned at the wall, bracing themselves for what they might find behind the corner.

The gates were open with gusts of fog rolling out onto the sidewalk. A scattering of costumed characters lurked at the entrance, daring partygoers to enter. Michael Meyers, wielding a knife, sat perched atop one of the stone pillars, threatening to attack those who walked just below him.

The girls gripped onto each other a little tighter as they walked across the street. The sound of chainsaws revving in the distance had Kat digging her fingers deeper into Kira's arm. They stood at the sidewalk only a few feet from the gate. Fog machines lined the length of the drive, casting a menacing haze across the entire manor. The centuries-old oaks looming over the path appeared sinister against the flashing strobes. They watched from the outside as characters leaped out from behind trees terrorizing guests, sending them fleeing towards the house or out onto the grounds.

"Okay, are you guys ready to do this?" Kira asked, glancing up at Michael Meyers, who was still intently watching them. She swallowed back the lump forming in her throat as he lifted a hand slowly, offering a wave, the knife gleaming in his hand.

They took slow and cautious steps as they neared the entrance. All eyes were focused on Michael, who continued waving. Just as they passed under him, he lurched down from the pillar. They each screamed, running down the path several yards before turning back to find him still standing at the entrance, waving goodbye.

"Damn it! I can't run in these shoes. Poor choices," Kat whined as she worked to calm her breathing.

They all linked arms again, preparing themselves for the next foray of monsters and villains. Halfway down the path, the view of the house became clearer. Visions of the once derelict estate house flashed in Kira's mind. Windows were boarded up and LED projectors bathed the house in a dark and eerie glow. Special holographic effects of ghosts danced across the lawn.

They moved slowly, watching for movement around the edges of trees. It seemed most of the cast were chasing others. The girls all lunged back as two figures suddenly landed hard in front of them. They weren't expecting attacks from the branches above. Two characters from the Purge inclined their heads, sizing the girls up before pulling knives from their inner pockets.

"Hell, no!" Kat called out, pulling Kira by the hand, skirting around them.

Nadia pulled Jade in the opposite direction. Unlike Michael Meyers, these guys were not quick to give up, chasing the girls all the way to the porch. Even then Kat continued to pull at Kira's arm, desperate to be out of their sight.

The inside was just as elaborate as the outside. The foyer was dim and washed in a faint red glow as a light fog rolled across the floors. The front rooms were usually open during parties, but the doors were closed. Projectors from inside those rooms created grim displays of creatures trying to get out. Everything was designed to lead guests through the center halls towards the back of the house.

Outside, the pool lights burned red while candles floated atop. Stepping off the veranda, their attention was immediately drawn to the raging bonfire blazing in the distance. A lined path of intricately carved pumpkins illuminated the way. The detailed and curated gardens gave way, opening up to a small field on the property's far-left side. Several conversational seating areas were set up on the outer edges, each boasting comfortable outdoor sofas and loungers, along with their own personal fire pits.

"This is freaking amazing," Jade said, soaking it all in.

"What is that?" Kat asked, pointing to a small building centered amongst the seating area.

Kira took a few closer steps. "Huh?" It was all she could manage as she realized what it was. *Has that always been there?* It wasn't any building, but instead a stone mausoleum. She led the girls in that direction, noticing a handful of guests entering and exiting the front gates.

"Ha!" Kat beamed as she pushed past the others, walking inside. The mausoleum was retrofitted into a bar. Black-lights illuminated the interior. She saddled up at the bar, smiling brightly at the vampire who was pouring drinks behind the bar, flashing his fangs. "Four shots of tequila, please."

"Well, well, well. If it isn't Miss *Katia*, the great, herself."

Kat furrowed her brow, turning to find Larz sitting on the stool next to her. "Well, well, well, *Drake*. You're looking very . . ." She stilled, tilting her head as she took in his costume. Her eyes widened as she turned back to Kira. "Do you see this?"

Kira pressed her lips together, trying to contain her own laughter. "Oh yeah, I see it alright."

Larz got a good look at Kat's costume. "I think this means we are destined for each other."

"And who exactly are you?" Nadia cut in as she reached for the shot Kat was passing in her direction.

Larz stood, flexing his muscles proudly. "Geralt of Rivia. Don't forget to toss a coin to your Witcher. Or your panties."

Nadia pursed her lips. "Yeah, I have no idea what that means, but it looks good on you."

"From one superhero to another, you make a very convincing Wonder Woman. Whoever gets to use that lasso later tonight will be a fortunate man," Larz smirked, leaning closer into Nadia.

Kat moved in between them. "The Witcher is not a superhero. He's a mercenary," she corrected.

"I'm pretty sure Yennifer would disagree with you."

"Yeah, yeah," Kat said, dismissing his comment as she turned to the girls, shot glass in hand. "Cheers to a fun and fabulous night."

"Cheers!" All four of the girls clinked their glasses together before turning them up.

"Drinking without me?" Blake whispered in Kira's ear as he crept up from behind, wrapping his arms at her waist, and pulling her into his chest. He nuzzled his face in the crook of her shoulder, pressing light kisses along her neck.

Kira melted into his touch. The tequila warmed her cheeks, but Blake's touch, as it did from the beginning, set her whole body ablaze. She twisted in his arms to face him and placed her hands on his shoulders. She pulled back slightly, taking in the sight of his costume, or in his case, lack thereof. He wore a sleek black three-piece suit, a crisp white-collar shirt, and his hair coiffed to perfection. Blake was always handsome and well dressed, but he was especially dapper and regal tonight down to the Louboutins on his feet.

She ran a single finger through his hair as she tried to place him. "I thought you were going to be the Devil?"

"I am the Devil." Blake reached into an interior pocket of his jacket, pulling out a pair of red devil horns and placed them over his head. "I'm Lucifer bloody Morningstar," he added in his best English accent.

"Hmm . . .," she murmured, running her hands down the length of his arms, pressing herself closer to him. "I think I like it. Maybe you should wear this more often."

"I think I can arrange that."

"But maybe we nix the accent. You sound too much like Larz and that's not an image I need popping into my head."

Larz doubled over, straining to get the words out between the roars of laughter. "She said it bro, not me."

Blake glared, flipping him off. He gave his brother several seconds to gloat before he took a step back, still holding Kira's hands. His eyes roamed over her frame, finally landing on her chest, specifically the necklace that rested atop it. His lips twitched as he took another slight step back, taking in the dress, his eyes wide and jaw tightening.

Larz's laughter quieted. "Hey, man. I forgot we need to get that keg from the house," he interrupted, pulling at Blake's arm. "You don't mind, do you, Kira? I promise to bring him back. Felix, these ladies are our special guests. Get them anything they want."

Blake blinked several times before pressing a quick kiss at her temple. "You look beautiful. It won't take long."

Kira's brows knitted in confusion as she watched him walk

away. Nothing about her relationship with Blake was normal. Because of that, they'd had more than their share of unusual interactions. But none of their experiences helped her decipher the expression she just witnessed on his face. The man who seemed to have everything together appeared confounded and uncomfortable.

She looked over her shoulder as the girls partook in a second round of shots, oblivious of the exchange. Kira stepped to the entrance, glancing down the dim path back to the house, unable to see him. With her hand grasping at the pendant, she searched for that little flutter within her, wondering if it would shed any light.

To her surprise, it responded.

THIRTY-TWO
SHE'S A GHOST

He could see her. Even with his eyes closed, he could see her standing in front of him. Guests were still arriving, getting in his way as he backtracked towards the house, racing to put distance between himself and the images that were still currently haunting his vision. No matter how fast he moved, he couldn't outrun them. They were a part of him. Taking two steps at a time, Blake bolted up the stairs in a panic.

Larz followed a few feet behind, staying quiet until they reached the confines of Blake's room. "*Silentium*," speaking the incantation with a wave of his hand as he closed the door behind him. No one needed to hear this conversation.

Blake paced the room, his hands folded together behind his head. He felt Larz's eyes boring through him, but he didn't have any words for him. At least not yet. It didn't matter. He knew Larz had heard enough of his panicked thoughts outside. It was why he'd made an excuse to pull him away.

"Who is Natalia? Or is it Rose?"

The sound of her name made him pause. Everyone in her life knew her by her first name. But he always called her by her given middle name. It had seemed fitting to him from the moment he first met her. He stumbled upon her as she sat alone in a garden, reading, surrounded by English roses. Even the rarest and most beautiful of which could never compare to her. He opened his eyes, looking down at the glowing red pool below. Guests still flowed in from the veranda doors, rollicking in the atmosphere and debauchery he and his brothers had crafted. He hadn't successfully forgotten her name since it bubbled to the surface in Tahoe, but he had managed to avoid it, pushing it to the deep fringes of his mind. But then, just like that night at the lake, it came screeching to the forefront, crashing into him without warning.

He searched for words, but there were none. What could he possibly say about a woman who, until recently, hadn't existed in his memory for more than four centuries? The pressure in his chest grew as he clenched his jaw. He sat, dropping his head down, his hands rubbing at his neck, desperately trying to alleviate the tension, to shake free from it. It wasn't working.

"Brother?"

"Fuck! Fuck! Fuck!" He jolted back up, grabbing the lamp from the nightstand at his side, launching it across the room.

"Bloody fucking hell . . . there goes another damn lamp. The housekeepers are going to think you have anger issues."

Larz's jovial nature wasn't going to help him today but smashing something expended some of the strain rolling through his muscles. He continued to slowly pace, staring down at the floor, silently prying at old memories. It was an otiose attempt. His mind was a tumult of thoughts, like an impossible tangle of wires with no beginning and no end.

Several minutes passed. Blake knew Kira was still outside

waiting for him. He finally turned to his brother, who was being far more patient than he deserved.

He dropped onto the bed, defeated. "She . . . she's a ghost from my past," he stated, looking up at him. "Before I knew you, before I ascended."

Larz pulled up a nearby chair, his brows furrowed. "Before me? You never mentioned a girl."

A faint laugh escaped his lips. If it weren't so brutal, it would be funny. "I would have if I had remembered her." He took a sobering breath before continuing. "I don't know how I ever forgot her. Maybe it was the dark magic. Years upon years of dark magic. I told you this before. There is no room for love when your heart is black."

"You loved this girl?"

Blake took a moment, allowing his brother's question to sink in. *Did I?* He scrubbed his hands across his face, pushing himself to his feet before crossing the room to the bar cart. He knocked back a double shot of bourbon, immediately pouring a second along with one for Larz. "Maybe," he finally managed, leaning against the window watching guests come and go below.

"What do you remember?"

A vision of her face flashed in his mind, causing his eyes to instinctively shut. His fist tightened around the tumbler, feeling the bend of glass beneath the force of his grip. He wanted to shatter it but knew the alcohol was better suited to calm his nerves. "Enough."

Larz stifled a small laugh. "Would you care to elaborate?"

He took another long drink. "I think I loved her. I think I was going to marry her . . . but . . . but then she died," he explained. "It was why I left England. It was years before I went back and found you."

"I'm sorry, brother," he replied. His tone was softer, sincere. "How did she die?"

Blake turned back to him, taking his seat on the bed again as he searched his memory. "I can't remember . . . she." His gaze rested on the floor between his feet, willing himself to pull back the veil. And then he felt it. Looking down at his open palm, he felt Kira's light. The same current of electricity that he felt the night they made love for the first time. He had felt it every time since then, but never had he sensed it like this. Her magic gave him clarity. It made him remember. His words were barely a whisper under his breath. "She drowned . . . I pulled her from the water."

He clenched his fists and cracked his neck to the side, trying to shut it down. The darkness could keep that memory. He didn't want it. The image of Natalia floating atop the surface of the water seared into his brain like a hot branding iron. He wondered how much darkness it would take to erase it again. And then he saw Kira. He knew it was her by the tinge of emerald-green that reflected in her eyes. Her hair was a dark cloud floating around her head. She stretched her arms above her head, eyes wide and filled with fear as she reached for the surface. She was reaching for the light, reaching for air. He watched the final remnants of breath bubble up from her lips. He saw her die.

Blake shook his head. Her magic was pulsing through him again, giving him access to her memories, just as it had once before. "But that's not how it happened? She was in the water, but she didn't drown," he whispered to himself.

"What the fuck was that?"

Larz's stern voice brought him back to the moment. It didn't take him long to realize what his brother was asking. "You read my thoughts?"

"Sort of." Uncertainty clung to his words.

"Why don't you stay the fuck out of my head!" He bolted from the bed.

"Then keep your bloody fucking walls up," he asserted, straining to keep his own composure. "But I didn't just read your thoughts, brother. I fucking *saw* it. It was like watching a fucking movie. So, again I ask, what the fuck was that?"

Blake stopped pacing to look back at him. "You saw it?"

Larz nodded, his expression unusually tense, his muscles rigid.

That wasn't how their connection worked. Their thoughts were audible, even generalized down to a base sensation or emotion, but they couldn't visualize them. "What did you see?"

"Kira drowning," Larz answered, clearly struggling with the concept almost as much as Blake was. "But like you said, that's not how it happened. I was there. Kira didn't die that day."

"No."

"So what the fuck was that?"

Blake stared him down, unsure of how much he should share. His brother knew him better than anyone, and a part of him feared the truth might reveal something he wasn't prepared to hear. But he couldn't change what Larz had seen.

"Her magic." His words hung in the air like a thick fog, evident and obscure all at once. How could he explain it? It was nearly impossible to put into words. He pulled off his suit jacket, tossing it across the bed as he rolled his shoulders. He waited for the question he knew was coming. The one he didn't have answers for.

"Natalia . . . How did she die, and what does that have to do with Kira?"

"You only saw my vision of Kira? Not Natalia?"

"No. Did you see her . . . just now?"

He watched Larz's confusion settle even further. His brother hadn't seen both women. He hadn't seen the obvious connection between them. The resemblance. He nodded weakly, lacing his hands across the back of his neck. "Yeah. I couldn't remember how she died, and then I suddenly felt Kira's magic, and everything became clear," he explained, pausing as he rubbed his hands across his face as if he could erase the images in his mind. "And then I saw Kira in the water."

"I don't understand. Is there some kind of link between Kira and this other woman?" Larz asked, waiting, and watching as his brother struggled to answer. "What are you not telling me?"

His questions bore into him like a dagger. They didn't lie to one another. With more than three hundred years together, they'd built a brotherhood built on trust and loyalty. "When I completed the Second Order . . . when I had her blood in my veins, I experienced one of her memories. Once the Blood Oath was complete, I didn't feel her magic anymore."

"What was the memory?"

Blake smirked, shaking his head. "I'm a man of many horrid and unspeakable deeds, but with this, I am a gentleman. I know I'm the bad guy, pretending to be the good guy, but you'll never hear that one from me."

A smile broke across Larz's face, slightly easing the tension that had been building between them. "Understood."

Blake paused for several seconds as he considered his words. His brothers knew the First Order was now complete, but they hadn't spoken about it. They had talked, joked, and shared stories hundreds of times about their conquest and the women they'd slept with. A part of him knew why they hadn't said anything. It was because they all suspected he had real feelings for her.

"In Tahoe, when I completed the First Order, I felt her magic again. It was . . . it was amazing. It's like electricity running through you. She's light, Larz. A fucking bright light."

Blake flexed his hand at the memory of its strength. He could still feel it faintly. His mind briefly recalled how it felt in those first few moments of the Blood Oath ritual. He wanted to rid himself of her magic, and yet he desperately wanted to cling to it as it drained from his body.

"After that first night we were together in Tahoe, I saw something. Kira has a small tattoo on her ankle. It's in memory of her birth mother," he said, turning to Larz, looking him straight on. "Her name was Natalia."

His brother's quiet expression wasn't what he wanted to see or hear. It only reaffirmed his emotions, his concerns, his confusion. He needed Larz to crack an inappropriate joke or to mock him with his crass language. But he didn't. Instead, he sat quietly, without a doubt, searching his own mind for answers.

"I felt something the moment she spoke that name, but I couldn't place it. I had completely forgotten about her. Later, in the middle of the night, I had a dream, a dream about Natalia, about Rose, I couldn't remember everything, but it was enough to scare the living hell out of me."

"What scared you?"

Blake pinched the bridge of his nose. "Kira looks like her . . . *Exactly* like her. Almost as if they are one in the same."

Larz leaned forward, pushing a hand through his hair as he worked to compose himself and mitigate his reaction. "Fuck . . . so what do you think that means? Is Kira some descendent of Natalia? Was she a witch?"

"No. No, she wasn't. And she never had any children before she died."

"Is it possible you're wrong? The name could just be a coincidence. And maybe hearing it stirred up buried memories. Four hundred years is a long time. Maybe she just bears a resemblance. Plenty of time to shift your memory."

Blake stifled a nervous laugh. "No. It's not a coincidence. Don't get me wrong. I've tried to convince myself of that for weeks now. But after tonight, I know there is some sort of a connection."

"What did happen tonight? You were with her for one minute, and suddenly, all I could hear were your thoughts screaming the name Natalia Rose. And of course, the look on your face wasn't exactly comforting."

He pictured Kira in his mind. The image of her in that dress would likely haunt him forever. Not because she wasn't beautiful in it, but because it appeared to be the same dress Natalia wore as her lifeless body floated atop the water. But he didn't know that at the time he first saw her tonight. Something else had convinced him of the divine connection between them. "The necklace she wore . . . it was Natalia's.

Larz's jaw slackened at the revelation. "Are you sure?"

Blake nodded. "I am . . . because I'm the one who gave it to her."

IT HAD BEEN NEARLY HALF an hour. And he knew Kira was likely looking for him, but he couldn't bring himself to leave yet. Larz had gone back ten minutes ago, leaving him alone to process through his thoughts. It didn't help. His heart, black as it may be, interfered with every attempt his brain made to make sense of it.

Blake walked across the room; past the broken lamp he'd thrown earlier. The record hadn't been changed since the first time he played it months prior. It was the only one of its kind. He had commissioned it special after watching her dance to this one song that day in the studio. He placed the stylus on the vinyl, watching it spin, listening to the crackle before the music began.

Those sounds brought him back to that day when she stood here in his room, dancing for him. He eased himself into the same chair, his eyes roaming the same space she once stood as he recalled the moment. The lines of her body and the way she moved were unlike anything he had ever experienced. She was pure grace. And then there was the kiss. He ran his hands over the soft leather arms of the chair, his eyes closed. He remembered how she crawled into his lap, pressing her body and her lips onto his own. His dick got hard at just the thought of it.

"Fuck," he groaned, deep and low in his throat. He was feeling things again. Just like before, she was making her mark on him. Another thing he didn't like. *Bloody hell.*

Blake looked down at his hands, balling them into tight fists, the whites of his knuckles showing. Hints of her magic, of her light, still ran through his system. It was a lecherous drug, making him feel things that were alien to him. The more he focused his thoughts on it, the more out of control he felt. His breath quickened, his vision becoming spotty.

The hum of the turntable and the click of the stylus brought him back to the moment. The song had finished, leaving him in turmoil. Maybe he had moved too early. Being with her was incredible, but, like an addict, he wasn't sure he could endure it much longer without losing himself entirely. They still had months before her twenty-first birthday, before the Third Order could be completed. How was he going to manage this?

He pushed himself from the chair to make himself another drink. He would never be able to make a rational decision or get clarification on Kira's links to Natalia if he couldn't control his own emotions. He crossed the room, drink in hand and gazed back down at the party outside. She was waiting for him somewhere out there. Looking down, he caught sight of a girl sitting alone in one of the patio chairs. The glow of her phone and the movement of her hands told him she was texting, but that wasn't what caught his attention.

He noticed her because he felt the hint of power within. *She's a witch.*

He smiled, looking at the framed image on his wall. "A perfect, delicate, crucial moment. Kairos, indeed."

Blake whistled to himself as he slipped his jacket back on, his posture and gait more relaxed as he made his way downstairs and outside onto the veranda. The witch was sitting in the same place; her head still ducked down, looking at her phone. Her magic was minimal at best. Blake guessed that she only practiced as a form of rebellion or for the sake of deviating against the norms. Normally, he wouldn't waste his time or energy on something so paltry, but he needed a fix.

"Hello."

Her initial look was one of indifference. But after catching sight of his eyes, she did a double take, smiling back at him. "Um . . . hi."

"The party is that way," he said, pointing down the lined path towards the bonfire. "Why are you out here all alone?"

"Oh, I'm waiting for some friends."

"Who are your friends? This is my house. Maybe I know them?"

"You live here! Wow! This place is sick," she said, stuffing her phone into her pocket. "Do you know Akesha Karvana?"

Blake's smile widened. Getting into bed with those witches was really paying off. "Yeah, I do actually. She's friends with Rayna and Tatiana, right?"

"Yes. Have you seen her tonight?"

Blake shook his head. "No, unfortunately, I haven't," he lied, having seen all three of them earlier before Kira had arrived, giving Rayna an order to keep their distance for the time being. "How about I give you a private tour of the grounds, and then I can help you look for her?"

The young witch was hesitant, glancing back over her shoulder at the darkened gardens, opening her mouth to refuse, but quickly closed it. Like most humans and witches alike, she was easily swayed by his charm and sex appeal, rendering her unable to say no. It was a natural gift. He could have used magic if needed, but over time he learned that his good looks and smile were just as beneficial.

He indulged her in light conversation as they walked, casually making his way to the far side of the gardens where the lights from the house or party didn't reach. Even then, he needed to be careful. There were hundreds of people here. They were on the farthest path, on the opposite side grounds yet still at least forty yards from the stone wall surrounding the property. He eyed it thoughtfully as she spoke, before placing an arm at her side as the other waved a hand across her plane of view.

"Requiem." The incantation's effects were immediate, allowing him to guide her off the path towards the outer wall without any difficulty. From there, they would be well out of sight.

Blake didn't look at her as he continued to speak, his arm laced around her back, forcing her to move along with him while keeping her upright as she stumbled on the uneven ground. "I'm sorry. I know this is not what you expected the night to be. It wasn't what I expected either. But I need this."

Reaching the exterior wall, he lifted the girl into his arms. He could move more quickly if she weren't on her own feet. "It's her magic. It's making me crazy. Every time we fuck . . . it's . . . it's like an incredible high. Sometimes it stays in my system for days. And since I don't want to go days without her, I never truly get it out of my system. It just builds up. Layers upon layers of her light, just annihilating me from the inside out," he ranted, confessing everything in a torrid stream of consciousness.

Groaning, he turned the corner at the back wall, backtracking towards the first of two gates that led to the ruins. The bonfire was a blaze of orange in the distance. He'd been gone for so long now. What would Kira think? How would he explain his disappearance?

"*Ingress.*" The gates opened at his command. Blake carried her through and placed her back on her feet at the base of the stairs. He watched as she took in her new surroundings. It was darker here, the tree's foliage blocking out most of the moonlight. "You see, I had her blood in me once before. It made me fucking insane," he explained, looking up at the invisible cistern beyond the rise of the stairs. "But then Khalida took it away. She took it all."

He reached out, turning her towards him, looking directly at her. "And now I need you to help take it away." He stilled. The fear in her eyes distracted him. His grip on the sides of her shoulders tightened, causing tears to break free and roll down her face. "Stop. Stop it." His voice low but strained.

Blake released her, removing his jacket before pulling out the chest hidden beneath the steps. His fists tightened around the fabric of the linen pants as he heard a faint whimper break from her lips.

He looked back at her with gritted teeth. "I said, stop it!" he growled, stretching his fingers as he rushed towards her, pulling her back to his chest. His once empty hand now held a dagger, summoned there by his magic. He held the blade to her throat, his hand trembling. He smelled the blood welling around the cold metal of the tip as he pierced her flesh. His chest heaved and his heart pounded. The dagger scattered to the leaf-covered ground as he pushed out a heavy breath. She fell, catching herself on the stone steps.

He took several long seconds to collect himself. "Fuck! Fuck!" He rushed to her, pulling her up to face him, his eyes meeting hers. "You were not here. You did not see me. You are going to go home right now and forget this night ever existed . . . *Obliviscatur.*" The words left his lips with a swiftness as if he feared he might change his mind mid-sentence.

Blake watched as she quickly made her way through the gate, collapsing on the stone steps once she was out of his sight. There were many things he'd done in his long life. Terrible things. And all with no remorse, never once regretting any of them. But standing there at that moment, her fearful tear-soaked eyes looking back at him, he saw something that terrified him. Regret. He knew if he killed her, he would live to regret it.

Even if Kira's light did finally leave his body, it had irrevocably altered a piece of him. The acceptance of that put him at ease somewhat. It didn't stop him, however, from rationalizing his actions. Maybe his reluctance came from knowing that the young witch's magic was weak and insignificant. The situation would be vastly different if there was true power to be garnered. He risked a backward glance behind his shoulder up the stairs. The Brethren still needed to grow their strength. Maybe having his brothers with him would make it easier moving forward.

Blake looked at his watch. Time had gotten away from him. It had been nearly an hour since he left the party. He grabbed his jacket, pushing the chest back under the stairs before exiting the gates. He was adjusting the collar of his jacket and smoothing out the material when he heard Kira's voice.

Fuck!

He quickly ducked out of the gate into the main garden, making it several feet down the path before she spotted him.

"Oh my gosh, where have you been? I was beginning to think you ditched me."

Blake pushed out a heavy breath before baring his devilish smile. In that short amount of time, somehow, he'd forgotten just how beautiful she was in that gown. It terrified him, digging up old ghosts from his past. It rendered him incapable of doing the very thing that gave him his power. And yet, all he wanted to do was hold her. He pulled her close, pressing a kiss onto her temple. He would have held her longer had he not felt the necklace she wore boring into his chest.

"I'm so sorry. I know I kept you waiting. But some stray guests were lingering out here. It's a liability, so I was trying to corral everyone back to the party." It was plausible and she seemed to believe him. People did tend to wander sometimes, though they were the only ones there now.

Her smile did something to him. He'd been lying to himself for so long. Even in the dark, he could see her light. It radiated out of her. He ran his hands up her back, his fingers twining into her hair, cradling her head as he stepped closer into her. He wanted to kiss her but didn't. Instead, he stared down at her, his thumb caressing the line of her jaw.

She furrowed her brow playfully under his scrutiny. "What?"

He considered her question, answering honestly. "You're good."

The little crinkle in her forehead deepened, her smile uncertain. "I'm good? What does that mean?"

"It means you're good. Probably too good for me." He felt her body tense slightly at his words. Statements like that usually don't end great. It lived in the territory of; It's not you. It's me. "But you make me want to try and be better."

It was the truth. His words put her body at ease, but it was his own that tensed under the admission. How were his head and his heart at such far ends of the spectrum? Maybe it was karma. Falling for a woman he was destined to kill seemed richly deserved after centuries of misdeeds and death.

And then she responded with a statement that caught him off guard once again. A statement that pierced into his heart like the very dagger he used in the rituals: "Dark is not evil and good is not nice."

He stared back at her as his mind raced. What made her say

that? What did that mean? What did she know of darkness? What did she know of evil? She was pure light.

It was then he realized it. That he was falling for her.

Holding her there in the darkness, he didn't care if it was her magic.

If he was already lost in her light, did it matter if he never found himself again?

THIRTY-THREE
SOON

The cooler air was beginning to set in. Kira wished she hadn't forgotten her jacket. It was getting darker earlier now, and the sun would be long gone by the time she finished in the studio this evening, dropping the temperature even further. A cold breeze whipped between the buildings, scattering brittle leaves across the quad. She pulled her cardigan tighter as she quickly made her way across campus.

It felt abnormally eerie and desolate. Usually, the quad was teeming with people at this time of day, but most students had left yesterday for Thanksgiving break. Kira was one of only a few that remained. She wanted to take the opportunity to get as much studio time in as possible before finals.

She stopped as she made her way up the stairs at McWilliams Hall, turning to catch the sun as it dipped behind the large oaks, setting the crimson and amber leaves afire. It was a beautiful sight, but it reaffirmed her sense of being alone. From that vantage point, she didn't see a single soul.

Her steps echoed, bouncing through the empty halls. She

clutched her duffle bag close to her body, swallowing hard as she listened for any stray sounds. As she made her way up the stairs to the second floor, she noticed the dimness of the hall leading to Studio C. She paused a few steps down, craning her neck to peer down the length of the corridor. The dark never scared her before. But the past year and a half had birthed some new fears within her. It had been more than three months since the funhouse incident, and she still found it hard to sleep in complete darkness.

Kira stepped into the hall cautiously, watching her shadow stretch and move across the floor with each step as the last few minutes of sunlight beamed through the window at her back. The crashing of a door below on the first floor sent her heart racing. She pressed herself into a wall, listening and waiting. The casual sounds of two students talking floated up the staircase before she heard them exit the front doors.

She dropped her head against the wall, shaking it as she silently chided her own foolishness. She pushed out a breath and continued her way to the studio she reserved. With the sun finally dipping below the horizon, there was no light at the far end of the hall. She ran her ID badge over the security sensor, the loud beep granting her access. With no windows, the mirrored room was darker than the hall. Flipping the switch, she was grateful to be illuminated in the light again.

The stillness and silence of the room pressed into her chest like a boulder. She glanced over her shoulder through the narrow window in the door. Dancing was a thing of solace for her. She wasn't about to allow her fears to creep into this space, quickly scrolling through her phone and selecting a playlist with loud, upbeat music.

It worked. Time melted away the darkness that crept outside the studio door.

Kira kept her focus on the music. On her body. On the movements.

Her technique wasn't as strong as it should've been at the start of the semester. She'd lost a piece of herself over the past year; to what, she still did not understand. But slowly, over the past couple of months she found something that helped her stay grounded, something that gave her a sense of purpose again.

Blake.

She was happy. He made her happy.

And to her surprise, dancing was once again making her happy. It felt good to have something to strive for once more. It energized her, giving her clarity and a sense of self-worth. She had uncovered a lot over the past few weeks. None of which was rational, but dancing helped her find some balance. It allowed her the time and space to clear her mind, to find her center.

It also gave her time with *him*. Well, an admittedly abnormal version of him. It had almost disappeared altogether. She'd felt it in those fleeting moments before the accident at the lake. Outside of that day, she hadn't felt that delicious pulse in her palm for weeks. But on that first day of school, when she returned to dancing, she sensed it again. It was faint at first, like a whisper across her skin. But with every passing day, it grew a little stronger. Now, she felt it as confidently as she did that first day during her final exam. It was as if he was dancing with her; his hand wrapped firmly within her own. The sensation was singular and breathtaking, as if it were a drug, enveloping her in a state of euphoria and contentment.

It was an inconceivable idea. One that she still held tightly to herself. There was no way she could ever explain it. Not to Blake. Not even to Kat. She'd barely been able to accept it herself, but with time, she finally recognized these extraordinary occurrences as genuine truths.

There were three things she knew for certain.

One, there was something within her, a light that spoke to her. It came to her the morning before Blake was shot. It burned bright when she found the necklace in the attic and when she tried on the dress in the costume shop.

Two, she had a preternatural connection to Blake. What she felt was real. He had marked her the first night they met in the parking lot when he ran a single finger across her open palm. And somehow, that faint touch had linked them inexplicably.

And three, these two mysterious truths were working in tandem, along with her dreams, giving her the gift of foresight. For months, she'd worked to shove those feelings aside, to bury them. After the dream about the mirror, she began to spend hours combing through her journal, putting together small pieces of her memories, analyzing every word. Each one was a bread crumb, creating a road map to the answers.

Kira didn't consider herself psychic, but she came to accept that she could sense things before they happened. Acceptance of the idea didn't come easily, but there simply wasn't any other explanation. Her visions were not entirely accurate, but their essence came to fruition. It happened the day of the shooting, when she found the dress in the costume shop and again moments before she nearly drowned. She recently began to wonder if meeting Blake in the parking lot was real. Her memory of that night had always been cloudy, as if it were a dream. It was the reason why she had never brought it up to him. Maybe it was a premonition of what was to come.

She'd been working in the studio for nearly three long hours, though it didn't feel that way. He was there with her. Those beautiful brushes against her palm created a fire within her, propelling her to push herself farther and harder. Ballet was an art that required discipline and passion, two things he brought out in her.

Kira spent much of her time working on her fouetté turns, a

pinnacle element to the piece she was working on. Standing at the bar, she moved into passé, with her right foot pulled up against her left leg, knee facing outward before extending it forward, falling into fondu and whipping it out, her leg fully extended ninety degrees to the right. She repeated the sequence over and over, committing the movement to muscle memory. It was a brutal assault on her body, but she blocked out the pain, keeping the focus on the exquisite sensation that flowed from her hand, stretching up through her arm and radiating out to the tips of her toes. She only stopped at the sound of her phone buzzing.

It was a text from Blake: *Still at the studio? Don't overdo it. You'll need some energy for what I have in mind for you later.*

Her smile was immediate. *Promise?*

I am a man of my word.

In that case, I'll leave soon.

I'll be waiting.

Kira clutched the phone in both hands, holding it to her chest, while visions of what was in store for her later flooded her thoughts. Blake was only the second man she'd ever been intimate with, but she knew without a shred of doubt that no one would ever make her feel the way he did. She sometimes wondered if he felt the same. When they were together, his physical response seemed to suggest that he did, but she was curious if it went any further than that. Did he experience a similar otherworldly connection? Her mother often used the expression, 'your ears must have been burning' which meant someone was possibly talking about you. Maybe there was something to that old turn of phrase. Perhaps she could feel his touch when he was thinking about her.

It was just past nine. She'd already spent more time here than she initially anticipated but wanted to run through the full piece just once more before leaving.

She felt his presence flair within her palm once again as she settled into fourth position, staring back at her reflection through the mirror. That fire ignited something within her as the music echoed across the room. She rose on pointe before moving into a bourrée, shimmering across the floor effortlessly. Her movements mirrored the delicate and tranquil melodies of the music as if she floated on the very air around her.

Kira felt that same connection to her body as she did that day so many months ago when she stood in that stale room in front of a panel of professors for her final exam. His touch did that for her. It brought her back from the brink of something that had threatened to steal this passion away from her. Before that day, she had drifted in and out, unable to truly engage in things. Unable to engage with the people that brought her true happiness.

The music rose in tempo, the energy building. Her leg stretched high behind her in attitude derrière before advancing across the floor, leaping, and twisting in mid-air with a tour jeté. That fire burned hotter; she could feel it erupting inside of her, the music seemingly growing louder with every beat. She could feel his hands gliding across her hips and his lips along the line of her shoulders. Her eyes moved to the mirror, ensuring that she was still alone in the room. A bright white room stood in deep contrast to the darkness and silence that waited outside the door.

She kept her eyes focused on her reflection, finding her center. The music swelled as she moved into relevé, high on her toes as she began the series of fouetté turns.

One turn. Two. Three.

She had successfully completed seventeen full rotations last spring.

Seven. His lips trailed across her collarbone.

Eight. His hands fisted into her hair.

The principal dancer in the iconic Swan Lake does thirty-two rotations.

Twelve.

Her calves burned, and her heart raced wildly in her chest. She lost count. It didn't matter. With each turn, her eyes whipped back to her reflection. Her body still moved in rapid succession, spinning fervently, but her focus was no longer on the movements. She was fixated on the sheer rapture of his touch and what it was doing to her.

The music disappeared. The song was over, but her body wouldn't quit. Absent of her pounding heart and gasps for air, the room was utterly silent. On another quick turn, she caught sight of him in the reflection. Startled and distracted, she fell to the floor - hard, her muscles spent. Her breaths were shallow, and her chest heaved, desperate for oxygen. The cool hardwood floors were a welcomed respite against her flushed skin.

Kira opened her eyes. Her cheek still pressed to the floor as she looked back to the mirror. He wasn't there. She was alone.

Her mind worked to make sense of what she'd seen. It happened so quickly, possibly just a trick of the mind. She began to relax, and then she felt him, her palm pulsing as she kept a steady gaze on her reflection. She felt his fingers skim across her skin, tucking away stray strands of her hair that fell against her face. His touch, light as a feather, trailed the length of her arm. A slow burn immediately followed the chills coursing and churning through her body.

Kira slowly rolled to her back, her eyes searching the empty space above her. Gently, she reached out with an unsteady hand, curious if she could feel him. *Are you here?*

As if he were answering, she felt his fingers twine within hers, pushing her arm back to the floor, pinning it above her head. Her free hand flexed at her side in response, unsure if she should touch him again, ultimately deciding against it. Instead, she closed her eyes, basking in the ardency of the moment.

She writhed beneath him, his touch much too slow, taunting and teasing her. "Please." Her voice sounded foreign in her ears, a pleading and raspy whimper. "Blake, please."

A low growl filled the room as his hand squeezed tightly around her own, crushing it into the hard floor beneath them. His response to her plea sent a rush of adrenaline down her spine, frightening and exciting her all at once. She felt his free hand drift down across her torso, fingers splayed as they reached her hips, digging into her skin. His touch was no longer gentle. Despite not seeing him or even being able to feel the weight of his body atop hers, she could sense the fire burning inside of him. He wanted this as much as she did.

His finger grazed that sensitive spot between her thighs. Her feet flexed and arched against the floor, raising her hips to meet his touch. Her leotard suddenly felt confining and hot, but she made no attempt to remove it. As if he could read her very thoughts, he finally released her hand, his fingers hooking the strap, dragging it down her shoulder. His hand traced across her breast, kneading deeply into her flesh. His other was still working slow and vicious circles, driving her mad. He pressed his palm hard against her as his teeth raked across her shoulder, causing her to shudder.

He was coming undone; she could feel it. "I want you. Please, Blake." She could hear him groan in her ear, his hands hardening against her, before suddenly easing back.

"Soon." It was a faint whisper at her ear, and then he was gone.

Kira pushed up, sitting on the floor, her eyes scanning the room. The sudden absence of his hands was merciless.

And then it went dark. The shadows outside the room had claimed the space, drowning out every ounce of light.

She didn't have time to react. Her silent scream caught in her throat as strong hands gripped her shoulders painfully, pushing her back. Her head hit the hardwoods with force.

The light that flared within her was trapped, fading into black.

Darkness consumed everything.

"KIRA . . . Kira, darling, you gotta wake up."

She could hear his voice, feel his hands cautiously holding onto the sides of her face. Her eyelids fluttered, but the bright fluorescent lights above were painful. She could hear an audible gasp of relief from Blake. The back of his hand caressed her cheek before pushing back strands of her hair.

Kira smiled as his face finally came into view. "Hi."

Blake released another heavy breath, his chest visibly rising and falling as if he'd been deprived of oxygen. "You're okay," he said. His tone made it difficult to decipher if it was a question or statement.

She slowly pushed herself up, immediately regretting it as pain rolled through her head, radiating down her neck and shoulders. She winced.

"Easy." His words were soft and wary. "What happened?"

Kira glanced around the room, realizing she was in the studio. Her eyes moved to the door, noticing the dark hallway. Memories of the night crept back into her mind slowly. She'd been training. She bit her lip as she silently recalled her last run-through of the dance. "How are you here? What time is it?"

"I got worried. I was expecting you hours ago. It's almost midnight."

Her eyes moved to the clock hanging on the wall in front of her. The last time she checked, it was only nine pm. "I'm sorry," she said, her eyes cast down, still searching the corners of her mind, trying to piece together what happened. She looked back up to his face; a vision of his shadowy reflection filled her thoughts. "I fell. I was doing a series of turns, and I lost my footing." She paused, her hand moving to the back of her head, again, wincing at the touch. A large knot had formed across the back of her skull. "And I fell."

"I'm so sorry, I didn't come sooner. I should have."

"No," she said, her brows knitting together as she shook her head. "No. It's not your fault. I'm fine."

"You're not fine. You could have a concussion."

Kira shook her head more vehemently. She hated hospitals. "No. I promise I'm okay."

"No, you're not," he stated, his tone more rigid. "I found you passed out on the floor. You've likely been unconscious for hours."

She stared back at him, taking a steadying breath. "Please don't make me go to the hospital."

She didn't explain why she didn't want to go, but she saw a shift in his body language that told her he understood her reasons. She hadn't been mentally prepared that day when Blake was shot. Being back in the hospital, the same one where her parents died, was painful. She couldn't bear to go back again so soon.

She watched him tentatively as he considered her plea, his eyes searching the room, searching for the right answer. He yielded. "Okay. But you're coming home with me. I want to keep an eye on you. And if I see any signs that you might be injured, I'll toss you over my shoulder and carry you there myself."

The corners of her mouth tipped up in a weak smile. "Thank you."

Blake moved closer, his hands cradling her face as he rested his forehead against hers. His breathing had relaxed, but she could still feel the tension in his body. Her mind raced through those final moments of her memory as they sat together on the studio floor. She had felt him. It was as if he'd been in the room with her. His touch was as real as it was in this very moment. But it was more than that because she'd seen him. It was a fleeting moment, but she remembered it. She saw his reflection.

Kira pulled back, taking in his face. And now he was here. Another premonition had come to fruition. "How did you even know where to find me?"

His jaw clenched, briefly looking away. "I knew you were on campus. When I got here, I saw that your car was still here. I started to call Kat but decided against it. I didn't want to cause unnecessary panic."

Kira pushed out a breath. "Thank goodness. I think I've given her enough heart attacks this year."

"Same here . . . so I looked up what building the dance studios were in. I was prepared to break in, but surprisingly the main doors were unlocked. I searched the first floor. When I got up to the second floor, I saw the light and ran down the hall."

His words both broke and healed something within her all at once. He'd saved her from a broken heart. He'd saved her from that hellish funhouse. He'd saved her life the day he pulled her from the water. And here he was, saving her again. It took her several long moments to distinguish the emotion, her heart clenching within her chest at the realization.

She loved him.

Kira searched his face, unwilling to say the words. It was too much, too soon. She could wait. "Thank you." It was all she could manage; fearful those words might tumble out.

His hands moved down her neck, brushing across the top of her shoulders, causing her to flinch. His eyes narrowed as his fingers gently moved the strap of her leotard an inch to the side, his thumb tracing over a tender spot. She followed his eye line, stretching to view the spot he was so delicately tending.

It looked like a bite mark.

THIRTY-FOUR
SHE'S AT THE GATE

This was a definite first. Even after four hundred plus years, Blake had successfully managed to avoid the holiday known as 'Thanksgiving' for his entire existence. He found the whole spectacle abhorrent and out of touch with the real history of that time. He would know since he was alive when the so-called first Thanksgiving took place in 1621 in Plymouth, only sixty miles from his home at that time in Salem.

Blake was semi-curious if any of the people in the room were even aware of the Wampanoag Nation's fate and the ensuing war that followed. Were they aware that it didn't even become a national holiday until the civil war? Likely not.

Vincent was the only member of the Brethren, who had any experience with family holidays and the subsequent traditions. As a Native American and part of the Sioux Lakota tribe, known then as Nakoma, Armand never celebrated the holiday. To him, it was a celebration of the arrival of men who ultimately committed a grand act of genocide against his people. It was one of the reasons he had turned to black magic, with hopes of helping his tribe. And Larz, being from England, had also never suffered through this holiday. Given their lack of familiarity, they leaned heavily on Vincent when it came time to host the event.

Regardless of his disdain, it made Kira happy. And as much as that bothered him to admit to himself, it was all that mattered to him right now. He paused at the cased opening that led to the kitchen, watching as she sat quietly, a befuddled smile playing at the corner of her lips. He snuck up from behind, wrapping his arms tightly around her, his lips at her ear.

He loved how she automatically settled into him as if it were the most natural thing in the world. "What are you doing?"

Her smiled grew, her voice barely above a whisper. "Do you see this?" Blake followed her gaze. Kat and Larz stood on the opposite side of the expansive kitchen island, both wearing silly novelty aprons that said; *Let's Get Baked* and *If You're Reading This, Bring Me A Beer.*

"Drake Larson, don't you dare touch it!" Kat warned, smacking the back of his hand.

"You're doing it wrong! And stop calling me that. You know bloody well I don't like it!"

Blake inclined his head. He hadn't noticed it before, but Kira was right. They were fighting like school children. "Hmm . . . maybe he should just pull on her pigtails already."

Kat's eyes darted to Blake's as he and Kira both failed to stifle their laughs.

"Still doing it wrong," Larz continued to scold.

"No, I'm not."

"You need to soak the dates before you chop them," Larz griped, reaching out to take the bowl of fruit, retreating as she smacked at his hand once more.

Kat turned to Kira, pointing with the large knife in her hand, ignoring Larz. "Can you tell me again why I'm making this? Why can't I just make my usual chocolate pecan pie?"

"Because I thought it would be nice to include something special for Larz since nothing on our menu really hit any of the English classic comfort foods. I mean, it was either sticky toffee pudding or minced meat pie. I chose the lesser evil."

Larz chuckled with a smug face.

Kat scrunched her nose and stuck out her tongue but didn't argue.

"And I'm making cherry pie per Vincent's request, and we brought Armand a bottle of scotch."

"Well, what about me?" Blake asked, nuzzling further into the curve of her shoulder, pressing light kisses to her skin. "You didn't ask me what I wanted to eat."

"I asked several times, and you never answered me."

Blake cocked an eyebrow, and grinned. "That's not true. I'm pretty sure I gave you a detailed list of what I wanted last night."

"Gross! We can hear you. Get a room," Kat and Larz moaned in agreement.

It had been four weeks since Halloween night when Blake finally confessed to his brothers about the connection between Kira and the woman from his past. Since then, they had been working non-stop to better understand any connection and the potential obstacles that it may create. So far, they had found nothing. From what he could remember, Natalia's line ended with her.

Khalida would have known her. She was physically present at that point in his life, but he was hesitant to reach out to her. Fearful of what she might say or do if she were to learn about the growing feelings inside him.

As for his brothers, Larz knew most of it, but he held firm on the decision to continue. The mission hadn't changed. Or had it? Later, Halloween night, after he found himself unable to sacrifice that little witch, someone with whom he had zero connection, he began to doubt his ability to fulfill the Third Order. He thought about how much he would miss Kira when and if she were gone.

Each and every day, he woke up telling himself he had time. They were still months away from her ascension. He would eventually wrap his mind around his feelings and get them under control. But then something new would happen. Something that would edge its way into his heart. Occupy it without mercy and overwhelm it with a tenacity that told him it was here to stay. It was a persistence he feared even a blood ritual would not dissolve.

That's how he felt two nights ago when he went searching for her on campus. He felt her magic the moment he pulled into the parking lot. He had told her that he'd searched online to determine which building she was in, but he hadn't needed to; he could feel her so clearly. He told her all the doors were unlocked. It wouldn't have mattered if they were. He also didn't search the first floor; her magic was so salient at the time it wasn't necessary.

The energy he felt from her didn't give him any indication that something was wrong, but his heart did. He'd taken the stairs three at a time as he made his way to the second floor. That small sliver of light beaming from the door window had sent a wave of nausea through his stomach. He ran the length of the hall, pausing for only a brief second to mentally prepare himself.

Stepping into the light, his eyes searched that bright space, finding her draped across the floor unconscious. His stomach dropped, and his chest tightened. It was a miracle he hadn't accidentally ripped the doors from their hinges in his effort to get to her.

He'd barely let her out of his sight since then, with the small exception of allowing her to go grocery shopping with Kat. She spent that night as well as last night with him. This morning when he woke up, he found her standing at the foot of his bed, using the back of a chair in place of a ballet bar, moving her body through several fluid motions before repeating them over and over. His heart did that same thing again, breaking and soaring all at once.

"Come on, I have something I want to show you," he said, pulling her up from the barstool.

"Dude, she's already seen it."

Blake turned to Larz; his brows drawn. "What?"

Larz smirked, but kept his eyes focused on his current task of chopping vegetables. "Your manhood. I think it's safe to say she's been there, done that. Let the woman start on the cherry pie already."

Kira was already tugging at Blake's arm before he could respond. "My pie is good, but it's not that good."

Still so full of surprises. He loved those moments. Especially the priceless expression upon Larz's face. They'd spent a great portion of their three centuries together attempting to one-up the other. And these tiny triumphs were golden. Before rounding the corner, he caught sight of his brother flipping him off as Kat slapped at his hand once again.

He allowed her to lead the way, only stopping when she turned right at the top of the stairs towards his room. He smiled, inclining his head the other direction, pulling her into his side. "I'm glad your head isn't hurting anymore. You terrified me the other night."

"I know. You've told me many times."

Blake opened a small door at the end of the hall. Behind it, a narrow staircase led to the third floor. *She's right;* he thought to himself as he held her hand, leading her up. He couldn't help it. It was all he thought about since that night. And waking up to find her practicing in his dimly lit room, the sun barely risen, he realized she would be back in that studio sooner rather than later.

"What's up here?" Her voice trailed off once her eyes caught sight of the space as a whole. She took several cautious steps into the middle of the room, her fingers splayed across her face.

The third floor was broken into two very large rooms covering the expanse of the entire house. The ceilings were vaulted. The aged planks were left exposed and painted white, as well as the heavy beams that stretched across the space. Transforming it from an attic, the ceiling boasted a large skylight with antique finishes, making the room bright and airy. The wooden boards along the floor were old, brittle, and pulling up in some areas. They must have been there since the day the house was built more than a century ago. But a large section had been refinished, returning it to its once former beauty, the wood now polished and smooth. Full-length mirrors stretched across the far wall, along with a ballet bar.

Blake kept his distance, his hands fisted in his pockets, allowing her to explore it on her own. It was difficult to gauge her reaction with her back to him and her hands at her face. The silence filling the room suddenly began to make him feel uncomfortable. It was another feeling on a long list of emotions that were outright foreign to him. *What if she doesn't like it? Am I overstepping?*

"I wish I'd finished a few days ago. Maybe you wouldn't have gotten hurt," he said, the quietness of the room finally getting under his skin. It was a lie, of course. He had only just started the project this morning after seeing her in his room. Fortunately, he knew a little magic to help speed things along.

He had a deep respect for her fortitude and ambition. She was fierce and independent. She reminded him of himself on some levels. And like him, she likely valued her personal space, her alone time. He also had to consider the downside of having her here more - the rituals.

How would they continue sacrificing witches to Khalida if she were there? It would be risky. But for him, it wasn't as dangerous as losing her to something else. She insisted that it was a simple fall and fully believed she was speaking what she perceived to be the truth, but he knew there was something more. Her magic was screaming out that night, the same as it had out on the lake.

Power only did that with two things. One, it sensed danger. Two, it was magnified by another magical or supernatural force. *Was this other force me? Did it sense me?*

He was about to plead for her to say something. Anything. But he closed his mouth as she stepped out of her shoes and took several tentative steps with her bare feet onto the dance floor. Her hands dropped to her sides, allowing him to finally see her face in the reflection of the mirror, but her expression still gave nothing away. And then, rising to the tips of her toes, she quickly kicked her leg out, spinning in place, before falling into a lunge. It wasn't until she landed the turn that he saw the smile on her face, releasing all the pent-up anxiety he felt.

Blake couldn't help the sudden thought that in over four hundred years of life, he hadn't come across anything as beautiful as the giddy smile she currently wore across her face. It made him feel the same. Ancient warlocks don't do giddy. He would need to lock that feeling up behind the highest and thickest walls to ensure Larz didn't find out. He wasn't sure what was worse, revealing the true nature of his feelings about Kira or listening to his brothers talk shit.

His smile widened as she darted across the room, jumping into his arms, wrapping her legs around his waist. He spun her around, resisting the urge to press her up against the wall and take advantage of the third floor's seclusion.

"I can't believe you did this for me," she said, breaking away for brief moments between kisses. "It's perfect."

"I just want you to have a place to practice. I don't like the idea of you roaming around on campus late at night by yourself."

Kira slid down his body but remained close, her hands clinging to his shoulders. "I'm not usually alone. This week was an exception. Regardless, I really do love it," she said, turning to take another long look. "It's stunning up here. What's in there?"

Blake shook his head. "It's the other half of the attic," he said, leading her to it. "It's just a bunch of old stuff . . . See. Furniture, antiques, some old books."

Kira walked a few feet into the room, brushing her hand across a banquet table half draped with a drop cloth. "I forced Kat to go up to the attic with me a few weeks ago. She couldn't wait to get out of there. If it looked half as good as yours, I'm pretty sure she'd call dibs and move her room up there."

"Why were you in the attic? Were you looking for something specific?"

"Yeah. Do you remember that necklace I wore on Halloween?" she asked, her fingers gliding across her collarbone.

His chest squeezed at the mere mention of it, but he maintained a passive expression. "Yes. You found that in your attic?" He had a lot of questions about the necklace, but his emotions were too raw that night. He wanted to give himself some distance and a chance to think about it rationally. Afterward, he never found an opportunity to ever broach the subject.

Kira nodded. "It was kind of weird, actually."

Blake followed her to one of the small window seats that looked down over the gardens. He pulled her close with her legs draped over his. "How so?"

"The night before the party, I had this really vivid dream about my mom."

Her eyes searched the small space between them, peeling back the layers of a memory. It was one she probably hadn't thought twice about since, but to him, her recollection of that dream meant everything. It meant possible answers to the link between her and his past. He suddenly wished he knew how her magic had invaded his own memory that Halloween night, granting him a sudden clarity of events that occurred centuries before.

"I was young, maybe like five or so. I was sitting at her vanity, playing in her makeup. She caught me. And instead of being upset, she helped me put on lipstick. And then she opened up her jewelry box and pulled out a necklace. It wasn't the one I wore that night. I think it was a strand of pearls or something. And then we danced . . . as always, I was wearing a tutu."

Blake tilted his head. "I don't understand. Did you dream about the necklace you wore?"

"No . . . It was kind of strange. I woke up, trying to commit it to memory because I don't often dream about my parents. I like to hold on to those whenever I can. But for some reason, I kept seeing that other necklace. Like it was in my peripheral vision. I used to play at my mom's vanity all the time . . . and somehow, I just remembered it. I thought it was weird when I woke up, how my mind clung to that one insignificant detail. That's odd, right?" She paused, looking to him for validation.

His jaw flexed, taking her hand in his before shrugging. A million thoughts raced through his mind, making it difficult to focus. He leaned in, trying to block out all the outlying questions that popped into his head. He needed to let her keep talking. He had questions, and here she was, putting it all out on the table. This opportunity wouldn't present itself again.

"The next morning, it just stuck with me all day And I had that amazing dress that I found in the costume shop . . . I thought it would look perfect. So, about an hour before we came here that night, I forced Kat to go up with me and rummage through my mom's boxes until I found it."

He knew it wasn't a coincidence that she found that dress in some costume shop or that a dream led her to that necklace. Something was fueling it. He didn't have answers for any of it, and he sure as hell hadn't thought of any way to ask. If he was honest with himself, he knew he'd been avoiding it. "So, it was your mom's?"

Kira nodded. "Yeah . . . but I don't ever remember her wearing it. I mean," she said, scrunching her nose and face, "it's not the most subtle piece of jewelry. It wasn't really her style. She probably just hung onto it because it was an antique."

"You don't know?" He regretted the question as soon as it came out. Her expression told him she was curious about why he was interested, but she didn't say anything. She simply pursed her lips and shrugged before taking another long look at the room.

"I don't want to leave, but I think I have a pie to get to."

Blake wanted to say that the pie could wait. He wanted to kiss her, pull her onto the floor and make love to her beneath the skylight. More than anything, he wanted to forget everything she had just shared. Despite everything he didn't know, there was one thing he was certain of. Her magic had sensed the dress and the necklace, and it sought them out. It led her to them. It was piecing things together that did not need to see the light of day.

THANKSGIVING COULDN'T BE all bad. Walking downstairs, his senses were inundated with the smell of cinnamon, allspice, and warm bread. As he walked into the kitchen, he was surprised to see three new guests.

The witches.

His jaw tightened at the sight of them, feeling Kira briefly tense beside him. But he didn't get the chance to see her face. She was already walking ahead of him.

"Hi. You must be Rayna," she said. He thought she was leaning in to shake her hand, but instead, she just went in for the full hug. "And Akesha and Tatiana, right?" She embraced the others just as genuinely.

Another surprise. He was sure he would never tire of them. A slight grin broke across his features at the sight of Rayna's surprised face. She was polite, though, hugging her back. He'd spoken to her at length weeks before, explaining that he was in a new relationship. He had only assumed she had returned to Larz's or even someone else's bed since then, but it wasn't something he cared to ask about, nor did he ask Larz to offer the information. As a whole, she seemed to take it well.

"It's nice to meet you. Blake talks a lot about you. And I'm so sorry we just barged in on Thanksgiving. I know the guys don't celebrate it." Her voice faded, turning to Blake as if she realized she may have just stated a truth he hadn't yet shared.

Kira turned to him as well. "Wait, you don't celebrate Thanksgiving?"

Blake took a small breath and smiled. It was too late to stuff the genie back in that bottle. "Not really. No."

He saw Kat's jaw drop from across Kira's shoulder. "What! What are we doing then?"

Kira approached him, her eyes soft, her hands running up and down the sides of his arm. "You didn't have to do this. Why did you invite us to dinner?"

"For the free food, of course," Vincent chimed in around a mouthful of bread.

Blake couldn't help the small laugh that escaped him. Vincent wasn't known for his jokes or comedic timing, so he felt it all the more when he landed one. Larz and Armand were also not immune, working hard to contain their own laughter.

"I'm sorry, Kira. It's my fault," Vincent amended, as he perched himself up on one of the barstools, popping some of the finished hors d'oeuvres in his mouth. "I grew up with the tradition. My parents were still around until I was a teenager, and then when I went off to college, I met the guys. Of course, Larz is a British douchebag, so he didn't celebrate it. Armand," he gestured across the room, "is a Native American, so . . . you know that story. And then there's Blake . . . well, he's all broody and shit."

"What the . . . I don't brood," he huffed.

Larz and Armand both faked a cough. "Bullshit."

"Long story short," Vincent continued, "I thought it would be nice to celebrate it this year. It feels like we all have a lot to be grateful for. I mean, Armand, I know this doesn't change the mass genocide of your people, but you know, Jade is hot and clearly too good for you. I'm sorry she's with her family and not here. And Larz, Kat is fucking slaving away to make you that sticky toffee pudding mess for you. That's friendship, dude. And Kira, Blake is a much more tolerable version of himself now that you're around."

Kira inhaled deeply, her hand pressed at her stomach before crossing the room and wrapping Vincent in a hug. "Oh, my gosh. Thank you." She turned back to Blake, her eyes a little misty but still playful. "I'm so glad you wanted to do this today. But dude, a simple heads up would have been nice. Now I feel bad for being so insensitive," she added, hooking a thumb towards Armand.

Blake glanced over to his brother. "Trust me. No one likes free food more than him."

"And scotch," Armand added, raising his glass.

"My goodness, we are so sorry. I think we should head out." Rayna said, finding an opening to leave.

"No, wait . . . you all should stay. We have more than enough food," Kira offered, reaching out, her hand at Rayna's elbow. "Please. I insist."

And there she is again. Always with the surprises.

DINNER WAS A SUCCESS. Despite being the better cook in the house, Kat and Larz prepared the majority of the food. And somehow, even with their constant bickering, they managed to make a good team.

And Kira continued to amaze him. She sat next to Rayna at the table, chatting away with the witches. She made a genuine effort to get to know them. It wasn't something he expected or even necessarily wanted. But it was the mere notion that she did that for him. She was putting her trust in him in a way that no one outside of his brothers had ever done.

The sun was setting, the glow of it brimming behind the oak trees, shining through the branches. Everyone was curled up in Adirondack chairs with blankets circling a fire pit outside just off the pool patio. Blake returned from inside, carrying drinks for the girls.

"I know I'm new to this, but is it normal to eat dinner at three o'clock in the afternoon? I feel like someone's grandpa. Does someone need to make it back to the senior center before dark?" Larz asked. He was joking of course, but there was also some genuine curiosity.

"I think you actually kind of nailed it. You're not just a pretty face, after all," Kat teased, playfully patting his cheek.

"My face isn't the only thing that's pretty, *Katia*."

Kat scrunched her nose. "You know, you're really gross sometimes."

"Speaking of pretty faces. Where's your boy toy? Is he off saving turkeys this time?"

Her eyes narrowed on Larz as she reached out for the drink Blake offered. "No. He's in Florida with his family." She pressed her lips together in a hard line, resisting being baited by him again.

Blake looked around, ignoring everyone's banter. "Where did Kira go?"

"Oh, she's fine. She walked out into the garden to watch the sunset. I would have gone with her, but dude, it's getting cold."

From his viewpoint, it was hard to see past the wisteria laden arbor that separated the gardens' two main sections. He handed the second drink to Kat, walking away before she could refuse it.

Blake reached out from within, sensing her magic, following it. He found her standing on the same path she'd found him a few weeks ago on Halloween night, but this time, she was much closer to the gate. "Hey, you! What are you doing?"

"Exploring," she answered, purposefully walking away from his grasp. "How many times have I been to your place and not taken the time to walk around out here?"

"Well, that's because we typically have more fun inside."

She was even closer to the gate now. He felt her magic pulsing harder.

"Exactly! I thought I would give myself a chance to walk around before you could distract me," she said, pointing an accusatory, but playful finger up and down in his direction before stepping to the edge of the rectangular pond. The gate was just at her back, but the sun was dipping further behind the trees, casting the stone wall in darkness. "It's so pretty here."

Blake swallowed hard. Her magic led her to that necklace, to that dress. What if it was leading her here? *No, the gates are heavily runed. She shouldn't even see the gate. And if she does, she can't pass through it.* "It is. But you'll have an amazing view of the entire garden from your new space upstairs."

That caught her attention. She looked back up to the house. From here, you could see the outline of the windows along the top floor, the disappearing sun barely touching it now. "Really? Oh my goodness, I think I was in such awe earlier that I didn't even look."

"Come on, it's cold, and it's getting dark. Plus, I'm pretty sure

Kat's stealing the last piece of pie." As he reached out his hand to lead her back up, his stomach dipped.

Her arm was stretched out, but just before her hand met his, she turned her head slightly, brows drawn in, almost as if she'd heard something from over her shoulder. "Wait, what's this?"

He was frozen for only a matter of seconds, but it felt never ending. She was at the gate, her hands fisted around the ornate iron bars. Her magic pulsed again. He could feel it. He could hear it. He blinked several times. *Can she see it?* It was faint, but something within her was glowing. It was her light. That beautiful light. It knew exactly what was behind that gate. "It's nothing, really. Just a part of the gardens that was never finished." The lie tumbled out of him with little finesse.

It was rather dark back there during the day. The sun was almost completely gone now. Surely, she couldn't see much. He was still frozen in place, several feet back, hoping and waiting for her to step away, to walk back to him.

And then his heart stopped. The shock of it paralyzed him. The brassy groan of the iron bars as they opened pierced him. *She can't do that. How the bloody hell did she do that?*

She was already a few feet inside before he found the ability to move again. "Oh, my gosh. Wow! Blake, this place is amazing!"

His breaths came fast and shallow as his heart thundered in his ears. Fortunately, she was too enamored by what she saw to look at him, giving him time to process and ease the horrified expression he knew was plastered across his face.

"It's like a fairytale back here. What is this?" she asked, the excitement in her voice rang through as she made a quick move to the stone stairs.

Blake had to think fast. "Hey, be careful. It's dangerous back here," he told her, gently gripping her at the elbow to keep her from stepping up onto the structure. He was thankful his voice didn't sound as shaky as he felt. "That's why we keep it locked up. Those things aren't stable."

He looked to her expectantly, waiting for her to turn back, but she seemed just as frozen and silent as he had been moments before. Something was off. He took a tentative step to face her. Her expression was blank, void of anything discernable. He'd seen it before. Once, the night he found her in the funhouse. Again, watching her at the bar after her breakup with Colin. He was cloaked in magic at the time, making her utterly unaware of his presence. And then again, most recently, at the party after the shooting.

"Kira?"

She didn't say anything. She was a statue. That bubbly and exciting moment was gone. The blood drained from her face, turning the color in her cheeks white. The Kira he knew had retreated to another place deep inside. What stood in front of him now was something different. Her magic was here.

Blake stiffened, his hands fisted at his sides, and jaw clenched. Part of him thought of tossing her over his shoulder and carrying her back. His own fear was taking over. What was Kira experiencing right now? What could she see? Was she dreaming? Was her magic communicating something to her, something that could potentially ruin all of his plans? Something that could destroy them all?

"Kira?" He finally reached out, softly placing his hand along her lower back.

His sudden touch broke through the trance she was locked in. Her muscles relaxed all at once, causing her knees to buckle underneath her. Blake moved quickly, his other hand wrapping around her to protect her head as it rolled back before easing her to the ground.

Blake's eyes remained steady; his jaw ticked as he watched her.

He put a hand to her cheek. It was cold out, and despite the loss of color in her face, her skin was warm. Too warm. He needed to get her back to the house.

His hands were beneath her when her eyes fluttered open. "Kira? Hey, be careful," he warned as she eased up onto her elbows. "Are you okay?"

Kira was quiet for a moment as if she were unsure of what to say. "Yeah, I think so. What happened?"

"You fainted." She still seemed foggy, but he could see the wheels slowly turning in her mind. "Maybe you do have a minor concussion."

"Oh . . . yeah, maybe."

"No, you don't. Don't even think about it," he challenged, pulling her into his arms as she attempted to stand on her own. "I've got you." Kira didn't argue. Instead, she leaned into him, wrapping her hands at his shoulders.

"You know, this is getting a little embarrassing. You keep rescuing me like I'm some sad damsel in distress."

"Well, don't forget, you saved me once as well."

"Yeah. Maybe I can get Larz to shoot you in the foot or something so I can reclaim my superiority on this front."

Despite the thoughts currently screaming in the back of his head, he laughed. "Please don't suggest that to him. I'm pretty sure he'd jump at the chance."

The sound of the metal gate grinding as he closed it behind him sent another chill through his spine. *This should never have happened.* He saw her that first night she was in their house. *She saw that door.* He knew then. He should have been better prepared for this. *It's my fault.*

More distressing was the look on her face when she came to. He recognized it immediately.

It was fear.

THIRTY-FIVE
SOON IS HERE

A few weeks had passed since Thanksgiving. December rolled in, bringing along cooler, brisker days along with an array of bright and cheery twinkle lights and front doors bedecked in holly wreaths. As a child, she loved taking rides with her parents after dark to view the neighborhood's festive holiday decor. But that child-like joy that once wedged its way into her heart at the sight of porches and yards lit up in lights was nowhere to be seen. Instead, her mind barely registered those scenes as she drove through the city on her way to meet up with friends.

Her thoughts were somewhere else.

With Blake.

After Blake and his brothers' confession about their lack of holiday traditions, she was hesitant to bring up any talks about Christmas, but then she woke up to the guys setting up a tree in the main foyer. Once again, he had done it for her. He was always so thoughtful, constantly looking ahead and thinking about her.

She loved him. Her heart solidified the emotion a little more with each passing day. Unfortunately, the words wouldn't come out.

She felt them on the tip of her tongue more than once over the past several days. It was too soon. Too fast. Colin probably wasn't even fully unpacked in his new apartment, and here she was contemplating whether to say 'I love you' to a new man.

And then there were the other issues. The ones she'd been working to avoid for days on end now, pretending they did not exist. Blake and ballet served as solid distractions but driving alone in the car proved to be a difficult place to ignore those problems.

Her mind wandered to the incident in the studio. She never saw him that night before she passed out, but then again, she never physically saw him in those moments. He was as visible as the air, but his touch was as keen as a knife. He was there, and yet, at the same time, he wasn't. It didn't make sense.

It never had, but somewhere along the way, she'd grown accustomed to it.

Accepted it as truth.

And then it was gone again. She'd danced nearly every day in the studio he had built for her, but not once did that delicious touch appear within her palm. Like once before, it simply drifted away. It wasn't until several days had passed without it that she realized how much she missed it, but it was more than that. She needed it. She craved it.

Being intimate with Blake was better than anything she had ever experienced. He made her body feel things she never knew were possible. There was an assertiveness to him, but it was always laced with a kind gentleness. Maybe it was the strength and size of his hands and how easily he molded and moved her to fit him, yet somehow his touch always remained so delicate and tender.

It was a sexy contradiction.

But that night in the studio was a completely different experience. Sure, it was entirely preternatural, something that most people would cling to as being the oddity of the whole incident, but she was beyond that now. Instead, as she drove, she focused on his touch and the guttural sounds that escaped him. There was an eagerness and intensity within him. It was fierce, brutal even. And she liked it.

Kira glanced at her hand, gripping the steering wheel a little tighter. It was dark, but she knew the faint yellow bruise still lingered there. The memory of her hand pinned above her head, and how he'd pressed it into the hardwood floor flashed across her vision. It was a physical reminder that what she experienced was real, that she wasn't crazy. And then there was the mark on her shoulder.

The bite mark.

Like the bruise on her hand, it was a physical representation of what she experienced, but with one crucial difference.

It frightened her.

She'd always felt a connection between the physical, present Blake and the invisible, absent version. She was never sure if he was fully aware of those moments or if something he had done incited them, but the expression on his face that night made it clear he was not. It was brief, but she saw the anger flash behind his eyes and the tightening of his jaw.

It pained him.

But as quickly as that emotion came, it was gone. He reverted to protective boyfriend mode, scooping her up and taking her back to his house where he kept a watchful eye on her.

He never said anything. Neither did she. Did he think she was with someone else? Did he think someone hurt her while she was unconscious? Was it possible she could pass it off as a prank between her and Kat? None of those options seemed as bad as telling him she was having a rough make-out session with an invisible replica of him who regularly manifested himself by stroking her inner palm.

Two things worried her more than anything now.

First, her own mental health. Every time she worked through the possible scenarios in her head, she envisioned Kat and Blake committing her to a place with padded walls. *You're not crazy, Kira. You're not crazy.* She had bruises. Blake saw the bite mark himself. It wasn't as if she could bite her own shoulder.

It was real. It had always been real.

Secondly, she feared her sexual predilections had shifted. Even as Blake made love to her last night, she found herself fantasizing about his invisible touch, imagining him fucking her on that hard studio floor. She squeezed her thighs together, the mere thought of it sparked that internal flame inside of her.

Her foot arched, and then flexed involuntarily as she attempted to get her body in check, hitting the gas pedal, the engine revving, and launched her car forward at high speed. Just as she moved her foot to the break, something flew across the windshield.

The car fishtailed on the wet pavement; both hands gripped the steering wheel, getting the car back under control.

Several seconds passed. The only sound she heard was her own heart thundering in her ears, and the gentle hum of the car's wheels on the asphalt before a weak laugh escaped her. "What is wrong with you?"

Just as she began to settle back into thought, she realized no other cars were on the road. None. No buildings. No street lights. Just darkness. Picking up her phone, she double-checked the address that Nadia texted her. She was meeting them at a new restaurant in the lower Ninth Ward, but that wouldn't take her anywhere outside the city.

The address was correct. Her eyes roamed across her GPS. It showed her in the city. *I should be driving past Jackson Square at this very moment.* She most definitely was not where her GPS said she was.

Kira slowed to a stop, flipping on her bright lights in an attempt to see more of her surroundings. She frowned and her eyes narrowed as she stepped out of the car, turning in all directions. The rain was barely a drizzle now, but thunder still rolled in the distance. Tall trees stood like inky shadows against the sky. It was all she could see. She jumped back into her car to call Nadia, Kat, or anyone who might help, but she had zero reception. *Maybe that's why my GPS isn't working.*

She ran her hands through her hair, searching every corner of her memory, wondering what she remembered last? "Did I make a wrong turn? Did I go over the bridge and head out of the city?" Her eyes scanned the dash of the car. It was almost eight pm. She'd been driving for nearly forty-five minutes. Wherever she was, she couldn't be too far outside the city. "I'll just turn around and go back the way I came." Saying her plan out loud didn't have the soothing effect she'd hoped for.

Kira drove for several minutes in the direction she initially came, keeping a watchful eye out for anything familiar. She straightened in her seat. Craning her neck, she tried to catch a glimpse of the distant glow of city lights on the horizon, but there was nothing.

She reached out for her phone, checking to see if she had driven back into an area with cell reception, but just as she took her eyes off the road, another thud skipped across her windshield. Her heart leaped into her throat, but she managed to maintain control. She leaned forward, searching for signs of what she may have hit for the second time when the sky lit up, bright white, followed by an explosive crack. Lightning connected with a nearby tree, toppling a massive branch directly in front of her. She reacted fast, turning the wheel to dodge it, but the roads were still wet. The car came to a haltering stop, pitching her forward, the seat belt cutting into her chest. Even a highly skilled driver would have been hard-pressed to avoid the ditch she now found herself in.

Kira dropped her head back against the headrest and blew out a heavy breath. She was silent for a long minute, gathering herself. The longer she sat there, the more frustrated she grew. "Shit!" She put the car into reverse and eased onto the gas. There was no movement, just tires spinning. She threw it into drive, attempting a different maneuver. The car didn't budge.

She jumped out to survey the situation, finding herself wedged on an embankment. Her left front tire wasn't even touching the ground. "Fuck. Fuck. Fuck!" F-bombs were not part of her regular vocabulary, but there were times when no other word in the English language would fit the bill.

Out of nowhere, what appeared to be a bird, flew down and perched itself upon the hood. It was so close. It looked like a large raven. It just stood there, almost statue-like. Kira expected it to fly away when she moved to close the car door, but it didn't. Even when she opened it again and violently slammed it shut, the bird remained planted in the same spot.

"Are you the blackbird from hell that got me into this situation?" she accused, ranting at the bird. It remained motionless as if it understood her. "Have I seen you somewhere before?" *I think I have.*

She looked into its eyes. The bird seemed to be looking directly back at her. Moving slowly, she got a little closer. Carefully, she raised her right arm and cautiously stretched her hand toward it. Almost close enough to touch, the bird suddenly cawed, shrill and loud, flying directly at her face.

Kira screamed and fell backwards on her ass. "Son of a bitch!" she shouted with ridicule from the cold, wet ground. She slowly pushed herself back to her feet, checking her phone once again. Still no service. Her options were limited. She could stay put and wait, or she could walk. There was no way she was that far from the city. Maybe if she walked a couple of miles, she could get a bar of reception.

Staying and waiting could take hours, and as it was, Kira had already exhausted any remaining patience she had left. At least if she was walking, she would be doing something pro-active. She opened her trunk and grabbed the emergency kit her father had bought her the day she got her first car. Jumper cables, tire jack, first aid kit. None of those things would help her in this situation, but she was grateful to find the flashlight.

Kira took a sobering breath. "You've got this." Her first several steps were slow and measured. She was no more than ten yards from her car when she looked back, her muscles tense and her stomach heavy with uncertainty. Anger and frustration had dominated her emotions since the moment she realized she was lost, but leaving the safety of her car suddenly allowed something new to creep in.

Fear.

The clouds had parted enough, allowing the moon to soften the darkness. Kira blew out a heavy breath, one she hadn't even realized she was holding. Standing in the middle of the road, she focused her eyes on the reflective lines painted down the center. *Just follow the yellow brick road . . . it worked for Dorothy, right?* She followed the path, silently counting her steps as she went. *One. Two. Three . . . Thirty . . . Forty . . . Fifty.*

She didn't allow herself to glance over her shoulder until she hit one hundred steps. Her eyes narrowed. The darkness seemed heavier at her back. Even the blinking of her hazard lights was no longer visible.

Kira cast her eyes down to the pavement, unable to see the next dashed yellow line behind her. She turned back in the direction she'd been walking, her eyes taking in the long stretch of road, the moon glowing down on several lines of the road. The brightness ahead was a contradiction to the blackness behind her. It was odd. It was as if the power of the moon had hit an invisible wall, and she stood at the very edge of it.

She pulled the flashlight from the back pocket of her jeans, pointing the narrow shaft of light down the center of the street. A rich, inky blackness surrounded the bright beam.

Is it moving?

Darkness is an inert thing, but it didn't feel this way; it seemed almost sentient.

Her chest tightened, squeezing her from within and her breath quickened. Something was out there. Instinct told her to run, but the fear was paralyzing. She swallowed hard, taking a single step backward away from the dark wall, but the blackness followed her, moving fast. She backed away quickly, nearly stumbling as she watched it swallow the reflective beam, obliterating every ounce of light. It grew closer and closer, finally reaching her outstretched hand, snuffing out the remaining glow of her flashlight.

She dropped it and ran.

Her eyes focused once again on the yellow lines. The darkness was overtaking her, moving over her, shrouding her in bleak shadows. She couldn't see the lines directly in front of her anymore, but she could see them several yards in the distance. *Faster. Must go faster.* Her utter fear propelled her, allowing her to finally catch back up to the light. But she didn't stop. She didn't look over her shoulder.

Kira ran until her lungs burned, and her muscles ached. Finally, after what felt like a mile, she slowed, looking back to see that she was well within the glow of the moonlight. Those dashed yellow marks stretched out in both directions. Her chest heaved as she sucked in air, her legs collapsing underneath her. She laid back on the cold, wet pavement as she tried to get control over the rise and fall of her chest.

A small laugh finally escaped her. "Fuck . . . You're fine." She convinced herself it was a trick of the light. That her imagination had taken over. *The darkness isn't chasing me.*

Kira cast her gaze directly above her, watching the moon as the remaining few wisps of gray clouds faded into the night, revealing a brilliant speckle of stars. She basked in that extra grain of light as if it were the sun itself. The city lights always blinded out the stars, so seeing them shine so vividly was an exceptional sight. The brightness seemingly chased away the fear as much as it had the darkness.

She got lost in it. It reminded her of that first night in Tahoe, high above the lake.

With him.

Everything else faded away. The tree, the road, the accident. Her fear. It was all gone. The only thing left was her, and a velvety star-streaked sky.

And then she felt it. Her hand flexed, her fingers pressing into the asphalt. He was with her. She kept her eyes steady on the sky above as he brushed beautiful circles into the heart of her palm.

"I've missed you."

The unexpected sound of his voice sent a new wave of adrenaline through her. His hands were at her face, gently caressing it as he pushed back her hair, pressing kisses along her jaw. She could feel the warmth of his body melding into hers. Sandalwood and citrus invaded her nostrils.

He pulled back the collar of her denim jacket, his mouth finding the skin along her collarbone. "Take this off." His voice was heavy and rough, laden with desire as he lifted her, pushing the material off her shoulders.

Kira obeyed, shaking it off. She had questions, so many

426

questions. Just as she opened her mouth, his lips were on hers. They were forceful. Unrelenting. Searing. And just like that, all her questions faded, lost to the unknown. Those frightening moments just minutes before were forgotten. She lived only within this moment. This second. This heartbeat.

His fingers softly skimmed the exposed skin between her jeans and the hem of her cropped sweater. Her breath hitched and her pulse thrummed at the sensation, her gasp breaking their kiss. She couldn't see him, but she felt his lips curl into a wicked smile.

Kira risked reaching out as she felt him move down her body. Unlike the last time, he didn't stop her. Her hands were in his hair when his mouth found that same sliver of bare skin just above her navel. He took his time, taunting and teasing. She arched her back slightly, urging him to keep going. A low, almost inaudible growl escaped him.

With one hand, he slid it under the material of her sweater. His fingers curled over the lacy fabric of her bra, jerking it down, palming her bare breast. His other hand traced down; his thumb and forefinger slowly and deftly working the button of her jeans as his lips continued their assault across her rib cage.

The crashing sound of thunder in the distance sparked something inside her . . . a tug from somewhere within. She ignored it, wanting to keep her focus on this moment, on this feeling. "Please." Her pleas were barely a whisper.

His gentle touch evaporated, both hands gripping the fabric of her jeans, yanking them down. Kira kicked her legs, eager to be rid of them. The rough, harsh texture of the road scraped against her bare skin.

There was a pause in the moment. She didn't feel his hands on her, but she knew he was there. An unnatural silence consumed everything. She sat up, searching the space between them. His breath hung on the air as he exhaled. It was the only thing she could

427

physically see that told her he was real. The moment felt so familiar. Tentatively, she reached out, her hand only inches away.

And then there was that spark again. It was stronger this time, distracting her. It was like a flicker of light in the corner of her eye. She turned away, looking into the darkness, but before she could focus on anything, his hand was wrapped around hers, pushing her back down, pinning it above her head. She could feel the weight of his body and his erection as it pressed into her.

His mouth was at her ear. "I'm done waiting. Soon is here."

That one word hammered into her consciousness. *Soon?* The word was another tug from within. She shook it off. It didn't matter.

He was done waiting.

And so was she.

His hand dipped below the fabric of her panties, a single finger gliding across her sex. "You are always so ready and willing." He worked in slow, meticulous circles.

Kira writhed beneath him, her free hand splayed across the back of his neck, pulling him closer to her. "Yes," she moaned, her lips finding his. Her eyes fluttered open at the feel of raindrops beating against her face. That beautiful starry sky was darker now, with heavy clouds that threatened to swallow the moon whole.

Soon was here. Soon was now. She could feel the heat boiling inside of her as she moved under that delicious touch. Soon was beautiful and rich. Soon was raw and eager. It was a keen rapture on her body. An exquisite assault on her senses.

Her nails dug into the skin at his shoulders as a soundless cry ripped through her body, shattering her entirely. She was limp beneath him; the rain soaking into her skin, luxuriating in the afterglow. The sound of thunder crashing overhead broke her from her reverie. Lightening followed, casting his body as a shadowy silhouette against the sky.

The sight of him caused her to snap up onto her elbows. It was dark. Darker than it had just been moments before. He was less than an arms-length away, but most of his face was still concealed in darkness. "Blake?"

The shadows moved with him like inky wisps floating on air. She could see his face now, that devastatingly handsome face. But something was different. Those oceans of blue that always regarded her with such warmth were now black and cold.

He moved closer, his lips now at her ear. "Run."

That one syllable fell off his tongue with a foul hiss, terrifying her to the core. She shuffled back, rough asphalt scraping the back of her thighs as she scrambled to her feet before launching herself into a full-out sprint. She hadn't even considered which direction she was going until she felt the cold wet grass beneath her feet.

Kira slowed, turning on her heel, pacing backward as she searched the darkened field she stood in. The rain was picking up as a familiar cold set in. Images of her time in the funhouse flooded her vision. She shook her head vehemently, tears spilling over. "No. No." Her protests were barely a whisper.

His laugh carried across the open field. "Yes! Yes! At least that's what you were just saying a few minutes ago."

She continued moving back, her eyes finally catching sight of him just ahead. "Blake, please."

"I do like it when you beg."

He moved with an otherworldly magnetism, arrogant, yet charming all at once. He was the same cloaked figure from the funhouse. She could see it now. She saw it in his walk. She heard it in his voice. Her eyes remained fixed on the billowy shadows that floated around him.

Blake.

The Shadow Man.

How had she not seen it before? Blake *was* the Shadow Man.

"You know," he drawled, his lips curling, "you should be more careful when you talk to strangers in the street."

Her chin trembled, fighting back tears. She clutched her fist tightly at her chest but didn't feel the sting of her nails digging into her palms. Denial was a boulder in the pit of her stomach.

He smiled . . . that beautiful arrogant smile. "You should also be more careful where you step."

Kira motioned to look across her shoulder, but it was too late. She was already falling, expelled by the cliff's edge, and claimed by a merciless gravity. She never looked down, her eyes fixated on the sky above, her hand outstretched as if the moon and stars might pluck her out of thin air.

Time is an ambiguous thing. It's constant. Trustworthy. It comes and goes, always moving at a steady pace. But it's also cruel and deceptive. Time took her parents too soon. As the wind rushed around her, she accepted it would take her as well. She squeezed her eyes shut to avoid seeing her own clock run out. *Will I feel pain? Will Kat be okay? Why? Why did Blake do this to me?* She had so many questions.

Blake. Her mind drifted to thoughts of him. The way he kissed her the first time, soft and sweet before turning more fervent. She thought about the first time he made love to her, the feel of his skin against her own. A silent cry caught in her throat. She thought of how his thumb always stroked her skin wherever his hand rested against her, as if he craved the feel of her as much as she did him.

Blake. I loved you.

And then . . . silence.

THIRTY-SIX
FOREVER MINE

Her eyes were still closed, and arms outstretched towards the sky, but she could feel the floor beneath her as she knelt back onto her heels. *I'm not falling. Am I dead? Was I dreaming?* Her current state of undress told her she was not.

She dropped her hands to her sides, her fingers tracing the familiar threads of the heavily worn rug on her bedroom floor. Her bare knees arched over the edge onto the hardwoods. Music from Kat's bedroom filtered through the walls. All these things told her she was home, that she was not splayed out over the rocky bottom of a cliff's edge.

Kira may have somehow found herself back in the safety of her room, but she was convinced that what had happened was real. She glanced down at the crescent shaped slivers that stung at the center of her palms. For once, she knew this was no dream.

The realization was a tsunami of emotions, raw, consuming, and lasting. She curled in on herself, her fingers clawing into the woven rug, clinging desperately to the memory of him. The good memories. His devilish smile. The way his thumb stroked the back of her hand while he held it. The serenity written across his face when he watched her dance.

When I dance . . . When he dances with me? Kira flexed her palm, silently willing that familiar flame to light up. *It was him. It was always him . . . Always.*

Another wave hit. She twisted tighter into herself, hushed screams clung to her lips as the pain ripped through, shredding her sanity. Visions of him taunting her in the funhouse flashed in her mind's eye. The magnitude of her sobs made her body quake. Should it hurt so much? Had anything she ever experienced hurt this way? The loss of her parents? Colin? She couldn't lose anyone else. Not him.

She would have walked through fire for him. Maybe she had. Her heart felt like ashes.

Kira remained on the floor, her cheek pressed against the hardwoods, until her sobs softened. Fatigue set in, leaving her muscles achy, but the numbness radiating from her heart left her feeling nothing. She was hollow. Broken. Alone. Her blank stare remained fixed on the narrow strip of light at the base of her door. Kat's feet pattered by several times, each an opportunity to call out, to seek some form of comfort, but the words never formed. What would she even say? Even the little flame she'd often felt burning from within had retreated. There wasn't even a flicker. It was simply gone.

Time passed. How much, she wasn't certain, nor did she care. The faint sounds of Kat's music had long faded into silence, and the thin beam of light that had offered her a scant amount of sanctuary had disappeared, hurling the room into an even deeper stillness. The sound of her alarm clock was her only companion. She kept her focus there, each tick echoing in her mind, lulling her into resignation.

Physically, her body was there in the room, but

mentally . . . emotionally, she was still outside lying on the cold wet pavement. Still there with him. Sleep was looming. She was eager to escape this moment, this feeling, but also feared what waited on the other side. The dreams. The nightmares. He would be there.

Did it matter? He was always there.

A swift and unexpected hush filled the space. She hadn't even realized her eyes had drifted shut until now, opening them quickly at the sudden shift in the room. The darkness was heavier, thicker, opaque even. She could feel the weight of it pressing into her skin. It was cold, like an icy gravity pinning her to the floor. Sucking in a breath, she continued to focus on the steady thrum of the clock, counting along with it in her mind. *One, two . . .*

But she couldn't count along. The sound evaporated. The constant tick of the clock had been the source that grounded her, kept her calm. There was only silence now. But it wasn't the silence that frightened her, it was the total absence of sound. There was nothing, as if the space around her was completely devoid of anything earthly.

Kira stilled, listening vigilantly as her eyes adjusted to this new darkness. The only thing she heard was her own breath.

No . . . not her breath.

Despite the protest of her muscles, she sat up quickly, scanning the room. No one was there. It was just her. Swallowing hard, she worked to control her increasing heart rate as she shifted, her body stiff from lying on the hardwoods for hours. She wrenched her hands at her heart, eyes closed once again, listening intently.

She turned slowly towards the sound, her eyes opening to her own reflection.

It was the mirror. The mirror was breathing.

Fear would have been the normal response, but she was well past normal. Instead, she rose to her feet, taking a step closer, a hesitant palm stretched in front. Her eyes roamed the mirror as a whole. It was old and grandiose; an antique she had come across more than a year ago in a small shop tucked away deep in the Garden District. It stood tall, nearly 6 feet from the floor and edged in iron and gold resin with ornate gilded leaves and rosettes. The glass itself was distinctly old and visually distressed. It was color washed along the outer rim, showing faint gleams of blue and green. Where some saw it as dated and garish, to her it was simply beautiful.

It was like him. Beautiful.

She paused for a brief moment, her hand hovering a mere inch away, desperate to reach out, desperate for answers. An audible gasp escaped her lips at the feel of his touch in the center of her palm. It wasn't the subtle touch that she'd become accustomed to. Instead, he entwined his fingers around her hand entirely, pulling her closer, her palm now pressing against the glass.

She sucked in another deep breath as she used her free hand to wipe away new tears that were forming. Feeling his touch again tore at any resolve she may have formed in the hours she spent crying. Leaning in, she rested her forehead against it, feeling the movement of the glass beneath her as it contracted in and out just as if it were the rise and fall of his chest.

A weak laugh broke free as she realized she could hear its heart beating.

His heart beating.

"Blake?" Her voice cracked, unsure yet still hopeful.

"I'm here. It's okay. I know you're afraid. But you don't have to be anymore. You can come to me." There was an energy and authority in his voice she didn't recognize. Commanding. Enthralling.

She stared back at her own terrified reflection. "Where are you?"

"I think you know exactly where I am."

She couldn't see him, but she could hear the devilish grin in his voice. She could still feel the heat from his hand wrapped around her own. And she could still feel and hear the beat of his heart. He was right there. Beneath a layer of glass and polish.

He angered her. Tormented her. Terrorized her. And yet she still loved him, still needed him.

"Come to me."

She should be running as fast as her feet would carry her. Instead . . .

Deep breath in . . . Deep breath out.

Kira stepped through the mirror.

Her leg's crumpled beneath her, hitting the stone floor with a thud. Heaving for air, her eyes scanned the space around her. She was alone. It had felt as if she were falling again. Stepping through the mirror into a void of nothing was the exact same as stepping off that cliff. Except this time, it was worse, so much worse. This time, she took that step willingly.

She heaved for air, searching for him, but she saw no one. The silence was heavy and thick.

The room was circular, not overly large but with an impressive domed ceiling. The walls and floors were constructed with large sandstone slabs. The edifice was rather austere with simple candlelit sconces around the perimeter. There were only a few small round windows set high along the walls. The moonlight that poured through did little to illuminate the space.

A wide arched doorway crafted from heavy wood and braced with large iron hinges and bolts stood directly across from her, flanked by two smaller doors. Behind her, an ornate altar crafted from carefully etched stone and marble insets sat atop a dais.

She approached it warily, unsure of where she was or how she got there. She ran her hand across a worn inscription, engraved into the stone. *Domus Asmodeus Kane.* She didn't know what that meant.

She turned again, taking another long look around the space. A lone round water basin perched upon a pedestal sat at the foot of the altar. She'd seen these in churches before. Maybe that's where she was . . . in some type of sanctuary. Her eyes narrowed at the grim hue of the water, dipping a single finger into the liquid.

Not water.

Blood.

"Hell, no." She ran for the large double doors, pulling and pushing, but it wouldn't budge, immediately switching to the door at the right. It opened easily, leading her into a long, wrapping corridor. She ran until she found another door, but it only led her into the same room. Her time chasing herself in circles in the funhouse flooded her thoughts.

"There you are. I've been waiting for you." His tone was smug, almost condescending. "I forget how long it takes to fall here from the other side."

Kira whirled around at the sound of his voice. Her instincts were all over the place. Her heart and mind were lost somewhere between running for the doors again and running into his arms. "Where am I?"

"Isn't it obvious?" he asked, leaning down, his lips at her ear. "You're in Hell."

She shook her head, taking several steps back, putting distance between them. "You're lying."

"Would I ever lie to you?"

Kira didn't answer. Everything had been a lie. And yet, somehow it hadn't. A part of her had always known. That flutter from within . . . it tried to tell her so many times. She sucked in a breath, protesting the tears that threatened. She had lied to herself.

He took one step towards her, his hands resting casually in his pockets, his expression unflappable. "Are you scared?" A spark of excitement flashed within his eyes. "Yes, you are. And I like it."

She shook her head, lips firmly pressed together. "I'm not afraid of you."

He regarded her for a long moment. "I almost want to believe you . . . But you don't realize I can hear how fast and how hard your heart is beating . . . I can feel your fear . . . and it fucking gets me off," he groaned deep in his throat as he closed the gap between them, his hand extending out, brushing his index finger across her open palm. A shrewd smile stretched across his face. "Then again, maybe that's not fear . . . Maybe you just want to have more fun."

His touch, as faint and terse as it was, sent a wave of electricity through her, melting away her resolve.

He stepped behind her, pulling her hair back before pressing a soft kiss to her shoulder. His hands raked down the sides of her arms before twining his fingers with hers, his grip firm. "I think we should put it to the test. Shall we?"

Kira stiffened as he trailed her hand along with his own across her stomach, reaching lower and lower, slipping between her thighs. He pressed her palm against her sex, applying gentle friction, coaxing her along. Her body immediately relaxed, dropping her head back against his shoulder as the pressure from his movements intensified.

"See. Always so ready."

He guided her, curling her finger, pushing it further down until she was deep inside. He led her through the motion for several long seconds before joining her, pressing his own finger inside. Unsure that she could withstand the sensation, she rose onto her toes, but he clearly knew her body better than she did herself. Within moments, she was riding both of their hands.

She bit at her lip to control the sounds threatening to escape her. Her head lolled against his shoulder, and though she felt as if her legs would buckle at any moment, she continued the frenzied movements of her hips, unwilling to give up on the exquisite fire that was building inside.

Her free hand stretched up, searching for him, wrapping behind his head. She was blind from the pleasure, but she wanted to kiss him. Needed it. Her lips crashed against his. It wasn't soft or tender. It was heady and scorching. It was a kiss that left you breathless and bruised, shaking and wanting.

And then she fell apart.

"*Requiem.*" His lips brushed against her ear, his words barely a whisper.

KIRA'S EYES FLUTTERED OPEN, squinting against a narrow strip of light that stretched across her face. She sat up. She was in a bed. Her bed. Her pillows. Her blanket. But this wasn't her room. She was still in the sanctuary. His sanctuary.

Looking down, she realized she was no longer wearing the same clothing, only a simple white linen shift. She slid to the floor, the patter of her bare feet against the cold stone was the only sound. Her eyes searched the room. It was mostly dim, but a bright light poured from the small windows placed high against the ceiling. It's daylight? *How long was I sleeping?*

Other than the bed and her clothes, everything appeared the same. But then she looked closer at the light and the way it stretched across the duvet. She tugged at the fabric at the foot of the bed, smoothing it out so that the light and shadows fell evenly across. It formed a series of lines, swirling together, creating an image. She didn't recognize it, but it felt heavy and unearthly, causing a stone to settle in the pit of her stomach.

"It's a sigil. A seal."

Her breath hitched slightly at the sound of his voice. "What is it for?"

"It's for you. For us."

"How?"

He stepped closer in behind her, his hands at her hips, his head resting against hers. "It connects us. To make you mine. To make me yours."

Kira didn't say anything as he led her away, pulling her toward the altar. She didn't flinch when he pressed a knife into the palm of her hand or when he did the same to his own. Instead, she looked on with full curiosity as he held their entwined hands over the basin, their blood mixing and dripping into the bowl.

Blake dipped his thumb into the warm liquid before dragging a smear of red across her brow. He did the same to his own. The controlled arrogance he always wore on his face was fraying. There was an eagerness, a hunger in his expression as if waiting was a form of torment.

He held his hands at the sides of her face, blood from his palm smudged along her cheek. He leaned in close, his mouth barely brushing against hers. "*Meus in sempiternum.* Forever mine." The incantation had scarcely left his lips before he kissed her. Hard.

Kira's arms wrapped around him as he lifted and carried her back to the bed. Soon was over. No more waiting. What followed was as impalpable as the stars plucking her out of the sky. At least that's how it felt.

An impossible pleasure. A soul-searing rapture. Euphoria. Heaven? *Maybe it is heaven. Maybe I did die when I fell from the cliff. No, no. Not heaven. He said it was hell.*

Kira searched within herself, seeking out the light that lived there. The one she thought would give her answers. It fluttered ever so briefly, but the sensations that were raking through her body snuffed it out.

They were a tangle of limbs and sheets . . . Sweat and blood . . . Rippling muscles, tongue, and teeth.

He was inside of her, shredding apart the very fabric of her being. Consuming it entirely. He emptied her. Filled her with something new.

If this was hell, she would gladly burn with him.

THIRTY-SEVEN
HOW WILL THIS END

K ira woke in her bed, her eyes scanning the room. The white ceiling above told her she was in her bedroom. She was no longer in the sanctuary.

She sat up, her muscles crying out from the movement. It hurt. Her entire body did. *Did I dream it? Was it all just another terrible dream?* She sat in her bed for several long minutes. *Terrible? Was it terrible? No.*

Some parts were. Some were beautiful.

Kira rubbed at her eyes, feeling the sting in her palm. Looking down, she saw the inch long cut in the center. Dried blood surrounded it and smeared down the length of her wrist. Fragments of last night came into view. She searched for the piece within her. That little piece she knew nothing about, but yet somehow recognized as important.

The piece she somehow knew was there to help her. It was gone. He took it.

She felt numb and frozen. Alone. Betrayed.

He made love to me. He fucked me. Over and over. But it

was . . . it was different. She slipped from her bed to retrieve her journal. She needed to write down what she could remember. While crawling back into her bed, she caught a glimpse of herself in the mirror. A smear of dried blood stretched across her forehead and cheeks. She stared back at her reflection. *Not a dream. It was never a dream.*

Kira opened the journal, writing feverishly. The words poured out. But it was the last three words that stared back at her now, breaking her from the inside out. Her fingers curled at the sides of the paper, crumpling the edges. She was tempted to rip the page out entirely. Burn it. Rid herself of the evidence of how she could think such things about someone she loved. Someone she still wanted. Still needed. But she didn't destroy the page. Those words remained, staring back at her in black and white.

She shoved the leather-bound book from her lap, disgusted with herself. Even as she wrote those last words, her body deceived her, lighting up with heat at the mere thought of how he touched her. How it made her want it again. Right here. Right now. She bit at her lip. *What is wrong with me?* Things had been going so well. She was happy again. Happy with him. And now she didn't know what she was, or how to feel.

It was difficult to focus. She caught a glimpse of her journal on the floor where it had fallen. Her eyes roamed it as she reached out tentatively. It was open to the first page, the same first page she'd ripped out and burned so many months before.

But it wasn't ripped. And it wasn't burned.

It was there.

Kira picked it up, running her finger along a faint jagged line near the binding. She could smell the smoke. The corners of the page were lightly singed and blackened, but not entirely damaged. *This page shouldn't be here.*

She remembered it clearly as she silently read the entry.

442

He carried me through double doors. From his sanctuary to my bed, he carried me. How long I was there, I can't remember. When I woke up, I immediately needed to see him again. I went to him. I needed answers. Needed him.

He's beautiful. I don't know how I know. I've never seen him. I can see his smile in the way he kisses me. I can feel his strength in the way he touches me. And somehow, through that dark hood he wears, I can see his ocean blue eyes and the way he looks back at me. He loves me. And I think I love him.

And so I drove to him. And then . . . I felt it. The impact. The pain. His screams. I don't know what happened. I only know that he killed me.

Kira flinched at the teardrop that splattered across the page. It was tinged with red, mixed with the blood from her cheek. She jumped up, running to the bathroom, scrubbing away the evidence of last night. Even after the last traces of red swirled down the drain, it wasn't enough to wash away the shame she felt.

She turned on the shower, peeling away the white shift she wore. She held it in her hands for a long moment. It was also stained with smears of blood. More importantly, this didn't belong to her. She'd never seen it before. Or had she? She wasn't sure. She wasn't sure of anything anymore.

"Kira! Kira, sweetie, you're here!"

Kira dropped the shift on the counter and grabbed the towel hanging on the wall, draping it around her naked body. She watched Kat's face fall from relief to utter horror.

"Sweetie, what happened? Who did this to you?"

Kira glanced back at the mirror. She'd been so focused on

removing the stains of blood from her skin that she didn't notice the gray and yellow bruises that covered her body. Some looked like handprints. She looked back to Kat, unsure of what to say.

"Are you bleeding?" Panic rolled through her as her eyes skimmed the red stained fabric. "Kira, tell me who did this to you!"

"I can't talk about it right now, Kat." Tears were already spilling down her cheeks as she tried to push her away.

"No!" Kat's screams were frantic. "You don't get to do that! Everyone has been freaking out since you disappeared."

Kira opened her mouth and closed it again. Kat was crying, really crying. She was so used to her being the rock. The peppy, happy rock that kept her grounded. Instead, she stood before her trembling. Confused. Scared.

"Kira, who did this to you?" she pleaded, her voice cracking.

Kira recoiled back, not wanting anyone to touch her. "It's nothing." She shoved her aside, leaving the bathroom. Forgetting her need for a shower, Kira slipped on jeans and a sweater, feeling Kat's eyes on her.

"Please talk to me. Blake is really freaking out, too. Does he know you're okay? Have you called him?"

Kira froze at the sound of his name. "Is he okay?" Her voice was strained. The fact that she still cared so much, after everything, sent daggers into her core.

Kat shook her head, her eyes wide. "No! No, he's not okay! None of us are okay!"

She stood, frozen in place. She wanted to go to him. Hold him. Kiss him. Kill him.

"When the police found your car, everyone assumed the worst. That you'd been taken or," Kat's voice broke, her eyes cast down. She took a sobering breath before looking up again. "It doesn't matter now. You're here."

Kira inclined her head, processing the words she'd just heard. "The police? You called the police?"

"What? Of course, I did. Why wouldn't I?" The look upon Kat's face was bewildered.

A question lingered in the corner of her thoughts. The police. The frantic nature of her friend. The discoloration of her bruises. "How long have I been gone?"

Kat swallowed and bit her lip as she collected herself. She sat softly at the edge of Kira's bed. There was something grief stricken and fractured behind her eyes. "Five days."

Kira sucked in air, reaching out for her dresser for support.

"Please tell me what happened? Let me take you to the hospital. I'll call Blake, and he can meet us there."

"No!" The volume of her voice shook Kat. It shook her. She calmed herself. "Please don't. I just need . . . I just need a minute."

What she truly needed was five days. The five days that she lost. The five days that he took and locked away somewhere in that sanctuary.

Blake? Kira wanted to go to him. It wasn't him. And yet somehow it was. *Why?* She wanted to scream that question to him over and over.

Kira crossed the room and sat beside her friend on the bed. "The last thing I remember, I was driving to meet up with you, Jade, and Nadia."

Kat's forehead creased. "Where? I don't remember that?"

"Nadia texted me and told me we were meeting up at some new place in the lower Ninth Ward . . . but I must have taken a wrong turn, and my GPS quit working and then my phone died."

"Sweetie, no . . . I," she stuttered, pausing briefly before she walked across the hall, returning quickly with her bag in hand, pulling out Kira's phone. "The police gave this back to me yesterday. They'd done everything they could with it."

Kira took her phone. She couldn't quite remember the last time she had it.

"The police found your car the night you went missing. It was in a ditch somewhere off Highway 300. It looked like you somehow avoided a tree that fell. But your phone, your purse . . . everything was there."

Kira scanned through her text messages, but there was nothing from Nadia indicating their plans that night. The last thing she saw from her was a text asking if she could borrow her cashmere sweater. There were no plans for dinner in the Ninth Ward. No address that led her astray. It didn't make sense. Kira frantically searched through Kat's texts and then through Jade's. Nothing.

She purposefully avoided Blake's texts, tossing the phone to the middle of her bed and out of her reach.

"The police also released your car. They couldn't find any evidence of foul play. They were mostly worried that you might have hit your head, became disoriented, and wandered off," Kat said, her last words coming out as a sob. "They've been coordinating search parties every day . . . We've been looking for you every single day."

Kira wanted to reach out for her friend, but she felt so adrift with her own emotions that she couldn't bring herself to be there for someone else. Instead, she simply watched Kat as she pulled herself together, keeping a few feet of distance between them.

"Armand came by yesterday and fixed the axle. He was confident you would come back, and he wanted to have it ready for you. The guys have been trying to stay positive for Blake. He's been an utter mess."

She tried not to react to his name, but she felt the prickle dance across her skin. She was unsure if Kat had noticed.

"Please let me take you to the hospital. You look like you need medical attention. I can call him on the way."

446

Kira only shook her head, backing away another step.

"Stop it now! I don't know why you are doing this. I should have made you go to the ER the night after the funhouse, but I knew how much you hated it. Every fiber of my being told me something was off that night, and every night when I heard you crying yourself to sleep. I told myself you would come to me for help when you were ready. But no more! I'm done waiting, Kira. I'm done!" Kat's tears flowed freely now. Tears made up of anger, concern, guilt and desperation. "I love you. Please don't make me drag you there. If I can't, I know Blake will."

"I am fine! I just need you to leave it be, for now, Kat!" she shouted, passing by her before making her way down the stairs. She would have taken Kat's car, but she saw her own keys on the table at the front door.

"Kira! No! Don't you dare walk out on me! You can't do this!" Kat screamed, reaching out to grip Kira's arm, but immediately ricocheted back, slamming to the floor - hard.

Kira jolted back, looking at her hands. She took a tentative step towards her friend. "Kat?" She could feel the electricity pulsating within her own arm. *Did I do that?*

Kat said nothing, rubbing the back of her head, looking back at Kira with bewilderment.

Instinct and years of friendship told her to go to Kat to make sure she was okay, but the frantic questions and emotions that coursed through every vein in her body told her otherwise. It terrified her to face him, but she knew exactly where she needed to go. She needed to see Blake.

Kira was barreling down his drive within a matter of minutes. She didn't even bother to turn off the ignition or close the door behind her as she sprinted for the porch. "Blake?" She was cautious as she entered the front door, taking only a few steps into the foyer. "Blake?"

The front door was unlocked. *Someone has to be here.*

It was still early that morning; maybe they were still asleep. She made her way to the stairs, but just as she took the first step, a familiar pulse came to life. It wasn't the twinge she often felt in the palm of her hand. It was the one she felt inside. It was that piece she thought he'd taken away.

Kira's hand flew to her mouth, tears welling in the corners of her eyes. She didn't realize how beautiful the sensation was until now. It was a light that brought her clarity. It told her things. And right now, it was telling her to turn around.

She backed down the step, turning to the door beneath the stairs. It was the same massive door, crafted from reclaimed wood, incredibly tall and nearly half as wide. Standing there now, she suddenly remembered when she'd been here before. She remembered it all now. It was that first night, the night of that first party. This light within her, a light she didn't even know of then, had led her to this very spot. There was something behind this door that it wanted her to see.

Kira stretched her arm out, tracing a single finger along the markings etched deep into the grain. She recognized them from somewhere else, though she wasn't sure how or from where. There was something behind it. She was anxious to know, but also scared of the answers she might find.

The door opened, and her heart sank.

She took a few cautious steps into the room, her eyes glancing from wall to wall, taking it all in. Pictures of her lined the walls. Images of her and Colin. Of her with Kat. Images of her home. A blueprint of it. Images of her at school and at the coffeehouse. "What is this?" Her voice was barely a whisper.

She eased down on the leather sofa, noticing an assortment of files strewn across the coffee table. The papers included everything from her school schedule, dance rehearsals, birth certificate, and newspaper clippings from her parents' car accident and subsequent deaths. Tears rolled down her cheek once again. She had wanted so badly for Blake to be good, for her dreams to be wrong, but the longer she sat here, the further away that possibility grew.

She was blind with rage and tears now as her eyes scanned another page.

I now love to play with you while you dream
I love it when I make you beg, and even more when you scream
I am lost, dead with no soul
Because of you I have only temptation and have lost all control
You were both my Heaven and my Hell
Your hot flesh I have now cast my spell
Because of you, I am now insane
As I make your reality and my fantasy the same
I give it all to you as you crave the pleasure, and you scream out my name
This creature has now tasted you and is no longer tame
You look into my eyes and are scared of what you see
But your hungering lust grows beyond your fear as you continue to beg for me
This fight you will lose and only I will win
How will this end

There were more, but she pushed them away, unable to continue reading, but then one stood out beyond the others. It stared back at her like a beacon. The light within her grew; a simmering fire ready to burst.

The Order of Three.

One. Take Her Body.
Two. Take Her Blood.
Three. Take Her Life.

Kira clutched the page tightly between trembling fingers. *Not Blake. Not my Blake.* She clung to that tiny feeling within her, the one that told her he loved her. The one that made her feel safe and special. He was the one that seemed to keep the nightmares at bay.

And now she knew the truth.

Blake was the nightmare.

THIRTY-EIGHT
BETRAYAL

"I'm sorry, brother. I thought that would work," Armand said as he made his way past Blake, clasping his shoulder with a gentle squeeze.

Blake barely acknowledged the gesture. His elbows were propped up on his knees, his hands fisted in front of him as he stared out past the foliage at nothing in particular. It wasn't possible. Even if she were dead, he should have been able to locate her by now.

And so far, everything they'd tried had failed.

"We'll find her."

Even Larz's commanding tone did little to sway him. Was it her magic? Did it sense something? Did it take her into hiding? It seemed unlikely. She was still months away from her ascension, but her power was growing. Maybe it was protecting her.

"She was here, you know." He watched his brothers' questioning expressions. "Here. Right here."

Larz stepped towards him. "What do you mean, right here?"

"At Thanksgiving. That night, she came out here for a walk. I

451

found her just outside the gate. She said she was just exploring . . . looking around." Blake pressed his palms to his brow as if he were trying to rid the memory from his thoughts. "I watched her waltz right through that fucking gate."

"That's not possible."

"Larz, I fucking watched her do it!"

His brothers were quiet, each looking to the other on how to proceed.

"Why didn't you say anything?" Vincent asked, always the one of reason and calm. "You know we would do whatever we needed to help."

Blake shook his head. "I don't know. Like he said, it shouldn't have been possible. Further, more, I should have known. I saw her that night. That first night she was at the house. She was at the door then, too. She was so close to it. The runes made it invisible to everyone, but she saw it. Her magic is stronger than we think it is."

"What did she do when she got back here? What did you tell her? Could she see the cistern?" Vincent asked.

"No, she didn't see it. And I made up an excuse. Told her we kept it locked up because it's unsafe . . . but then," his voice broke off as he stood, pacing down the last few steps of the ruins, turning back towards them as his feet met the ground, "she was standing here, and she just . . . froze. The look on her face . . . I've seen it before. So have you," he said, glancing at Larz. "The look she had that night at the funhouse, it was the same. When I reached out for her, she collapsed."

"She fainted? What did she say when she came to?" asked Vincent.

"Nothing. She didn't seem to know what happened."

"Do you believe her?" Armand asked.

"Yes . . . and, no."

"I don't understand."

Blake looked to the ground, unable to find the words he needed. To find the words he should have shared with them weeks before.

Larz stepped closer. "He thinks her magic is calling the shots. That it's manifesting itself into something sentient."

Vincent and Armand looked to one another. "Is that even possible?"

"I'm a four-hundred-year-old warlock. I live in a world where anything is possible. I," Blake's words caught in his throat as his eyes turned to the sky. The shadows grew darker beneath the canopy. The winds were picking up, the branches swaying heavily as the trees bowed over in defiance. His eyes darted back to the gate. He held his breath as he took a few tentative steps, pausing for a split second before he broke into a sprint. "She's here."

He didn't look back as he ran, knowing his brothers were on his heels. The sky grew darker. Blake looked up at the ominous clouds rolling in overhead as he moved across the garden grounds. It only took him a matter of seconds before he was charging through the back doors off the veranda. He slowed, moving deliberately, listening for her.

Kira's doing this! She's alive. His first instinct was to run to her, hold her, kiss her, but he stopped himself. *She's crying.* He could sense her hurt, her sadness, her resentment. Mostly, he felt his betrayal. And as he took another step, the open door beneath the stairs came into view. He now understood the reason behind those tears.

Blake glanced behind his shoulder, giving Larz a silent order to let him go in alone.

The room buzzed with an angry energy. He could feel it. "Kira, darling?" He said her name, flinching at the sudden crash of the thunder outside.

Easy, Blake. I think she's upset. He heard Larz's mental suggestion from outside the room.

No shit. "Kira?" She turned to face him. There was nothing but horror and sorrow in his eyes when he saw hers. He noticed the flush in her cheeks and the tension in her body. She was feeling something entirely different. Anger.

Kira glared back at him. "What is this?" she demanded, gesturing to the entire room with her hands.

The crack in her voice, along with her tear-soaked eyes, nearly brought him to his knees. He remembered how it made him feel to watch her cry in the car the day she broke things off with Colin. It was something he had wanted so badly, but the moment he got it, it crushed him. This was a million times worse.

"Kira, let me explain," he said, making a move towards her, but stopped dead in his tracks as a wall of flames shot up from the floor drawing a line between them. *Her magic.* It shouldn't be possible. She hadn't ascended.

"Don't touch me," she spat, backing away towards the door.

"Kira, please don't go. I need to explain."

Glass tumblers and bottles from the bar cart shattered, crashing to the floor behind him. "You can't explain this away!" she bit out.

"You're angry. I understand, but things are different," he said, feeling the pressure building within the room. "Please. It's not what you think." He could hear the chandelier now violently shaking just above him, but he didn't dare take his eyes off her. "We need to talk about this."

Kira forced a weak smile, flipping the paper she was holding to face him. "Why? So you can finish me off? You can already check one and two off your list." The tears rolled freely now.

"That . . .," his voiced cracked. "That was before." It didn't matter what he said at this point. A violent rush of air whipped through the room. Tendrils of hair danced around her face as the wind tore away the images tacked to the wall. The papers from the coffee table flew through the air.

"How could you? How could you use me like that? Lie to me . . . do those . . . things, those terrible things to me? Get into my dreams? Why? How?" She looked down, the fury in the room softening slightly, the images and papers drifted to the floor as the wind evaporated. The anger in her voice transformed into something different. Anguish. Regret. "I loved you."

Blake fell to his knees. It pained him to look her in the eyes, but he didn't dare turn away.

I loved you.

Her words were an echo imprinted in his mind and heart, shredding apart every piece of him. He wanted to reach out for her, to stop her from leaving, but she was already turning towards the door. He watched as Larz attempted to block her exit, but she waived a hand in a fluid motion, violently launching him backwards through the wall.

Thunder crashed outside, but the sound was muffled by the cascading shriek of glass shattering throughout the house. The chandelier above collapsed, knocking him to the ground. He tried to call out to her as he heard her footsteps heading out the door, but he couldn't find his voice.

Bloody hell! I think Kira's power has come forth; Larz's thoughts invaded his mind.

It took Blake several seconds before he was able to move. Her magic had held him there, caged like an animal beneath the chandelier. He continued pushing against it with his full force until her magic finally lifted, causing it to soar across the small space and crash into the wall.

He ran out into the foyer to find Larz and Vincent pulling a large shard of window glass from Armand's shoulder blade. "Are you okay?"

Armand laughed, shaking it off. "I'm fine. I just watched a tiny girl throw Larz across the room and through a wall. I can die happy now."

"Vincent, take care of Armand. Larz, we have to go after her." She was already peeling out onto the road by the time they made it down the front porch.

"Looks like we're taking mine," Larz said, a twinge of irony in his voice, pointing to the car upside down against Blake's. "She flipped it like it was a bloody matchbox toy. That won't go over well with Armand."

Blake said nothing, barely glancing at the once newly restored Trans Am now on its hood as he crawled into the passenger seat of the Audi. "Full speed. She just took a left."

It was quiet for several long seconds. Blake felt Larz's eyes drift back and forth from him to the road. They hadn't caught up with her yet, but he could feel her. "Go ahead. Come out with it. Say what you want to say."

Larz's tone was even and calm given the situation. "She's strong. Her magic shouldn't be that strong yet."

Blake struggled with his words. His emotions were all over the map. He was happy to see her safe. Horrified that she knew the truth. Confused by her early ascension. And then there was the anguish. The look on her face would haunt him to the ends of the earth.

"No, it shouldn't be. But then again, she's the *Supra*. We've never dealt with someone like her before. Maybe we don't know everything we think we do."

"That's true. You've also never dealt with anyone who's loved you like that before."

His words stung. They hadn't said those words to each other. Not yet. He knew Larz had heard her, what she'd said; *I loved you.* Armand and Vincent likely did as well. He kept his eyes on the road ahead, waiting for her car to come into view.

"And you love her."

Blake swallowed. It wasn't a question. It was a statement. "Yes." His admission was like an explosion ringing in his ears. His words were an affront to everything they had worked toward. He clenched his jaw, waiting for Larz to speak. Anger was a rare emotion from his brother, but it was the only sentiment he could fathom. When he didn't say anything in return, Blake risked a glance, noticing a slight curve playing at the edge of his lips. "What the fuck? Are you smiling?"

A grin broke across Larz's face. "I'm sorry, man. I'm not trying to make light of the situation. I know this is serious, but dude . . . I called it."

His brother's words eased some of the tension. "You did." Blake sucked in a breath. "I'm sorry, brother, but I can't kill her. I think I've known it for a while now."

A small laugh escaped him. "Bloody hell, I've known it for a quite a while. Nice of you to finally catch up."

The corner of Blake's lips turned up slightly. The fact that his brother had known his heart better than he did shouldn't have been so surprising. "How long have you known?"

"Oh, fuck. Maybe since that night you waltzed up the drive with stars in your fucking eyes. Perhaps it was when you launched yourself onto the rocks to save her life. Or maybe it was after the second or third antique lamp you destroyed. Take your pick."

"There she is!" Blake sat up tall, mentally reaching out to her. He didn't know if it would work. He'd never attempted to communicate with her in such a way. This type of connection was delicate and mostly used within one's own Coven or Brethren.

Kira, it's me. Please listen. I'm so sorry.

She heard him. He felt it. She also sped up, changing lanes. Her magic turning all the lights ahead to green. He pushed harder. She couldn't see him, but he was right there with her.

Please. I know you're scared.

"Leave me alone!"

He could see her. It was as if he was sitting right beside her. Her screams tore through him. He watched her face wrench in agony. The realization of how much he'd hurt her was a knife piercing and turning in his gut. The need to reach out, touch her face, and steady the tremor of her lower lip was strong and keen. He searched within himself. Were there any words he could say? Could he fix this? He opened his mouth, prepared to say the only thing that mattered, but the words didn't come. It was as if everything suddenly stopped.

No . . . not stopped.

Everything was moving in slow motion.

He watched her head extend far to the left, bending at an odd angle as her body jolted slightly towards him to the right. The seat belt kept her in place as glass exploded all around her, inward from every angle. He cringed, seeing it slice the delicate curve of her cheek and along her jaw, forming red lines. He saw a blast of white shoot forth from the steering wheel. He wanted to stretch an arm across that space, protect her, but he wasn't in the car. Not really. Not physically.

And then she was flying.

Glass and tendrils of her hair floated up around her face.

No, not flying. Falling. *No! Kira, no!*

"Fuck!"

Larz's voice jolted him back to their car, where he saw the full damage of what had been done. A truck driving in the opposite direction crossed the center line, slamming into Kira's driver's side at high speed. The guard rails were no match against the force of the impact. The mangle of metal and glass that was now Kira's car was slipping across the edge.

Blake only paused for a second, but the crush in his chest made it feel like it would never end. "Kira!" He was at the edge of the bridge, looking down before the car hit the water. "*Respirare.*"

And then he jumped.

His incantation to allow her to breathe beneath the water would only work for so long. And it would do nothing to stem the other injuries that she endured from the impact. He swam down, following the car as it sank to the bottom of Lake Pontchartrain.

Blake made it to the driver's side. The window was gone. He stretched his arm in, cradling her face as his other ripped at the door. The water's pressure should have made it impossible to budge, but his anger and fear fueled his power. His spell wasn't working; she wasn't breathing. Her lungs had collapsed. He ripped away the seatbelt, gathering her into his arms before he swam back to the surface.

He moved fast. But there were already several people running down the embankment to the shoreline to help. Larz was there.

Blake was stunned. Almost frozen. He handed her limp, broken body to his brother. *Save her.* He gave his silent command and turned away, crouching to the ground, his hands coiled in fists at his head. He still stood knee-deep in the lake, afraid that if he moved, he would shatter entirely.

Seconds passed. Minutes, maybe. Someone reached down, placing a hand on his shoulder, breaking him from the calm he had crafted around himself. He shot up, walking past the person, paying them no attention. His eyes searched for Kira and Larz, but he didn't see either of them. More time had passed than he'd thought.

Panic struck him as he ran up the embankment. He never heard the wail of the sirens when the ambulance arrived. He must have blocked it all out. Larz stood at the back of it, watching closely as the medics lifted her, sliding the stretcher inside. He glanced back at Blake for only a second, jumping in the back of it moments before the doors were closed.

Blake stood, rooted to the spot as he watched it drive away. He saw the look on Larz's face. He knew his brother. He knew what that blank expression meant.

Kira's dead.

BLAKE UNDERSTOOD HER NOW. He understood why she'd pleaded for him not to take her to the hospital that night. Standing against the muted colored walls with his arms folded across his chest, he stared blankly at the double doors. The doors where doctors in white coats and green scrubs walked through, sharing news that ended with either tears of joy, or earth-shattering cries.

The opening and closing of those doors would haunt him forever.

Kira's doctor hadn't walked through yet. It didn't make sense. He'd been there for over an hour. Kira herself would have been there for much longer. He'd spent a long time pacing along the bridge, his heart and stomach tied in knots. He didn't drive to the hospital until a crew began making an effort to pull her car from the lake. He couldn't be there for that.

Larz, Armand, and Vincent were all there when he arrived. They didn't speak to him, remaining quiet, but giving their support.

Larz texted Kat several times, but she never responded.

"Mr. Michaelson?"

Blake jumped at the sound of his name. "Yes?" He didn't recognize his own voice. It sounded weak. Broken. He wasn't ready to have her death confirmed, but he knew it was true. She was in this hospital, but her power most certainly was not. That magic was gone. It had died with her on that bridge.

"I am Dr. Orlovsky. I was given your name. Are you a family member of Miss Lockwood?"

He shook his head. "Kira doesn't have any family. I'm her boyfriend."

"I see. Normally we don't share information with non-relatives, but I do see in her medical chart that she recently donated blood to you for emergency surgery, so we'll make the exception."

That memory hit him like a wrecking ball. That was the day she kissed him for the first time. Nodding his head, he said nothing, gritting his teeth. He worked to bite back the scream building inside of his chest, knowing he wouldn't be able to bear to hear what he was about to be told. He couldn't feel that light within her anymore. He leaned against the wall and steeled himself for the horrid words he was about to hear. The words that would destroy his entire being.

"I don't want to lie to you. Miss Lockwood suffered extensive damage. She has several fractures and broken bones, as well as a punctured lung. There was also significant damage to her head, including several cuts and contusions. The greater fear is if there is any major injury to the brain."

Blake's brows narrowed as he worked to comprehend her words. "Wait." He choked, his mouth bone dry as he tried to swallow the knot in his throat. He dragged a hand across his face and through his hair. He squeezed his eyes shut as he steadied himself against the impact of what he was hearing as it rippled through every part of him. "You're saying Kira's alive?"

The doctor paused for a moment. Her tight-lipped smile gave little away. "She is alive. But I need to warn you, her condition is critical. We did lose her for several minutes. CPR was initiated to continue blood and oxygen flow, but with every minute, there is still the risk for brain damage. Right now, we just have to wait for her."

He stretched his hand over his face, unable to speak. His chest heaved as a wave of relief overtook him. He felt Larz's hand at his shoulder giving him a light squeeze.

"Can we see her?"

The doctor opened her mouth to speak, but Larz moved fast, waving a hand across her vision. "*Assentior*." It wouldn't have mattered, but he didn't want to give her the opportunity to say no.

She smiled. "No more than two at a time, guys."

Blake and Larz silently followed the doctor through the double doors. The emotions that raked through his body were foreign. It was an odd mixture of elation and consternation. It felt wrong; the sensation clawing at his insides.

But the hurt only magnified when he walked through the door. The sight of her broken body, the bandages, the tubes . . . it was his undoing. He doubled over at her side, his head resting on the mattress at her hand. "I'm so sorry. This is my fault," he confessed. His voice was quiet, and his words were genuine. "I would denounce all that I am, and all I ever wanted to become to take this all away. I would be nothing, less than normal, less than human to trade places with you right now. It should be me lying there. Not you."

And then Blake did something he couldn't ever remember doing.

He cried.

Tears. It was another odd sensation.

Larz was at his back. "She's going to be okay."

He nuzzled his head into her hand, his tears pooling in her palm. "I'm so sorry, Kira."

Larz turned at the sound of the door opening.

"Hello, I'm Dr. Kane. I think you spoke with Dr. Orlovsky. She assisted me with the surgery, but I'll be taking over her case now. Did she explain Miss Lockwood's condition?"

Blake sat up for the first time since he walked into the room. The sounds of the machines were suddenly louder. Her skin seemed so pale against the bandages. "She did, but do you think she'll wake up soon?"

"I'm sorry, but this is a question I cannot answer. Cases like this are hard. But it's important to stay positive. Some experts believe that patients in comas can often hear the people around them. So, if I were you, I'd start there," he said, noting some of the stats on the monitors. "Things seem to be stable. I'll check back in later."

Blake thought about what the doctor had just said. *Can she hear me? Will she even want to listen to what I have to say?* "Do you think she'll forgive me?" Larz's silence sliced through him. "You don't think so."

"I don't know."

Honesty. For centuries he'd been grateful that he could count on his brother for the truth, but for the first time, he wished like hell that Larz would lie to him. "I can't feel her light anymore."

"I'm sure it's there. It's probably just taking a break. I mean, it did drop a chandelier on your ass today."

Honesty with a side of humor. Classic Larz.

"Get away from her!"

Blake and Larz both whipped around, turning to the door. "Kat?" Her eyes were puffy, and red rimmed from tears, but it was the anger that rolled off of her that confused him. "Kat, I'm so sorry, we tried to get in touch with you," Blake said, his tone apologetic.

"I said, get the hell away from her!"

Her words were laced with disdain and disgust.

"Kat, what's wrong?" Larz reached out, placing a hand at her shoulder, but he quickly jerked it away as if she had burned him. He turned to Blake, his eyes wide. *I think I know where some of that light went.*

Blake's eyes narrowed, brows furrowed. *Not possible.*

Then be my guest . . . reach out and shake her hand. Just don't come crying to me if she drops a chandelier on your ass, too.

Blake took a step forward, holding his hands up in defense. "Kat, please. What's wrong?" He barely had time to react to the book she launched at him, but he caught it as it slammed into his chest.

"I know everything. And I do mean everything. You're never going to touch her again," she gritted out the words as she moved closer, wedging herself between him and Kira's bed. "You need to go. If you don't, I'll scream."

Blake felt Larz's hands at his shoulders, pulling him towards the door, but he couldn't look away. He couldn't turn away. "Kat, what do you think I've done?"

"Security!" Kat wailed, glaring at him with rage.

He could see the hostility in her eyes, feel it radiating from her with so much fierceness, he flinched. "Kat, please," Blake begged. "Just talk to me."

"I need help in here, please!" Kat's voice was louder, more frantic now.

Larz pulled him further to the door.

Two nurses, followed by Kira's doctor, entered the room. "What's wrong?"

"These men need to leave. Kira wouldn't want them here."

Blake heard the doctor whisper to one of the nurses to retrieve security. "What's the problem? I thought *you* were the boyfriend."

"Ex-boyfriend."

"Okay. And *you* are?"

"Her roommate."

"Look, this is a hospital. I'm not here to mediate anyone's relationship status."

"He raped her."

Kat's words ripped through him. His head spun around on his shoulders, staring her down. He opened his mouth to respond, but he couldn't form words. He felt Larz tense at his side. *She thinks I raped her.*

Larz didn't respond.

The doctor took a slow step in his direction, his tone soft but commanding. "Okay, I think you two should go."

Blake was hesitant, but finally allowed Larz to pull him away. Kat blocked Kira from his view, but he kept his eyes pinned on her until he was entirely through the door. Air left his lungs in a heavy whoosh as he braced himself against the wall. *Kat thinks . . . Kat thought. How? Why?*

And then his eyes focused on the brown leather-bound book that he still held in his hands.

He raced through the hallway of the hospital, waiting until he was outside to read anything. His brothers followed close behind, listening to his thoughts.

"It's Kira's journal." He immediately skipped to the last entry, hoping it might shed some light on where she had been over the past five days.

For months I've told myself I'm dreaming, that these are just nightmares. That I'm stressed. Overworked. But I know none of that is true. Everything I've experienced has been real. I know that now.

From that very first night when I met Blake in the parking lot at the club, he's had some supernatural hold over me. I've denied it. I've accepted it. I've denied it again. There were moments when I wanted it to be him. There have been moments I've pleaded that it wasn't.

After last night, I can only wish that it wasn't Blake. Not my Blake. Because the man from last night stole something from me. He stole my choice. He made my body betray me. He raped me.

I shouldn't sill want him. I shouldn't still need him. I shouldn't still crave him.

God, help me, but I do.

Blake slammed the book closed, a silent inferno building within him. It was a fury that burned white-hot behind his eyes. He looked to his brothers. The faces that stared back at him told him they heard every word he silently read.

Larz swallowed, his eyes narrowing as he looked at the book in Blake's hand. "But you didn't meet her for the first time in some parking lot."

"No. No, I didn't."

"So, who the bloody hell did she meet?"

Blake worked his clenched jaw, his teeth grinding. "I don't know. But I'm going to find him." Sucking in a breath, he cracked his neck to the side, gripping the book, his knuckles white. He needed to harness the anger he felt raging within him.

"And then?"

"And then I'm going to fucking kill him."

EPILOGUE
NECESSARY EVIL

The rhythmic hum and beep of the monitors was the only sound in the room. The roommate had finally left in search of food and coffee.

He ran his finger lightly over her bottom lip, paying extra attention to the cut that split along the right side. "I'm so sorry about that, my love. I take no pleasure in hurting you. Especially not now." He leaned down and pressed a soft kiss to her lips. "But it was a necessary evil."

Running his hand through her hair, he grazed her ear with his lips. "I don't want you to worry anymore. Blake Michaelson will never hurt you again. He's gone. You'll wake up soon on my command, and then we will be together just like I promised from the very beginning. From that first moment I crawled into your bed and made you beg for me. To the moment we were finally together, and you agreed to be mine."

He smiled at the slight movement of her fingers, attempting to twine with his. "There she is. There's my dark angel. I told you I would see you again one day. *Meus isempiternum.* Forever mine."

The sound of footsteps drew his attention. *The roommate.*

"Oh, hi. Any change?"

The doctor turned at the sound of Kat's voice in the door, a wicked grin curling at his lips. "Yes, actually. I think she can hear us."

I know she can hear me.

THANK YOU

This book was truly a labor of love. Time. Sweat. Tears . . . More tears. It's been an amazing experience and I'm so excited to continue Kira & Blake's story in the upcoming book.

As a first time author, I've learned a lot. Much of that comes from my readers and the reviews they've given me. Reviews are a huge part of what will continue to make this series thrive. I would so greatly appreciate it if you took a few minutes to leave me a review and let me know what you thought of the book.

GoodReads
Amazon

SPECIAL DEDICATION

I want to dedicate this book the best man in the world, the man I call my daddy:
DONNY WAYNE ROGERS 7/3/1951 - 1/2/2021
You were so proud of me, and were so excited for the book to come out this year. But I know you are in Heaven watching over me, along with my grandmother, Wilma Rogers. It was because of this wonderful and unique woman, that I became interested in poetry and writing from the beginning. You were a true and genuine inspiration to me and so many others.

My mother n' law, that I only knew as my second mom, Betty Cagle.

My cousins, Jeannie Click and Danielle Thacker. We lost you both much too soon.

ABOUT THE AUTHOR

B.L. Cagle is from Lewisburg, Tennessee. She currently lives in South Carolina with her husband, teenage daughter, and their fur baby. She is the proud mother of an MP Soldier in the Army.

She is a huge Tennessee Volunteers fan, loves animals, and both dirt track and drag racing. When she's not writing or reading, you can find her on the trails riding her RZR with her family, or at muscle car shows.

The love of writing began in the 4th grade after winning a short story contest, and has continued writing short stories and poems for her family, and friends.

After having recurring dreams, she began writing them down. She turned them into a chilling tale leading into the paranormal world, and how dreams can overtake the mind.

You can visit her website for news, upcoming events, sneak peeks to the upcoming novels and more on the blog.

www.blcagle.com

facebook.com/BLCagle

twitter.com/blcagleauthor

instagram.com/blcagleauthor

ACKNOWLEDGMENTS

A special thank you to my husband, Mike Cagle, and my daughter, Krista, for putting up with me through all of this. Thank you both for giving me the time I needed to write and the support, even though there were times you both wanted to take my computer away and smash it.

Thank you to my sister, my business partner, and my editor, Sammie Brown. You were the one that not only encouraged me to go back to school, but also start this writing journey. Thank you for helping me through the process. I also want to thank you for helping me with the book and going through it line by line.

Thank you from the bottom of my heart to Sonder Press for publishing my work, and taking on this project. And thank you to our amazing narrator, Stina Nielsen, for gracing this story with your voice and talent for our audiobook. You are absolutely amazing.

I want to personally thank my mother, Kathy Rogers, and my other sister, Kimberly Rogers, she is an amazing artist, and hope to see her artwork published someday.

I can't forget my neighbor that I have adopted as another family member, Miss Terry Orlovsky! She has rooted for me since day one!.

I also want to thank my co-workers at Tidelands Health Family Medicine at Prince Creek in Murrells Inlet, SC for their support and encouragement. The providers: Dr. Epperson, Dr. Hess, and Michelle (Shelly) Rottner; ARNP, FNP and the nurses: Carla Vereen, Amanda Compton, Lisa Frierson, Jamie Luciani, and my (Ying) Lois Vasalka, and our front staff: Charlene Jones and Kelly Flynn-Gregga. I also want to one of our Pre-Med interns, Emma Morel, that is from NOLA for sharing notes of the area with me. Thanks Kathy Dowling for all your advice.

Thanks to all my friends from my hometown of Lewisburg, TN, and my new friends here at the beach in SC and especially and most importantly, my "TWITTER" #WritingCommunity family. Without all of you, this wouldn't be possible. I thank you all.

A SPECIAL ACKNOWLEDGEMENT TO THE BEST DUCKING CRAZY WOMEN I KNOW: THE COVEN

I want to not only recognize, but also acknowledge some very special women that I have come to know over the past year. I never knew I would meet so many and interesting people on Twitter, but out of thousands of people, I was lucky enough to come across a few that will forever change my life. It all started on #ShirtlessThursday while on Twitter and somehow we all got together, and we just clicked. From that day on, we became not only friends, but we became each other's extended family. I have met a lot of people in my life from moving to another state and traveling all over to different places for work with the opioid epidemic, but never have I met such an amazing group of women that I will forever hold dear to my heart. I want to thank each of them personally for everything they have done for me, for their advice and constant encouragement. They have been my lifeboat in times of stormy seas, and nothing but positive and uplifting, but mostly, inspirational. These are the kind of people everyone should have in their lives. Even though some of us are close by while others are on the other side of the world, we all will one day soon come together and meet face to face. Eva Alton, Wendy Bayne, Mariah Bottaro, Ainsley Elliott, Hattie Hart, Bonnie Mackenzie-Smith, and Elsie McArthur

INSPIRATION AND SPECIAL ACKNOWLEDGEMENTS

My inspiration not only comes from my own mind and imagination, but also from my dreams. Some are even from my own past encounters, but they also come from music: just the words alone from the songs gave me ideas. Movies and TV Series also came into play within my story.

I want to add thanks and give recognition to the bands/artists and their music that I have listened to continuously over and over for inspiration, along with movies and TV shows: I have gotten so much inspiration from them all and felt that they needed an acknowledgement. Some may also show my age, but that's okay.

ARTISTS AND BANDS

Criss Angel, Beastie Boys, Alice Cooper, Anberlin, Arctic Monkeys, Ariana Grande, Better Than Ezra, Billie Eilish, Breaking Benjamin, Bush, Candlebox, Chevelle, Christina Aguilera, Creed, Crossfade, Damn Yankees, Chris Daughtry, Def Leppard, Deftones, Diamante, Dio, Disturbed, Dokken, Evanescence, Fozzy, Giant, Godsmack, Great White, Guns N' Roses, H.I.M., Haunted, Imagine Dragons, Jennifer Lopez, Jonathan Davis, Journey, Judas Priest, Keel, Kendrick Lamar; The Weekend, The Killers, Kingdom Come, KISS, Korn, Linkin Park, Lita Ford, Marilyn Manson, Maroon 5,

Mcauley Schenker Group, Meg Myers, Megadeth, Motley Crue, Muse, Nickleback, Nine Inch Nails, Oasis, Ozzy Osbourne, Paramore, Prince, Puddle of Mudd, Queensryche, Quiet Riot, Rainbow, Ratt, Rob Zombie, Saliva, Scorpions, Seether, Sevendust, Shinedown, Slayer, Stabbing Westward, Staind, Taylor Swift, Thirty Seconds to Mars, Three Days Grace, TOOL, Usher, Vinnie Vincent Invasion, Warlock, Wild Blue, Winger, Vaults, Vixen, W.A.S.P., Whitesnake, 3 Doors Down, 5 Seconds of Summer, 38 Special, and 10 Years…

MOVIES AND TV SERIES

Halloween, Lucifer, Interview With the Vampire, Star Wars, The Fast and the Furious, The Purge, The Witcher, Wonder Woman

Made in the USA
Monee, IL
18 August 2022

f7c13188-8a7a-4bd1-990f-7217c37062cdR01